A KILLER
WHO LEAVES NO CLUES

"You're suspicious that murder has taken place, but what evidence do you have?"

"Evidence?"

"Well, yes. There has to be something to make you think that a murder has taken place—like a corpse with a smoking gun lying next to it. Or at least a corpse that looks as though it would have preferred not to have ended up the way it did. You don't have that, Amanda. You have three people who died as a result of serious life-threatening illnesses, who up until a decade or so ago, *would* have died of their illnesses."

Amanda tried to convince herself that what Lydia said was true. Logically, her fears were groundless. Nevertheless, she couldn't put it out of her mind. Three deaths, so sudden, so unexpected, so wrong . . .

Diamond Books by
Margot J. Fromer

SCALPEL'S EDGE
NIGHT SHIFT

NIGHT SHIFT

MARGOT J. FROMER

DIAMOND BOOKS, NEW YORK

This book is a Diamond original edition, and has never been previously published.

NIGHT SHIFT

A Diamond Book / published by arrangement with the author

PRINTING HISTORY
Diamond edition/May 1993

ISBN: 1-55773-895-5

Diamond Books are published by The Berkley Publishing Group, 200 Madison Avenue, New York, NY 10016.
The name "DIAMOND" and its logo are trademarks belonging to Charter Communications, Inc.

PRINTED IN THE UNITED STATES OF AMERICA

10 9 8 7 6 5 4 3 2 1

This book is for

MARTHA ELLIOTT

ACKNOWLEDGMENTS

My thanks to Helen Michalisco, M.S.W., and Sharon Owens, R.N., of Johns Hopkins Hospital for introducing me to the intricacies involved in the care of organ-transplant patients.

═══ PROLOGUE ═══

Aaron Zurman lay dying. To his surprise, he found that it didn't matter much. In fact, it didn't matter that he was being murdered.

He chuckled, but of course no one heard the sound because he had been rendered voiceless by the endotracheal tube inserted deep into his throat. The only thing that could be heard in Aaron Zurman's room in the intensive care unit at J.F.K. Memorial Hospital was the beep, beep, beep of the cardiac monitor and the hypnotic whoosh of the ventilator. Even his mother sitting in a chair, swaddled in a green paper coverall and matching paper cap and shoe covers, was silent.

Zurman was awake, but he kept his eyes closed so his mother would think he was asleep. He was sick of his mother. Sick to death.

What the Nazis had tried and failed to do those long years ago was now being accomplished by someone so diabolically clever that even Aaron Zurman, who didn't admire many people, was impressed. Zurman prided himself on being a crack diagnostician, but even he couldn't figure out how they were managing to kill him right here in the middle of one of the busiest intensive care units in the city, with the constant stream of people flitting about and the unending glare of lights and hum of machinery twenty-four hours a day. Even so, he knew it was them, all right. No question about it.

He was too tired to figure it all out. And he didn't really care. Finally, he didn't care. This, they would never believe, he thought. Who would think that Aaron Zurman, M.D., board-certified in three medical specialties, physician-turned-politician, would give up the control he had clung to so tenaciously for so long and just lie back and let them kill him.

This effortless sliding toward the place where there was no thought of control was delicious. It reminded him of winters

1

in Bunnik when his mother would take him and his two sisters gliding on the frozen canal. When the sled got too heavy for his mother to pull all three of them, she would tell the girls to get out and walk alongside, and Zurman would have it all to himself. He and his mother would go whooshing along atop the thick ice, just the two of them, the wind stinging his baby cheeks.

He shrieked with delight.

At the sound of her son's gargling moan, old Mrs. Zurman struggled awake and leaned forward in the plastic-covered armchair that was pulled up next to the tangle of tubes and machines connected to her son. *"Was ist das?"* she asked. She spoke mostly Yiddish or Dutch now. It was too much trouble to try to remember the English she had never really made the effort to learn. Her son was too sick to care what language she spoke. She wasn't even sure that he cared anymore what she said. She thought that perhaps he had never cared.

Zurman looked at his mother. She was no longer pulling the sled, and on his cheeks lay a heavy coat of uremic frost, not the flakes of a light Dutch snow. He closed his eyes against his mother's questioning, demanding gaze. This time she would not be able to save him. This time he would not have to be beholden to her for the rest of his life. The weight of the gratitude that had obliterated everything else and turned him into an emotional cripple would finally be lifted.

His mother would have to deal alone with the fact of his death, with the consequences of his murder. He would no longer be there to shield her against the reality that, for as long as he could remember, she steadfastly refused to acknowledge.

A great gust of relief blew through him, and he allowed himself to slide back into the dream-fantasy that sometimes brought him comfort but equally often turned into quaking panic. Please don't make it the hiding dream this time, he prayed to the God that was no longer there for him. Please, please not the dream where the boy cringed suffocating and terrorized in the dark cellar, listening to the thundering boots of the searchers above.

But this time, no dreams came, and he lay watching the nurses tend to the machines and tubes that connected him to the life that someone had decided to end.

Aaron Zurman looked like death itself. His blood pressure had plummeted to the lower reaches of the ability to sustain life, and the drugs being pumped into him to increase the pressure were not working. He knew that. Zurman had spent enough time hovering over patients just like himself to know what he looked like, what was going on around him. He knew his bed was in the center of the room with plenty of space around it for the emergency team to apply the paddles and inject the drugs when his heart finally stopped. He knew that time would come soon, and he wished fervently that no one would notice.

Fat chance, he thought bitterly. The alarm would sound, the ventilator that even now pushed the breath of life into him at a steady fourteen times a minute would switch to a different ratio of oxygen and other gases, and the white coats would come running to apply the jolt of electricity that would prolong his dying for a few more hours or days—as he had done to others so many times.

The nurses were a long way away now, and he couldn't hear what they were saying. He knew, though, that they were worried about his new kidney, the one he had received only two days before. Or maybe it was fifty years ago. That was when his old kidneys had been kicked to shreds by the black boots.

No, it must have been just recently that he got the new kidney. Why else would he be lying here in a hospital not his own, where the nurses never once looked at him—only at the machines and tubes that they fiddled with? He knew that they were concerned about his electrolytes, which were so far out of balance that they could never be set right. The errors in his body's chemicals would soon throw his heart wildly out of rhythm, the alarms would go off, and after two or three times his heart would stop for good. He knew that. *Baruch ha Shem*, he prayed. Make it soon.

He looked again at the woman who had thrown him from the train into six years of more horror than it was possible to endure, but which he had endured. The years that had turned him into the kind of person that someone would need to murder. He wondered which one of them had the balls to do it.

Zurman smiled inwardly. What an ingenious son of a bitch, he thought. I could have used a guy like that.

Aaron Zurman spoke none of these thoughts aloud, not just because he was beyond speaking, but because they weren't the kind of thoughts he was used to. He had always been unaccustomed to facing himself and his feelings, and now he was rather enjoying the clarity of reality. He had considered the fact of death many times; after all, he was a doctor and a politician. But he had no idea what it was really. It had never occurred to him that he would enjoy it, that he would be so relieved. It didn't hurt. He wasn't sad. He liked this drifting about in the benign Dutch winter, watching the back of his mother's fur coat as she pulled the sled over the frozen canal.

He lay in the sled looking up at the low sky, grey now with the storm to come. He thought about the hot chocolate that *Mutter* would make for him and his sisters and the cinnamon pastries that she would take from the oven. Bobbie would be crouching under the table waiting for his share. He and Bobbie had a system all worked out: the little brown and black dog lay at Aaron's side until exactly the moment that *Mutter* turned her back, then quietly, so as not to jingle the tags on his collar, Bobbie stood up under the table at Aaron's feet and closed his mouth ever so gently over the snack. No gulping, no smacking of lips. Bobbie wasn't one to spoil one of the best things he had going.

The sled glided to a halt under the little bridge over the canal near their house, and his mother turned to him with a smile as he got out and helped her pull the sled up the bank of the canal. "Are you frozen solid, my little pumpkin?" she asked, wrapping the coat around him so that they were snuggled together under the fur. "Are your cheeks like cherry ice cream? Is your nose a strawberry tart?"

He giggled as she kissed the parts she named, and he and his mother and sisters walked up the lane toward the shelter of home in the gathering storm. He turned at the slight sound behind him, and there was the black boot, whooshing out of nowhere and slamming into his side. Aaron grunted as the dream pain exploded in his side and ricocheted around his belly.

Again and again the black boot smashed. Bunnik was gone. His mother was gone. He lay in the mud of the pigpen at the side of the Belgian farmhouse, so close to the sea, so close to escape. The mud sucked at him, the boots pounded and pounded; the pigs pushed him deeper into the mire, snorting and poking him with hairy snouts. The pain was gone now and he opened his eyes. Through the red haze, he saw *Mutter* crying, her frightened doe-eyes opened wide. The pigs wore white uniforms as they poked at him and turned him this way and that. He heard them say, "Stand clear," and he knew what that meant and waited for the agony of the electricity to course through his chest. Nothing happened. He felt nothing. He saw them, of course, and he heard everything as though from a great distance, but he felt nothing.

"Enough now," he said, but of course no one heard. "Leave me be. Let me go now," he pleaded.

It occurred to him that he ought to recite the *Sh'ma Yisroel*, the Jewish prayer of affirmation, the prayer traditionally on the lips of the dying. But Aaron Zurman had nothing to affirm, so he rejected this final supplication, and thought with grim satisfaction that there is indeed a reason why there are so many atheists in the foxholes of high-technology medicine.

Finally, the white coats left, the boots stopped their incessant kicking, and his mother picked up the rope of the sled. "Come, popsie," she said, wrapping him in a blanket as she settled him into the sled. "We'll go for a nice ride to where it's warm and safe. I'll protect you."

═══ CHAPTER 1 ═══

Two men and a woman stood in the parking lot of the Riverside Funeral Home in the sweltering August afternoon. They were dressed almost identically in navy blue suits. The men had on white shirts and dark ties, and the woman wore navy pumps with her suit, a pale pink silk blouse, and a small tan shoulder bag. They were all sweating, but no one was willing to make the first move to remove a jacket, so everyone remained stuck in their hot, constricting clothes. No one suggested they sit in an air-conditioned car, though all wanted to.

The short man was annoyed by the name of the funeral parlor. The nearest river, the Potomac, was at least ten miles away, much too far for anything even remotely resembling a breeze to refresh the three of them. The taller of the men looked around before he spoke. "So we're rid of him. Finally."

The other two looked uncomfortable. It was one thing to exult in the death of a hated and feared colleague privately, even to have had a hand in engineering it. But it was something else entirely to speak those thoughts aloud. The woman believed it was unseemly and stupid, and the short man felt his heart lurch in panic as he remembered why they were here.

"Should we go to the cemetery and then back to the house?" he asked the others.

"We might as well carry this charade all the way through," the woman said.

"I was watching you in there," said one of the men to the woman. "Why were you playing it so grief-stricken? You didn't need to pretend to be quite so overcome." He watched the woman's face suffuse with anger. "Is there something you're not telling us about your relationship with Zurman?"

6

The woman's face reddened further. "Why, you two-bit lousy shit. It's none of your goddamn business what my relationship . . ."

"Hey, hey," said the short man, relieved that he wasn't the only one having second thoughts about what they had done. "Let's not get into that here. Or maybe you want to put on a show for all these people. Maybe you'd like to start a little investigation, get people suspicious. They're already starting to stare."

"Let's just get through this with as little fuss as possible," said the tall man. "We'll go to the grave and the house, pay our respects to the mother, and then get on with replacing the bastard. That's what we went to all this trouble for in the first place, isn't it?"

The others agreed. Getting rid of Zurman, getting him off the county council was what they had set out to do. The trouble was that none of them had realized how easy it would be, and now they felt the first little stabs of fear.

The short man voiced what they were all thinking. "I just can't believe no one will ask questions. Everyone knows how we felt about Zurman. And now that he's dead, we're the ones they'll come snooping around first. I just wish we hadn't . . ."

"Don't be a jerk," said the woman sharply. She was still irritated by his implication that she had been something more than a fellow council member to that creep, Zurman. "Everyone knows that he was walking around half dead for years. The guy even looked like a corpse most of the time. His death can't possibly be a surprise to anyone. I mean, all those years on dialysis."

"But he finally got the kidney transplant," said the man. "That was supposed to have cured him."

"Well, it didn't, did it?" she snapped. "Why don't the two of you just shut up and get in your cars. I've managed everything up till now and I've done exactly what we agreed had to be done. We're rid of him, and you two can go home and put the finishing touches on your get-rich-quick fantasies. You've got a free hand now to build anything you want, but you had damn well better remember who gave you that freedom."

The woman was almost snarling now, and a few people walking through the parking lot stared curiously at her and her two red-faced companions. No one wanted to linger in the sun that beat down onto the shimmering asphalt. Everyone was too anxious to get into their cars and turn on the air conditioning full blast.

The tall man made an effort to smooth things over. The last person he wanted to be on the wrong side of was this ball-busting bitch who, now more than ever, had his tender parts very neatly squeezed in her voracious grasp. He glanced down at her long, witchlike fingernails and imagined them raking across his testicles. He shivered despite the searing heat as he thought, not for the first time, that whenever she wanted to, she could send him to the place where Aaron Zurman now rested.

"Look," he said to the woman. "Let's not get into an argument here. Too many people know who we are."

The other two had no choice but to agree with what the tall man said, and as they turned to move to their cars, the woman cursed in frustration, causing several heads to turn. "My fucking shoe is stuck."

As she stood awkwardly on one foot, leaning against the taller man for support, the other bent down to dislodge the woman's shoe which had indeed imbedded itself an inch into the melting asphalt. He handed it to her wordlessly.

"Fuck, it's ruined," she said, and strode off to her car.

"Didn't your mother ever tell you to say thank you?" the man muttered quietly, so the woman wouldn't hear.

"What that bitch's mother taught her doesn't bear thinking about," said the other. "I'd stay the hell out of her way, if I were you. Far, far away."

CHAPTER 2

Amanda Knight lay in bed with the covers tucked up under her chin against the blast of the air conditioner. She was watching her husband through barely open eyes which she wanted him to think were still closed.

Ken James was standing in front of the mirror knotting his tie. He had on a light blue shirt with a fine maroon stripe, navy blue socks that stretched to his knees, the maroon and navy patterned tie that he was weaving into a knot—and nothing else. No underpants. And his shirttail wasn't long enough. In the mirror, he watched his wife watch him. He knew she was awake, and moved so that his shirt rode up even higher over his hips.

Amanda smiled despite her effort to feign sleep, and the grey cat that was snuggled into the valley between her pillow and Ken's stepped up her level of purring as she saw Amanda's smile broaden. "Ken, have I ever told you that you have great legs? Not to mention everything else that's swinging in the breeze!"

Ken grinned at her in the mirror. He loved it when she looked at him. All his life, he had dressed the way most men did: shorts first. But soon after they began their love affair, Amanda had rearranged his order of dressing to her satisfaction, and now the silly game of peek-a-boo meant as much to him as to her.

"Do you really think so? No one's ever told me that before," he said as he did every time she commented on his legs. He sat down on the edge of the bed. "Aren't you going to work today?"

"Of course, I'm going," she replied. "But I don't have to spend half an hour in front of the mirror admiring my body, so I'll be ready before you leave the house."

"That's because you have me to admire it for you," he

9

said, whipping off the covers and planting a kiss right in the middle of her belly. Her whole body responded to the touch of his lips.

"Oh, no you don't," she said, getting up and walking toward her bathroom. "Will you put your pants on and turn off the damn air conditioner?" She decided to have just cereal and coffee this morning, mindful of the squeamishness she had felt in a bathing suit this weekend when she and Ken were at the beach.

Amanda poured a cup of coffee from the pot in their bedroom and drank it as she put on her makeup and talked nonsense to Shadow, who sat on the vanity shelf next to the sink. Just as Amanda was streaking eyeliner across her lids, the cat pricked her ears, leaped off the edge of the sink, and shot out of the room.

"Shit," she said as she wiped the streak of dark brown off her cheek, then went to her closet to look for something to match the weather which the radio announcer said would hit 100 degrees today. She finally chose a kelly green and white print dress with a wide green patent leather belt that set off her chin-length dark hair, green eyes, and newly replenished tan. She smiled at herself in the mirror. "You don't look too bad," she said to her reflection.

"Honey, I'm leaving now," called Ken from the bottom of the steps. "I fed the moose."

Amanda smiled. So that was what had made the cat leave the side of her beloved: the sound of a cat food can being opened. Ever since she had told Ken what the vet had said during Shadow's last checkup, he had adopted numerous pet names for the cat.

"She's not a moose and she's not fat," Amanda yelled back. "She's just big-boned."

"She's a hog. Love you, bye."

The veterinarian had been more diplomatic. "Do you think she could manage to lose a few pounds?" he suggested.

Fat chance, thought Amanda as she walked into the kitchen to eat cereal with skim milk and black coffee. Shadow was standing next to her empty bowl, meowing piteously. "You're such a liar," said Amanda to the cat. "Ken fed you. You haven't even finished cleaning your whiskers. You *are* a pig, and you're lucky I love you so much that I won't ever admit it to him."

Shadow conceded defeat and jumped onto the kitchen table to interfere with Amanda's breakfast and newspaper reading. Ken wasn't there to protest the presence of an animal on the table, so Amanda and Shadow passed a companionable fifteen minutes until it was time for each to attend to the day's business: Shadow jumped onto a sunny windowsill to supervise the growing of the grass, and Amanda drove to work.

Mornings still weren't the same without Bill Cerri. The radio announcer, who hated bagpipes and the harpsichord, but loved all other classical music, had died recently after twenty years with WETA-FM, and Amanda felt a longing for the familiar voice as the replacement announcer told her what she already knew: the traffic was hideous and the weather was worse. So what else is new? she grumbled to herself. It's August in the nation's capital, and just because the monkeys on Capitol Hill have gone home doesn't mean the rest of us aren't in full swing. Not everyone in Washington is a politician, she thought grimly.

But Amanda knew that wasn't really true. Everyone here was a wheeler-dealer of some kind. In a city that was as much a company town as any turn-of-the-century steel or fabric mill town, almost everyone worked either directly for the federal government or for a business or organization that received most of its income servicing the government or lobbying the government or needing to be near those who ran the government. And half of them didn't do anything worth doing, she thought as she finally made it through the light at Wisconsin and Van Ness.

The neighborhood in which she worked was typical. The narrow, crowded streets of Georgetown were clogged with morning traffic, and as she endured the stop-and-go marathon, she once again marveled at the houses and the people who lived in them: incredibly wealthy lawyers, ambassadors, lobbyists, journalists, and politicians. Then too, there were group houses overflowing with Georgetown University students, and other houses in which young lawyers and aspiring politicians lived, two to a bedroom, in a welter of cheap furniture, no privacy, and constant noise just to have a "good" address and to be near those they imagined might do them some political good. Amanda shuddered at the thought of living with a front door directly on the sidewalk, no room to grow grass and flowers, and the Saturday night revelers throwing up on the doorstep.

She watched the men and women leave their houses, dressed for success in suits even on this boiling hot morning, the women all wearing running shoes and ankle socks over their pantyhose. Politicians and lawyers off to screw things up even more, she thought with some derision.

But then she smiled to herself. Even she was a politician. As director of nursing at J. F. K. Memorial Hospital, named for a President whom no hospital could have saved, she had met a number of times with people from the Secret Service to work out the details of care in case the President had a medical emergency. J. F. K. Memorial was one of the major hospitals in the city that was designated a presidential emergency center, and her fervent wish was that the incredibly complex mechanism would never have to be activated.

"It's not that I care all that much about some politician getting shot," she had once said to her best friend and absolute confidante, Glencora Rodman. "There will always be another one to take his place, but I don't think I could live through the media and political circus." Amanda, who thought that the last decent President had been Harry Truman, remembered the horror stories told to her by the nursing administrators at George Washington University Hospital when President Reagan and Jim Brady were brought in. The director of nursing hadn't slept for three days in a row.

"The Secret Service guys wore those little walkie-talkie things in their ears when they came to the hospital to talk to us," she told Glen. "What do you suppose they're listening to?"

Glen snorted. "Probably Muzak! Or maybe they need regular doses of the 'Star Spangled Banner' to keep up their patriotic fervor. Who else but a complete dork would deliberately choose to put himself between a bullet and a politician!"

Amanda breathed a sigh of relief as she inserted her card into the entrance gate of the employees' section of the hospital parking garage. She squeezed her bright red Honda Accord into her very own reserved parking slot. Ken's salary was about twenty times what she earned, and he was president and CEO of the largest computer manufacturer in the world, but he didn't have a reserved parking space. Years ago, in a burst of what Amanda called pseudo-democracy, Naylor-Noyes Corporation had abolished reserved parking for their executives. Now Ken didn't want to incur the employees' outrage, so free-for-all parking remained in effect at Naylor-Noyes and the head honcho, her own sweet love, sometimes got wet tootsies on his way to work.

In a city like Washington, where a strip of asphalt with two white lines sold for $35,000, a reserved parking slot was the stuff of dreams. She had once heard a man on the street say that he would sell his soul to have a reserved parking space. He didn't sound as though he was joking. But Amanda's job required her to be in the hospital at odd hours, so she had convinced her boss, David Townsend, to give her a spot three cars down from his.

The hospital's multilevel garage was covered but otherwise open to the elements, and as she got out of the car, Washington's swampy August heat, mixed liberally with exhaust fumes, hit her in the face like a suffocating blanket. It's a good thing the patients don't get discharged through here, she thought. They'd have a relapse right away.

"Did you have a good weekend?" her secretary, Louise, asked.

"I had a great time," Amanda replied. "But I think Ken still feels uncomfortable that I'm such good friends with gay men. In a million years he wouldn't admit it, though."

"You were lucky to be at the beach," said Louise. "This weather is the pits. Here are the weekend reports," she added, handing two one-page summaries to Amanda. "It seemed pretty quiet. No one fell out of bed—for a change—and the only death was a man on the transplant unit. Two days post-op."

"Two days! My God, what's the new chief doing to those poor patients up there? This is the second death on the transplant unit in a month."

"But Amanda, they're not exactly in tip-top shape when they're admitted," Louise pointed out. "In fact, they're about three-quarters dead."

"You're right," replied Amanda, "especially the heart and liver patients. They're actually more dead than alive if they get to the point where they need a transplant. But these two patients were kidney transplants, and neither one of them made it out of the hospital alive. I want to go to the M and M on this new one, Aaron Zurman. Will you let me know when it is? I'd hate like hell to find out that there was something the nurses could have done to prevent this."

"Okay, I'll call pathology. Don't forget the department heads meeting today. Noon in the boardroom."

"Great," said Amanda. "There goes my diet!"

"A diet," replied Louise in dismay. "Not another one! Does this mean you're going to be all grumpy and cranky again?"

"Probably," said Amanda grinning as she went into her office. But her smile faded when she realized that Louise was seriously worried about her mood. Last spring, in her annual panic about how she was going to look in a bathing suit, Amanda had decided to confine her entire menu to skinless chicken breasts, yogurt, and salad with no dressing. After a week, she started to feel incredibly deprived and had yelled at Louise twice, the second time because the automatic pencil sharpener didn't work. Grimly pointing to the plug lying on the floor, Louise had slowly bent over, plugged in the sharpener, put on her jacket, and said, "I'm going shopping for the rest of the day. Call me at home tonight and let me know if you're going to be a bitch tomorrow too. My house needs cleaning, and frankly, Amanda, I'd prefer scrubbing floors to working for you when you're nasty."

Amanda had not called Louise that evening. Instead she went to her secretary's house with an armload of spring flowers from the most expensive florist in her neighborhood. The two of them had gone to an ice cream parlor where Louise had a single scoop of sorbet and Amanda had a hot fudge sundae. Then she went home and seduced Ken right in their backyard behind the hedge he had been clipping in the fading May light.

Sitting down now behind her desk, Amanda smiled as she remembered the scratches on her buttocks and the hedge clippings in Ken's hair. But she worried too about her dependence on sweets and what a bitch she became when she tried to diet. "Maybe I should go to a shrink," she had told Glencora after last spring's attempt at dieting.

"Maybe you ought to learn how to moderate your behavior so it's not feast or famine all the time," said Glen.

That was one of the troubles with Glen. She actually talked like that: moderate your behavior. Another trouble was that

Glen's own behavior was always completely moderated. She never pigged out, she never drank too much, and her clothes were never wrinkled—even on a day like today. And Amanda had never seen Glen's hair messed up, even when she first woke up in the morning. But her apartment was always a mess. There were magazines strewn about, dirty dishes in the sink, and clothes lying on every chair. Once when Amanda had slept over, she had found a shoe under the pillow of the guest bed.

"Oh, thanks," said Glen. "I was wondering where that was." No apology, no sense of shame for the mess, no sense of remorse that sometimes there weren't any clean towels for guests. That was one of the things that endeared Glen to Amanda: the freedom to be herself—that and her absolute loyalty to the friendship.

Amanda sighed over her problem with dieting as she prepared to read the weekend report compiled by the three nursing supervisors. The catered lunch at the department heads meeting would be delicious and she would eat everything and then consider her diet blown. But maybe this time she'd take Glen's advice and try to get some perspective on the problem of the extra fifteen pounds that had been plaguing her since high school.

I'll think about it later, she vowed.

If you're going to talk like Scarlett O'Hara, said the voice of sweet reason, *then the least thing you could do is get down to her waist size.*

Oh, shut up, replied Amanda, who never would have the body of Scarlett O'Hara and who was married to a man who hated skinny women—thank God.

As she read the report, which was indeed relatively uneventful, perhaps because half the doctors in town were on vacation in August and patients didn't want to spend the waning days of summer in the hospital, Amanda was bothered by the fact that the transplant patient had died only two days after receiving a new kidney—a procedure now so common that almost no one died in the hospital.

Amanda knew that of the 9,000 or so kidneys transplanted in the United States each year, about 85 percent are successful over the long haul. And the rest of the patients don't necessarily die. Most often they reject the new kidney and have to go back on dialysis for a while until they can receive a second transplant. Some people have had three or four kidney transplants. Almost no one dies two days later in the middle of the transplant center's intensive care unit right under the noses of doctors and nurses who do nothing but take care of transplant patients.

Even among those who had liver transplants, a far more complex and risky procedure than a kidney, 70 percent survived the first year.

What the hell had gone wrong with Aaron Zurman? The report noted that he was a physician, and Amanda visualized the lawsuit that would surely follow the death of a doctor. She began to have a very strong feeling that the quiet, uneventful August weekend at J. F. K. Memorial would spawn a legal nightmare.

She buzzed Louise. "Will you get me a copy of the autopsy report on Aaron Zurman?" she asked.

Amanda turned on her computer and worked on one of the tasks she hated: staff evaluations. As she had worked her way up the nursing administration ladder, the problem of evaluations became easier to deal with because the people directly under her were competent for the most part. But many years ago, when she had gotten her first promotion to head nurse and had to judge all the staff nurses, licensed practical nurses, and nursing aides on her unit, she had assumed that honesty and reality were the way to go. She well remembered her shock when, following a poor evaluation, she'd been accused of racism.

The nurse in question complained to the director of personnel that Amanda was unfair and didn't like blacks. Amanda had been outraged. "Lillian O'Brien let a dying man lie around in his own shit. She said she was too busy to change his sheets and clean him up," Amanda had sputtered when she was called on the carpet for alleged unfairness.

"Well, was she busy?" asked the director of nursing at the hospital where Amanda had worked then.

"That's not the point," replied Amanda. "Nurses are always busy. No hospital on the face of the earth ever has enough nurses to go around, especially now that the only patients who get to stay more than two or three days are the very sickest ones.

"They're more than busy," she fumed. "They're run ragged. They're pushed and pulled in a million different directions, but that doesn't excuse cruelty to patients."

"Oh, come on, Amanda," said the director, who hoped with all her heart that this wasn't going to turn into a major fight. "O'Brien wasn't being cruel. She just forgot to change some poor guy's sheets. It happens all the time. It's not that big a deal.

"Look, you're new at this. This is your first time doing staff evaluations. O'Brien says she's going to file a grievance if you don't change her evaluation, and I believe her. You just got promoted yourself; do you want everyone to think you're a troublemaker?"

That was more than a dozen years ago, and Amanda had caved in and changed the nurse's evaluation. She regretted it to this day. For an entire year, O'Brien had taken advantage of having Amanda over a barrel, engaging in minor infractions of the rules, coming to work late, taking more than her share of time for lunch, calling in sick the minute snow was forecast.

That was when Ken had given her the first of many lessons in management tactics. "You're smarter than all of them, honey," he had said. "So the trick is to figure out the game and then beat them at it."

And now he was CEO of a giant computer conglomerate and she the director of nursing at Washington, D.C.'s most prestigious hospital. Machiavelli and his missus, she said to herself as she recommended a raise for one of the six nursing supervisors. I hope David Townsend is as generous to me as I am to Betsy, she thought.

Ruth Sinclair, the hospital's director of dietary services, poked her head into Amanda's office shortly before twelve. "Ready for the monthly pep talk and skull bashing?" she asked cheerfully.

"God, is it noon already?" said Amanda. "How time flies when you're having fun!"

Amanda grimaced at her own remark. It was fun to give someone she liked and respected a big raise, but the nurse who had left her office just moments before Ruth arrived had not created a barrel of laughs with what she had come to say.

"Having a rough morning? How was the ocean? Boy, have I got some juicy gossip for you!" said Ruth all in a rush.

Amanda's face lit up. She could tell from the way Ruth was smiling that this was going to be really good. "Quick, tell me," said Amanda. "On second thought, wait here one second. I have to pee before the meeting."

"I'll go with you," said Ruth. "I have to go too."

The two women entered the ladies room in the administrative wing, and without having to discuss it, they poked open the doors to all six stalls to make sure they were alone.

"Have you met the new chief pharmacist?" asked Ruth.

"I've seen her once or twice," said Amanda. "Eddie pointed her out to me the first time, and I guess I've seen her in the cafeteria. "She's quite attractive, don't you think?"

"She's smashing," replied Ruth, one of the few plain women Amanda knew who was not jealous of women better looking than herself. Ruth reminded Amanda of one of the cafeteria ladies who used to serve lunch to her and several hundred other screaming animals at Brighton High School. The only difference was that Ruth smiled a lot, and she didn't wear a hairnet or a white nylon uniform. Amanda wondered if they still wore hairnets.

"Do you know how she got the job here?" asked Ruth.

"Because she's the best qualified and counts pills better than anyone else, and the whole American health care system is guilty because there are no women heads of pharmacy. And it doesn't hurt that she looks like a million dollars," replied Amanda.

"Right. All of that, I'm sure. And probably to keep the two of us company in the midst of all these high-powered men," said Ruth, who paused for dramatic effect because she knew that Amanda was dying to hear the rest. "But the real reason is that she was screwing some big cheese surgeon at St. Jude's, and his wife found out and stormed down to the pharmacy and wrecked the place looking for her."

"Wrecked the place?" asked Amanda, incredulous. "You mean she did actual physical damage?"

"I heard the pharmacy looked like a snowstorm of pills," replied Ruth. She dearly loved a good drama. "Thousands of dollars of medication scattered all over the room. They had to appeal to other hospitals to replace some that patients needed right away. In one instance St. Jude's had to pay for a drug company's corporate jet to fly all the way from upstate New Jersey with a one-of-a-kind drug for an emergency.

"It was a mess. I heard they still find pills lodged in odd corners, and this happened weeks ago," said Ruth.

Amanda shook her head in disgust. She knew what was coming. "So a big surgeon's wife tears up a hospital pharmacy to get at the other woman . . . Did she ever find her? What's her name, by the way?"

"No, she never got her," said Ruth. "She was in a meeting. Her name is Evelyn Portman, and if I were her, I'd keep close tabs on my rear end. Too many people get ideas from revenge movies these days!" Then Ruth became more serious. "But I know what you're going to say, Amanda. The wife does all the damage and the 'loose' woman gets fired—and of course nothing happens to the man.

"I don't think Evelyn Portman was exactly fired, though. I think the doctor cooked up something with his buddies here to get her a job."

Amanda was disgusted. "So she didn't get canned officially. Maybe they let her quit with a big wad of cash in her hand, but I'll bet there are serious footprints in her butt! Is she still screwing the guy?"

Ruth giggled. "Now, how would I know that?"

"Well, you knew all the other stuff. How did you find out, by the way?"

"Through the food-service grapevine," said Ruth. "Just like you find out stuff through the nursing grapevine."

"Well, here's to grapes," replied Amanda, going into a stall and closing the door. "Fermented, as well as on the vine!"

Ruth and Amanda walked together in companionable silence toward the boardroom at the end of the administrative corridor. "Are you responsible for this lunch, or are we going to have real food?" asked Amanda.

"I beg your pardon," replied Ruth in mock indignation. Bad jokes about hospital food had long since ceased to bother her. "We're having Hopewell's cater this lunch. This is their first job for us. I'm trying them out, so be sure to let me know what you think."

Ruth pulled open the heavy wooden door to the conference room, but Amanda put a hand on her arm, restraining her. "I have to ask you something," she said. "Do you remember years ago those ladies in white nylon who used to serve meals in the high-school cafeteria?"

"Do I remember!" replied Ruth. "I used to be one of them. Yuk, what an awful job. All those disgusting steamed vegetables without a single nutrient left in them. And the screaming adolescents with their hormones run amok." She shuddered at the memory. "What about them?"

"Do you think they still wear hairnets?"

Ruth stared at Amanda in amazement. "Do you know how weird you are?" she asked finally.

Amanda grinned. "I know," she said. "That's why you love me. So do they wear them?"

"I haven't the foggiest idea," said Ruth. "And I have no intention of setting foot in a high school ever again, so if you want to know, you'll have to do your own research!"

As soon as it got dark, Amanda and Ken went skinny-dipping in the pool in their backyard. Now they were lying on lounge chairs, each draped in a towel, wrapped in silent thought. Amanda had known Ken for fourteen years and had been married to him for two, and she was still not sure what he thought about at times like these. Was he plotting another corporate coup? Was he indulging in a romantic fantasy? Was he thinking about how to fit a haircut into his schedule? She turned to face him. "You need a haircut."

He sighed and put his hand to his head. "I know. It's so hard to make the time. I'll do it this week."

He lapsed into silence again, sighed, and reached for her hand.

"What's wrong, sweet love?" she asked.

"Nothing," he said. "I wish I had more time to do things like this. Just lie here and relax."

Amanda wasn't sure he meant that. They had done nothing but relax all weekend at the beach with Eddie and Donald, and Amanda didn't think that Ken had enjoyed it all that much. And she didn't think that being in the house with gay men was the only problem, because he liked and respected both men. Amanda suspected that Ken was uneasy without the security of having his briefcase near him for two whole days. She had talked him out of bringing it. "It's rude," she had said. "You're guests in their home. How would you like it if one of your corporate commandos brought his damn cellular phone to the dinner table in your home?"

"I wouldn't mind as long as he didn't put it down in the mashed potatoes," he had teased. But he had given in and left his briefcase home and then regretted it.

"Do you think you'd enjoy it as much if you were able to rest and relax more?" she asked. "It wouldn't be such a treat—it would be like eating chocolate every day of the week; you'd get tired of it real soon."

He squeezed her hand. "You always look at things so philosophically," he said. "That's one of the reasons I love you so much. But you're wrong about one thing: I'd never get tired of chocolate!"

Amanda laughed and squeezed back and didn't bother to mention that the reason he admired her sense of perspective was that he looked at things from a much more rigid point of view. Only in the past several years had Ken learned to add shades of grey to his previously stark black and white view of human behavior.

Amanda changed the subject. "I want to tell you something strange that happened at work today."

"Shoot," he said.

"There was a death over the weekend on the transplant unit, the second one in a month, which is very unusual. A man rejected his kidney after only two days, and that's almost unheard of nowadays. In fact, it's so out of the ordinary that Townsend brought it up at the department heads meeting today. He was not a happy camper. And of course, the PR office is all a-twitter. They had made such a big deal out of stepping up the transplant unit's technology and capabilities. Huge, expensive party for the new chief and all that kind of hoopla."

"Someone has to start making money for that place," said Ken, who thought that all institutions and organizations were essentially businesses.

"Right," she replied, always uncomfortable talking about the money aspect of taking care of sick people. "Anyway, unless some nurse screwed up, which is entirely possible, I don't get any of the fallout because the transplant unit isn't my direct concern. What was odd was that the head nurse up there came down to see me this morning and told me that the guy's mother had said that her son had been murdered."

"Murdered!" said Ken. "Right in the middle of the hospital?"

"Well, not your basic garden-variety murder with a gun or anything obvious like that, because no one could get in to do it, and even if they did, there are always lots of staff people floating around any ICU, especially the one on the transplant unit. I suppose you could actually kill someone on a unit—stranger things have happened—but they'd never be able to get away with it. Besides, the nurse said the mother is old and senile and barely speaks English and was all broken up over her son's death. It seems they were refugees and had a bad time during the war. World War II, that is."

Ken smiled. The fifteen-year difference in their ages was, at certain times, more apparent than at others.

Amanda thought back to the conversation late that morning when Bonita Elliott had come into her office apologizing for bothering Amanda with something so silly. But she was clearly concerned.

"What exactly did the mother say?" Amanda had asked.

"It was hard to tell," Bonita had said. "She has this incredibly thick accent, and I got the impression that she was speaking a combination of English and German or something, all in the same sentence. But she was *real* upset and she kept clutching at my arm *really* hard, Amanda. It was obvious that she wanted me to take her seriously.

"So I listened to her, but all she said was, 'They got my Aaron. They killed my Aaron. Finally they got him.' She went on and on like that, crying and on the verge of hysteria.

"One of the interns gave her a shot to calm her down and then someone came to take her home. We got her son wrapped up and sent to the morgue, and then I got busy and didn't think about it anymore. But it's been bugging me all weekend, Amanda. I mean, I'm sure it's nothing. I had talked to Mrs. Zurman often before, and it's obvious that she's not playing with a full deck. She's pretty fogged in and upset, but I can't stop thinking about it. I mean, what if . . ."

Bonita's voice trailed off and she shrugged.

Great, thought Amanda. Another murder at J. F. K. Memorial. Last year the chief of medicine was found with a scalpel imbedded in his throat, now patients were being offed. No wonder the public relations people were upset. She wasn't sure what to do. But when in doubt . . .

"Write an incident report," she told the head nurse. "It's hard to believe that a kidney transplant patient was murdered right in the middle of the hospital. It's so ghoulish that I don't *want* to believe it, but you had better write it up to cover your ass—to cover all our asses."

Amanda smiled to soften the sarcasm, but Bonita understood the need to protect herself legally. Every person working in every hospital in every state in the Union understood that need. "Write it in as much detail as you can, and use Mrs. Zurman's exact words as much as possible. Put it in his chart, and give me a copy.

"And, by the way, Bonita, I've asked to see a copy of Mr. Zurman's autopsy report just because it's so unusual to have a patient die so soon after a transplant. I'll let you know if anything looks fishy to me," said Amanda. "Thanks for telling me about this."

"So what do you think?" she asked Ken now.

"I'm not sure there's much to think," he replied. "A patient died; his senile old mother is hysterical; a nurse who likes drama thinks she hears something she probably didn't hear. Did you give the report to the lawyers?"

"Yes, but we have a few layers between the lawyers and us peons. Risk management, they call it now. But I sent it to the right people, along with a cover memo detailing what Bonita told me."

"So you're off the hook. Let's go to bed."

"Let's do," she agreed.

CHAPTER 3

Roberta Garfield let herself into the empty house and sank onto the couch with a sigh. Andy threw himself into her lap, scattering the handful of mail onto the living room carpet. She let it lie on the floor while she hugged and petted the dog. "I know you want to go for a walk," she said to him. "But it's so hot out there and I'm so exhausted. Just give me a few minutes, okay?"

She remained where she was, letting the air conditioner dry the sweat on her face while she stared vacantly at the envelopes on the floor. One was from the Smithfield Research Group, and she knew immediately that she didn't get the job. Job offers came by phone; rejections were mailed—if the places were nice enough to let you know at all.

She closed her eyes for a moment against the pain of another rejection, and when she opened them, dusk had fallen and Andy was whimpering seriously. "Why didn't you wake me up?" she said to the dog. "You must be ready to explode."

As she and Andy walked in the quiet evening, Roberta felt the despair returning. For a while, she had thought it would be all right. The new doctor who had replaced the surgeon who had operated on her three years ago was young and encouraging. This afternoon, when she had gone to the hospital for a routine checkup, she told him how depressed she had felt recently. She didn't tell him that she was exhausted all the time, because she believed it was only part of the depression—and this incredible heat that threatened to last forever.

"Roberta, you can't expect to go back to being your old self," Dr. Zyrwynsky had said. "You're whole now. You're complete. You're healthy."

"Then, how come I'm so miserable?" she had asked, hearing a whine creep into her voice despite her efforts to suppress it. "How come no one will give me a job? Why are most of my friends scared of me? Every man I meet leaves as soon as he finds out what I had done. One of them actually said that he was afraid I'd have a heart attack and die in bed."

She had begun to cry then, and could see right away that her tears made him uncomfortable. William Zyrwynsky, like most surgeons, hadn't been much help when it came to dealing with anything other than the mechanics of surgery. "Do you want to see a psychiatrist?" he had asked.

"I don't need a shrink," she had replied, crying even harder, hating herself for exposing her fear to a stranger, hating Dr. Zyrwynsky for his insensitivity. "I need a job. I need people to stop thinking of me as a cripple. I need a man to look at me as if I'm a woman. A sexy woman!"

And, she said silently to the brown and white Shetland sheepdog who was walking more calmly now that his initial frenzy to go for a walk had been satisfied, I need to stop feeling so tired and washed out all the time. "It's this damn heat," she said aloud, starting to feel dizzy again, refusing to acknowledge that twilight had brought with it a refreshing breeze and that her dizziness had nothing to do with the weather. "Let's go home and get supper."

The dog seemed to think that was a fine idea.

Roberta picked two tomatoes from her garden and snipped off a few fresh basil leaves. In the kitchen, while Andy sat with his rump on top of the air-conditioning vent in the floor, she sliced the tomatoes on a plate, shredded the basil leaves on top, and sprinkled the red and green salad with a little sugar. To this she added a liberal portion of shrimp salad she had bought the day before at Sutton Place Gourmet (Glutton Place, her friend Sally called it), put a Schubert piano sonata on the CD player, and sat down at the hand-crafted antique inlaid wood dining table that her mother had given her when her parents decided that their furniture was too old-fashioned.

The music and the presence of the dog lying quietly under the table, from time to time licking her bare feet, calmed her so that she felt strong enough to open the letter from Smithfield. This is what it said:

Dear Ms. Garfield:
Thank you for talking with us about a position with the Smithfield Research Group. We reviewed applications from many highly qualified individuals, including you.

Unfortunately we cannot offer you a position at this time. However, we were very impressed with your credentials and your demeanor, and would like to keep your materials on file in the event we have an opening for someone with your experience. Again, thank you for your time, and best wishes in your future efforts.

Demeanor. Christ! Roberta felt the familiar humiliation well up and turn to anger. Demeanor—what was this: grammar school where she was given an A in conduct but flunked arithmetic?

The rejection came as no real surprise, though. She knew she wouldn't get the job the minute she saw the president of Smithfield's face close when she told him about her operation.

"Why do you tell them?" Sally had asked. "After all, it's not as if it showed. And you're all better now. You're as healthy as most people, and you probably have less likelihood of dropping dead on the job than all those people who smoke and stuff themselves with doughnuts every morning and go to McDonald's for lunch."

"It's not dropping dead that they're concerned about," Roberta replied. "It's health insurance. No small company will hire me because the health insurance premium rates for the whole company will go up because of me; they think I'm a big risk—preexisting condition and all that. And no big company wants me because they think I won't be eligible for insurance."

"That's so unfair and it's not always true, is it?" said Sally.

"No, it's not fair. But who said life has to be fair?" Roberta replied. "It's also not true because some big, rich insurance companies would give me a policy—at greatly inflated rates and a big loophole for them to jump through if I ever have heart problems or anything even remotely connected to my heart. But it's not always the insurance companies; most of the time it's the employers."

She hadn't told Sally about the time she actually did get a job because she lied about her past health history. Well, she didn't lie exactly; she just neglected to mention that three years ago she had lain on an operating table at J. F. K. Memorial Hospital with a huge, gaping hole in her chest. Two weeks after she had gotten that job she had been fired because the giant computer that all the insurance companies were hooked into had revealed the fact that into that hole in her chest had been placed the heart of someone who had died too young, someone who had been perfectly healthy except for the little matter of a fatal car crash.

Her boss had looked like a wounded buffalo when he called her into his office. "You should have been honest with us," he had said. "You should have told us the truth."

"Would you have given me the job if you had known about my heart transplant?" asked Roberta.

"Of course," he said. "We're firing you because you lied, not because you're sick."

Using a choice selection of very short words, Roberta had called *him* a liar, challenged him to give her the job back if "being sick" wasn't a factor, and then, when he wouldn't reconsider, she described in her most colorful language what he could do with the job. She took quite a while telling him off. After all, she was a writer and could do it with a sophisticated vocabulary and perfect syntax.

Roberta had been furious at the unfairness of the discrimination, and she was still angry when she thought about the episode, but although she would never admit it to anyone, she wondered if perhaps that man had been telling the truth: that she hadn't been fired for having had a transplant—but for being naive enough to get caught in such an obvious deception. So now she told prospective employers right away—and had been unemployed for five years, two of them because she was too sick to work and three because people were scared to hire someone who couldn't get full health insurance coverage.

There was something else that she had never told Sally. She had never told anyone because no one had ever asked. Roberta laughed with a sound that didn't seem funny even to her own ears. Where did people think she had gotten the money to pay for the transplant? No one, not even those quintessential busybodies, the hospital social workers, had ever mentioned money.

Prior to the operation, Roberta had been too sick to work for two years and had no health insurance. And people with no money and no insurance received no transplanted hearts. The "green screen" she had heard it called. Even if you passed all the medical tests—and Roberta knew how stiff they were—

if you couldn't pay for the surgery and the care afterwards, too bad.

She had rented out her own house and moved in with her parents for most of those five years, at first because she was too ill and weak to take care of herself. It was only this past winter that the doctors and nurses on the transplant team had agreed that she was well enough to live alone, so as soon as the tenant's lease expired, she and Andy had moved back into her own little house on Grace Church Road.

And never once in all that time had anyone asked where she had gotten the money to pay for the incredibly expensive care. The hospital and doctors had simply accepted her checks, which never bounced. The bills came and she paid them on time. Money was never discussed.

The doctors and the people who worked at the organ bank made such a big deal out of the generosity of the donors. "Your new heart is free," they had told her over and over. "We don't charge people for organs. That would be unethical."

Big deal. Of course the heart was free. The person it had belonged to had no use for it. What was he going to do: set up an organ swap shop in the Great Beyond? It was all the rest of it that wasn't free. Medical care could cost her about $250,000 all told. Where did people think that an unemployed writer got a quarter of a million pictures of George Washington?

Roberta lay on the couch in her living room listening to the cicadas sing their song of summer, absently scratching Andy's ears. She opened her shirt as she did so often and looked at the long scar that ran down the center of her chest from the hollow of her throat almost to her waist. She put her hand under her left breast and felt the solid thud thud of the heart that should by all rights have been beating in someone else's chest.

That night Roberta dreamed she was dead. God, it was lovely.

It wasn't at all the way it had been when she was really almost dead. That time it had been screaming fear and clawing pain. This time it was peace.

When she woke from the dream, she looked out at the moon shining on Robert and Shelly's roof across the street and felt again the oppressive weight of the loneliness and unhappiness that had driven her into the oblivion of the dream. And so she let herself drift back into its comfort.

Only it was gone.

This time there were two puppies. One was bigger than the other, but they were both black and they lay sunning themselves on the stump of the black locust tree that had recently been cut down in her front yard. Only it wasn't her yard, and neither dog was hers. She saw that right away; neither puppy was Andy, who now lay stretched out next to her on the bed.

Nevertheless she had to kill one of them, so she chose the smaller of the two. It was an ordinary little pup, not much bigger than Andy as a baby.

She approached it gently. *Here doggie, doggie. Nice puppy*, she said in a soothing, coaxing voice. So perfidious.

Roberta picked up the little animal and stroked it for a moment, and then she began to strangle it.

But it wouldn't die. It didn't want to die.

It fought back, turning and twisting and scratching and clawing to get away from the terrible pressure around its neck.

Roberta couldn't understand it. The dog ought to want to die. At least it ought to be willing to accept its fate. It ought to have known that it was time for its life to end. Why was it fighting so?

The puppy escaped—or did she release the pressure and allow it to jump from her arms?—and ran into the garage, and now Roberta felt that it was maimed from what she had done to it. Maybe it had brain damage. Maybe it would be crippled. Maybe it was in pain. Surely it was terrified.

She ran into the garage, frantic now to get to it. To do what? To kill it? To save it?

To apologize to it. God, she needed to tell the dog that she was sorry, that she didn't mean for it to die, that the dog wasn't the one that needed to die. *Please, puppy, puppy, where are you? I know you're in here. Please come out and let me tell you how sorry I am. Please. I didn't mean to do it.*

Roberta sensed rather than heard the dog in a far corner of the garage and she knew that it was alive and meant to stay that way. Then she began to cry and knew that it was all hopeless. The dog didn't understand. It would never understand. Roberta knew she would never get over the guilt of having tried to kill it, of having hurt it. She went back outside and sat on the tree stump where it all started, put her head in her hands, and sobbed.

"Why are you crying?" her real dog seemed to ask as he rubbed his cheek into Roberta's tear-streaked face and pressed his body close.

Roberta put her arm around Andy, and with her heart pounding from the terror of the dream, lay watching the dawn change the moonglow on Robert and Shelly's house from glistening white to a dull grey.

This is too much, she thought and rolled over and felt under the skirt of the night table for the two small plastic bottles she kept there. Eighty capsules of oblivion and the detailed book of suicide instructions from the Hemlock Society, which espoused "peaceful self-deliverance" for people with cancer.

The fact that the capsules were there comforted her. She kept them in case this new heart should fail. She had long ago decided that she couldn't face another ordeal like the one she'd been through. Four times her first heart had stopped beating. Four times the doctors and nurses had rushed to her side, placed the paddles on her chest, sent the current coursing through her body, and jolted her back to life.

Twice she had been prepared for surgery, and twice it was canceled at the last minute, once because the new heart wasn't as good a match as the doctors had thought, and once because the donor family had changed their minds.

But the third attempt had been successful, and now she was perfectly healthy. She was forty-eight years old; she worked out at the gym three times a week, and she looked good. In fact, she was in better physical condition than she ever had been, and except for having to take antirejection drugs for the rest of her life and having to have a heart biopsy every six months or so, she was in good shape. Except for facing constant job discrimination that wasn't covered anywhere in any law. Except for the nightmares, of course, and the fatigue and depression that had become her constant companions in the past week or so.

But it wasn't time yet for the capsules, so she returned them to their hiding place and went back to sleep without explaining anything to the warm animal snuggled next to her.

CHAPTER 4

"That's one of the strangest things I've ever heard," Amanda said to Louise. "Buried the very next day? That's barely enough time to call all the relatives, let alone get them to come to Washington for the funeral."

Louise shrugged. She had just told Amanda that not only had there been no autopsy performed on Aaron Zurman, his body had been whisked out of the hospital morgue the very night he died. Apparently Mrs. Zurman had explained, through a relative who had accompanied her to help her wade through the intricacies of dying in a hospital, that her son was to be buried on Sunday.

"I got the impression," Louise went on, "that they would have put him in the ground the day he died except for some religious restriction. But maybe I'm getting the story wrong. It sounds kind of odd, so I'm probably mistaken. You could talk to the people on the transplant unit or in the morgue. They're the ones who dealt with the family."

"It doesn't really matter," Amanda replied. "All I wanted to do was read the autopsy report. I wonder if there's one on the other patient who died on the unit. I'll wander up there some time and see what the story is."

Amanda had not told her secretary what Bonita Elliott had said about Mrs. Zurman's accusations, since she hadn't given the incident much thought after the nurse had left her office. Far stranger things had happened at J. F. K. Memorial. In fact, after telling the story to Ken last night, she'd decided to put it out of her mind. But now, two days after she had filed a copy of the incident report and given another one to the chairman of the risk management committee, her radar turned on with a loud click. Hearing that Mrs. Zurman had taken her son's body out of the hospital morgue after business hours, her imagination began to fill with dark Victorian images, com-

31

plete with a steady rain and a sea of huge black umbrellas, of body snatchings and dead-of-night burials to cover the tracks of murder.

What a jerk you are, said the no-nonsense voice of what she always hoped was her better self. *Why are you looking for trouble?*

I am not looking for trouble.

Yes, you are. Look where your hand is.

Amanda's left hand was on the telephone, and her right hand was punching in the numbers of Eddie's page code.

I just want to have lunch with my buddy, said Amanda to the voice.

Bullshit. You want to start . . .

"Hi, Amanda," said Eddie Silverman into the phone.

"How'd you know it was me?" she asked.

"It's these new phones," he replied. "They tell you who's calling if it's from inside the hospital. How come you don't have one? I thought all the big cheeses got the expensive equipment right away."

"I forgot about that," Amanda replied. "Louise has one, but I don't. I guess the theory is that your secretary is supposed to screen your calls, so the 'big cheese' can be above all that. Anyway, do you want to have lunch?"

"Sure. In or out?"

"In" meant the hospital cafeteria which, except for the salad bar, was the same as hospital cafeterias everywhere: depressing food in a depressing atmosphere, but with the compensation of a foot-thick grapevine. "Out" meant Giovanni's, the Italian deli across the street where at lunchtime the customers were almost entirely hospital staff, and the gossip possibilities were almost as good as the cafeteria.

"In," said Amanda. That way she could avoid the temptation of her favorite Italian tuna, tomato, and provolone submarine sandwich and be virtuous at the salad bar. "Do you want to stop by my office or meet me there?"

"I'll meet you there at twelve-thirty," he said.

"Okay," replied Amanda and put down the phone, which rang immediately. Someone was calling on the line that came directly into her office, bypassing the hospital's central switchboard and Louise's desk. She had given the number only to Ken and a few close friends.

"Amanda Knight," she said into the phone in her crisp professional voice.

"Hi, Amanda, it's Lydia."

"Aha! Washington D.C.'s finest lady detective."

"I wish I had as much confidence in me as you do," said Lydia. "In the murder capital of the country, the unsolved cases are getting out of hand. God, this city is drowning in its own blood.

"But don't get me started. I didn't call to complain to you. I called to see when we could get together for dinner. Just us, not Ken and Sal."

"How about brunch on Sunday? We can go to that place way out on MacArthur Boulevard and maybe if it's not too hot we can eat outside."

"Okay," said Lydia. "What's the name of it, and is it going to cost me a week's salary?"

"I can't remember the name, but I know how to get there, so I'll pick you up about eleven-thirty, and it's not expensive during the day. It's one of those places that jacks up its prices the minute the sun goes down."

"I've never been able to understand that," said Lydia. "It's just a rip-off. It doesn't cost them any more to cook and serve the food at night than it does during the day."

"Lydia, you're too logical. You had it right the first time; it's a way to gouge the customers."

"Well, so you see, I *am* the best lady detective in Washington."

Lydia's voice didn't sound right. "Is something wrong? You sound down," said Amanda.

"Love troubles," replied Amanda's friend.

"Oh no. Did you and Sal break up?"

"More complicated than that. He wants to get married."

"Oh, God," said Amanda, who knew exactly why Lydia was more worried than ecstatic at having received a marriage proposal from the man she was crazy about. "You're right," she said. "We have to talk seriously without any men around."

"I've got to run, Amanda," said Lydia. "My illustrious partner, Paul, who really is the best detective in town, is hopping up and down here. See you Sunday. I'll wait for you downstairs so you don't have to look for a parking spot. Bye."

Amanda hung up the phone, looking forward to having

brunch with her friend. She could understand why Lydia was nervous about the idea of getting married—and possibly ruining the lovely relationship she had with Sal Mateo, who was the chief medical examiner for the nation's capital. Sal looked like a giant teddy bear and was very fond of telling people that most lovers' eyes locked over a glass of champagne, but his and Lydia's had done so over a corpse.

The conversation with Lydia started Amanda thinking about how her own relationship with Ken had changed in the two years that they had been married. In many ways it was better. The legal commitment she and Ken had made to each other, the one that Amanda saw as irrevocable, was a steadying influence on her fear of permanence. And not having to worry about money anymore was a relief; there was no denying that. Neither did she have objections to the beautiful house in Bethesda with the swimming pool in back and the woman named Lucille who came in twice a week to deal with the dust and the laundry.

But, by the same token, there was the physical presence of Ken every single day of her life. He was always *there*. She had to think about getting a real supper on the table every night—or at least arranging for them to eat. It wasn't that she loved him any less than she did before their wedding, it was just that it was hard getting used to his being around most of the time. The fact that he traveled so much on business didn't bother her. In fact, she enjoyed those times of solitude and believed that it eased the transition from single woman to wife.

And it wasn't as though Ken demanded her presence every moment. He was quite content if they spent entire evenings in separate rooms. But, like most men, he expected Amanda to arrange for his comfort, and she wasn't always pleased to do that. Take the matter of having dinner with Lydia, for example. Amanda would have done it any evening, but she suggested Sunday brunch because she knew that Ken would be out playing tennis and would eat lunch at his club. He wouldn't pout and say, "But what am I going to do about supper?" when she told him that she was eating out with Lydia.

He was perfectly capable of making a sandwich, or cooking real food for that matter, or getting himself to a restaurant. He did, after all, run a gigantic and immensely profitable corporation. And neither did he worry about her dinner plans when he worked late or had a business function that involved dinner. He had fended for himself perfectly well in the years between his divorce and his marriage to Amanda, but now that they *were* married, he assumed that things would be a certain way.

But then again, she loved the security of sleeping with him every night, of knowing that his body was always there next to her, of being able to reach out any time she wanted to feel the solid strength of his presence, of knowing that he wanted to be with her. It was nice. It was better than being alone.

She dialed Ken's private number, keeping her fingers crossed that he would be at his desk. "I just wanted to tell you how glad I am that I finally agreed to marry you and how much I love you," she said when Ken picked up the phone.

"You're just deciding that now?" he asked, not knowing whether to be pleasantly surprised at the compliment or puzzled at the way his wife's mind worked, a phenomenon that he had never fully understood.

"No, I figured that out a long time ago," Amanda replied. "I just wanted to make sure that you know it—that you're properly grateful."

"Oh, I'm grateful, all right," he said. "You always make sure I am. And I love you too, but why this sudden spurt of marital introspection—in the middle of the workday?" Ken was very single-minded about his work; messages of love and devotion were not generally a good cause for interruption.

"I don't know," she replied. "Just like that. Probably to delay doing these evaluations." She didn't want to tell him about Lydia's call and the thoughts it had stirred up.

And then he asked the question that men have been asking their wives since the beginning of time: "What are we having for dinner?"

Amanda laughed with a certain tone that Ken didn't know how to interpret. "Bread and water," she said. "Go back to work, and I'll see you later."

Amanda was torn between finishing the evaluations and going up to the transplant unit to find out why Aaron Zurman's body had been taken from the hospital and buried so quickly.

Leave it be, said the voice of practicality. *Undertakers probably work all shifts just like nurses, and even if he was murdered, which is just too farfetched to be true, the undertaker didn't have anything to do with it. So mind your own business, finish the evaluations, and don't you dare have dessert at lunch.*

Amanda sighed and did what she was told. As she was pushing open the door to the ladies room before going to the cafeteria to meet Eddie, she bumped into Evelyn Portman coming out. Ruth Sinclair was right. "Smashing" was the perfect word to describe the new chief pharmacist. She was taller than Amanda who was five feet eight. Evelyn had thick auburn hair, with precisely the right amount of grey sprinkled through it, cut into a feathery style that suited her perfectly. Her navy silk dress had wide lapels and gold buttons and was cinched at her slender waist with a navy leather belt. The dress cost a fortune, the gold earrings and necklace were real, and the navy and white spectator pumps looked like they were brand new.

"Hi, Evelyn," said Amanda. "How are you enjoying your new job?"

"Fine, thank you." Neither friendly nor unfriendly.

"I've been meaning to call you to see if you'd like to have lunch together soon. Maybe we can get out of the hospital and go someplace nice in the neighborhood," said Amanda. "Ruth's a wonderful person, but you know hospital food . . ."

Evelyn looked at Amanda expressionlessly. "I'm usually pretty busy at lunch," she said. "Maybe after Labor Day. I'll call you." She let go of the ladies room door so that Amanda had to catch it with her shoulder to prevent it from swinging shut.

"Kind of an arrogant type," she said to Eddie when they had set their trays down at a table. As they'd filled their plates at the salad bar, she'd told him about bumping into Evelyn.

Eddie shrugged. "Maybe she's banging the guy at St. Jude's every day at lunch."

"How did you know about that?" asked Amanda in surprise. "I just found out about it on Monday."

"Come on, Amanda, this is a hospital. Everyone knows everything about everyone, and they know it even before it happens—even if it's not true. Look what they know about us!"

Amanda laughed. Rumors about her and Eddie had waxed and waned for the six years that Eddie had been at J. F. K. Memorial. She had been a nursing supervisor when Eddie had come to the hospital, a green intern fresh out of medical school. He was new in Washington and seemingly friendless and alone. Her affair with Ken had been in one of its several shaky periods, and she was lonely and in need of male company.

The fact that she was eight years older than he and miles ahead of him in her career didn't seem to make a difference, and almost immediately they thought of each other as contemporaries. He was not like the dozen or so other interns who started at the hospital that July. He actually cared about his patients as people, and she never heard him refer to a patient as "the stomach in Room Two-twelve" or "the emergency gallbladder," as did most of the doctors and nurses. He referred to his patients by name, and Amanda liked that. She also liked his asking for help when he didn't know something, instead of bumbling through and causing trouble for everyone.

They'd started having long talks at Giovanni's and in the cafeteria, seeking each other out at lunchtime. Once in a while they had dinner together after work, but even after two years of increasing emotional intimacy, there had been no hint of sexual desire—from Eddie. Amanda would have gone to bed with him in a minute if they had not worked at the same hospital—and if she had felt any inclination on his part for a physical relationship. But she never had.

Glencora had an explanation for the absence of sexual sparks. "He's gay," she had said.

"Now, how do you know that?" Amanda had demanded, her heart sinking with disappointment. "You've never even met him."

"Amanda, don't be so naive. A good-looking guy who's smart, single, friendly, and sexy, who doesn't make a pass at an attractive woman he likes—what would you think? Does he have a girlfriend? Does he talk about women?"

Why had it bothered her so much that Glen thought he was gay?

"Oh, shit, Glen," she said, when the answer struck. "I'm in love with him. How can I be? I'm already in love with Ken."

Glencora didn't like Ken, so she ignored the last part of the remark. "Of course you're in love with Eddie. Any fool can see that. But what are you going to do about it? You could ruin a really nice friendship by trying to seduce him, or you could just go on as you are and consider yourself lucky."

So Amanda had done the smart thing, and the friendship had deepened and grown stronger. Their careers had flourished together. Eddie was now chief medical resident, which meant that he was assured a place in the private practice of his choice in Washington—a city where there were pots of money to be made as a physician.

One day Eddie and Amanda had eaten lunch in her office, surrounded by the fragrance of Italian sandwiches. He had been limp with fatigue, sprawled out on her office couch, his white shirt a wrinkled mess and his trousers splotched with blood and other stains that it was best not to think about. His eyes were closed, and thinking he was asleep, she prepared to tiptoe out of the office and let him sleep for a while.

"You know about me, don't you, Amanda?" he had asked out of the blue.

That was the first time he had ever mentioned it, and Amanda thought for a moment about playing coy, but that seemed pointless and childish—and too much effort, given the exhaustion etched onto his craggy features.

"Yes, I've always known," she replied. "How do you think I restrained myself from jumping on your bones all these late nights here and in the cafeteria!"

He had laughed, relieved that it was okay with her. He told her later that he had thought it would be, but still it was a relief to have it out in the open.

Now they laughed again over their salads at the capriciousness and frequent inaccuracy of the hospital rumor mill. She had been married for two years, and Eddie and Donald had been living together for three, although Eddie didn't advertise that fact. Yet the rumors of an affair between them persisted.

Amanda changed the subject first. "You're going to get an official thank-you note, but I just wanted to tell you what a nice time we had this weekend. Donald is a fabulous cook."

Eddie patted his stomach. "He is, isn't he? And you and Ken are good eaters. He appreciates that. He hates cooking for people who are always kvetching about calories and cholesterol.

"And I'll say something to you that you can't repeat: Ken James looks great in a bathing suit—for an old guy!"

Amanda choked on some lettuce. "Old! He's fifty-two—and you keep your grubby little paws off him. You have your own man!"

Eddie smiled. "Don't worry, Amanda. I'm not interested in Ken. I think in his heart of hearts he's a homophobe."

That stung, probably because there was some truth to it. "Eddie," she replied seriously, "I don't want to get into a discussion of homophobia with you right now. Just let me say that Ken believes in justice; he just has a hard time when faced with the reality of two homosexual men who are basically the same as he is. He has come to like you and Donald, and now he has no real way to set you apart as 'different.' You and Donald as people are no longer a part of some faceless group to whom he has to apply an *idea* of justice. You're my good friend, so an injustice done to you would be an injustice done to me. So that puts the whole thing in a different perspective. It's new and it makes him uncomfortable.

"And besides, Eddie my love, who gave up his tennis game on a Sunday morning last October and marched with us in the gay rights parade in damp, rainy, yucky weather, not to mention in front of TV cameras—when some of *your* faggy friends stayed home in bed because they didn't want to mess up their hair!"

Eddie said nothing for a minute. He didn't like Ken James. He thought that Amanda's husband was arrogant and supercilious, although he had to admit that Ken was obviously head over heels in love with Amanda and that his manner softened somewhat when he was with his wife. But he had to give the man credit: for a person in his position, marching in the gay rights parade took guts. Even though Amanda probably forced him to go, Ken was not one to give in if he had made up his mind not to participate.

He squeezed Amanda's hand. "I'm sorry. I didn't mean to hurt your feelings."

She squeezed back. "It's okay. Listen, speaking of minority groups, I want to ask you something about being Jewish. Actually, I guess it's about Judaism in general, not about your being Jewish."

"Oh, is the great atheist ready to get religion?" he asked.

"I am *not* an atheist," she replied. "I haven't actually decided that there is no God; it's just that I have a lot of serious doubts about what kind of God it is that makes people suffer the way you and I see them suffer all the time. . . .

"Oh, come on, don't get me started on that again. I want to know about Jewish funeral practices. For instance, is it usual to bury someone the very next day?"

"Amanda, in olden days—I mean three or four thousand years ago, not just before the Pilgrims came to the New World—if a person died early in the day, the burial took place the very same day. If he died late in the day, he was buried the next morning. Why do you want to know all this?"

"I'll explain in a minute," she replied. "But what about today? This is the age of embalming and refrigeration and people having to come from miles around to get to the funeral. There's no reason any longer to have to move so quickly."

"Amanda, there are basically two reasons why Jews do everything they do, at least all the Jewish things they do: it's either a law or it's a tradition—and sometimes both. There are all kinds of laws concerning death and burial: who is allowed to touch the body, how it has to be prepared for burial, and what can be done to it and what is not permitted. To tell you the truth, I'm a little rusty on that stuff, and I'd have to look it up if you really want to know. Why don't you ask the hospital rabbi?"

"I don't need to know all the religious details, and I hardly know the man," she replied. "Besides, I only want to know one thing really: why would a corpse be removed from our morgue on a Saturday night and then buried the very next day?"

"Amanda, you're making this sound like a body-snatching. It's really quite simple. If the man is an Orthodox Jew . . . Was he?"

"I don't know."

"Who was he? What are you talking about?"

"A guy named Aaron Zurman who died on the transplant unit on Saturday, whose old, senile mother said something strange to one of the nurses who told me, and I just sort of wondered . . . Oh hell, Eddie, I don't know what I'm wondering about. I'm always curious, you know that. So just tell me, okay?"

Eddie shrugged. He knew Amanda would keep hounding him until she got what she wanted. "Okay, let's assume the guy was very orthodox, very traditional. If he died on a Saturday, he couldn't be buried the same day even if he died early in the morning because it's against Jewish law to bury people on the Sabbath. So the funeral home wouldn't be allowed to pick him up until the Sabbath is over, which is officially when the first three stars appear in the sky on Saturday night."

"No kidding?" said Amanda. "That's really romantic. But what if it's cloudy? How do you know when the Sabbath is over?"

"It's all worked out ahead of time. There are Jewish astronomers who sit around and figure this stuff out," Eddie replied. "For every single Sabbath, there is an official starting time on Friday evening and ending time on Saturday evening. So it would be all right to pick up the body after the Sabbath is over in order to prepare it for burial the next day."

"But there's still the same question: why the rush? I can understand not wanting to keep someone in the hospital morgue, and I can see wanting to get them somewhere so they can be watched over by family, but why does the funeral have to be so soon?

"I've been to Jewish funerals," she added. "Sometimes they're two or maybe even three days after the person has died."

"Amanda, we're talking about only the more traditional practices. Not too many American Jews outside of New York City still live like that. And you certainly don't see many of them in Washington.

"Anyway, you want to know why. There are many reasons, but I was always taught that it was for humanitarian reasons: You have to provide enough time for the family to make funeral arrangements, but you don't want to delay so long that the mourners are in unnecessary pain from not having the dead person properly laid to rest. And of course, embalming is not permitted, so for aesthetic and health reasons, you can't let a corpse lie around for very long—even with refrigeration."

"Why isn't embalming allowed? I thought it's required by law."

"It's not absolutely required in most states. That's just a funeral directors' scam. Anyway, the casket is always closed at a Jewish funeral, so there's no reason to embalm. Jewish funeral directors understand all this, and don't give the families any trouble about embalming."

"How do you know all this stuff, Eddie?"

"Amanda, I'm gay. I go to a lot of funerals, and there have been some problems about morticians not wanting to handle the bodies of people who have died of AIDS."

Now it was her turn to squeeze his hand. "I'm sorry. I forgot. Although God knows how anyone could forget about AIDS for more than a minute." She paused for a moment and then asked, "So, why isn't embalming allowed?"

"There's a prohibition against mutilating the body even after death. The physical body is considered sacred; therefore it's against the law to cut into or alter it for no reason. I think Catholicism has much the same rule."

"Wait a minute," she said. "If it's against the law to mutilate the body, what about a kidney transplant? Wouldn't that be considered mutilation? Removing a vital organ is pretty drastic."

"In Jewish law there is no higher obligation than to save a life, so healing disease and preventing death would supersede the restrictions against mutilation. But then when the person has died, the issue of preserving life is moot, so the law against mutilation comes back into play. It's all pretty complex, and I'm not exactly an expert on the finer details. What's this all about, Amanda?"

"The patient's mother, this Aaron Zurman, said to Bonita Elliott that her son was murdered. Or maybe she didn't really say that; Bonita admitted that the woman barely speaks English, and she wasn't sure what she was saying. And then he was whisked out in the middle of the night and stuck into the ground so fast that I sort of got suspicious."

Eddie rolled his eyes. "Amanda, you have to stop reading those murder mysteries. This is a hospital. People die. And anyway, now that you know there's a perfectly good reason for taking Zurman out at night, you can give up your fantasies of murder and mayhem."

"You're right," she said. "Thanks for explaining it to me."

"You sound disappointed," he said. "You're a ghoul!"

"Right again," she replied with a grin.

CHAPTER 5

William Zyrwynsky and Eddie Silverman were pouring antibiotics and antihypertensive drugs into Roberta Garfield's veins. They were frantic.

"This shouldn't be happening," said Zyrwynsky. "I saw her just a few days ago. She said she was fine."

Well, she's not fine now, thought Eddie. She's dying. He wouldn't say the thought aloud, partly because to voice what he knew to be true was to make it come true, but mostly he refused to speak aloud because he believed that you never knew what comatose patients could hear. It was well known that hearing was the last sense to leave a dying person, and more than one patient had told him that they had heard everything when they were supposed to have been unconscious. Even patients deep under anesthesia were reported to have heard things that had been said in the operating room.

Besides, it wouldn't score him any brownie points to register a lack of confidence in the new chief of the transplant unit. He had come highly recommended to J. F. K. Memorial only two months before, and as far as Eddie could tell, he deserved the good reputation. He was an excellent doctor, but no amount of medical skill would save this dying woman.

Eddie thought that God himself could not save Roberta Garfield.

He had never seen such a rapid onset of massive infection. Roberta's body temperature was beyond the ability of ordinary thermometers to register it, and she was sweating profusely despite the automatic hypothermia blanket in which she had been wrapped in the emergency room. And they had no idea what was causing the infection.

Zyrwynsky must have been thinking the same thing. "Where the hell are those lab reports?" he said, more to himself than to anyone else. "If we knew what bugs were floating around

43

in there, we could get a little more specific with the drugs. Damn! I've never seen anyone get this sick this fast."

Bonita Elliott went off to pretend to call the laboratory. There was no point in actually nagging them. The people down there were working as fast as they could, and would get the results up to the unit the minute they knew anything. She knew that Dr. Zyrwynsky's anger wasn't directed at her. It was more a reflection of the frustration he felt at not being able to save his patient.

Bonita had gotten to know Roberta during the several speaking engagements they had done together on behalf of the hospital's transplant unit. She liked the woman, who was one of J.F.K.'s most successful and politically active transplant patients. They had gone to Richmond together only last week for a meeting at the United Network for Organ Sharing. The hospital had paid for the trip and had sprung for a big room at the new Omni International, which they had shared. After treating themselves to a huge dinner in one of the trendy new restaurants in an upscale neighborhood that had just a few years before been a slum of unused warehouses and whorehouses, they came back to the room and charged a movie to the hospital.

Then they had lain in the dark and talked far into the night. Roberta cared about the volunteer work she did for UNOS, and Bonita was always amazed about how open and frank she was with the audiences. She seemed to have no fear of revealing her feelings about the transplant, about having come so close to death, about her gratitude toward the donor family, and about living with someone else's heart. She seemed to believe that all the public needed was more information about organ transplantation, and people would line up in droves to donate everything in their bodies.

Bonita didn't believe that people were that altruistic. "A few months ago I had to go through that whole rigmarole of having my picture taken and eyes tested to get my driver's license renewed," she had said to Roberta that night in Richmond. "Now they ask everyone who gets a license if they want to sign up for organ donation—you know, in case you get creamed on the highway. I told the woman at the counter that I was already a donor, but I decided to hang around for a while to see how many people signed up. Guess how many?"

"Zip," Roberta had replied.

"Right," said Bonita. "People aren't as good as you want them to be."

"I don't buy that," Roberta had replied. "Soliciting organ donation like that is going about it the wrong way. I mean, think about the kind of mood people are in by the time they get to the head of the motor vehicle line. They wouldn't give a penny to a little beggar child.

"Besides, look where they are. They're in an automobile environment with safety posters all over the place. Then some clerk says, in essence: 'Sooner or later you're going to disregard our warnings, or some drunk is going to smash into you, and there you'll be, spread out all over the interstate, and we'd like to come over and cut out your heart and kidneys and your eyes.' "

"That's gross," Bonita had replied. "They don't do it that way. If anything, the clerk is bored and doesn't seem to care one way or the other. They certainly don't make a big pitch for donation."

"No, but I'll bet that a lot of people won't donate because they can't bear to think of themselves squashed like bugs on the highway. Or they have some kind of vague idea that that's the way it will be. Or they're in a rush to get out of the motor vehicle bureau and don't want to make that kind of decision in that atmosphere. Or they don't understand what the clerk is asking. Whatever—it's the wrong time and place to recruit donors. No wonder hardly anyone signs up.

"The public needs to be really educated about organ donation," she had said. "People have all kinds of strange ideas about why they 'can't' donate. It's weird that otherwise reasonable people think that they can't get into heaven if they don't have all their body parts, or if they think about donation, somehow they'll hasten their own death."

Bonita understood what she meant. She had heard dozens of irrational reasons for not donating. "You know," she had told Roberta that night, "last week when Bill Zyrwynsky asked a man for his sister's kidneys, the guy accused him of murder. He made a real scene; we had to call security to get him out of the hospital. It gave me the creeps—like he was calling us grave robbers."

"All that ignorance makes me so mad. I'd like to slap some sense into their heads. Did you know that as of the beginning of this year, more than twenty thousand people in this country were waiting for organs—and those are just the ones that UNOS and the transplant network knows about. God knows how many thousands of others there are. Just because people are so stupid and insensitive."

The two women lay silently in the darkened hotel room, and then in a soft voice, with no trace of the outrage of a moment before, Roberta said, "But they're afraid, and I understand that too."

Bonita remembered the passion in Roberta's voice as she had said that, and she remembered how eloquently she spoke to audiences about her own experiences with heart disease and the need for donors. And now she lay dying—and no one knew why.

"What did the lab say?" asked Dr. Zyrwynsky as he and Eddie Silverman approached the nurses' station.

"Nothing," said Bonita, not really lying. "Give them a chance, Bill. Those people bust their asses for us."

"I know, I know. I'm sorry," he said. "Maybe I should call and apologize," he added, reaching for the phone. "I don't want to get them aggravated with me. After all, I'm the new kid on the block."

"They're not mad at you, Bill," said Bonita, pushing his hand away from the phone. "But you have to give them time."

Zyrwynsky smiled a little. "I'm not used to working in a place where people are actually nice to each other. Johns Hopkins is such a mean-spirited environment." He sighed. "Did Roberta seem okay to you when the two of you went to Richmond? Sometimes women tell each other things that they don't tell their doctors, you know—that maybe they don't think are important."

"She seemed depressed and kind of tired," said Bonita. "But I'd be depressed too if I were unemployed for that long. And she gets very worked up over these UNOS meetings. She said she was too tired to run the next morning, but I chalked that up to the heat and the fact that we had been up till all hours talking."

Zyrwynsky sighed again. "I've got to get something to eat and some coffee before I pass out here. We'll keep pouring the Keflin into her, although if she has viral cardiomyopathy again, a whole truckload of Keflin won't do any good. I'll be in the cafeteria. Page me the second anything happens."

Eddie Silverman left with Zyrwynsky, to attend to his other patients, and Bonita went over to sit by Roberta's bed for a few minutes. The change was shocking. If she hadn't known who was lying there, she would not have recognized the woman who only last week had sat across the dinner table from her, a little flushed from a half bottle of wine, but gloriously alive.

The woman in the bed was deathly pale, but with the bright spots of color on her face that were indicative of dangerously elevated blood pressure. Roberta was a big woman, tall and husky, but now she looked small and lost, hidden as she was in the hypothermia blanket among the tubes and machinery that monitored her every body function. She was clad only in a thin hospital johnny and nothing else. Bonita got a sheet and covered Roberta's feet, leaving the blanket unimpeded. She checked the cardiac monitor and noted the unnaturally fast but still regular beat of the heart. The alarm would go off if Roberta slipped into cardiac arrhythmia or ventricular fibrillation.

What really worried Bonita, though, was the fact that Roberta's kidneys were barely working. The drip of dark yellow urine that flowed through the catheter from her bladder to the plastic bag hanging under the bed was much too slow. Above Roberta's head were two bottles of fluid flowing into the vein of her left arm. One contained dextrose and water, and the other was a solution of Keflin, the antibiotic that was effective against a wide range of bacteria. It was one of the most potent broad-spectrum antibiotics around, and doctors often used it when they didn't know exactly what they were trying to kill. Bonita imagined it as spraying shotgun pellets at noises in the night instead of taking careful aim with a rifle at a known intruder.

But as Dr. Zyrwynsky said, if Roberta had another bout of viral cardiomyopathy, the disease that had slowly destroyed the muscles of her heart five years ago, only another transplant could save her. As Bonita well knew, Roberta had about as much chance of being eligible for another heart as she had of becoming President of the United States.

Bonita checked all the plastic tubes and lines that connected Roberta to the most modern life-support system available and then slipped her own hand into the pale one lying limp on the sheet. She closed her eyes for a moment and was surprised to find tears sliding out from under her lids.

She sensed someone watching her, opened her eyes, and saw Amanda Knight regarding her curiously. Shit! The director of nursing had caught her with her emotional pants down.

"Don't be embarrassed," said Amanda. "I've always thought that this business of not getting involved with your patients was utter nonsense. If you don't care about them, how can you care *for* them?"

Bonita smiled gratefully. "True, but you're not supposed to sit around sniveling over everyone."

"But Roberta Garfield isn't just anyone, is she? I understand the two of you did a lot of work together for the transplant unit," said Amanda.

"I liked her," said Bonita. "She gave a lot of herself. She really cared about the program."

Amanda noticed that Bonita was speaking of Roberta in the past tense, but she said nothing. It was her experience that when the nurses talked like that about a patient, they had unconsciously given up and knew that death was inevitable.

"Do you have time to talk for a few minutes, or are you too busy now?" asked Amanda.

"It's okay. I just need to be where I can keep an eye on Roberta."

"I read your incident report and sent a copy to the risk management people," said Amanda.

"What did they say? They probably think I'm crazy."

"I haven't heard a word," replied Amanda. "I didn't actually hand it to them personally. I sent it through the interoffice mail, but my guess is that someone glanced at it and then filed it somewhere very deep. It probably didn't get a second thought."

"But you thought about it," said Bonita.

"Actually, I did," Amanda replied, a little sheepishly. "And then I stopped thinking about it after I talked to Dr. Silverman and he explained why a Jewish person's body would be taken out of the hospital so soon and why the family would refuse an autopsy. But now with this . . ." Amanda waved her hand vaguely in Roberta's direction.

"I know," said Bonita, who was much more worried than she wanted to admit to her boss. "This is the third transplant patient to go bad when there was no reason for it."

Amanda winced at the expression. She hated it when doctors and nurses talked about patients "going bad," as if they were vegetables left out in the sun too long. Everyone used the expression. Even she did, when she let herself lapse into lazy speech patterns, and it disgusted her.

"What do you think is going on?" she asked.

"I wish I knew," said Bonita. "First, there was that guy, what's-his-name, the construction worker, whose brother gave him a kidney. It was an almost perfect match, about as close as you can get without being an identical twin, but he rejected it in four days—and so suddenly and massively that we almost didn't believe it. That kind of rejection hardly ever happens anymore. I know it sounds almost complacent, but now that we have cyclosporine, and we've done so many kidneys, it's become routine. It's like having a post-op appendectomy die. It just doesn't happen—at least not on day four.

"Bill, I mean, Dr. Zyrwynsky, was all broken up about it. It wasn't a real good way for him to start a new job. Then Aaron Zurman died *two* days post-op the same way: sudden massive rejection."

"But he got a cadaver kidney, right?" asked Amanda.

"True, but it still shouldn't happen," said Bonita. "Unless, of course . . ."

"He wasn't murdered," said Amanda. "Think about it. How could anyone have gotten into the unit to do it? And even if they could—after all, this isn't an armed camp—there was no sign that he was murdered: no knives, no guns, no nothing."

"I know," said Bonita. "I guess I just hate to face the fact that maybe we're doing something wrong. *Very* wrong. And now there's Roberta."

"But that didn't happen here," replied Amanda. "It's not the same thing at all. She's not connected in any way with the other two." Amanda was afraid that Bonita would start blaming herself for what was happening to her friend, and that would lead to an erosion of self-confidence, which could undermine her ability to take care of patients. Amanda did not want that to happen to Bonita. Good nurses were too hard to find.

"Just the same . . . Hang on a minute. I think this is the lab."

Bonita picked up the phone in response to the unit secretary's signal. "Hi, Dave. Got something for me?"

"Hang on to your hat, Bon-Bon," said David Brandon, the lab technician. "Your lady has galloping PCP."

"No kidding! Are you absolutely positive?" asked Bonita. *Pneumocystis carinii* pneumonia was seen almost exclusively in AIDS patients, and Bonita would have bet a year's salary that Roberta Garfield, who was always complaining about not getting any sex, didn't have AIDS. "Are you doing . . ."

"I'm way ahead of you, Bon-Bon," said Dave. "We're running the Western Blot right now."

"Thanks, Dave," she said. "It's nice to deal with someone who has a brain. But if you call me Bon-Bon one more time, I'm coming down there and stick one of your big glass beakers right where it'll hurt the most!"

She heard a lewd chuckle on the other end of the line. "Just be gentle with me, Tootsie Roll," he said and hung up.

"Asshole," she muttered as she punched in the numbers of Dr. Zyrwynsky's page code. He answered right away. "Roberta has pneumocystis," she told him. "I know, I can't believe it either," she said in response to his exclamation of surprise. But I've never known Dave Brandon to screw up. He's running an AIDS test to double-check."

As Bonita talked to the transplant physician on the phone and then made another call, Amanda heard the patient moan. Roberta's eyes fluttered open, and she looked wildly around the room and struggled to sit up. Amanda leaned over the side rails and put her hand gently on Roberta's shoulder. "Lie still, Roberta. You have an IV in your arm. You're in the hospital and we're taking care of you. You'll be fine, but you have to lie quietly."

Roberta relaxed her body but looked worried. "Andy," she said. "Where's Andy?"

"Who's Andy?" asked Amanda. "Do you want me to call Andy for you?"

"Andy, Andy, where's Andy?" Roberta said over and over. She began to thrash her head back and forth on the pillow, and it took all of Amanda's strength to hold her still.

Suddenly Bonita was at her side. "It's okay, Roberta. Andy is fine. He's with your parents. Can you hear me, Roberta? It's Bonita. Andy is fine. Your parents are taking care of him."

Roberta relaxed and sank back into unconsciousness. "I hope she heard me," said Bonita. "Andy's her dog; she lives alone and she was always so worried about what would happen to him if she got sick again. He's such a sweet dog; he's going to be so lonesome without his mom."

"You have your hands full here, so I'm going to leave you alone now," said Amanda. "Do you need anything from me?"

"Not right this minute," said Bonita. "But maybe later you could find out why they're giving me such a hard time in Pharmacy. There's someone new running the place, and she's got all these bureaucratic rules. Like, for instance, I just ordered ten 5 cc vials of Bactrim, and the clerk put me on hold and then said I could have only two now, and they'd send the other eight up later.

"They're just making life hard for everyone doing it in two batches like that, and I'm afraid they'll forget and then I'll have to call again because we'll run out or Dr. Zyrwynsky will want to up the dose or something. It's just a nuisance having all these stupid rules."

"Are two vials enough to get you started?" asked Amanda, not knowing why she was asking, since she had no jurisdiction over another department.

"Oh sure, it's plenty for a few hours," replied Bonita. "It's just that the bureaucracy gets me down sometimes. Things are never easy. Thanks for your help."

"I didn't do anything," said Amanda wryly, half to herself, as she pushed through the double swinging doors that separated the transplant from the other surgical units on the floor.

You wouldn't know what to do if a sick person jumped up and bit you on the ass, said the part of herself that occasionally missed doing bedside nursing. *You don't even understand how all these fancy machines work*, the voice added.

You're right, she retorted. But I could learn if I had to, and I know how to run the nursing department of the whole hospital, and I run it damn well.

The truth was that on the rare occasions when Amanda had to pitch in and take care of sick people—usually when

Washington was paralyzed by an inch and a half of snow that any normal city would take in stride—she didn't like it much. Every now and then she could see that she had been able to help someone feel better, to speed recovery, or to alleviate pain. But for the most part, it was boring, repetitive work that didn't require a college education and two masters degrees.

On the other hand, the feeling of truly being able to help someone was like nothing else. It meant something. It was good and satisfying. Amanda sighed. Those occasions were too rare, and interspersed among the satisfying moments was an inordinate amount of frustration, annoyance, and the unpleasantness of having to deal with idiotic, unthinking people. Amanda sighed again, almost a shudder this time; if the general public realized the disasters that could happen in hospitals—and frequently did—they would choose to stay home and have their surgery on the kitchen table. Hospitals were dangerous places.

Amanda remembered a conversation she and Glencora had had a long time ago. "There you are, lying in bed, stark naked except for that stupid little hospital nightshirt that barely covers your ass, in a room that doesn't even have a lock. Anyone could come in and do anything they wanted," said Glen.

"Come on, Glen, there are people all over the place watching the patients," she had replied, knowing as she said it that it wasn't true. Many times, maybe most times during the evening and night shifts, the patients *were* basically unguarded.

"Bullshit," said Glen. "Remember when you burned your hand?"

Involuntarily Amanda looked down at her right hand, which was smooth and unscarred. Six years ago she had spilled a pot of boiling water on it, and as she remembered the long and painful treatment, it seemed almost miraculous that the skin had grown back as healthy as it had ever been. She had spent one night in the hospital after Glen had rushed her to the emergency room.

"Remember when I came back later that night to visit you?"

"Not really," Amanda replied. "I was pretty out of it. All those delicious drugs."

"Well, that's exactly my point," Glen had said. "I just waltzed right into your room. It was late in the evening and there was no one around. No one asked who I was. No one said anything. And there you were, all alone in there, snoring away . . ."

"I was not snoring," said Amanda indignantly.

"Actually, you were," replied Glen. "I stood there and watched you for a while, amazed at how much noise you were making. But that's my whole point. You were out cold, and no one knew I was there. I could have done anything I wanted to you. If I were a man with nasty, sick little sexual proclivities . . ."

Glen had left the rest to her friend's imagination. Now, walking back to her office, Amanda's thoughts drifted to what might have happened to Aaron Zurman. Even though he'd been in the intensive care unit, something could have happened to him in the same amount of time that, not twenty minutes ago, she had stood alone at Roberta's bedside before Bonita had come over to reassure the patient about her dog. A quick injection of something was possible. You could even slip it into the intravenous tubing, and it wouldn't leave a needle mark. Although in Aaron Zurman's case, one more needle puncture wouldn't have made any difference. All hospital patients looked like pincushions by the time they were discharged.

Aaron Zurman wasn't murdered, said the voice of logic, *so just forget it and go back to taking care of your department.*

All right, all right, she said testily, as she settled down to compose a recruitment brochure in an attempt to solve the chronic shortage of nurses at J. F. K. Memorial. But how do you know? He *could* have been killed.

Amanda was trying to think of reasons that J. F. K. Memorial was a better place for nurses to work than other hospitals in Washington. She had to come up with something for the brochure before the meeting with the advertising people. (*No, you cannot say that it's because you are the most wonderful boss who ever lived!* chided her conscience.)

Louise buzzed to say that Betsy Murdock was on the phone. "Hello, Betsy," she said to the supervisor for whom she had just recommended a raise.

"Hi, Amanda. Do you have some time to talk? I think we have a serious problem."

"That's good. We haven't had one for a full five or ten minutes! Do you want to talk in the office or over lunch?"

"Your office," replied the nursing supervisor. "This has to be kept quiet."

"Come on down now, then," Amanda told her while she pictured a black cloud of doom forming above her head. Unlike some of the other supervisors, Betsy usually solved her own problems, so if she was bringing one to Amanda, it meant that it was serious.

She was right. The supervisor's normally placid and pleasant expression now registered worry. Betsy Murdock was in her early fifties and, like thousands of other women, had returned to work when her youngest child entered high school. Four years ago she had applied for one of the staff nurse positions that were always available in any hospital in any American metropolitan area, and Amanda knew right away that she would quickly promote this woman who had the precise combination of brains, compassion, and common sense that Amanda wished she could instill in all nurses. She remembered telling Ken about Betsy's job interview. "I felt like handcuffing her to the chair," she had said, "just to make sure she accepts my offer. If she decides not to take the job, I'm going to go to her house and kidnap her!"

But Betsy had taken the job, and now she was supervisor of all the surgical units in the hospital. She flopped down on the couch in Amanda's office and groaned with the pleasure of sitting on a comfortable piece of furniture. "I might as well just blurt it out," she said. "There's no way to ease into this."

Amanda said nothing, but the black cloud grew more ominous.

"Someone is stealing narcotics, and they're doing it in the most despicable way."

"Damn," said Amanda. "The old give-half-to-the-patient-and-save-half-for-yourself trick?" she asked.

Betsy nodded. This method of stealing hospital narcotics was one of the most common—and one of the most difficult to stop. It was also supposed to be prevented by unit-dose medication administration. No such luck.

When Amanda had first begun nursing school medications would come up to the patient floors in large stock bottles and vials, and nurses would take the correct number of tablets out of the giant bottle and put them into little paper cups and give them to patients. In the case of an injectable drug, the nurse would fill a syringe with 1 or 2 cc from a common bottle that contained 50 or 100 cc. Stealing was rampant. Sometimes it was "benign" rather than malicious. It was never right, but Amanda could understand a nurse helping herself to a handful of tetracycline for a child at home with bronchitis when such drugs were still horribly expensive. She herself had taken her share of hospital aspirin and vitamin pills.

But stealing narcotics was a different story. She remembered an incident many years ago when she worked at her first staff job. One of the nurses had a thriving business going. She would transfer small amounts of Demerol, Dilaudid, and other potent painkillers from the large stock bottle to a smaller vial and sold them to God-knew-which-junkies at a clear profit for herself. She had apparently been doing it for years before she was caught.

Unit dose was supposed to change all that. Drugs—pills, tablets, liquids, and injectables—all came individually wrapped from pharmaceutical manufacturers, and all the hospital pharmacy had to do was stick on a label with the patient's name and the time at which the drug was to be administered. Every patient in the hospital had a little drawer in the nurses' medicine cart with a day's supply of each drug. The system was supposed to be foolproof and theft-proof, and it had cut down a great deal on errors because all a nurse had to do was be able to read the name of the patient and the name of the drug. Of course, she had to give that drug to the correct patient, and Amanda shuddered to think how many times patients swallowed drugs that were meant for someone else. But that was a problem of stupidity and carelessness. Betsy was sitting on her couch telling her about pure maliciousness.

Amanda knew almost without being told what was happening, because it was an old trick, developed almost immediately after the advent of the unit-dose system. A nurse who wanted to steal narcotics could insert a hypodermic needle into the individual vial of, say 100 mg of Demerol, and draw up part of the dose to give to the patient. The rest of it she could do with as she pleased. She could take it into a bathroom and inject it into her own vein. Or she could put it into a rubber-stoppered larger vial.

There were variations on this ugly theme. A nurse could steal an entire unbroken vial of a drug, which would be worth far more on the black market, and give the patient nothing more than sterile water. She could give the patient part of the dose ordered by the physician, save the rest for another patient and do the same thing, and then steal the leftover vial. Or she could give a patient an injection of absolutely nothing—just stick him with a needle.

But whatever the method, the patient wasn't getting the full dose of the drug needed to control pain, and the nurse was violating the sacred trust placed in her by the patients who depended on her honesty and professionalism. A nurse who stole narcotics from patients in pain needed to be strung up by the thumbs—or preferably, a more delicate part of her anatomy—and left to rot.

Betsy felt the same way. "When we catch this bitch, I am personally going to drag her by the hair to the electric chair," she said to Amanda.

"Not if I get to her first," Amanda replied. The two women smiled at each other to ease the tension of their rage, and then they got down to the business of discussing who the culprit might be and how they could go about setting a trap.

═══ CHAPTER 6 ═══

That evening as Amanda lay in a tub filled with cool water reading a novel, three people—two men and a woman—sat on the side porch of the woman's house in a housing development of mini-mansions in Potomac, Maryland. The shorter of the two men had been depressed and frightened as he drove through the quiet summer streets to this meeting. He regretted the death of Aaron Zurman. It was true, he thought, Zurman was becoming a nuisance, a dangerous nuisance, and his death had been necessary both for the party and for the plans of the triad, but he wondered if there hadn't been another way to have eliminated the doctor. Death was so . . . excessive.

The woman's husband was out of town, and the maid had been dismissed for the evening to give the three of them the privacy they needed, so the woman herself had to mix the drinks and fill the ice bucket. While the woman was in the kitchen, the other man said to the short one, "Nice house, huh? Her old man must be cleaning up."

The short man shrugged. "Yeah, great." He didn't like the house or the neighborhood. These tract mansions had become all the rage in suburban Washington where people would pay almost any amount of money to buy a big house, no matter how badly it was built, as long as it was in the right ZIP code. And 20854 was one of the zippiest.

The dwelling he now sat in seemed to have been put together with paper clips and chewing gum. The brick facing was only for show. Each "brick" was only an inch thick and wouldn't support the weight of even these flimsy walls. The walls themselves were made of the cheapest wallboard, and when a toilet was flushed overhead it sounded like Niagara downstairs.

The woman came onto the porch with a cheap plastic bowl filled with pretzels and dropped it on the glass-topped wrought-iron coffee table. He knew how expensive the table and the matching chairs and sofa were, and it amused him to contrast the costliness of the furnishings with the rude meagerness of the food offered.

"What's the matter, Mark?" she asked. "You look like you could use a good high enema."

Mark Cipriotti blinked and looked at the woman with a puzzled expression. He said nothing.

"Full of shit, that's what you are," she said and laughed in a way that reminded Cipriotti of a woman he had met when he was fifteen years old and driving with his friends to the lake every Saturday night to drink beer, pick up girls, and make general fools of themselves. The woman had been a waitress at one of the lakeside restaurants. He thought of her as an older woman, although she was probably no more than thirty. She had very dark hair, wore very red lipstick and lots of heavy blue eye shadow, and she opened the top of her uniform to the extent that would have a maximum effect on fifteen-year-old hormones. He used to sit there staring at the tops of her breasts until his aching balls forced him into a booth in the men's room where two or three strokes on his cock would be enough to bring him to miserable lonely orgasm.

That waitress used to laugh like this woman, as she watched him and his friends hobble off to the john, the front of their pants bulging with the desire she had created.

It was not a pleasant laugh.

Sarah Castle was not a pleasant woman. Mark knew she saw the thin film of sweat on his upper lip, and he saw the contempt on her face. Not a pleasant person at all. Frightening, in fact. He shivered a little, despite the warmth of the evening, thinking about what had happened to Zurman, thinking how easily Sarah Castle accepted it.

"Let's get on with it," she said to Cipriotti and Allen Hackett, president of the Montgomery County Council. He intended to stay president for at least a decade, now that Zurman was out of the way. "How close are they to signing?"

"Before this happened, they had their pens out ready to seal the deal," said Hackett about the developers who planned to build an office and hotel complex at the southern end of the county. Ten million square feet of space was involved, as were thousands of new jobs—as well as crushing traffic jams, the bulldozing of old, established neighborhoods, and the eradication of an old and gentle way of life in that part of the county.

Zurman had exploited the anger and fear of the residents and whipped opposition to the developers into a frenzy. He organized demonstration marches, got people to sit down in front of rush-hour traffic on Georgia Avenue, got arrested for civil disobedience twice—and had his name in the newspaper two or three times a week. The three people on the porch did not believe that Zurman cared one way or the other about the new development; he was simply using the issue to get on the fast track to a seat in Congress next year.

They had no illusions about Zurman's political zeal; they knew he would use whatever information he needed to stop the development, to expose the relationship between these three and the developer, and to carry himself to Capitol Hill and a hero's victory. This could not be allowed to happen. Now it would not happen.

"They're feeling a little skittish now," Hackett went on. "They think that maybe Zurman's death will galvanize this grassroots movement and then there will be more opposition than ever."

"Bullshit," replied Castle. "The people who live downcounty don't care about anything more than getting reservations at whatever this year's trendy restaurant is and getting their kids into private school. You'll see—the minute they get over the shock of Zurman's death, they'll cave in and sell those houses they say they care so much about. After all, they're going to get top dollar for them, and they ought to be grateful for that in this soft real estate market."

"I'm not so sure," said Hackett. "This could backfire on us. You know, Zurman being a doctor and a refugee and all. And having had a kidney transplant . . ." His voice trailed off. He didn't know what he meant. He knew only that he was plagued by second thoughts. By third, fourth, and fifth thoughts. He knew that he didn't sleep well anymore, and he knew why.

"What the hell has all that got to do with anything?" asked Sarah Castle. She was genuinely at a loss to explain why these two men were behaving so strangely. She thought of them as wimps. "Weenies," her teenage daughter would call them.

She did not understand human sympathy, and it never once occurred to her that Zurman's death might produce a sympathetic backlash. She was not able to make the connection between the death of Zurman and the reluctance of the developers to sign the agreement. The political and personal obstacles that Zurman created were gone now, and she could see no reason for the developers' new balkiness. Not understanding human nature is a fatal flaw in a politician, but Sarah Castle couldn't recognize that defect in herself.

CHAPTER 7

Amanda lay in a lounge chair on the wide flagstone patio between the house and the swimming pool. Her eyes were closed and she hovered on the edge of sleep. The heat wave had finally broken and she let the warm, dry breeze that had blown in from Canada during the night wash over her. The Sunday papers were stacked neatly on a glass-topped table beside the chair, but she made no attempt to read them. She was exhausted, and the thought of devoting energy to Lydia's conflict about getting married tempted her into a deeper sleep. Marriage was a sore subject with her this morning.

Neither did she feel much like playing hostess to Lydia and Sal for the rest of the afternoon and evening. When she had told Ken that she and Lydia were having brunch together, he suggested that the detective and the medical examiner be invited to a cookout, and Amanda had agreed enthusiastically, so she had called Lydia and reversed the driving arrangements and issued the invitation for swimming and a grilled meal afterwards.

Ordinarily she would look forward to such an evening, but the fight with Ken last night, and the energetic way they had made up, had left her emotionally drained and seriously short of sleep.

It was a stupid fight, one of their most childish. To make matters worse, it had taken place in a fast-food restaurant within earshot of half the other patrons in the place.

"Don't eat this shit," she had said to Ken as he pulled into the Roy Rogers on Wisconsin Avenue near Van Ness Street. "You'll clog your arteries. I'll make you a peanut butter and jelly sandwich when we get home."

It was the wrong thing to have offered.

"Great compromise," he had replied sarcastically. "Peanut butter instead of fried chicken. I'm eating here. You can sit in

61

the car if you want to." And he had gotten out of the car, closed the door none too gently, and stalked into the restaurant.

Amanda had planned to sulk in the car while her husband stuffed himself with food that she knew would give him pangs of remorse before they even got home. The idea of moral superiority was pleasant to contemplate, and she smiled smugly to herself. The feeling lasted about two minutes—driven away by her rumbling stomach and anger at Glencora. She decided to blame her friend for what was rapidly taking on the characteristics of a comic opera. Mozart could have composed some spectacular music for this stupid libretto, she thought, as she got out of the car and followed her husband inside.

"I'll pay," she had said to Ken as he took out his wallet when they reached the cashier. She knew it would irritate him. He didn't mind that she earned a good salary; he just couldn't get it into his head that the man didn't always have to pay. Usually, she didn't make a fuss, but this time she took the wallet out of his hand, shoved it back into his pocket, and said, "I *said* I'll pay." She was really angry now.

They sat in the ugly plastic booth, grossly overdressed for a fast-food place—she in a silk dress with multicolored tulips on it, he in one of what he called his "going to church suits" and an expensive tie that she had bought for him at Bloomingdale's—not on sale. She waited for him to drop a piece of the greasy chicken on his tie. They devoured the chicken and french fries, glaring at each other, neither one willing to admit how much they liked it—and how much more satisfying it was than the meal they had just eaten at Glencora Rodman's house, the meal that Glen had spent all day preparing.

"I told you to eat something before we left," she had said. "You've been there before; you know the portions are too small."

"Too small!" Ken had retorted. "Even Shadow wouldn't be satisfied. How does she expect to keep her new boyfriend happy if she feeds him enough for a goldfish. Of course, he has the brain of a goldfish, so maybe he won't notice that he's being starved!"

The annoying thing was that Ken was right on all counts. Glen was an excellent cook, but she believed that quantity spoiled quality and consequently served portions that satisfied no one but herself. And Glencora, with an IQ that was off the charts, was undeniably attracted to big dumb men who were easy to control. They evidently satisfied her emotionally and sexually, but they didn't add much to the conversation at dinner.

The boyfriends all left eventually, probably because Glen wasn't rich enough to turn them into real gigolos, and they got sick of being patronized at the same time as they were thrust into her group of painfully trendy friends. And, Amanda admitted to herself, they were probably starving to death.

But she refused to concede any of this to Ken, and she argued against his threat never to go to Glen's house for dinner again. "Yes, you will," she said angrily. "Glen is my friend and I love her, so you'll go just because of that—not to mention that I put up with a hell of a lot of jerks you associate with. And stop blaming me because you were too stubborn to have a snack before we left. I warned you."

"I don't even like her," said Ken.

"No kidding! You don't make much of an effort to hide that fact," she retorted. And then she said something that escalated the fight into a higher, more serious gear: "She doesn't like you either."

There was shocked silence. A deep, angry flush rose under Ken's tanned cheeks, accentuating the sharpness of his cheekbones and the aquiline perfection of his nose, and his blue eyes turned hard. Amanda didn't know if he was angry because Glencora didn't like him or because Amanda had told him so. It was obviously a shock. Ken had trouble seeing himself through other people's eyes.

Amanda reacted to his anger with fury of her own, and by the time they stalked back to the car for the drive home, phrases like "stuffed shirt," "pompous bastard," "arrogant, supercilious shithead," and "egotistical maniac" were bouncing around the walls of the dark green Saab that was now traveling much too fast. They entered the house yelling at each other, and Shadow, who met them at the door, put her ears back and streaked for safety under the couch.

Amanda had turned the shower on full blast and stood under it, sobbing. She was old enough and wise enough to have known that marriage would not be all sunlight and roses;

she knew that she and Ken would fight; and she knew that eventually they would make up. But she was never prepared for the intensity of the pain and the fear that each fight would drive him away from her permanently. She thought that she didn't understand the rules of marital fighting, and that made her frightened and insecure. She believed herself to be at a disadvantage because Ken had been married before, and she saw herself as a novice compared to his twenty-two years of experience. Usually she thought about this when she was more in control of her emotions, when there was an opportunity for it to occur to her that if his first marriage ended in divorce, he might not be any better at coping with relationships than she. But now, standing in the shower crying, she couldn't think clearly enough to realize that he was as miserable as she.

When she was dried, perfumed, teeth brushed, and getting into bed, she immediately saw his unhappiness in the way he curled into himself as he lay on his side. As she crawled in next to him, she put her arms around him and kissed him on the soft vulnerable spot under his jaw. He opened his arms, and she pressed herself close to his body, feeling his penis respond to the touch of her lips. "Now," she had demanded, her need and urgency surprising her as much as it did him. "Go inside me now," she demanded. "Don't make me wait."

She wrapped her legs around her husband as he plunged into her with his full strength, and with great convulsive gasps, she came almost the moment that he was completely inside her.

His blue eyes, soft now with desire, passion, and surprise, widened with understanding as she held him inside her while she regained her breath, and then they began a slow, deliberate journey to the kind of totally uninhibited sexual fulfillment that can come only with someone completely loved and trusted.

Now she sat in the lounge chair and smiled as she remembered last night's lovemaking. Amanda had had her share of lovers and her fill of sexual experimentation by the time she made a commitment to Ken, and sometimes she was embarrassed by just how much experimenting she had done, but she had never found anyone with whom sex was so consistently exciting and satisfying as with Ken James. She had no illusions about the role that sex played in her decision to marry him, tacky and shallow as that sounded. But good sex was hard to find, especially in Washington, a city filled with self-centered, self-absorbed men who came to the capital to climb the ladder of political power and had little energy left for pleasing the women in their lives.

"Hi. Were you asleep?" asked Lydia as she walked across the patio to where Amanda lay. "I saw your note on the door and walked around. You know, that's an open invitation to a burglar. You could be cleaned out while you lie here taking a sun bath."

"Yes, Miss Detective," said Amanda. "You're right, except that I put the burglar alarm on."

"Okay, I'm sorry. I forgot that Ken is into all this high-tech gadgetry. But it's *Ms.* Detective. I'm a liberated woman," said Lydia Simonowitz, who looked to Amanda as much like a policewoman as Elizabeth Taylor looked like a professional linebacker. Her hair, topping a body that seemed too fragile for the work she did, stood out like a flame against her pale skin, and her perpetually mischievous expression, now in a wide smile, did not go with interrogating criminals. But she must have been good at it because she had been promoted to detective after only six years on the Metropolitan Police force.

Amanda laughed. "Sorry, Detective. Oops! *Ms.* Detective." She stood up. "I was just lying here thinking about what assholes most men are."

Lydia rolled her eyes and the women laughed together. "Dump your stuff in the house and let's go eat. Did you bring your B-suit?" asked Amanda.

"Yes, I did. The pool looks delicious. I can't wait to jump in. I may not come out until I turn into a prune!"

When the women were settled at a table under a tree on the terrace of the Old Angler's Inn in Potomac sipping Bloody Marys, Amanda said, "Both of us may be liberated, but we are definitely not trendy. No one eats quiche anymore, and in a million years I wouldn't admit this to Glencora."

She told Lydia parts of last evening's experience, turning the fight with Ken into an amusing scrap and describing in full delicious detail the intellectual and conversational inadequacies of Glen's new playmate.

Lydia laughed at the picture that Amanda painted and then said, "If quiche isn't trendy and no one eats it anymore, why do you suppose it's on the menu at a restaurant like this?"

Amanda stared at her friend. "That's a remarkably sensible observation."

"That's all it is," said Lydia. "An observation, coupled with common sense."

"No wonder you're a good detective. You see things so clearly," said Amanda.

"I'm not sure it's a matter of clarity," said Lydia. "It may be simply seeing things and then putting your observations together with things you already know and drawing a logical conclusion. You don't have to be Danny Detective to do that."

"Maybe not," said Amanda. "But you have to have a certain sort of mind, a way of thinking."

"That's true," replied Lydia. "And I suppose I do have that kind of mind. And maybe that's why I *am* a good detective. But if there's someone who really thinks like a house afire, it's Paul Bandman."

Bandman was Lydia's partner whom Amanda had met several times, a few of them in an official capacity. She remembered the encounters with no pleasure at all. "When Paul Bandman grills you, you *feel* like a house afire," said Amanda with a little grimace.

"Well, you didn't exactly start out very cooperative," said Lydia, and the two women smiled as they remembered how they met—as a result of the murder of J. F. K. Memorial's chief of medicine last year.

"Getting back to what you were saying," said Amanda, changing the subject to possibly current murder. "If you observe things and then put them together with things you know, you ought to come to a correct conclusion—or at least something that seems reasonable. Right?"

Lydia looked at Amanda. "What's on that devious mind of yours?"

"Weird things have been happening in the hospital in the past month or so—to be specific, in the transplant unit.

"If I do what detectives do and start out with what I know and then add things that I observe, I come up with the conclusion that something is very, very wrong at J. F. K. Memorial.

Frighteningly wrong," said Amanda.

Lydia perked up. She was off duty and glad of it, but as she had said to Amanda, she was indeed a curious person. "Tell me everything," she commanded.

Amanda described the mysterious deaths of the three patients: first the construction worker whose name she now knew was Jack Sherwood, and then Aaron Zurman and Roberta Garfield, who had died yesterday, less than twenty-four hours after an ambulance had brought her to the emergency room. Bonita had called her at home while she and Ken were dressing for Glen's party. The transplant nurse also had the results of the autopsy, which Dr. Zyrwynsky had demanded be performed right after Roberta died. Apparently the hospital pathologist hadn't been pleased to be dragged off the golf course on a summer Saturday.

She described Mrs. Zurman's suspicions that her son had been murdered and what she had told Bonita Elliott. She added that Roberta had died of massive PCP infection, a type of pneumonia seen almost exclusively in AIDS patients— but that Roberta's blood test had come back negative for human immunodeficiency virus, the microorganism that causes AIDS.

"The autopsy on Roberta revealed nothing particularly wrong with her new heart," explained Amanda. "It hadn't been rejected; it had none of the signs. It was working perfectly—until it stopped. Most of the organs that depend on good blood circulation to function were okay. Her kidneys weren't too great, but they started shutting down while she was in the intensive care unit, so that came as no big surprise when they looked bad at the autopsy. The thing that was really wrong— and I acknowledge that this was a biggie, it's what killed her— was that her immune system was almost totally shut down."

"I don't know much about organ transplantation," said Lydia. "But I do know that the people have to take drugs for the rest of their lives. Maybe she wasn't taking hers."

"You're on the right track, but it's the wrong train," said Amanda. "If Roberta hadn't been taking her cyclosporine, her immune system would have gone into overdrive and possibly rejected the heart. And there would have been obvious physical signs of rejection at the autopsy. But there weren't. No thick-

ening of the heart muscle that indicates that it's been straining
to circulate blood; no general system shutdown from a lack of
oxygen; no brain damage. Nothing."

"Amanda, to carry your transportation analogy a little further," said Lydia, "are you sure you're even in the right
station? What makes you so suspicious that these people—
all or some of them—didn't die naturally?

"Maybe 'naturally' isn't the right word. Maybe I should
have said that they died 'medically,' as opposed to having
been murdered, which is what I think you think. After all,
you work in a hospital. People die all the time."

Amanda sighed. "That's what Glencora said when I told
this to her. That's what Ken said. That's what I thought too
when Bonita first came to me with what Mrs. Zurman told
her. But it's not logical. What I *know* doesn't jibe with what
I've seen."

"What do you know?" asked Lydia.

"I know that people don't die in hospitals at the rate that
the public thinks they do. We try real hard to keep them alive
and send them home under their own power. Most of the time
we're successful.

"And I *know* that almost no one dies two days after routine
surgery."

"But Amanda," protested Lydia. "A transplant is hardly
routine surgery."

"Not to the patient, of course," she said. "And certainly not
to the donor and the family. But in terms of surgical technique
and the postoperative course, it is routine. Okay, hearts aren't
as ho-hum as kidneys, and livers are still pretty tricky. But
none of those considerations apply here. Both the kidney
patients died right away; and that never happens anymore.
Or it happens rarely enough that when you have two in a
row in a hospital noted for its success, you ought to sit up
and take notice. And I went to the M and M conference on
Zurman and Sherwood," she added.

"M and M?" asked Lydia. "I bet it doesn't mean sitting
around eating little candies."

"You *are* a first-rate detective," said Amanda with a smile.
"M and M is morbidity and mortality," she explained. "Any
decent hospital has an M and M when there's an unusual or
unexplained death or illness. Anyone interested can go, but the

pathologist is always there as well as the doctors and nurses who took care of the patient."

"They sit around and discuss what went wrong?" asked Lydia.

"That's about it," Amanda replied.

"So, what happened?"

"Nothing much, that's the problem," said Amanda with a sigh. "Nobody could contribute anything significant. They *assume* that Zurman died of massive rejection, but there was no autopsy to prove it. Sherwood died of what's called hyperacute rejection. And so far, Roberta's official cause of death is massive PCP infection, and no one seems to think that her death is worth further investigation. As long as the pathologists find a causative organism, that satisfies them.

"There will be an M and M on Roberta, probably this coming week," Amanda continued. "But I bet it will be short and routine." She sighed heavily.

Amanda explained PCP to Lydia and then added, "It will probably never occur to anyone to ask *why* Roberta died of such an unusual disease."

"But it has obviously occurred to you," said Lydia. "Do you think the doctors were trying to cover up one of their own screw-ups?"

"Now you sound more like a malpractice lawyer than a detective," said Amanda with a wry smile. "That's where my mind usually jumps first also," she admitted. "But in this case, there was nothing to cover up. Roberta didn't come to the hospital until she was deathly sick, and by that time, it's not likely that anyone could have saved her."

Amanda barely noticed that the waiter was taking away their empty plates. "Roberta had her transplant three years ago, and she was fine. There was no reason for her to die the way she did. No reason at all," she added. "Something is going on here, Lydia."

"And you think that something is murder?" asked Lydia, serious now. "Let's look at what there is: you have the ramblings of an admittedly confused and senile old woman, the perplexing deaths of two people that you believe shouldn't have died in the circumstances they did . . ."

"Three."

"What?" asked Lydia.

"Three people died when they shouldn't have. Don't forget Jack Sherwood."

"Okay, three," said Lydia. "You're suspicious that murder has taken place, but what evidence do you have?"

"Evidence?"

"Well, yes. There has to be something to make you think that a murder has taken place—like a corpse with a smoking gun lying next to it. Or at least a corpse that looks as though it would have preferred not to have ended up the way it did. You don't have that, Amanda. You have three people who died as a result of serious life-threatening illnesses, who up until a decade or so ago, *would* have died of their illnesses.

"And you can talk about 'routine' all you like, an organ transplant is not an everyday occurrence. It is *not* like getting a tooth filled. It's not even like any other type of major surgery. It's almost like dying and being reborn, for God's sake."

Amanda looked at her friend. "I thought you didn't know anything about transplants."

"I don't," said Lydia. "But I read the papers. And I do hang around with a doctor," she added with a smile. "Even though his patients are all corpses!"

"Oh God, I'm sorry," said Amanda. "We were supposed to talk about you and Sal, and here I am whining about my troubles, which I admit, in the clear light of day, don't look like what I thought they did."

Amanda tried to convince herself that what Lydia said was true. Logically her fears were groundless. Nevertheless, she couldn't put it out of her mind. Three deaths, so sudden, so unexpected, so wrong, so . . .

". . . all confused," said Lydia as Amanda jerked herself back to the Old Angler's Inn and her friend's need to talk about love and marriage.

"Do you love Sal?" asked Amanda.

"Very much."

"Do you respect him?"

"Absolutely."

"Do you trust him?"

"As much as I trust anyone—any man."

"Do you want to have his children?"

"Yes, but not right away," replied Lydia. "I've never met anyone like Sal," she continued, "and I've been around the block a few times. He's the most interesting man I've ever known, and he wants to make a commitment to me."

"So, what's the problem?" asked Amanda.

"You make it sound so easy," replied Lydia. "But it's a big step, a huge risk. I'm not sure I'm ready for it. My career is going well, and I'm happy to give that a lot of energy right now. I don't know if I want to devote the time to the responsibilities of marriage."

"It does take time," Amanda admitted. "You're not alone as much. You always have someone else's needs to consider, and someone else's laundry and meals and a bigger house and all that stuff. I'm not saying that you'll become a domestic slave, but let's face it, no matter how modern men think they are, the responsibility for keeping the home fires burning still falls on women.

"Ken may earn a lot of money, and I don't actually have to scrub the floors because we can afford to pay someone to do that, thank God, but the house would be damn cold if I didn't keep that fire going," she said. "I'm the one that arranges everything, and although I don't love it—I didn't love it when I had to do it for myself—I don't really mind it. And at least I don't have to do as much physical work now."

Lydia said nothing, and the two women drank their coffee in companionable silence. Finally Lydia said, "It would be such a huge change."

"Change is scary," Amanda admitted. "But as I told you, I was thinking just this morning that most men are such jerks, and you're not going to find one much better than Sal."

"You're right about that," said Lydia. "How long do we have to wait before we can jump into your pool?"

"Let's go!" said Amanda, signaling for the check.

When they had paid and were walking to the car, Lydia asked, "How far in advance do you have to plan a wedding?"

"We could drive to Elkton after supper. That's where all the teenagers go because you don't need a blood test in Maryland, and there are lots of those little wedding chapels—like in Las Vegas. Ken and I could be witnesses, and then you and Sal can check into a sixteen-dollar-a-night motel."

Lydia laughed. "Oh gross," she said. "Don't you want me to have a nice wedding so you can get a new dress?"

• • •

Amanda lay in the sun next to Lydia, both women slathered with sunscreen, listening to the snip-snip of the hedge clippers as her husband gave the "green kids" their last pruning of the season. She thought remotely about murder and mayhem, about what she would cook for the evening meal and about lovemaking with Ken. But even that faded into fuzzy images as she drifted into lethargy born of peace, contentment, and a full belly.

The Reverend Caspar Torrey was not at all contented. Nor was he at peace with himself or with his world. On this Sunday afternoon he sat in his home office with the windows closed, refusing to allow himself the pleasure of the soft summer weather that he believed was given by God. He did not deserve one single shred of God's grace. It was unlikely that he would ever again be in a state of grace.

That thought filled him with the same sense of grief and loss that Roberta Garfield's family was surely feeling at this moment. At the same time, though, Caspar Torrey felt the first stirrings of relief—and the guilt that accompanied it. The sin was over.

No, that wasn't right. The sin itself would go on forever, but the sinful action would not continue, and that was almost as good. Never as good in the eyes of God, but nevertheless a relief in the real world where Caspar Torrey spent most of his time.

Of course, he had exchanged ongoing small sins—well, relatively small—for that one large one. But that's the way it was in the real world. And come to think of it, that's the *only* world in which he would be permitted to spend time now.

"Open the windows, Cass," said his wife on her way into the room to do just that. "Take advantage of this beautiful weather. In fact, why are you sitting cooped up in here? Go out and sit on the lawn."

The Reverend Caspar Torrey and his wife looked remarkably alike. In fact, many people mistook them for brother and sister. Both were blond and pale with washed-out, almost colorless eyes that, in certain types of light, made them seem almost ghostlike. The way they dressed completed the shadowy image. Even now, in the privacy of their own home after

Sunday services, they dressed as though they might at any moment be called by their parishioners to sartorial judgment: he in grey twill slacks and a white dress shirt open at the throat, she in a beige skirt (with pantyhose on underneath even on a summer Sunday afternoon) and a plain white blouse with a small round collar that could as easily belong to her husband. Her only jewelry was a gold wedding band, and her only makeup was a pale pink lipstick of the shade that mothers pick out for their little girls' first lipstick.

The house in which they lived adjoined the Presbyterian church and was as modest as most such dwellings are. Caspar and Leona Torrey could have afforded something far more sumptuous, and Leona resented the meagerness of the lifestyle that her husband believed was obligatory. She had believed that too, in the beginning, but not any longer. She didn't believe much of anything anymore.

"Leave me alone," said the clergyman in a more acerbic tone than he usually used with his wife, or with anyone. "If I want to be stuffy, I'll damn well be stuffy."

Leona Torrey shrugged. Although he rarely snapped at her, she was familiar with, and growing tired of, his increasing moodiness. This had been going on for too long now—at least a year, and she no longer tried to get to the bottom of it. Her sensitivity and patience were growing thin and she was beginning to look critically at the marriage. There were days when she thought about helping herself to some of the money that Caspar had stashed away over the years, but she was frightened. Where would she go? What would she do? Who was she without Cass and her identity as a minister's wife? As Caspar Torrey's wife.

What Leona didn't know was that even if she could have gathered the courage to leave her husband and the parsonage walls that were closing in on her, she would not have access to the money, which she thought of as millions, but which in reality was far less. Still, the account held a lot of money for a minister who sprang from the lower middle class and had never risen beyond the confines of a medium-sized Presbyterian church in a suburban community where hardly anyone left anything bigger than a ten-dollar bill in the Sunday collection plate.

Leona could get her share of the money only with the help

of a clever lawyer—a clever, expensive lawyer—because the Reverend Caspar Torrey's secret account was in his name only, and in recent years it had been diminishing almost as fast as he could replenish it.

Leona knew none of this.

"Suit yourself," she said and closed the door to his den with harder-than-necessary force. "Screw you," she said aloud as soon as she was well out of the range of her husband's hearing. "Screw you right into the wall of your precious church."

The Reverend Caspar Torrey was aware of his wife's anger, and he was aware of the reason for it. He didn't blame her. He deserved it. He deserved a great deal more than her anger. He deserved a vengeful God to come riding in on that nice summer breeze, causing all hell to break loose in the soul of the Reverend Caspar Torrey.

He sighed. Come to think of it, all hell had already broken loose. He had been a resident in Hell since the morning he had shaken Roberta Garfield's hand after Sunday services. It was a brief touch, no different from that given and received by the hundred or so other congregants who had attended the service that day. No different, but after the electric shock that flowed from her hand to his, his life had changed irrevocably.

He had loved her from that moment. He had hated her from that moment. He had been consumed by her from that moment. And now he was cooped up in the self-enforced stuffiness of his office planning her funeral. A funeral that would not be taking place were it not for his actions.

══ CHAPTER 8 ══

You are despicable, said her conscience.

How was I supposed to know that the woman was falling to pieces? Amanda asked, somewhat petulantly because she knew her conscience had her over a barrel this time.

Because Bonita told you so, that's how.

Bonita said that Mrs. Zurman was confused and had trouble speaking English, and maybe was a little senile, Amanda retorted.

Well, what other information did you need? asked the voice sarcastically. *What does it take to make you understand that a senile old woman who's just gotten off the boat and has lost her only child isn't going to be able to sit down and talk rationally?*

She didn't just get off the boat. They've been here for more than thirty years, Amanda said in her own defense. And stop making me feel worse than I already do.

You should feel like a first-class shit. You caused that woman more pain that she already has.

Now, wait a minute. That's not true. She was glad to see me, and it was obvious that she wanted to talk. And she sure as hell was clear about what she thought when the word 'murder' came up, Amanda retorted.

It was true, Amanda reflected as she drove home in the late August evening, the windows of her car open to the continuing freshness of the breeze. She had been unable to understand most of what Mrs. Zurman had said because the woman spoke a mixture of English and another language that Amanda didn't recognize but thought might be German or Yiddish. But it was clear that she was glad to see Amanda, and also clear that she believed her son had been murdered.

Amanda had taken Lydia's advice and tried to add knowledge to what she observed. "Tell me about the Holocaust," she had said to Eddie. "How would it affect survivors?"

Eddie stared at her across the cramped table they had shared that noon at Giovanni's. "Huh?" The enormity of the question floored him.

"I mean, what does it mean to have survived the worst experience that a human being can go through? What would someone be like after having lived through something like that?"

"Does this have anything to do with what you were asking me the other day about Jewish funeral practices and the transplant patient who died?"

"I guess so," Amanda had replied. "But I'm not sure how it ties in. I understand what you told me about needing to bury someone as soon as possible, and that seems perfectly rational to me. Good, in fact. But I wonder what might be going through the mind of someone like Mrs. Zurman, who everyone thinks is senile and maybe also not exactly in her right mind."

She held out her hand to stay what she knew Eddie was about to retort. "I know it's a mistake to think that all old people are senile and that because someone is overcome with grief means they can't think coherently," she said. "But by the same token, maybe she was beaten so badly in the concentration camp that she has some kind of brain damage. Or maybe what's wrong with her isn't the kind of senility we usually think of, but rather some type of permanent hurt caused by the Nazis. A sort of grief and loss that's impossible to recover from."

Now Amanda's hands shaped themselves into a gesture of frustration and futility. "Oh hell, Eddie, I don't know what I'm talking about. Never mind. Forget I asked."

Eddie sighed. "Amanda, thinking that you're going to drop this is like believing the jury will follow the judge's instructions to disregard what one of the lawyers said during a trial."

"I know it's an impossible question to answer," Amanda replied. "There is no one way to respond to something so monumentally devastating."

"That's true," said Eddie. "But I think that there is one generalization that can be made about all Holocaust survivors, and that is that they were irreparably damaged. No amount of time can heal the wounds. No amount of psychotherapy can put the experience into perspective, because there *is* no perspective for what the Nazis did to six million of my people—and millions of others as well. No amount of German financial reparations can soften the loss. Not even moving to a new country and starting a new family can erase the memory of what happened.

"I believe that the survivors are not the same people they were before the Nazis came for them, and that's all I can tell you, Amanda. If you want to know more, you'll have to do some reading." Eddie had tears in his eyes, and they walked back across the street to the hospital in silence.

"I'm sorry I asked," she said to him when they were ready to part company in the lobby. "I didn't mean to upset you. I didn't realize it would be so hard for you to talk about. I mean, you weren't there yourself, so I never thought . . ." Amanda was thoroughly confused and embarrassed now.

"Don't be sorry," he said. "It's good to remember. It's something that the world must never forget. It's good to know you care." And then he had added, with a smile and a quick one-armed hug: "Even if you asked because you have something weird going on in that diabolical little mind of yours!"

Don't blame either Lydia or Eddie, the voice said as she turned the corner into her own street. *Lydia didn't tell you to go bothering this poor old woman, and Eddie thinks you're bats. Lydia even called you this morning and specifically told you to be careful. So you did this all on your own. At least be honest about that.*

Amanda ignored the voice and continued her reverie. After work today she had driven up Georgia Avenue at the height of rush hour to Leisure World ("Seizure World," the hospital social workers called it) to see Mrs. Zurman. She had regretted it almost immediately.

The woman who opened the door to the apartment was as pathetic a creature as Amanda had ever seen—she looked like a pale raisin. Mrs. Zurman had been washing dishes, but as she rolled down her sleeves—not quickly enough to keep Amanda from seeing the dark blue number tattooed on her forearm—and invited Amanda into her living room, she seemed to straighten up and don a veil of dignity and pride. It was as if she were torn between the desire to keep intruders out of her world of grief and defeat and the need to tell someone about what she feared and believed.

As Amanda sat on the tan sofa strewn with needlepoint pillows, she thought of an evening in Amsterdam last summer and the woman she had seen at Il Gattopardo where she and Ken had taken Gordon Franklin for supper after the symphony.

There had been a black and white cat named Pedro in the restaurant. He lived there and as each table filled, Pedro greeted the new customers, all of whom returned the overture with a warm word or a pat. Pedro didn't beg food, and in fact, after he had said hello, he went to a chair in a little hallway that led to the restrooms, and curled up there until the next patrons arrived. Pedro did not linger over dinner with any of them.

Except for the old woman. When she came in, Pedro went to her table and stayed for a while, winding around her legs and talking to her in soft, pleasant chirrups the way cats do when they are engaged in serious conversation. The woman was not effusive to Pedro, but Amanda could see that the two had a relationship that was more than the casual encounter that Pedro permitted himself with the other customers.

The woman was alone and she ordered a half carafe of red wine—the house wine, not a bottle that would be uncorked especially for her—a plate of pasta with bright green pesto sauce, and coffee. She had done that every evening since she moved into the apartment building across the street, said Gordon, who knew the owner of the restaurant. Every evening she came into Il Gattopardo, sat alone at the same table, and ordered a small quantity of inexpensive wine and a plate of pesto.

Amanda watched her eat slowly, savoring her food. She sat up straight and kept a pleasant, if somewhat blank, expression on her face. Her hair was grey, and Amanda could see that it was very long because the bun at the nape of her neck was full. Her dress was unadorned navy blue with a high neck and long sleeves, and she wore a small pin of opals and coral on the lapel. Her purse, which she carried on her arm in the old-fashioned way, was equally staid and also navy blue. She was probably in her seventies, with a sweetness of expression and a clarity in her eyes that belied the suffering she had endured.

Amanda knew, without having to be told, what the woman had been through. She knew the tattoo was there under the sleeve of the plain, navy blue dress, and she was not surprised to see a similar brand on the arm of Mrs. Zurman who looked remarkably like the woman at Il Gattopardo.

From time to time she talked with the owner and the waiter, both of whom treated her with the same deference accorded the other diners. Il Gattopardo was a small and terribly elegant restaurant where dinner took two or three hours, and the patrons almost always ate all the courses and ordered at least a bottle or two of wine. The old woman's patronage represented a loss to the restaurant, but she was treated as if she spent as freely as everyone else.

Ken's car wasn't in the garage, so Amanda changed into bright red knee-length shorts and a red- and white-striped tank shirt, fed Shadow and started supper, still thinking about the woman who had lost her only son to what she believed was murder, not a failed kidney transplant.

When Amanda had asked Mrs. Zurman why she thought her son had been slain, she could say only, "They hated him."

"Who?" Amanda had asked.

"The bad people," said the old woman. "The people who are Nazis here." Then she had burst into tears, saying, through her gulping sobs, that the Nazis were everywhere. When Amanda had asked who would have had a motive for killing her son, Mrs. Zurman seemed not to understand the word. She tried again: "Who would have wanted to kill him?"

"They hated him."

"Who hated him?"

"The Nazis."

Amanda had been standing on verbal quicksand, and the longer she stayed, the deeper she would sink. But she didn't want to leave because this woman was so obviously trying to tell her something. Was Aaron Zurman really murdered by a band of American neo-Nazis, who Amanda knew were gathering strength and numbers in the increasingly conservative and right-wing political atmosphere in this country?

If so, why would they pick an ordinary suburban physician, a fine, respected doctor? The fact that he had served on the county council for two terms didn't make him much of a threat to a bunch of skinheads or a new breed of Brown Shirts.

Were the Nazis Mrs. Zurman spoke of really the same ones who had burned the brand into her arm so many years before and had done God only knew what else to her? Or was she confused about the decade in which she was living? Had the beasts destroyed the part of her brain that made accurate contact with reality?

Was the woman confused about where she was? Was she brain-damaged, or did she have a real senile dementia? Was her language problem so severe that ordinary conversation was impossible? Was she just plain dumb?

It could be all of the above, you jerk, said her conscience again. *So why don't you just butt out and leave the whole thing alone. It's not your business.*

Amanda sighed. Investigating death was not part of her job description as J. F. K. Memorial's director of nursing. Lydia had told her much the same thing on the phone that very morning when she had called to thank Amanda for the evening of grilled chicken and a cutthroat game of Trivial Pursuit afterwards.

"I've been thinking a little about what we talked about at brunch yesterday," said Lydia. "About what you think is going on at the hospital with the unexplained deaths."

"Yes?" replied Amanda expectantly, hoping that Lydia would say that she and Paul Bandman would be right over to open a full-scale investigation.

No such luck.

"Don't go getting yourself into trouble by stirring up things you have no proof about," warned Lydia. "People get sued for libel and slander by doing what I think you're thinking of doing. Don't open a can of worms unless you're pretty sure what those worms are doing."

Amanda had acknowledged the advice and thanked her friend—and then she had gone out and done precisely what Lydia had told her not to do, and had upset a grief-stricken woman in the process.

She sighed again as she washed lettuce, and resolved to leave the whole thing alone.

Shadow ran to the back door at the same moment that Amanda heard Ken's car crunching on the gravel driveway. She looked down at the tubby grey cat and wondered if she should get Ken a puppy for his birthday next month. Although he tried his best not to let the cat know it, because he was fond of Shadow and didn't want to hurt Amanda's feelings, Ken thought that cats were essentially inferior to dogs, and Amanda knew he missed not having one. But a puppy, no matter how sweet and adorable, was a nuisance, and a dog was a bigger responsibility than a cat. Ken went out of town often, and the thought of dragging a big retriever out in a blinding snowstorm at night was not at all appealing. Still, Ken would love a dog, and Amanda smiled at the thought of a silky black Labrador puppy playing with Shadow.

"Hello, Miss Elephant," he said to the cat as he came in the back door and kissed the back of Amanda's neck as he always did. To her he said, "You look like a candy cane."

"Maybe after supper, if you're a good boy, I'll let you lick me," she replied with a grin.

And he did. Oh my, yes he did.

"How dare you barge into my aunt's house and upset her? I have half a mind to report you to your superiors, and if you do it again, I'll have you arrested for trespassing!"

Amanda looked at the man across the desk from her and tried to equate the anger he was apparently feeling with the way he expressed it. The two did not jibe at all, and she had trouble taking him seriously. The man's name was Gerald Miller, although the minute Louise brought him into the office, Amanda mentally dubbed him the Chinless Wonder. He was Aaron Zurman's cousin.

Chinless wore a summer suit of tan broadcloth with a light blue shirt and a navy tie with a red stripe in it. Very preppy, she thought, until she glanced down at the tasseled loafers and noticed the line of skin above the too-short socks. Not preppy at all.

His face didn't match the outfit. It was weak and petulant with what her mother used to call a "hangdog" expression. His posture completed Amanda's initial impression of a tentative and uncertain man. He had the face and demeanor of someone who expected, and believed he deserved, to be slapped.

Despite the challenge of his words, he posed no real threat, and Amanda could see right away that he was a person who resorted to blustering and bullying to cover up his essential inadequacy. She immediately detested him.

"In the first place, Mr. Miller, I wasn't trespassing. I rang
your aunt's doorbell and she invited me in—just as you came
uninvited to my office and were asked in. In the second place, I
did not upset her deliberately, and I believe she was glad to see
me. It was she who first made the accusation of murder. And
in the third place, if anyone is going to call the police, it will
be me—to investigate the allegations made by Mrs. Zurman.
Are we quite clear about all this, Mr. Miller?"

Amanda's resolve to forget Mrs. Zurman and her dead son
went out the window the minute Chinless had sat in the chair
opposite her desk and opened his mouth. Now she watched
him deflate like a little kid whose temper tantrum runs out of
steam because he's forgotten why he started screaming in the
first place.

"I didn't mean to threaten you, Ms. Knight," he said. "It's
just that my family is very upset by this. What's left of the
family," he added bitterly. Only then did Amanda notice the
slight accent in his speech and the tears that glittered unshed
in his eyes.

"And I didn't mean to come back at you like such a shrew,"
she replied in her most placating manner, wishing at the same
time that he would go away, hoping that their mutual apologies
would end the encounter. But Gerald Miller sat like a lump
in the chair and seemed to cast about in his mind for what to
say next.

He gulped and said, "Do you think Aaron was murdered?"

Amanda felt herself being squeezed into a familiar, uncomfortable spot between a rock and a hard place. She spent
time there regularly and ought to be used to it by now. She
wasn't.

She knew that some diplomacy was called for. This man was
obviously concerned—as concerned as she was becoming. "I
honestly don't know," she said. "The only reason that this has
become an issue is that your aunt made an accusation to the
head nurse on our transplant unit when Dr. Zurman died.

"And perhaps 'accusation' is too strong a word," she added.
"It was difficult for the nurse to understand exactly what your
aunt meant, and frankly, I had the same problem last night."

"What precisely did my aunt tell you?" asked Chinless. Perhaps, Amanda now reflected, he wasn't as much of a hangdog

as he appeared. So far he had demanded answers to questions that in themselves were unclear, and he had volunteered no information—and no help. She would have to be careful of everything she said.

"Are you an attorney, Mr. Miller?"

"No, why do you ask?" he replied. He seemed genuinely puzzled.

"You burst in on me, hurled accusations—this time the word is quite appropriate—at me and have given me no reason to continue this discussion, now that the apologies have been dispensed with. I can't tell you what your aunt said to Ms. Elliott; that's privileged and confidential communication. I can only say, because it seems to be common knowledge, that your aunt believes that your cousin was murdered."

"That's true," said Chinless, angry again. "And if he was—and it's becoming obvious to me that you know a lot more than you're willing to say—then this hospital was at fault. If my cousin was murdered while he was a patient here, J. F. K. Memorial is going to have a lawsuit on its hands the likes of which you have never seen."

Shit, thought Amanda. The man is right. She stared at him in dismay. Be cool, she said to herself. Don't get him any more upset than he already is.

Aloud she said, "Unfortunately, you're quite right, Mr. Miller. Suing hospitals and doctors seems to be a favorite American pastime, and if your cousin was indeed murdered, I wouldn't blame you and your aunt one bit for suing us for everything we've got. We are supposed to be in the business of protecting patients, not exposing them to more harm. You would, however, have to prove that the hospital was at fault or, at the very least, negligent, and I have no doubt that our attorneys would give you a good run for your money."

Chinless stared at her, disarmed, Amanda hoped, by her candor, charm, sympathy—and unwillingness to put J. F. K. Memorial in any more legal jeopardy than she had to.

She pressed whatever psychological advantage she had won. "Look, we both hope he wasn't murdered, but let's try to be logical about this. Murder happens, unfortunately even in hospitals, so perhaps if I understood a little bit about *who* would want your cousin dead and *why* he would be a target for murder, we could go about figuring this out in a rational way."

Chinless seemed to think that was reasonable, but he could offer no clue and was of no practical help. According to Gerald Miller, his cousin Aaron Zurman was a paragon: a selfless healer, a devoted son, a refugee who had come to this country after having been tortured by the Nazis—"the worst kind of depravity in the history of mankind," was the way Chinless put it. Aaron Zurman and his mother, the only two survivors of a large Dutch Jewish family, had passed through Ellis Island with almost no money in their pockets. Zurman had become a successful physician and a popular local politician championing the rights of the common man.

Amanda imagined that she could hear violins playing in the background while Chinless painted this angelic picture of a murder victim.

But it didn't wash.

Lydia had once told her that people get killed for a reason. "There's always a motive for murder," she had said. "Even apparently random, pointless killings have meaning to them, and the killer is invariably connected to the victim, no matter how remote the connection may seem at first."

She had gone on to explain that when the police have absolutely nothing to go on—no clues, no leads, no evidence—they begin by looking at the victim's life. What had he or she been up to that would make someone else want—or need—to kill?

"It sounds as though you're saying that there are no innocent victims," Amanda had commented.

"Not at all," Lydia replied. "All murder victims are innocent. If I didn't believe that, I'm not sure I could function in this job."

"But surely," Amanda went on, warming to the topic, "some people do such despicable things that they deserve to die. They deserve to forfeit their life."

"But deserving to forfeit your life and deserving to be murdered are two entirely different things," said Lydia. "One is a function of a rational and civilized society that imposes certain punishments which, in theory at least, are supposed to fit the crime. And the other is personal revenge, taking the law into your own hands. It's anarchy."

"That's all very well and good," said Amanda, "if you have a society, specifically a justice system, that works the way it was designed to. But somehow I don't think the Founding Fathers ever envisioned a society that would fall apart at its moral seams the way ours has. The system just doesn't work any longer."

Lydia had admitted that things had indeed gotten out of hand, that too many people were getting away with murder— literally and metaphorically. But she would not concede that anyone, no matter how reprehensible, deserved to be murdered. "Amanda," she had said, "murder—the unwarranted killing of an innocent person—is *always* wrong. It is the one universalizable moral principle that I am absolutely positive about. I'm willing to debate anything else until we're purple. But not that."

Amanda had agreed in principle, but the thing about the conversation with Lydia that now clamored for attention, as Chinless looked at her from across the desk, was the detective's belief that there was always a motive for murder.

What had Aaron Zurman been up to that would make someone want to kill him? She said as much to Gerald Miller, who insisted that he had no idea why anyone would want to kill his cousin.

They stared at one another, neither of them knowing what else to say. Amanda broke the silence. "I have a lunch appointment," she said. "I suggest that if you really believe your cousin was murdered, you should go to the police with your suspicions, although I have a feeling they will ask you the same types of questions that I have. Other than that, I'm sorry that I have nothing further to offer you."

Just before Miller left her office, Amanda asked him one last question: "Why didn't your cousin marry?"

The answer came readily. Too readily. "Aaron Zurman was devoted to his mother. She saved his life, and he spent the rest of *his* life caring for her and protecting her. She needed him, and his obligation to her precluded a relationship with another woman. Too bad," he added in a voice that he tried to make sound ominous, "that she couldn't have saved him again."

Amanda didn't think he would go to the police. He didn't seem the sort to put himself at a disadvantage in front of quite so authoritarian a figure as a policeman. But then again, you never knew . . .

The minute Miller closed the door behind him, she dug through her files and found the incident report that Bonita Elliott had written at Amanda's request. This is what it said:

> *Mrs. Selwa Zurman, mother of Aaron Zurman, who died this afternoon on the transplant unit of J. F. K. Memorial Hospital, voluntarily told me that she believes that her son was murdered. She was not able to say who she thought killed her son, nor did she know how the murder was committed.*
>
> *In fact, she said little else than things like, "They killed him. They murdered my Aaron." It was difficult to understand what she was saying because she has a thick foreign accent and at times did not appear to be speaking English.*
>
> *Mrs. Zurman also appeared to be highly distraught and at times was crying in a hysterical manner that was disturbing to other patients on the unit and to staff. Her nephew, Gerald Miller, arrived shortly thereafter and took her home.*

The report was signed "Bonita Elliott, R.N." and told Amanda nothing more than she already knew about Mrs. Zurman's beliefs. *Did you expect some kind of revelation while the report was sitting in your files?* asked the inner voice, which was annoying in its stubborn insistence on reality.

Amanda shrugged. You never know . . . she thought, picking up the phone and dialing the hospital's general counsel, Rudolph Wilson.

"Rudy, can I assume you saw a copy of an incident report that I sent to risk management about Aaron Zurman's mother saying that he had been murdered here in the hospital?"

"It rings a small bell, Amanda. Why?" asked Rudy, his tone shifting immediately from friendly and collegial to neutral with overtones of suspicion. A typical lawyer's switch, thought Amanda.

"Well, her nephew, Zurman's cousin, was in my office just now repeating the accusations his aunt made," she replied. "He said that if his cousin was murdered here, he's going to sue us for everything we've got."

"What prompted him to say that?" asked Wilson.

Shit! Now you're screwed, said the voice, which forgot to tell Amanda to think before she picked up the phone and brought the damn lawyers into it. *You thought you were covering your ass,* said the voice in its most sarcastic tone, *and now all you've done is get your ass in a sling.*

Amanda thought furiously. She had to answer Rudy's questions without an obvious lie—at least not too big a lie, but she didn't want him to know what a fool she had made out of herself yesterday.

"Apparently he's been talking to his aunt and they both believe that Aaron Zurman was murdered," she replied. Not an out-and-out lie, but far from the whole truth.

"Why did he come to you?" asked Wilson. "Why didn't he come to my office? Why doesn't he report it to the police?"

This time she told a big, juicy lie: "I don't know, Rudy. Maybe because his aunt had originally talked to a nurse, Bonita Elliott on the transplant unit. Maybe because he wanted to go to Bonita's boss and get her into trouble. Who knows what goes through people's minds, Rudy?"

She allowed herself to be carried along now on her wave of righteous indignation and fell overboard: "Maybe the general public doesn't know that hospitals have huge batteries of lawyers sitting around waiting for people to make trouble."

She had gone too far. Wilson's voice changed again, from lawyerly neutral to frostily hostile. "If you hear from this man again, Amanda—or his aunt or anyone else having *anything* to do with this case—send them right to me. Don't talk to anyone connected to this family in *any* way, and that includes their attorneys. Do you understand, Amanda?"

"I understand, Rudy," she replied, "but there's no need to treat me like a five-year-old."

Now his voice took on a patronizing tone. "I'm not treating you like a child, Amanda. I just don't think you realize the gravity of this kind of thing."

Asshole, she thought. Aloud, she said, "Don't worry, Rudy. I'm not planning to take on your job as well as my own."

═══ CHAPTER 9 ═══

Amanda's lunch appointment was with Evelyn Portman, the new chief pharmacist, who had called the week before to make this date. She didn't actually apologize for her rudeness that day in the ladies room—Evelyn Portman didn't seem the type who would say she was sorry—but Amanda thought that the suggestion to have lunch was a way to smooth things over. She was positive that Evelyn would offer to pick up the tab.

They shared a taxi, which unfortunately was not air conditioned. "I'll bet the temperature is up twenty degrees since I came to work this morning," said Amanda rolling down the window next to her. "So much for the break in the heat wave!"

Evelyn looked annoyed and immediately put her hand up to her head in a futile effort to prevent the hot gust of air from ruffling her perfectly groomed hair. Amanda decided not to roll the window back up. Evelyn smiled grimly. "It *is* warm, isn't it?"

Amanda's heart sank. Lunch was going to be difficult. Evelyn Portman was no sparkling conversationalist. How could she be, Amanda wondered to herself, all bundled up in those heavy clothes in this weather? Evelyn did indeed look uncomfortable in a beige suit that she wore with a cream-colored, high-neck, long-sleeved blouse. She should have left it in her closet until after Labor Day.

Amanda took a guess. "That's a pretty suit. Is it new?"

Evelyn looked a little sheepish and made an effort to be friendly. "I ran out at lunch yesterday and picked up a few things. It's nice to work so close to a shopping area. St. Jude's is in the middle of nowhere."

Amanda smiled. "Off the rack and on your back!"

"I beg your pardon?" said Evelyn.

Amanda blushed. How could this woman, a clotheshorse if ever there was one, not know what she meant? Maybe she came from somewhere strange. "I do the same thing," she did. "If I buy a new outfit, I have to wear it right away."

"I see," replied Evelyn.

Oh God, thought Amanda. No sense of humor. No sense of the absurd. New in her job. A perfectionist. She wondered again how she would get through lunch with this woman who seemed a composite of Amanda's least favorite character traits, wrapped up as a typical Washington, D.C. career woman: an uptight go-getter who took herself deadly seriously and spent half her salary on clothes and the other half on a "good" address, leaving her in a perpetual frenzy of anxiety over the resulting debt.

The taxi pulled up in front of the restaurant. Amanda reached for her wallet, but Evelyn already had a five-dollar bill in her hand. She must have had it there all the time because Amanda did not see her open her purse. Either that or she was very good at sleight-of-hand. She shrugged. "I'll get it on the way back."

When they had settled into their table, Amanda followed up on the hunch that had struck her in the taxi. "Where do you live?" she asked.

"In Kalorama," replied Evelyn.

"Oh, that's nice, living so close. You can walk to work," she said, trying to keep her mind out of its financial computing mode. Kalorama was one of the most expensive areas in the city. Houses as well as condos there sold for upwards of a million dollars. There were no rental apartments. Renters, considered tacky and transient, were not welcome in an area inhabited by ambassadors, attorneys with six-figure incomes, and people who did nothing more than clip coupons for a living. The vehicles parked in the garages of Kalorama homes were mostly Jaguars, Rolls-Royces, and a few expensive American cars. The narrow, quiet streets were dotted with officers of the Secret Service Uniformed Division who stood guard outside the many embassies in the neighborhood. How could Evelyn Portman, pharmacist, even chief pharmacist, afford to live in Kalorama?

The perfectly groomed mannequin across the table raised her eyebrows and was the second person in an hour to patronize Amanda. "Walk to work?" she asked, as if the suggestion were too bizarre to even contemplate.

• • •

"The whole lunch was like that," Amanda said to Ruth Sinclair later that afternoon as they sat in a corner of the mostly empty cafeteria drinking iced tea. "She was scrupulously polite, but I had the distinct impression that she didn't want to be eating lunch with me, even though she suggested it. I am definitely not good enough for her."

"She sounds like a bitch," said Ruth sympathetically. "The kind of person to stay far away from." Ruth was a firm believer in remaining as untouched by hospital politics as she could. In her job it was relatively easy. There were not many commercial catering companies big enough to provide the wide range of special dietary needs required by a major teaching hospital like J.F.K., so when Ruth and David Townsend negotiated the contract every other year with Intercontinental, there was not much competition from other companies. Consequently Ruth was not subjected to the temptation of bribes, kickbacks, and other assorted shenanigans that went on in the housekeeping and maintenance departments.

"We're talking *very* sharp teeth," said Amanda. "What really frightens me is how closed and aloof she is. There's no way to know what she's thinking. She asked me absolutely nothing about myself or the nursing department or hospital gossip or the way the place is run or who has the real power and who gets things done. Nothing! It was eerie."

"Is she still screwing the guy from St. Jude's?" asked Ruth.

"That's what I wanted to ask you," replied Amanda. "I couldn't exactly come right out and say, 'So, have you been getting any lately?', could I?"

"No, but I'll bet you were dying to!" said Ruth.

The two women giggled. "I can't imagine Evelyn Portman having sex," said Amanda. "She'd get her hair messed up, and she might even sweat!"

They laughed again, and as Amanda looked at Ruth's open, cheerful face, she pictured her and her husband making love. She imagined two happy, middle-aged puppies romping around in bed, tickling and nuzzling each other and laughing. "You have to find out for me," she said.

"Find out what?" asked Ruth warily. She liked Amanda and respected the way she ran the nursing department, but

he thought that her insatiable desire for gossip would get her
into trouble eventually. "Your nose is twitching," she said.
"You look like your cat and you know what happened to the
cat who got too curious."

"But satisfaction brought it back," said Amanda, reciting the
second line of the nursery rhyme.

Ruth sighed. She knew that Amanda would pester her until
she got the information she wanted. "What do you want to
know?"

"Is she still sleeping with the guy at St. Jude's, and who is
he? Has she ever been married—and how can she afford to
live in Kalorama on her salary without insurance money or
alimony or something?"

"She lives in Kalorama?" Ruth's eyebrows shot up in surprise. "Wow!"

"Wow is right. And you know what else is interesting?" said
Amanda, who did indeed look a little like Shadow when she
was stalking an ant crawling across the kitchen floor, ears alert,
whiskers tense, body ready to pounce. "She wouldn't tell me
what street she lives on, and she isn't in the phone book and
has an unlisted number. I checked the minute I got back after
lunch."

"What's the big deal?" asked Ruth. "Why is she being so
secretive about where she lives?"

"That's what I want you to find out," replied Amanda.
"What's with this woman?"

"Why do you need to know all this stuff?" asked Ruth,
genuinely puzzled. After the way Amanda had described the
lunch with Evelyn Portman, she couldn't imagine why she'd
want to delve into the pharmacist's background.

"I don't *need* to know," said Amanda. "I'm just curious,
that's all. What is she hiding?"

"Maybe she's just a naturally reserved person," said Ruth.

"Maybe."

"Okay, okay! I'll ask around," Ruth promised, "because I
know you won't leave me alone until I do."

"Thanks," said Amanda.

"And meow to you," replied Ruth. "You ought to be drinking your milk out of a saucer!"

CHAPTER 10

"You are so beautiful, Amanda, and I love you so much."

Amanda smiled at her husband across the dinner table and told him that he wasn't so bad-looking himself. "And I love you too," she said. "And I respect you and admire you. And I have the hots for your body!"

"Do you want to go into the bushes right now?" Ken asked

She made a small motion as if to get out of her chair, and he instinctively reached out to restrain her. Then they both burst out laughing.

"I had you going there for a second," she said, and he had to admit that she did.

"You're such a sex maniac that I wouldn't put it past you to attack me right here," he said. They were on the patio of L'Auberge Chez François in Great Falls, Virginia, eating Swiss food by candlelight in the summer breeze.

"You didn't mind a little public demonstration of physical affection that time on the New Jersey Turnpike," she retorted with a sly smile, and Ken had the good grace to blush at the memory of what she had once done to him in full view of truck drivers sitting high in their cabs, as he had steered his big old Plymouth down the superhighway.

"I dream about that sometimes," he said, and she saw how much he wanted it to happen again. She simply smiled, took off one sandal, rubbed her bare foot against his pants leg under the table, and planned a nice little surprise for him on the ride home that evening.

Ken and Amanda ate in companionable silence for a while, enjoying each other, the food, and the elegance of the restaurant. She liked the way the breeze caressed her bare shoulders and ruffled her dark hair. It made her think of things she wanted to do when they got home.

But that was for later. Now she had her husband's full attention, and she decided to take advantage of it. "I want to pick your corporate executive's brain," she said.

"Always at your service, my love."

"It's about this new pharmacist, Evelyn Portman. Aside from the fact that she's a cold bitch, which doesn't affect me one way or the other because I'd rather go swimming in the ocean in February than have lunch with her again, she's giving my nurses a hard time, and I don't know how to handle it, since I have no authority over her department."

Amanda described to Ken what Bonita and some of the other head nurses had said about the new drug distribution rules. "She doesn't do it all the time," Sylvia Watson had said at a head nurses' meeting, "only when the patient is first admitted.

"When we send down the initial order for medications, the pharmacy will give us only the first dose, and then they make us fill out another requisition for the rest of the doses for that day. It's a nuisance, and there's no reason for it," said Sylvia. The other head nurses had agreed.

"It creates more paperwork," Bonita added. "And then on the patient's second and subsequent days of hospitalization, we get the full number of unit doses the way we always have. I don't understand why we have this stupid new rule that makes no sense and makes more work for everyone—them *and* us."

Amanda knew how angry they were. Anything that created more paperwork and increased the ever-burgeoning bureaucratic tangles of caring for patients made nurses' jobs more difficult. Keeping the "crap quotient" down was up to the director of nursing.

"Evelyn Portman made this ridiculous new rule," Amanda explained to Ken, "and the nurses want me to do something about it, but I can't tell her how to run her department. What do you think I should do?"

"Did you ask her why she has a new procedure?" replied Ken. "Maybe there's a good reason that you're not aware of."

"No, I didn't," she admitted. "Ordinarily, I would approach something like this informally, like the time I asked Ruth why lunchtime for patients was changed from noon to eleven-thirty.

"Actually when that happened, Ruth told me about it first because she knew that it would affect nursing, and she gave me as much notice as she could. But then, Ruth is a reasonable and intelligent person."

"And you don't think the new pharmacist is?"

"Oh, she's smart, all right," replied Amanda. "No doubt about that. But she's the kind of person who might interpret my asking a question about procedure as criticism, and she might go running to David Townsend to complain that I'm poking my nose into her business. I think she has friends in high places," she added, explaining to Ken the circumstances under which Evelyn got the job at J. F. K. Memorial.

"That's just gossip," said Ken, who was a scientist as well as an administrator and believed very little that he couldn't see or measure. "You have no idea what the real story is."

Amanda acknowledged that the story was gossip. "But I believe every word of it. It has the ring of truth," she said.

She didn't tell him that she was intensely curious about how Evelyn Portman financed a home in Kalorama and why she would not say exactly where she lived. Ken would just tell her that it was none of her business and that it had no bearing on the problem at hand. And he would be right.

"As I see it, you have three choices," said Ken. "You can talk to Evelyn herself—diplomatically—and ask her why she made the new rule. Are you sure, by the way, that the rule came from her and not from higher up?"

"No," said Amanda, who had not considered that possibility. But Townsend would have told her that he was changing the pharmacy procedure, and he would have explained why.

"I'd find out about that if I were you," he said. "Second, you can go to David Townsend and ask him about it, but that can backfire by casting you in the role of tattletale and bothering your boss with something you ought to be able to deal with yourself."

Also true, Amanda thought. "And third?" she asked.

"You can drop it. Do nothing and wait and see if the nurses get accustomed to it and stop complaining about it. They may be angry now only because it's a new rule, something different to get used to, and eventually they will simply accept it the way they accept everything else."

Amanda sighed. "I suppose that's the most sensible course of action," she said, and she saw on his face that he thought so too. Ken didn't get to be CEO of Naylor-Noyes by making a mountain out of every molehill that came his way.

"But I hate to do that," she said. "I hate to make the nurses come that much closer to drowning in paperwork. They have so much already that's important, and this new thing is completely unnecessary."

Ken had no response to that. She had asked his advice, and he had given it. And neither of them wanted to talk more about work. It was too pleasant an evening, too romantic a setting for anything other than enjoyment—and anticipation of what lay ahead.

"May I join you?" asked Bonita.

Amanda was sitting alone at a table in the cafeteria eating lasagna that had looked good behind the glass in the food line. It tasted disgusting. "Please do," she said to the transplant unit nurse, who also had a portion of lasagna.

Amanda put the bookmark back in her novel and watched Bonita take a bite. She laughed at the expression that crossed the nurse's face. "Revolting, isn't it?"

"Jesus, how can anything that looks so delicious taste like such shit?" asked Bonita, outraged.

"It's a culinary crime," agreed Amanda, and both women doggedly ate some of the lasagna, unwilling to stand in the long line at the salad bar.

"I was going to call you later this afternoon," said Bonita, "but then I saw you here and didn't think you would mind my joining you."

"I'm glad you did," replied Amanda, who really was glad. She often had to eat alone in the hospital cafeteria. Most of the staff nurses were reluctant to sit with the boss, and the supervisors tended to eat in a group that Amanda did not join unless she was specifically invited to.

"I went to Roberta's funeral on Monday," said Bonita. "It was strange."

"It must have been sad for you," replied Amanda.

"It was," said the nurse. "It's not that I lost my best friend or anything—Roberta and I weren't that close—but I liked her and I'll miss her. I feel terrible about the way she died. She was doing so well and had made such a good physical adjustment to her new heart."

"And the psychological adjustment?" asked Amanda.

Bonita shrugged. "It's hard to tell. I think she was depressed a lot, and she was angry about the way people treated her a lot of the time—like a cripple. She hadn't had a steady job for years, and I don't think she made much money as a freelance writer."

"It sounds like a good reason to be depressed. How did she support herself?"

"Beats me," replied Bonita. "I always wondered about that, but I never felt that I could ask her. We didn't have that kind of relationship. It occurred to me that, even though she was always complaining about being horny, maybe she had a sugar daddy."

"At her age?" asked Amanda. She was immediately ashamed of making what could be construed as an incredibly sexist remark. She glanced at Bonita to see if she was offended.

"I know what you mean," said the other nurse. "You usually think of kept women as young and dumb—bimbos—and Roberta was no bimbo." She shrugged again. "I probably shouldn't have said that. I don't have anything to base it on. It's just that . . ."

"Just that what?" asked Amanda, intrigued now.

"After she died and before her chart went down to Medical Records, I looked at the cover sheet, and in the space where the name of the health insurance company is listed, it said 'self-pay,' " said Bonita. "Now where would a woman who had no health insurance and no job get several hundred thousand dollars to pay for a heart transplant and all the aftercare and medications? You know that a transplant means never-ending medical expenses."

Amanda stared at her. "That would require a *very* sweet sugar daddy," she replied.

"So she had a sugar daddy," said Glencora Rodman to Amanda that evening over dinner. "Lots of women do, even though no one has used that phrase since 1945!"

Amanda laughed. "I'm just an old-fashioned girl," she said. "Do you want more chicken?"

"Yes, please. It's wonderful," she said, handing over her plate. The two women and the grey cat were sitting at Amanda's kitchen table, and Amanda made silent note of the two healthy portions of chicken salad with grapes and walnuts that Glen had consumed, not to mention an ear of corn, a large tomato, and two big glasses of Chardonnay.

Ken was off on a business trip to New York and was not witness to the amount of food that Glen was putting away. If he had been home for dinner, there would have been some sarcastic comments made the moment Glen had driven away. Amanda's husband had not gotten over the fact that his wife's best friend didn't like him. It didn't matter that he didn't like Glencora either.

"After all," Glen continued, "in a way, all women who are supported by men who have more money than they do could be said to have sugar daddies. Even you."

Amanda stared at her friend. "How can you say that? We're married. It's different."

"The only difference between you and that patient is that you had a wedding," replied Glen and then added, "and the fact that you're being supported by Ken is a matter of public knowledge and public record, and from what you've told me, this woman didn't say anything to anyone about what you call her sugar daddy."

"If she had one," said Amanda, who was beginning to be sorry that she had brought up the subject.

"Right," said Glen. "*If*. But where else would a sick woman get that much money?"

"She could have stolen it," said Amanda. "She could have had an inheritance. She could have been blackmailing someone."

"Who? Her sugar daddy?" asked Glen. "Come on, Amanda. Aren't you getting a little carried away with your fantasies? And besides, why do you care where this patient, who's dead now, got the money to pay for her medical care? Why are you so obsessed about it?"

"I'm not obsessed."

Yes, you are, said the voice, which always told her the truth about what she was feeling. At the same time, her best friend said nothing but sat across the table stroking Shadow, who purred in another chair waiting patiently for one of the women to slip her a piece of chicken. Glencora's expression clearly said: you're full of shit.

"Okay, you're right. It doesn't matter," said Amanda, who didn't believe that for a moment. "But that's not what I'm really worried about."

Glencora remained silent. She picked up a small piece of chicken and let the cat lick it from her fingers. Amanda rolled her eyes. "If Ken could see that, he'd have a heart attack. He doesn't even let her sit at the table when he's home."

"I can't imagine why," said Glen sarcastically. "You're such a pushover for that animal."

"But it wasn't me who fed her at the table," said Amanda testily. "She's supposed to eat out of her bowl—on the floor."

"Come on, Amanda. What's bothering you?"

She sighed. "Someone is stealing narcotics at the hospital."

"Oh God, no wonder you're upset. How do you know? Can you catch them?"

Amanda repeated to Glen what Betsy Murdock had told her on Friday. "It's not really a question of knowing for sure, as in having evidence of theft," she added. "It's more knowing because of experience.

"When, all of a sudden several patients begin to complain that their pain medication isn't working, you have to wonder if something is going on."

"But just because someone is in pain doesn't mean that nurses are stealing narcotics," said Glen. "Isn't that jumping to a conclusion?"

"Yes and no," said Amanda. "That's what makes this kind of thing such a pain in the ass. It's true that sometimes Demerol or morphine doesn't always relieve pain, especially really intractable pain from cancer or other awful diseases. But with 'routine' pain, like what you have right after an operation or a heart attack or childbirth—something like that, it's easier to predict what kind and how much of a drug will relieve it most of the time. That's why there's a standard range of doses of narcotics.

"For example, you give a patient 75 mg or 100 mg of Demerol or 10 mg or 15 mg of morphine every three or four hours for two or three days post-op, depending on their weight and what they've had done, and that usually takes care of them.

By that time, they're walking around pretty well and they can be switched to aspirin or Tylenol for a few days, and then they don't need anything for pain.

"That routine is known to work well, but when someone—or in this case, many someones—is still hurting a half hour or an hour after a big jolt of morphine, you have to start wondering if they really have gotten the medication."

"That's disgusting," said Glen. "Why don't you just call the police?"

"I could, I suppose," replied Amanda. "But if all of a sudden there are detectives swarming all over the hospital, asking questions and poking around in narcotics closets, whoever is doing it will stop for a while and get away with it. I'd rather lay a trap."

"What kind of trap?" asked Glen, very alert now.

"You're not going to write a story about this, are you?" asked Amanda. "Because if you're going to put it in the magazine, I'm not telling you any more."

Glencora was the editor-in-chief of *Style and Sense*, a local magazine that originally was devoted to fluff and gossip about rich and prominent Washingtonians, the ones who lived in Kalorama, Georgetown, and the tonier suburbs like Potomac, Maryland and McLean, Virginia. But she had quickly become bored with covering celebrity parties and writing articles about face lifts and home decorating, so little by little, the articles in *Style and Sense* had grown more serious and substantive. There was now real information among the advertisements for $2,000,000 houses and plastic surgeons who would reshape your entire body.

The magazine was beginning to attract national attention, and an exposé on narcotics thefts in a large university hospital, where many *Style and Sense* readers went as patients, was just the kind of thing that Glencora would like to get her hands on. The magazine would have to increase its print run for that issue, and Glen would score big brownie points with the publisher.

"I won't write about it until it's all over," Glen promised. "But if it turns out to be a real crime and a real problem in other hospitals, and if I think our readers would be interested, I might do it. But I won't do it now and I won't interfere with your investigation. Fair enough?"

"Fair enough," agreed Amanda, who couldn't imagine how anyone would not be interested in a scandal of that magnitude.

"So how are you going to catch the thief?"

"Betsy and I have figured out a paperwork trap," said Amanda. "We're going to keep a list of all the patients who complain that they're not getting relief from narcotics, and then we'll see if one nurse is common to all of them."

"Very clever," said Glen. "But how will you prove it? All she has to do is say that the patients had especially severe pain or that they were particularly whiny people, or that their operations were really difficult—or whatever."

"That's true. We haven't figured out that part yet," admitted Amanda. "One step at a time."

"What about asking Lydia for help?"

"She's the police. I just told you why we don't want to get them involved yet."

"But she's also your friend," said Glen. "Couldn't you just ask her advice in an unofficial capacity?"

"But I'd like to keep her as a friend. It wouldn't be fair to her to ask her to keep this quiet. If she has knowledge of a crime, she'd be obligated to report it and the police would have to take some action," replied Amanda. She did not add that she had already told Lydia about what she was beginning to think of as the transplant mystery. Even though the narcotics theft was "real," she had no proof of that either, and there was no point in having Lydia think she was completely crazy. No, the police were out.

Glen acknowledged that Amanda had a point. "What's for dessert?" she asked.

"Nothing," said Amanda. "Let's go for a walk and work off part of the dinner."

"Okay."

"Then we can go to Gifford's for ice cream," said Amanda.

Mark Cipriotti was scared. Things were not working out at all in the way the three of them had planned, and now he was as afraid of Sarah Castle as he was of being caught.

Either way, he was fucked.

The developers still hadn't signed the contracts to build the office-hotel-retail complex, and now, after that stupid, childish street demonstration, it looked as though the deal might fall through permanently. Television cameras had caught the full force of the demonstration, and it was the lead story on all three local stations on both the 6 P.M. and 11 P.M. news. It was on the front page of *The Washington Post* this morning, and Allen Hackett said he had seen a small piece in the *New York Times*.

"The *Times*! Jesus, Al," he had said on the phone to Hackett.

"The reporters love it," said Allen Hackett. "They probably think they're back in the sixties. It makes great copy."

It was even better for television. All those chanting yuppies, with their hundred-dollar sneakers and designer T-shirts, carrying homemade picket signs protesting the encroachment of big bad business chewing up their neighborhood.

And the signs. Cipriotti felt sick when he saw the signs. AVENGE AARON ZURMAN!—DON'T LET ZURMAN DIE!!—REMEMBER WHAT ZURMAN STOOD FOR. There was one that had scared Cipriotti more than all the others combined: ZURMAN DIED FOR YOU!

They were making a martyr out of him, out of plain, ordinary (but hot-to-trot-to-Congress) Aaron Zurman. That meant that his death would be examined and poked over and possibly investigated by the police. Cipriotti was positive now that the police would investigate Zurman's death.

He had been sweating when he picked up the phone to call Allen Hackett, and when they finished the conversation, his hands had been too slippery to hold the receiver. His heart was pounding so hard that he thought he would have a coronary, and fear had blurred his vision so badly that he didn't think he would be able to drive to the meeting place that he and Hackett had just agreed on.

═══ CHAPTER 11 ═══

"Jesus H. Christ on a goddamn crutch!" said William Zyrwynsky. "What the hell is going on here?"

The chief of J. F. K. Memorial's transplant unit said this to every single one of the team members who were gathered in the conference room for the emergency meeting.

He said it to no one in particular.

He was furious, but Bonita was pleased to see that he showed no shame over the tears in his eyes. "This is the third unnecessary reject since I joined this staff, and I will be goddamned if I'm going to let this little boy die!"

The little boy was named Billy Ockerson and he was two and a half years old. He lay not 100 feet away from the conference room, and he was even closer to death now than he had been three days ago when he had received part of his mother's liver.

Bill Zyrwynsky had been one of the pioneers of this type of transplant: removing a piece of tissue from a living donor who is a close genetic match and implanting it in a recipient who would die without it. Now it looked as though Billy would die anyway because he was in the throes of hyperacute rejection.

"How am I going to face this woman and tell her that not only has her son died, but that part of her has died as well, that her gift of life was not able to save her only child?"

Bonita spoke. "Bill, stop taking this so personally. We're all doing everything we can. We're pouring cyclosporine and Imuran and everything else we can think of into him. Billy is getting the best possible care. If we can't save him, he cannot be saved. If you were thinking clearly, you'd realize that liver transplant patients are damn sick people."

Bonita was afraid she had spoken too sharply to Zyrwynsky. He was a nice guy and one of the new breed of physicians who tried not think of themselves as gods, but he was still the chief of the unit, and as smoothly as the team worked, she was still "only" a nurse.

She was also afraid that the whole team had become contaminated by the hoopla surrounding Billy Ockerson's operation. The reporters were still pestering them, and even though the barracudas with their TV cameras and self-righteous demeanors were supposed to be sent to the hospital's public relations department, sometimes an enterprising one got onto the patient floors. Last evening a woman from *The Washington Post* walked right into the transplant unit itself.

Billy's parents, frustrated by the lack of an available liver donor for their child, had succumbed to the temptation of hiring a publicist, who managed to convince Channel 6 that an appeal on the evening news for a liver donor would be a good and public-spirited thing to do.

Unfortunately the backlash had been more vindictive than anyone had expected and the appeal had backfired. Groups of parents of children who were also waiting for a variety of organs, but who couldn't afford to pay for publicity, were furious at what they saw as favoritism for Billy Ockerson. The TV station had been obligated to interview many of them, and the tear-streaked faces they presented to the camera fueled more outrage, and the next day the *Post* in its lead editorial excoriated the Ockersons' "crass commercial pitch." So there had been no liver for Billy—whether because of the backlash or because of fate, Bonita had no way of knowing, but she was secretly on the side of the people who had protested.

The kind of media circus that the Ockersons had unleashed was bad for organ transplantation. Roberta Garfield would have hated it, and Bonita found herself with sudden and unexpected tears in her eyes as she thought of Roberta.

Zyrwynsky spoke again: "You're right. We can't let our anger cloud our professional judgment."

Bonita noted, with a combination of cynicism and amusement, that Bill Zyrwynsky was still "doctorish" enough not to apologize for his flare of anger and not to accept it as his own, but he was also human enough to acknowledge its presence at the conference table, even though he made an effort to spread it around. Better than the old school of physicians who ran their professional and personal lives like a slave ship, she thought.

". . . seems to me that we have two basic choices," Zyrwynsky was saying. "We can keep on with what we're doing, pray like hell—and then face the media music when Billy dies. Or we can convince his parents to start him on FK-506."

Eyes opened wide all around the conference table. FK-506 was a new and still experimental antirejection drug that had so far proved to be almost 100 times as powerful as cyclosporine, with far fewer side effects. It had been discovered as a common soil fungus, but when it was refined it turned into a veritable miracle for transplant patients. It was still in the research phase, and Zyrwynsky would not only have to get permission from Billy's parents, he would have to ask for emergency compassionate use from the Food and Drug Administration.

The press would surely find out, and that, Bonita thought, was the real risk. If Billy was saved, Zyrwynsky would be hailed as a hero and a daring medical pioneer. If Billy died, Zyrwynsky could easily be branded a Dr. Jekyll who experimented on innocent children and gave them unapproved and unproven drugs to further his own career. He would be raked over the coals in the press, and the hospital would suffer from the adverse publicity.

And that, Bonita knew, was something that J. F. K. Memorial tried to avoid at all costs. In fact, William Zyrwynsky was hired away from Johns Hopkins because he had received so much good publicity there, and J. F. K., as a private hospital, needed to beef up the departments that produced high revenue and good press.

The transplant unit was one of them. Organ transplants were expensive, almost always successful, at least for a few years, and the patients were so grateful that they tended to lavish praise on the doctors and nurses, who they perceived as having given them a new life. Sometimes they also made big donations.

Health care was big business now—at about $600 billion a year, just about the biggest in the nation—and private hospitals were becoming as competitive with each other as car dealers and department stores. Bill Zyrwynsky knew that. He was aware of his own reputation and knew that one of the major reasons he had been wooed to J. F. K. was to help fatten the coffers in the transplant unit.

Everyone else sitting around the conference table knew these things as well, but they were also aware of the conflict they faced. Where did their primary obligation lie—to the patient or to the hospital? Ah, there's the rub, thought Bonita as she watched the faces of the dozen others as they considered the risks of giving Billy FK-506.

"We could kill Billy in our zeal to save him," said Stephanie Dahlgren, who seemed compelled to point out the obvious at every opportunity. Bonita thought she was basically a decent nurse, but she had no tact.

Zyrwynsky flushed at her remark as well as at the rejoinder made by Jack Hillsborough-Joyce. The latter, a second-year surgical resident who was as pompous and silly as his name suggested—a name inherited from his mother, not foisted on him by a feminist wife—said, "The kid seems to be on his way out regardless of what we do."

The debate went on, but Bonita was no longer listening. She believed their obligation was only to Billy, not to the Ockerson family, not to the hospital and its damned bottom-line accountants, and certainly not to the media vultures.

Sometimes Bill Zyrwynsky was too democratic. Make a decision already, she thought. I have patients to take care of out there. I can't sit here all morning.

As if on cue, Zyrwynsky said, "I think we should go for it. Any serious objections to asking permission to put Billy on an FK-506 protocol?"

Ken was playing in the finals of a tennis tournament, and Amanda decided that she could not sit in the broiling sun for one more minute, watching people smash little green balls back and forth at each other. As long as she was going to leave the tennis club, she thought it would be a good opportunity to talk to Lydia alone, but arranging lunch with a detective, who could be anywhere in the city at any time, even on a Saturday, was almost impossible.

At almost the same time as the conference about Billy Ockerson was ending, Amanda fished a quarter out of her purse and called Lydia at her desk at the Second District Headquarters on Idaho Avenue, N.W. Her friend picked up on the first ring.

"Amanda! What a coincidence. I was just about to call you."

"Great minds run along the same track," said Amanda. "You first."

"Remember Sunday when we talked about your suspicions that something strange is going on at the hospital? Well, apparently you're not the only one who thinks so," said Lydia.

Amanda felt excitement and nervousness at the same time. "Tell me," she said.

"A guy came in here yesterday and talked to one of the other detectives and said that his cousin had been murdered at your hospital."

"Gerald Miller!" said Amanda.

"Right. How did you know?"

"Because he was in my office on Tuesday saying the same thing," replied Amanda.

Lydia was silent for a few seconds. "Okay," she said. "Your turn. Why did you call me?"

"I wanted to get together and talk about what Chinless said when he came to see me. I need to ask you some questions. Are you by any chance free for a late lunch?"

"Chinless?"

"Gerald Miller," explained Amanda. "Don't you think he's kind of wimpy-looking?"

"I didn't see him. I told you he talked to another detective."

Did Lydia sound just a little annoyed at becoming involved in a murder investigation that wasn't officially hers? Did she think Amanda was taking advantage of their friendship?

"I can't make lunch," she said, "but Sal and I are going out for pizza tonight. Why don't you and Ken come with us?"

Amanda wasn't sure how enthusiastic her friend was about the invitation, nor was she certain that Ken would be in the mood for anything more energetic than sitting by the pool and having her wait on him—if he could stay awake that long. She explained this to Lydia and added, "I don't want to be a third wheel."

"Don't be a jerk," said Lydia in a voice that erased Amanda's previous fears. "Put your jock husband to bed and be at my apartment at six-thirty. We'll talk more."

"Did anyone ever tell you that you look exactly like Paul Bunyan?" Amanda asked Sal Mateo as the three of them sat in a booth at Machiavelli's on Capitol Hill, sipping beer and waiting for their pizza.

Lydia almost choked. "More like the Jolly Green Giant— ho, ho, ho," she said.

"Do the two of you want me to leave while you discuss my physical charms?" asked Sal in mock outrage. "I could go out and pace up and down Pennsylvania Avenue while you amuse yourselves at my expense."

Sal Mateo, chief medical examiner for the District of Columbia, did look like Paul Bunyan, or maybe a benign brown bear. He was huge: about six and a half feet tall, and his face was dominated by a bushy brown beard and matching mustache. The ferocity was softened, however, by gigantic brown eyes that radiated warmth, humor, and intimacy. No wonder Lydia was ga-ga over him. He was dressed now in faded cut-off jeans, sandals, and a Boston Red Sox T-shirt. He had ordered a large pizza for himself while Lydia and Amanda would share a medium one. Amanda had never seen anyone with so prodigious an appetite. Lydia called him "the vacuum cleaner."

The first time Amanda had seen Sal Mateo had been in his morgue. He had been dressed then in green scrubs under an enveloping heavy plastic apron—and she had passed out practically in his arms.

"So what's with Gerald Miller?" asked Amanda.

"I don't know too much more than I told you on the phone," replied Lydia. "He walked into the squad room yesterday and said that he believed his cousin had been murdered at your hospital. Detective Len Agostino interviewed him and apparently couldn't get too much information. The guy, Miller, didn't *have* much information and said basically what you told me at brunch on Sunday about the victim, Aaron Zurman."

"Don't start calling him a victim until you know for sure that he was murdered," said Sal.

"Okay," said Lydia. "But anyway, Agostino went out to talk to Mrs. Zurman yesterday afternoon. He didn't think he'd get much because he didn't believe there was much of anything to get—but when someone mentions the word murder, you can't just ignore it." She smiled and held out her hands, palms up, in a gesture that expressed frustration with her job, the politics of the District of Columbia government, and life in general.

"I knew you would grill me about this tonight, so I talked to Agostino before I left work."

Amanda leaned forward. "Nothing," said Lydia. "He got absolutely nothing. The woman had such a thick accent that he couldn't understand anything she said—even if she had been making sense, which apparently she wasn't."

Amanda understood the detective's frustration; it mirrored her own. "But what if—" she began.

Lydia held up her hand. "Let me finish."

"Sorry," said Amanda.

"Agostino is going to get in touch with Miller when he comes back from a business trip, find out what language his aunt speaks, and interview the woman with an interpreter. Then at least he'll know if the problem is a language barrier or mush-for-brains."

"Whose—Agostino's or the old woman's?" asked Sal.

Lydia ignored the remark, but judging by the expression that crossed Sal's face, Amanda thought there might be some pinching going on under the table.

"So that's it?" she asked, disappointed that Lydia didn't have a dramatic cops-and-robbers story, with full sirens screaming, to tell over the pizzas that had just arrived at their table.

Lydia swallowed a mouthful of pizza, took a sip of beer to cool her mouth, and said, "What did you expect? An arrest, a conviction, and maybe the bad guy fried already?"

Amanda felt chagrined because Lydia had put words to her fantasy with uncanny accuracy. She smiled sheepishly. "I don't know. I thought maybe they would begin an investigation."

"They have," replied Lydia. "A case file has been opened. You'll probably have Agostino or his partner paying the hospital a visit in the next few days. He'll talk to Zurman's mother as well as to Miller again. They'll keep going until they either reach a dead end or until they make an arrest. It's too early to tell which it will be."

Sal had been working his way through the pizza without seeming to be paying much attention to the women's conversation, but he hadn't missed a word. "What did this guy Miller say was the murder weapon?" he asked them.

"He didn't say," replied Amanda. "In fact, he admitted that he had no proof that a murder had taken place. I told him that no one had done any obvious harm to Zurman while he was in the hospital. No one had shot his cousin or stabbed him, or anything like that."

"There's more than one way to skin a cat," said Sal. "Knives and guns are obvious, but they're not the only way to off someone."

"Poison!" said Amanda.

Sal merely shrugged.

"But he's been buried," she said. "If he really was murdered, it's too late to find the evidence."

"Dig him up," Sal replied matter-of-factly.

"You two are disgusting," said Lydia. "Can't we drop this, at least until after we finish eating? Besides, I have something to tell you, Amanda. Don't make any plans for New Year's Eve."

"Are you giving a party?" asked Amanda.

"Yes—in a church with a minister," answered Lydia with a smile so wide that it looked like her whole body was grinning.

While Sal and Lydia were making eyes at each other over the remnants of the pizza and Amanda was now definitely feeling like a third wheel, Caspar and Leona Torrey were having one of the worst fights of their lives. She wanted to kill him and thought that if one of them didn't leave the room, she might very well do just that.

"You were sleeping with her," Leona hissed. "Everyone in the whole church must be gossiping about the way you behaved. Bawling like a baby at that woman's funeral. You lost control and made a complete fool of yourself—and of me." She said this in a voice so venomous that Caspar took a step backward.

If she knows that part, what's to prevent her from knowing the rest? Caspar thought. His heart raced and he felt his hands begin to sweat despite the cold air blowing on him from the window air conditioner in the living room. But four years in the seminary and more than twenty years as minister to middle-class Presbyterians had taught him, at the very least, to show nothing of what he was feeling. However, all the years of keeping his upper lip stiff had blown sky-high at Roberta's funeral.

How had it happened? How had he let himself fall apart so totally? How had he allowed all those years of carefully nurtured discipline to fail him when he most needed it?

On Sunday evening, after he had prepared Roberta's eulogy, he had gone to the funeral home where Roberta lay waiting for her final ride to church the following morning, and then to her eternal resting place at Mt. Hope Cemetery. He had planned his visit for just before the mortuary closed to the public for the evening, but one mourner remained long after the other guests at the wake had departed.

The woman who stood quietly in front of the coffin did not question why Roberta's minister had come so late in the evening. That was one of the advantages of being a man of the cloth: people always gave you the benefit of the doubt, no matter what kind of mischief you were up to. Everyone wanted to believe the best of the clergy. It was how he might be able to get away with . . .

The Reverend Caspar Torrey shook his head to clear it of the memory of the last time he had seen Roberta alive, and concentrated on the problem at hand: his wife.

"How long?" she shrieked. "How long were you fucking her?"

Caspar was startled by the word. "Don't talk that way about her," he replied—and gave himself away.

"I'll talk any way I please," shouted Leona. "I'll say any words I want. FUCK. FUCK. SHIT. PISS. FUCK. ASSHOLE. FUCK. FU—"

"All right, Leona," he cut in in his soothing, placating minister's voice, suddenly weary, no longer caring what happened. He left the room saying, "When you're calmer, let me know," and went out into the garden, where he knew she wouldn't dare continue the fight, lest the neighbors hear.

The roses that bloomed late in the season filled the summer air with their heavy fragrance, and just for a moment he thought he was in Roberta's bedroom with her scent, so much like these dark red blossoms, lingering on his skin. He had always regretted having to take a shower before he left her and went home to Leona. But to return home with the smell of sex and roses heavy on him was unthinkable.

Again, he cried for his loss, for what he had done, for the way he had destroyed two lives. Again, he no longer cared. The Reverend Caspar Torrey thought he had stopped caring on Sunday evening as he sat next to Roberta's casket, open for the last time, and bade her farewell.

Before he sat down and placed his hand on the smooth mahogany of the coffin, he had not realized the depths of his grief. But when it flowed over him, engulfed him in its magnitude and finality, he began to cry. At first it was more a whimper than a sob, but finally he gave in and moaned aloud. He did not notice that the woman he had seen just a few moments before had returned from the parking lot to the room where Roberta lay in order to ask the minister a question. Neither did he notice that she stood in the doorway, staring in astonishment, and then quietly left—her question unasked.

When he finally left Roberta about an hour later, drained and shaken, Caspar thought he had gotten it all out in those racking sobs. He should have known better, he thought wryly as he walked in the rectory garden this evening. How many times had he counseled parishioners and explained the long, rocky, and unpredictable course of grief? How could he have been stupid enough not to apply those lessons to himself? Why was he so surprised when he was overtaken by a fresh wave of grief and had broken down sobbing in the middle of his carefully prepared eulogy?

Leona was wrong about one thing, though. The parishioners might indeed be talking about how he had cried—an uncharacteristic action for a clergyman. But in a million years, they would never know why. They took his tears for the concern of a truly caring minister. People commented on it, all right, after the graveside service was over and before they dispersed to their cars. But they were not the remarks that Leona imagined. "It's so good to see a minister who cares about his flock," said one.

Another mourner, his own eyes misty, said, "I'm not sure my own children will get that emotional when I die." A woman about Roberta's age took his hand in both of hers and held it for a long moment. "Thank you for caring so much," she said simply.

Leona would find out soon enough that she was wrong about the way people perceived his tears. But that would not be enough to heal the trouble between them. That had begun long before Roberta had shaken his hand on the church steps that first morning, and in the end it had nothing to do with Roberta and what they had done together and what he had been doing for her these past years—and what he had ultimately done to her.

It was a busy evening in the nation's capital. Crack dealers were killing each other in record numbers. Amanda Knight was talking about wedding plans with her friend Lydia and the city's chief medical examiner. Senators and representatives were sitting, as usual, in the deep leather chairs of the Metropolitan Club and the Union League Club, thinking of ways to further screw up their country's government. The Reverend Caspar Torrey, longtime minister of the Calvary Presbyterian Church of Gaithersburg, Maryland, was consumed with grief and guilt. And Evelyn Portman, she of the perfect grooming, expensive clothes, and every hair in place, had fallen apart, at least in a sartorial sense.

In fact, she was a mess. Her hair was in wild disarray, her clothes lay disheveled on the floor of her apartment on California Street, Northwest, and her makeup was hopelessly smudged. Evelyn herself was in the throes of lust. In moments, her lover would bring her to the third and final orgasm of the evening. Her bones would rattle beneath her skin.

Amanda would have been delighted to have been a fly on the wall in that bedroom on California Street, which was furnished meagerly compared with the sumptuousness of the living room.

If Amanda had been there, she would have had to retract the unkind remark she'd made to Ruth Sinclair about Evelyn not wanting to get her hair messed up by making love.

On the other hand, what Evelyn and her lover were making could not be classified as love, in the strictest sense of the word, because they did not love each other. Rather, they had formed a small and exclusive mutual admiration society, and at the end of these occasional sessions in Evelyn's bedroom each found a need fulfilled—a need that was much more than sex and quite different from it.

Now, after her lover had accomplished his goal of forcing her over the edge of rational thought, he and Evelyn lay silently for a while, their sweaty bodies not touching. She was thinking about what a technically expert lover he was—and how totally devoid of anything even remotely resembling emotion. She sometimes felt like a musical instrument, the way he stroked, plucked, tongued, caressed, and penetrated her to achieve the instrument's ultimate performance. But, she admitted to herself, feelings were not part of this bargain, and if she wanted tenderness and love, she would have to look elsewhere. The problem was that she did not know where or how to look.

Evelyn's lover was lost in his own thoughts too. He wondered how soon he could decently leave. He had patients to see at the hospital before he went home for the evening, and he wondered uneasily if his wife had tried to call him at his office and what kind of message she would have left with his answering service. The vision of what his wife had done to the pharmacy at St. Jude's crossed his mind, and he shuddered.

He felt trapped. Leaving his wife would cost him more money than he could afford. But staying married was getting more and more expensive because Evelyn Portman did not come cheap. Even if he could scrape together the cash and even if he could leave the marriage with his balls intact, Evelyn would be like a hawk circling with talons outspread the minute she heard the word divorce. He would have to leave the arrangement as it was for the present, although he wasn't sure how much longer he could keep it up. He was exhausted by Evelyn's sexual needs and frightened by her financial demands. He sighed when he realized that he had gotten himself into a mess, and there seemed to be no way out.

As if she had read his mind, Evelyn touched his arm and said, "The condo board is talking about raising the monthly fee."

Her lover pulled his arm away and said, "How much do you want this time?"

"You make it sound so cold-blooded," she replied. "I had thought we were more to each other than that."

Oh Christ, he thought. Here we go again. He rolled over, put his arms around her, and ran his hand along her flank, keeping his mental fingers crossed that she would not interpret the gesture as foreplay. "You know I care deeply about you," he said with as much sincerity as he could muster. "You know that I've made a commitment to you, and that if I were a free man, I would make my feelings more tangible and public. But for now . . ."

He let his voice trail off. They had been through this before. Every woman who slept with a married man had heard this before.

Evelyn got out of bed, put on a silk robe that he had bought her last Christmas, and went to the window, turning her back to him. "Twenty-five hundred should do it this time," she said.

"Christ, Evelyn, I can't come up with that much. You're bleeding me dry. It was the same amount last time." It seemed like only yesterday that he had gone to the bank, withdrawn the cash, and sent it to her by courier.

She shrugged and felt the panic begin to rise, but she managed to control her voice. "So let's end it then." There was no quaver in her voice. No whine. Good. Let *him* be scared for a change.

"Evelyn," he said, coming to stand next to her at the window and putting his arm around her, feeling the silk and the warm flesh beneath, growing rigid again despite his desire to be out of this apartment. "You know how much I care about you."

This time it was she who slipped from his grasp, but not before noticing his rapidly hardening penis. His continuing need for what she did for him—the important things, not the sex—emboldened her. "I'd like the money tomorrow," she said. "I'll be in my office all day."

Evening in Washington deepened into the dead of night. Evelyn's lover had left, seen his patients, and gone home to an empty house. He fell into a deep sleep, neither wondering nor caring where his wife was.

Evelyn Portman tossed and turned for a long time before she fell into a light, restless slumber. She woke briefly and took two aspirin for the headache she always developed after crying so hard.

Amanda and Ken were at home asleep. Shadow was pressed up against her woman, but the loud purring woke neither husband nor wife. The bedroom windows were open and the night breeze ruffled the cat's soft belly fur.

Lydia and Sal were asleep too. They looked like two forest creatures curled up in a snug nighttime hiding place—a big brown bear with its arm around a small red fox.

Even most of Washington's drug dealers and addicts were asleep now, or at least in a state that passed for sleep. Two of them had died this night. One lay under the harsh glare of police floodlights in an alley behind a housing project in a neighborhood called Anacostia. A good portion of his blood had flowed out onto the cracked, garbage-strewn pavement. The other one was alone in a crack house, abandoned instantly by his fellow patrons and not yet discovered by a human soul who would call the police.

The city had finally quieted for the night.

The residents of the suburban community of Rockville, Maryland had gone to bed hours before. But one of them, Mark Cipriotti, lay awake, more frightened than he had ever been in his entire life.

Sarah Castle had threatened to kill him.

CHAPTER 12

Amanda and Betsy Murdock sat in Amanda's office at her round conference table with dozens of patients' charts spread out around them. The door was closed and locked and Louise had been given instructions to hold all calls except for emergencies.

"Here's another one at the beginning of a shift," said Betsy. She put a stroke, with the date and time noted, next to the name Julia Finn on their master graph. It was the fourth notation for that nurse. "At seven-thirty in the morning this patient was 'in extreme agony' even though she had received a hefty slug of Demerol only an hour and a half before."

"I suppose it stands to reason that it's a night nurse," said Amanda. "Fewer people notice what you're doing."

"How many more charts do we have left?" asked Betsy.

"Many," replied Amanda. "Don't ask."

The two women doggedly read every nurse's note on every surgical patient's chart for the entire month of July. They were looking for examples of patients who complained that they were not helped by pain medication. Thus they limited their search to the three days immediately following the operation. They would widen the search if necessary, but Amanda thought it might not be. They had three "suspects" already, a fact that depressed her enormously. Three nurses out of a total of more than five hundred employed at J. F. K. Memorial Hospital who might be stealing narcotics was more than she wanted to deal with. The fact that they were taking drugs that rightfully belonged to sick people in pain made it that much worse.

Amanda and Betsy worked silently for a long while, putting the completed charts on the floor in one corner of the office. They had decided to start with charts of discharged patients so as not to raise suspicions about what they were doing.

116

Amanda had had to take Charley Boston, the chief of Medical Records, into her confidence. He had instructed his clerks to pull all the charts she had requested, and they made an amazingly large pile in her office.

"Are you going to tell Townsend about this?" asked Betsy.

"Sooner or later I'm going to have to," she replied. "I'd like to put it off until I have something concrete to tell him, but eventually he'll need to know. Maybe we can catch the culprit and he'll give us each a medal for keeping the police out of it."

"Better a medal than those stupid yellow ribbons that the nurses wore during the war," said Betsy dryly.

Amanda made no response, but a frown of annoyance crossed her face. When President Bush had sent troops to the Persian Gulf, many of the nurses sported yellow ribbons, some of them so big that they looked like corsages, and American flags pinned to the blouses and shirts that they wore over white pants or skirts.

Amanda hated it. It reeked of mindless, unthinking patriotism and jingoistic war-mongering that frightened and appalled her. Besides, it looked idiotic. One of these days she was going to have to figure out how to control the size and type of that kind of crap without alienating people who supported what was obviously a popular cause. But right now, finding the narcotics thief was more important than worrying about the "decorations" for whatever war was next.

When finally all the charts were stacked on the floor, it looked as if they had made some serious and disturbing discoveries. Julia Finn had seven of what Amanda was coming to think of as "strikes against her." Two other nurses had five apiece. All worked the night shift permanently.

She and Betsy looked at each other in dismay. "Do you think there's some kind of narcotics ring here in the hospital?" asked the latter. "Maybe we're supplying half the addicts in the District with a nice variety of drugs."

And a varied pharmacopeia indeed was involved: morphine, codeine, Demerol, Dilaudid, Numorphan, and Innovar. The last was by far the most potent, a combination of narcotic analgesic and tranquilizer. Anyone who received a shot of Innovar spent several hours in another solar system.

"It's beginning to look that way," agreed Amanda. "Do you

have any idea of how many times this might have happened
but went unrecorded: the number of patients who didn't complain, the ones who did complain but no one bothered to
document?"

"I'm not sure I even want to think about that," said Betsy.

"Luckily we don't have to," Amanda told her. "We can
work with what we have—and I'm not even sure what to do
with that. It seems to me we have a number of choices."

"Before we do anything drastic, like get Townsend involved,
let me do a little investigative work," said Betsy. "I was only
half joking when I made that remark about a narcotics ring.
What if these three birds are working together and have some
sort of organized scam going?"

"What if they're not?" Amanda reminded her. "What if
they're not guilty of anything more than being crazy enough
to want to work permanent nights? And even if they're guilty
as sin, even if they have direct links to the Mafia, we have no
proof of anything," she added.

"I wasn't exactly going to rush in and make a citizen's
arrest in the middle of the night," said Betsy, a little miffed
at Amanda for not giving her credit for more common sense.
"I was thinking more of trying to find out if these three have
any connection outside of work, or maybe if they knew each
other before being hired here."

Amanda shrugged. "It can't hurt, I suppose, as long as no
one knows what you're up to. But even if they do know each
other—if they give joint Tupperware parties every weekend—
it still doesn't prove anything. And if they have no connection
outside of work, that doesn't mean that they're not in cahoots
stealing narcotics."

"All true," acknowledged Betsy. "But it's a start."

Amanda sighed. "Okay, but you'd better do it soon. If someone really is stealing, we have to catch the thief right away, and
I have a feeling that Townsend will want the police or maybe a
private undercover detective involved. Probably the latter. You
know how the hospital is about bad publicity. He's not going
to want any shit to hit the fan before it absolutely has to."

The women gathered up all the charts and stacked them
in piles on the conference table. Amanda decided not to ask
Betsy how she was going to find out if the three nurses knew
each other.

Some things you just don't need to know, warned the voice that tried to keep her out of trouble. This time she listened.

Amanda returned to her office from lunch at Giovanni's with Eddie Silverman and picked up her pink message slips where Louise had left them stuck into a corner of her desk blotter. One was from the head of Housekeeping (probably a complaint that too many people were bleeding onto the sheets) and another was from Ken with the time his flight was arriving from a one-day trip to Chicago. At the bottom of the slip Louise had written, "Ken said not to bother coming to the airport but to meet him at that good pasta place in Georgetown."

Amanda knew exactly where he meant: Filomena's on Wisconsin, next to the store that sold upscale sex toys, where the pasta was homemade and the desserts were to die for. She called and made a reservation for an hour after his plane was due. Maybe after dinner they could peruse the stock at The Pleasure Chest.

The third message was from Bonita Elliott. Amanda decided to respond in person and took the elevator up to the transplant unit.

On the way she stopped for a surprise visit to the cardiac step-down unit. This was where patients spent a few days after leaving the cardiac intensive care unit but before going to a regular floor where the nursing care was not as intensive.

Amanda made unannounced inspection tours from time to time. She did it to check up on the nursing care, and it was the only way she could find out what was really going on. She looked in several patients' rooms, introduced herself and chatted with the occupants. All seemed pleased that she visited them. One middle-aged man flirted with her and she flirted back.

There were no full bedpans next to the hopper in the utility room, although she noticed that the trash cans were filled to overflowing. She realized that she had not returned the call to the housekeeping department. Maybe it was to tell me they're going on strike, she thought.

She checked the narcotic closet, counted every drug in it,

and compared the total to the running tally sheet sent up to each nursing unit three times a day by the pharmacy. Cardiac patients used few narcotics after the initial crushing pain of a heart attack had passed, so the stock here was meager. Everything seemed in order, but incorrect tally sheets were not how Betsy had discovered the narcotics thefts.

Leah Stambler, the head nurse, came out of one of the patient's rooms at the opposite end of the hall and paled a little when she realized what Amanda was doing. She ran a good unit, but an inspection made everyone nervous.

"It looks good," said Amanda, "but the dog who lives next door to me would love your garbage can. What's the matter with Housekeeping?" She was careful not to blame Leah for the mess until she knew what was going on, but she also wanted to find out what the nurse had done to solve a problem that would reach critical proportions by that evening if the trash were not taken away soon.

"I've called Housekeeping twice, and both times they said they'd be right up," said the head nurse. "I was going to call again, but then I got busy."

"I'll take care of it," said Amanda, walking toward the phone in the nurses' station. "I need to call them anyway."

"Thanks," said Leah, who was happy to be able to return to taking care of patients.

The call that Amanda made turned out to be one of the most gratifying interactions she'd had all day—all week maybe. It seemed that there had been some confusion about the scheduling of trash pickup with the new hauling company that the hospital had hired, and the housekeeping department was phoning everyone to apologize for the inconvenience.

Amanda hung up the phone and looked in patient rooms to find Leah Stambler. She waited in the hall until the nurse finished helping a very old woman back to bed, then told her what Housekeeping had said. "They actually apologized?" asked the head nurse incredulously.

Were working conditions on the nursing staff at J.F.K. Memorial so habitually unpleasant and morale so low that Leah Stambler was surprised at a positive interaction with another department? Amanda decided to pursue the issue, but this was not the time to think about how.

"Will wonders never cease!" she said aloud. "I think you'll

get rid of your garbage very soon, but if no one shows up by the time the day shift is over, let me know."

When Amanda arrived at the transplant unit, she found Bonita in the staff lounge with her shoes off and her feet up on a chair. She was drinking a Coke and looked as if she didn't have the energy to suck the liquid up the straw.

"Billy Ockerson died this morning," she said. "I can't handle this anymore, Amanda. The patients are dying like flies and there doesn't seem to be anything we can do about it." She burst into tears just as Bill Zyrwynsky came into the lounge looking, if anything, worse than Bonita.

"Is Billy Ockerson the little boy who got part of his mother's liver?" asked Amanda. "What's going on here?"

Slowly, and in excruciating detail, Bonita and Zyrwynsky told Amanda what had happened to Billy Ockerson and what was likely to happen if and when the press got hold of the story. "And they will," said Zyrwynsky bitterly. "They've been hounding us like dogs after bitches in heat ever since I did the transplant. The mother is still a patient here, although I think she'll be ready for discharge in a day or so.

"I just got back from Mark Sullivan's office, and he told me to say 'No comment' to everything and refer everyone to the PR people. But the hospital PR department can't control everything. That little boy's funeral is going to be a circus," he added.

Amanda knew, without having to ask, that both Zyrwynsky and Bonita would be at that funeral, and she knew also that they blamed themselves for his death—perhaps for all the recent deaths on the transplant unit.

When Amanda left the transplant unit, Bonita and Bill Zyrwynsky remained in the staff lounge, each with their shoes off and feet up on chairs. Neither spoke for a long time. Finally Bonita said, "This isn't a coincidence, Bill. We're not killing these patients. Someone else is."

"What?"

Bonita told him about what Mrs. Zurman had said to her after her son died, and she waved off the comments she knew would be forthcoming from the surgeon. "I know what you're thinking," she said, "because I thought the same thing too.

Actually I still think it. But still, if I hadn't seen that ministe
that night . . ."

"What minister, what night?" asked Zyrwynsky.

Bonita told him of having gone back inside the funera
home on Sunday evening after she had left the wake. "I knew
the minister would still be there, and I wanted to ask him
people in the congregation would have an opportunity to stan
up and say a few words about Roberta. I thought I'd like t
say something about the work she did for the unit.

"Anyway, when I went back into the room where Robert
was, there he was sobbing his eyes out. I've never seen a ma
cry that hard. You hardly ever see *women* cry that hard."

"So?"

Bonita stared at Zyrwynsky. Men were so dense. "Bill, thi
man was her minister. Ministers do not go to pieces when on
of their flock dies."

"So what are you saying?"

"I'm saying that he was more than her minister. He was he
lover."

"So?"

"Bill, for God's sake! A minister, a *married* minister, a pilla
of the community having an affair with one of his congregant
Can you imagine the scandal?"

Bill Zyrwynsky finally snapped to full attention and lis
tened to what Bonita was saying. "Are you saying he kille
her because of a potential scandal? That's crazy, especiall
here in Washington when members of Congress are screwin
teenage girls *and* boys all over the place. Who would loo
twice at some obscure minister having an obscure affair wit
an attractive woman who was not exactly a child?"

"Maybe he didn't kill her," said Bonita. "Maybe his wif
did. And I don't agree that just because people are used t
congressmen behaving like pigs that it's okay for the clerg
to do it. People are still basically puritans at heart. Beside
I think he was giving her money."

"Bribing her to keep her mouth shut?" asked Zyrwynsky
"Come on, Bonnie, you're going off the deep end."

"No, not bribing her. Just helping her out."

But she had to acknowledge that Zyrwynsky had a point
Perhaps she was letting her imagination run away with her
Still, there was the little matter of several hundred thousan

ollars of medical expenses paid in cash by an unemployed
rriter. She decided not to say anything about that. No point
a letting the chief of the transplant unit think she was losing
er marbles.

"Do you know how much Protestant ministers earn?" asked
yrwynsky. "About enough to keep a bird alive. If the church
idn't provide free housing and a free car and other benefits,
ley'd all starve to death. I know. My grandfather was an
piscopal priest, and things haven't improved all that much
a fifty years. If Roberta Garfield's minister was keeping her,
'll eat my scrubs," he said, plucking at the faded green outfit
aat looked like pajamas. "And I'll have yours for dessert!"

Bonita smiled and said, "Before or after they go to the
aundry?"

Then she changed the subject quickly and was relieved when
le trash men banged open the door and began emptying the
verflowing wastebaskets. She and Bill left the staff lounge,
ut before they parted company, she said, "I'm going to take
mental health day tomorrow. Now that Billy is dead, our
ensus is down and we have enough nurses to cover. I'll call
a sick in the morning, but I wanted to tell you so you wouldn't
vorry."

"That's a good idea," said Zyrwynsky. "I might do the same
nyself." He squeezed her shoulder in an effort to be comfort-
ng and encouraging, but it didn't help in the slightest.

═══ CHAPTER 13 ═══

That afternoon, Len Agostino sat in Gerald Miller's offic and tried to make sense out of what the latter was saying.

"Tell me again why you think your cousin was murdered, he asked the man. "Also fill me in on some other details: lik who do you think had a motive to kill him and how did the do it?"

Miller looked frightened, as if being face to face with real-live detective—whose open jacket revealed a .38 calibe police special tucked into a brown leather shoulder holster— was more than he had bargained for when he'd gone to th station house to make what Agostino now thought was a off-the-wall accusation. Maybe even a sick bid for attention

Agostino sighed in anticipation of spending time with y another nut case. The detective spent so much time with n cases that he thought he was turning into one himself. His wif definitely thought he was. When he looked into the mirro which he did as seldom as possible these days, he thought h looked more and more like a nut case.

"I don't know," said Miller. "All I know is that my aur told me that Aaron told her that he was being killed."

Well, that was a piece of new information, a tiny shred o something to go on. Something to be followed up this evenin when he and Miller, who would serve as interpreter, woul go together to Mrs. Zurman's apartment. Christ, he wasn' looking forward to dragging all the way up Georgia Avenu in rush-hour traffic. He wanted to be home, sitting in his back yard, drinking a beer and torturing himself with thoughts o where his wife might be—and with whom.

Neither was Agostino looking forward to the medium amoun of traffic he would encounter when he left Miller's office in high-rise building in Tyson's Corner, Virginia. He looked ou the window, and for as far as he could see, there were offic

buildings exactly like the one in which he was now sitting.
Behind him was Tyson's Corner Mall, a shopping complex so
big that it straddled both sides of Route 123. Agostino had gone
Christmas shopping there last year, and he had been so stupefied
by the immensity of the place and the overwhelming number of
goods for sale that he had left without buying anything.

A real nut case.

"When did Zurman say that he was being murdered?" asked
Agostino.

"I'm not sure exactly," replied Miller. "I think it was right
before he died, but you can ask Aunt Selwa that yourself."

You bet your sweet ass, I'll ask her, thought Agostino.
Aloud he said, "Tell me why you *think* your cousin was
killed."

"I don't necessarily think it. My aunt does."

"But it was you, not the dead man's mother, who came to
the police station," said Agostino. He was growing seriously
irritated with this man, but getting angry at witnesses—or
whatever this guy turned out to be—was not the way to do
a good police investigation. He fought down his annoyance
and looked around the office for something calming on which
to rest his eyes.

A police psychologist had once taught him that trick, and it
usually worked. "If you want to keep control of an interview,"
said the man who everyone in the department called Ziggie
because he tried so hard to look like Sigmund Freud, "take
the time to keep your feelings in check while you're talking.
What happens to your feelings afterwards is another story."

Ziggie had given Agostino a list of things he could do,
all of which involved short periods of silence. The one that
Agostino found the most reliable was to stop talking and
look for something pleasant, either in the room or outside
a window, to focus on until he felt control return. Silence
from a detective invariably scared people because they didn't
expect it, and Agostino found that when he returned from the
little mental vacation, his control had increased.

But there was nothing pleasant here. Miller's office was
all hard lines of chrome and glass with a glaring yellow and
orange rug on the floor. The two prints on the wall mirrored
the harsh tones of the rug and were done in the style that
Agostino thought of as "kindergarten modern." Outside there

was nothing but the glaring August sun burning on granite and glass architectural monstrosities.

When this happened, Agostino turned inward for peace and directed the yellow of the rug and prints into the warm rays of the sun on the beach at Rehoboth, Delaware. He listened to the surf for a few moments and paddled about in the salt water until he felt refreshed again. Then he said, "Let's start over. Your aunt was with your cousin when he died, and she told you that he said that he was being killed. Right?"

"Yes."

"Did he or she or both of them use the word murder?"

"I don't know."

"All right. We'll deal with that later. But for now, tell me what you can about your cousin Aaron Zurman. Forget about the murder part. Just tell me what kind of person he was, who his friends were, what made him tick. What he liked to do. That sort of thing."

Agostino knew, as did every detective in the world, that only when you knew what kind of person the victim was, could you begin to understand why anyone would want to kill him.

Agostino said nothing. He leaned back in the chair, crossed his legs, and forced himself to relax. Miller finally seemed to understand that Agostino was serious, that he was willing to sit across the desk—forever if necessary—to get the information he required.

Miller began. "When you looked at him from the outside, my cousin was a nice guy. Almost everyone liked him. He was a good doctor. I think he was one of the few who wasn't in it strictly for the money. Oh, he liked money as much as anyone, don't get me wrong, but he also cared about his patients. He even sometimes went to their funerals if he had gotten to know them."

Miller fell silent and stared at Agostino. "But from the inside?" the detective prompted.

"The inside?"

"Yes, you just described Zurman, a little sketchily I must say, from, as you yourself put it, the outside. Now I'd like to hear you tell me about him from the inside."

"You think you're pretty clever, don't you?" asked Miller in a voice that reminded Agostino of his son Joey when the boy had been about three or four years old. Agostino would tell his son to pick up his toys or put his dirty clothes in the hamper, and the child would plant his chubby legs wide apart, put his hands on his hips, and say, in perfect imitation of his mother, "You think you're so smart, but you can't make me!"

Agostino would laugh and tell him, "Sure I can make you. I'm your pop!" And eventually the little boy would do as he was told.

Eventually this grown man would do as he was told, but Agostino was annoyed at the idea of having to wait for him to grow out of whatever childish phase he seemed to be stuck in. Aloud to Miller, he said, "Actually, I *am* pretty clever. I solve the cases I'm assigned, and I'm going to solve this one—with or without your help. With or without a subpoena—that's up to you."

This case was nowhere near approaching the point where a subpoena was possible, but it never hurt to try a bluff. Agostino believed in giving everything his best shot.

Miller caved in like Jell-O set out in the sun. "I'm sorry. I didn't mean to insult you. It's just that I'm so upset."

Agostino sighed. Everyone was always upset. Everyone used it as an excuse for being rude and obstructionistic and selfish and stupid and pigheaded and a bad driver.

Again he swallowed his anger. "What was your cousin like on the inside?" he repeated.

"I think he was scared and lonely and angry most of the time, and he used up an enormous amount of energy pretending not to be any of those things," replied Miller.

Then, as if horrified by what he perceived as disloyalty, he added, "But he had good reason to be—because of what he had been through as a child."

"Tell me what he had been through," said Agostino, and then was almost sorry he'd asked. He heard a story of atrocities so bestial that even he, who had been a detective on the Metropolitan District Police force for twenty-six years, was shocked. Agostino, who was older than Zurman and thus had been alive during World War II, knew about the Nazis and had read his share—more than his share because of the line of work he was in—about what they had done. Agostino also believed, again because of his work, that he had heard of everything that human beings could do to one another.

He was wrong.

The story that Miller told about what Zurman had experienced was beyond anything the detective could imagine. It was beyond the child rapings and beatings and burnings that were the worst thing Agostino had to deal with. It was beyond the sum total of all the senseless slaughter he had seen in his years as a police officer.

What Zurman had lived through changed him forever into something different than he would have been, had not the Nazis come marching into the town of Bunnik when he was a child. Agostino did not know what Zurman would have been, or what he had become, but he believed that the person he was caused his death.

If indeed he had been murdered.

Agostino now thought that it was just possible that there was something to Miller's story, but if the captain had asked him why, he would not have been able to say. So he still would have nothing to report this afternoon when he returned to the squadroom. He would simply go back now and write up this interview on his wheezy electric typewriter, meet Miller at his aunt's apartment at 6 P.M., interview the old woman, write up that report, and not think about any of it until tomorrow.

That was his plan. It was a good plan. Too bad it didn't work out.

"I wanted to tell you that I'm sorry I lost my temper with you," said Sarah Castle. "This whole thing has gotten me terribly upset, but still, I shouldn't have said what I did."

Mark Cipriotti said nothing. He didn't feel like graciously accepting her apology, but he was too frightened of Castle to voice what was going through his mind: thoughts that terrified him in the amount of rage and violence they contained. The past three weeks had left him drained, exhausted, and petrified. Castle could apologize all she wanted, and he still would believe that she was capable of killing him—and he was afraid that he could do the same to her.

"Listen, let's forget all that," said Allen Hackett. The three were meeting late Tuesday afternoon in his office on the top floor of a complex of Montgomery County office buildings in Rockville.

"It's more than two weeks now since Zurman died, and unless the police are a lot more disorganized than any of us thought, we have no reason to worry. They don't let death get this cold before they come sniffing around, so let's get on with the more important thing—what the hell the developers are going to do now. I, for one, am worried."

"I think we ought to forget about it," said Cipriotti. "That demonstration killed whatever support we might have had. Leave things alone until the feelings die down. These people are not going to put on any more spontaneous demonstrations, so I think we should just leave things as they are and wait it out."

"Spontaneous, my ass!" said Castle, venom and bitterness once again strong in her voice. Cipriotti flinched involuntarily. Castle noticed it and shot him yet another glance of contempt. "There's no such thing as a spontaneous demonstration," she said. "You can't be naive enough not to know that. Someone's behind this, and I want to know who it is. Find out, Mark."

Cipriotti flushed but said nothing. To refuse her request would have been to incur more of her wrath, and that most assuredly was not a wise choice.

Hackett saved him. "I'll make a few calls, Sarah," he offered. "I know these people better than Mark—or you, for that matter."

Cipriotti was relieved. He was at the point where he would do almost anything to stay out of the path of Sarah Castle's wrath. Her threat to kill him was still fresh in his mind.

At the beginning of the meeting he had told her that he thought that one or two of them should go to the police and offer assistance in the investigation of Zurman's death. She had looked at him with an expression of enraged incredulity.

"You stupid, fucking numbskull!" she had shouted. "There *is* no investigation. Why should there be an investigation into the death of a man who spent the last few years of his life three-quarters dead? Why should anyone think twice about a death that occurred in a hospital?"

"But, sooner or later, there's bound to be . . ."

Castle had silenced him then with a raised hand poised to strike, her face mottled red with uncontrollable rage. Being struck by this woman was not what he feared, since he'd noticed that her fingers were outstretched and relaxed in the posture of an impending slap. If he'd been facing a man, the fingers would have been curled into a fist, and the physical menace would have been far greater. It was her words that chilled him through to his heart.

"Sooner or later there's going to be another death," she snarled. "And it's going to be you, you spineless, fucking little idiot."

CHAPTER 14

Amanda Knight and Len Agostino did not know each other, but if they had, they would have recognized how alike they were in many respects. They knew about each other through their respective relationships with Lydia Simonowitz, but when they eventually met they would each understand, if they thought about it at all, why each reminded Lydia of the other.

This early morning right after Labor Day, with the leaves drooping heavily on the trees and the air sultry, the director of nursing and the police detective were sitting at their desks, pertinent papers spread out before them, wondering what to do next.

Late last evening, after he had left Mrs. Zurman's apartment, Agostino had finally stopped kicking himself in frustration. Amanda had not yet started, because she didn't know what to kick herself for. She knew she was missing something, but she couldn't figure out what, and the frustration was almost worse than the guilt she might have heaped upon herself if she could think of what she ought to feel guilty about.

Agostino didn't deal as heavily in guilt as Amanda did, although the emotion he felt was surprisingly similar. Yesterday, as he drove around the beltway after leaving Gerald Miller's office, he'd felt like a rookie cop. He had allowed himself to become so submerged in the horror of what Aaron Zurman had experienced as a child and adolescent that he completely forgot to ask Miller about Zurman's immediate past life. He had rectified that omission last night at Mrs. Zurman's apartment, but it had been a slip in procedure that only a rank amateur would make.

What he discovered last night was that Zurman had been a pillar of the community—and an emotional cripple. Neither Miller nor Mrs. Zurman had said that, but Agostino had been around the block of human nature enough times to put together a picture of a man who was unable to form close relationships. Most likely, after what he had been through, he trusted no one.

Zurman had never married, and at first Agostino thought, as many others would, that Zurman was homosexual. A fifty-eight-year-old never-married, good-looking Jewish doctor was about as common as a black man in the Oval Office. But as Agostino looked around Mrs. Zurman's small living room, he saw the reason for her son's bachelorhood: he was too tied up in his relationship with his mother to have room for another woman—or a man. The pictures of Zurman and his mama that were all over the walls and the tabletops revealed a mother who had a tight grip on her son's balls.

The conversation added to this impression. "Tell me about Aaron," he said to Mrs. Zurman through Miller, who was translating from English to Yiddish and back again.

"He was such a good boy," said Mrs. Zurman. "He came to visit me every day. He went to shul with me almost every Shabbos. He loved me. He took care of me." Her voice broke then and Miller put his arm around his aunt and said something to her in Yiddish, and she made an effort to stop crying.

Agostino tried another tack. "You told a nurse at the hospital that someone killed your son. Why did you say that?"

This brought a fresh wave of weeping, and Agostino sighed inwardly as he thought about how difficult and useless this interview was turning out to be. But then she quieted down and came right out with it—in perfectly understandable English: "When my son lay dying, he didn't say the *Shema*. He said, 'They're killing me.' He died without *Hashem*. Instead he died with an accusation of murder on his lips."

Miller explained that *Shema Yisroel* is the central prayer of Judaism and many Jews, religious or not, believe it should be their last words as they take their dying breath. But Zurman, for some reason, had not recited the prayer and had died, according to his mother, without God. This seemed a significant thing to Agostino, himself long since estranged from God and the Catholic church, but he could not say why.

What he said was: "Who was your son talking about? Who is 'they'?"

But that was it. That was all the information Agostino was going to get out of this woman, who lapsed back into such heavily accented English, interspersed with Yiddish, that there could be no further direct conversation between the detective and Zurman's mother. Everything went through by Miller, and Agostino had no way of knowing how accurate the translation was.

He learned little else that he could not have surmised by himself. Zurman was indeed a fairly predictable sort of person, except for his involvement in county politics, which was unusual for a physician. But Miller explained that Zurman had recently become disenchanted with clinical practice, he had no wife and children to worry about, and had never had the out-of-control zeal for making money that many of his colleagues did.

"I don't think he cared much about whether the developers built or didn't build that huge complex on Colesville Road," said Miller in explanation of Zurman's active participation in the Montgomery County zoning fight that Agostino had read about with only marginal interest. "I think he got involved in it because it was a cause, and it gave a new purpose to his life. It was exciting, he got a lot of publicity, and it was something different. He was growing bored with medicine, and as I said, except for his mother, he had no family to consume his energy.

"Besides, he wanted to get reelected to the county council, and opposing the developers in a big way would get him noticed. He would have loved that demonstration the other day," added Miller with some bitterness.

"In a sense my cousin was like an actor, or at least what I've read about actors. A lot of them crave love and attention but they're not capable of getting it from close relationships with people, so they knock themselves out to win applause and good reviews from critics. That sort of thing. It seems a lonely existence to me, but he didn't seem to mind." Miller shrugged. "Then again, who knows? We weren't all that close, especially recently, and I have no way of knowing what went on in his mind."

So here was Aaron Zurman, an ordinary man with no close ties to other human beings, with the exception of his mother who surely did not kill him. A man emotionally removed from the passions that human relationships produce, removed then from the probability of murder for love or hate.

Agostino tried the other motive: "Who would benefit financially from Zurman's death?" he asked Miller, who in turn asked Mrs. Zurman.

She looked surprised and didn't answer. "Ask her if she knows what's in her son's will," Agostino directed.

"I don't have to ask her. I know what's in it, and she is not."

"He left nothing to his mother?" Now it was Agostino's turn to be surprised.

Miller sighed. "Things were more complicated than they appeared. A love-hate relationship, I think you'd call it."

And hate won, said Agostino to himself. Aloud, he asked, "So who benefits from Zurman's death and how does that leave his mother?" He had visions of another penniless old woman going on welfare when her son could have set her up for life.

"My cousin never supported his mother," replied Miller. "He didn't have to. She has plenty of money of her own." He held up his hand and answered Agostino's unasked question. "The German reparations alone would have kept her quite nicely, but my aunt is a shrewd businesswoman. When she and Aaron came to this country, they settled in Philadelphia and she got a job in a beauty salon giving massages and facials and other women's stuff. Eventually she opened her own shop and got a good stockbroker, and the rest you can probably figure out for yourself."

"Tell me about the German reparations," said Agostino.

"What does that have to do with my cousin's death?" asked Miller.

"Nothing. I like to learn about things that I don't know about," replied Agostino. "Do you mean that your aunt was getting money from the Germans all this time?"

"The West Germans," replied Miller. "Or what used to be called West Germany before reunification. East Germany never paid a nickel. After the war, an international agreement was drawn up so that the German government would pay the survivors of the concentration camps enough to live on comfortably for the rest of their lives."

"I never knew that," said Agostino.

"Most people don't," replied Miller. "Even a lot of Jews aren't aware of it. Most survivors don't talk about it. They see

German money as tainted with Jewish blood and some won't take it."

Agostino was silent for a while and then snapped back to the issue at hand. "So if Zurman left nothing to his mother, who benefits from his death?"

"He left everything to charities. I don't remember which ones—there are several—but you can eliminate money as a motive for murder."

Then if no one had a reason to kill Aaron Zurman for love or for money, if there was no murder weapon, and if the only person who had raised the issue of murder in the first place was a mother whose elevator didn't always go to the top floor, where were they? This was the question that nagged at Agostino this morning as he sat at his desk looking out the grimy window. He would have closed the file in a second if it had not been for one persistent thought: why would Mrs. Zurman, whose elevator *sometimes* made the complete trip, have brought up the subject of murder? There was no reason for her to have done so unless her son had actually said what she reported.

Unless, of course, she had not heard correctly. Do people with heavy accents also *hear* with accents? It was a new question for Agostino, an interesting one, if he said so himself. For instance, if a person who was born in another country said, *"I vant to go to de benk,"* instead of "I want to go to the bank," would they hear *"I vant to go to de benk,"* when an American-born person said, "I want to go to the bank"?

If Mrs. Zurman heard her son say, "They're killing me," did he say exactly that? And if he did, is that what he really meant? Or was he using a figure of speech that his mother could not understand because her English was so rudimentary?

When Agostino complained to his wife that his feet were killing him, he did not mean that one of his feet suddenly reached up, kicked him in the head, and gave him a fatal skull fracture. It meant merely that his feet hurt. Could Zurman have meant that one of the dozens of medical procedures to which he had been subjected had been especially painful?

Could he have said *billing* instead of *killing*? Was it something about pills? Could he have not said anything of the kind? Was Mrs. Zurman out in some left field of her own mind? Was she tilling that field?

Agostino had to tell the captain something. He had to report on what had happened, what he made of it all, and what he thought the next step would be. Agostino knew what the captain would say: "Close it out, you got nothin' to go on. Toss the guy's place if you want, but then close it out and get on your other cases."

Agostino had already asked Miller and Mrs. Zurman for permission to search Aaron Zurman's apartment in the unlikely event that something interesting would turn up: a threatening letter, an incriminating bank statement, evidence of blackmail—something, anything. He would do that before he went to see the captain and then he would close it out.

Agostino was disappointed because, despite the fact that he had no evidence, he believed Zurman had been murdered. He was disappointed because he *hoped* Zurman had been murdered. It wasn't that he wanted more violence in the District of Columbia. God knew, there was too much of that already, he thought, with only a small dose of guilt. It was just that this would be such a challenging case to crack.

That was the word all right: crack. Agostino would like to work on one great big juicy murder case that didn't involve drugs. Just one—to relieve the monotony of drug dealers, drug users, drug pushers, and drug wholesalers who dealt in crack, ice, cocaine, marijuana, heroin, uppers, downers, methadone, and God-knows-what-else. Agostino sighed and mentally crossed his fingers as he picked up his car keys and headed out of the station house.

Zurman had lived in Somerset House, the fancy new condo on Wisconsin Avenue in Chevy Chase, where the cheapest apartments were a million dollars, and where the doorman and resident manager would not be pleased to see a police detective. Zurman had lived on the 18th floor with a view north toward Bethesda—maybe $2,000,000?

Agostino decided to stop at his favorite deli for corned beef and a kosher dill before searching. And if the urge to take a crap came over him while he was at Zurman's apartment, he would use the toilet there. A $2,000,000 dump. He smiled as he drove out of the parking lot.

As Agostino drove east toward the Parkway Deli, Amanda began to read the four charts for the second time that morning.

The problem was that she had no real idea—aside from a gut instinct that was surprisingly similar to the one that Agostino felt as he drove through Rock Creek Park—of what she should be looking for. The instinct told Agostino that Zurman had indeed been murdered, despite all evidence to the contrary—despite no evidence at all.

Those feelings plagued Amanda also as she leafed through the charts. Perhaps when she got to the three autopsy reports that lay on her conference table she would be able to make sense out of these senseless deaths.

She was certain that the four, a construction worker, a physician, a writer, and a toddler, were connected, and their deaths had nothing to do with the quality of the nursing or medical care given at J. F. K. Memorial Hospital.

You think they've all been murdered even though there's absolutely no reason in hell to think that, said the voice, which was fighting a losing battle to keep Amanda out of trouble.

There's no reason not to, replied Amanda. There is nothing in any of this information that would point to malpractice of any kind, not even the slightest innocent mistake. I've gone over the information like the most critical hospital accreditor.

Even if no one here screwed up, that doesn't mean these people were murdered, said the voice of reason. *They could have died for any number of coincidental reasons.*

True. But they didn't, replied Amanda.

The problem, of course, was proving a gut feeling—and disproving coincidence. Here were three patients who had died of hyperacute rejection three or four days after a transplant—two kidneys and a liver—and one who had suddenly fallen desperately ill with a rare virus and had died despite immediate and massive treatment—three years after a heart transplant. A middle-aged man, a middle-aged woman, a young man, and a little boy who was still practically a baby. Two had received organs, in Billy Ockerson's case part of an organ, from close relatives and two had received cadaver organs. There were no common threads.

Amanda picked up the autopsy reports. Jack Sherwood had died of what apparently was a typical reaction to organ rejection. Roberta Garfield's autopsy, on the other hand, did not reveal a rejected heart. The organ itself had looked perfectly normal. Billy Ockerson's autopsy report said that his own liver had been almost totally nonfunctional practically since birth, and the piece that his mother had given him was far less than healthy-looking. The transplant had been initially successful. Then something had gone very, very wrong.

The three patients who had received recent transplants had gotten the usual complement of antirejection drugs, as well as the rest of the armamentarium given to postoperative patients: drugs to prevent infection, drugs to prevent undue clotting of the blood which could lead to a stroke, drugs to relieve pain—enough medication to float a battleship.

Amanda took her *Physicians' Desk Reference* off the shelf and painstakingly cross-checked every single drug that all four patients had received to see if the dosage was correct. She found no errors.

She learned nothing from almost three hours of reading. These four patients had nothing in common that didn't pertain to their medical problems. There had been no obvious violations of medical or nursing practice. There was no way they could have been murdered through some fault on the hospital's part.

I told you so, said the voice, which was growing increasingly irritating. *You know you can't talk to anyone at the hospital about your crazy suspicions. They'll think you're loony. We already know it, but why tell the whole world?*

Maybe not here at the hospital, Amanda thought. But there is someone I can talk to about this. She picked up the phone and called Sal Mateo.

"Hi, Amanda," he said, his voice sounding strangely booming and far away.

"Are you in a tunnel?" she asked.

"No, I'm on a speaker phone. Everybody in the room can hear what you're saying, so don't spill any secrets!"

Amanda realized where his hands were while he was talking to her on the phone and she felt her gorge rise a little. Now she couldn't tell him why she wanted to have lunch with him. "Would it be better if I called back later?" she asked, giving him a broad hint that she wanted to talk privately.

"No, you're not bothering me," he said cheerfully. "What can I do for you?"

Men were so dumb about some things. Any woman would have known immediately that Amanda wanted a private conversation, but there was no choice now but to blurt it out. "There's something I need to ask you," she said and then quickly added, "but not on the phone. Are you by any chance free for lunch?"

There was an awkward pause. Perhaps he was embarrassed to be asked to lunch by a woman who wasn't Lydia. Maybe he had plans for lunch. Amanda was a little irritated. If he had taken the hint and not blasted this conversation all over the morgue, he wouldn't have to be embarrassed. Men!

"I'm brown-bagging it today," he replied, "but why don't you come on down here and we'll find something for you to eat in the fridge."

Amanda laughed. "Sal, I would rather starve to death, crawling on bloody hands and knees in the middle of the Sahara Desert, than eat anything out of that refrigerator."

She heard a cackle and a voice from somewhere in the cavernous room: "Anybody for a chopped liver sandwich?" There was general laughter at the remark.

"You people are gross," she replied. "I'll bring my own sandwich. And the next time you and Lydia invite us to dinner, I want a written guarantee that she's doing the cooking!"

"You'd better ask to see the supermarket receipt too!" replied Sal. "Gotta go. My patients are dying for me to finish up here." Amanda heard more raucous laughter as the call was disconnected.

═══ CHAPTER 15 ═══

Sitting in the taxi on the ride back to J. F. K. from the District morgue, which was located in the far distant southeast quadrant of the capital, on grounds that it shared with the city hospital and the jail, Amanda thought about the conversation with Sal.

He was as pleasant and friendly as always, but unable to be of much practical help. "Amanda, I know next to nothing about the physiology and chemistry of organ transplants. Most of our clients haven't had the luxury of expensive high-technology medical care."

It was true. People upon whom Sal Mateo and his assistants performed autopsies were District residents who had been murdered or who had died under other suspicious circumstances. Most of the several hundred murders that took place in the nation's capital each year were drug-related, and drug addicts were never candidates for organ transplants.

"In all the time I've been here, I don't think I've ever done a post on someone with a transplant," he added.

"What would you do if you got someone like that?" she asked. "By the way, what do you call them?"

"Call whom?"

"The people you do autopsies on? Patients? Clients?"

Sal looked puzzled, as if he had never been asked the question, and Amanda was immediately sorry she had spoken. Her curiosity often made people uncomfortable, as it obviously had now.

Sal thought about it. "Sometimes we call them by name. Sometimes by their toe-tag number. Sometimes by whatever killed them." He shrugged. "Sometimes by names that aren't too polite."

She got back to the original point. "So what would you do if you opened a corpse and found an organ that wasn't the original goods?"

"It would depend on what it had to do with the cause of death," Sal replied. "If the cause of death was a slug in the heart or something equally obvious, I wouldn't do anything, just note it on the report and leave it at that—if I knew that the organ had been transplanted."

"Can't you always tell?" asked Amanda, surprised.

"If the transplant, say a kidney, had been done years ago, the suture lines may have become so faint that I wouldn't notice them, especially if I was concentrating on the slug in the heart: entrance wound, bullet path, exit wound—things like that."

"Oh," Amanda said, and then didn't know what else to ask. She was beginning to feel like a fool.

"Amanda, does this have to do with what we were talking about over pizza the other night?" asked Sal. "Why don't you tell me what's going on and then maybe I can be of some help to you."

So she told him—everything. About all four deaths, about what she had found and not found in the charts and autopsy reports this morning, what she believed, and what she knew. "I know I'm being a jerk," she admitted, "and I'd appreciate it if you wouldn't tell anyone about this. I don't mind if you tell Lydia, she already thinks I'm crazy, but no one else, okay?"

"Okay," Sal said. "But Lydia doesn't think you're crazy, and neither do I. After all, murder is our business, and if there's the slightest shred of evidence that these four have been murdered, we want to know. It'd be an interesting change for us down here. We get kind of tired of the endless stream of bullet wounds, knife slashings, and drug overdoses."

Sal looked downright wistful as he thought about a challenging forensic pathological puzzle.

Amanda pursued her line of questioning. "So if you don't know too much about organ transplants and if you got a body in here that had had a transplant and you thought that somehow it might be connected to the cause of death, what would you do?"

"I'd give myself a short course on organ transplantation," he replied. "I'd go to the library and read, and I'd probably call your guy—what his name, Warshawski?—he's supposed to have written the book on organ transplantation."

"Zyrwynski," said Amanda, "but I can't exactly go bouncing into his office and say that I think that four of his patients got knocked off. I'm not *that* tactless!"

Sal laughed. "You're not tactless. Just enthusiastic! So what about that guy at St. Jude's? The one who lost out to Zyrwynsky. I can't remember his name. Something German. He's probably a Nazi."

"Now who's jumping to conclusions?" said Amanda. "What do you mean, lost out to Zyrwynsky? Were they competing for the job at J. F. K.?"

"I don't think it was a heavy-duty, cutthroat competition," replied Sal, "but you know how some doctors are when it comes to prestige and money and all that good stuff that comes with the territory when you treat people who can pay their bills. Unlike my patients!" He laughed ruefully.

"So what do you know about this not-so-heavy-duty competition?" asked Amanda, who once again looked like Shadow with her eyes open wide and her whiskers bristling.

"Not much," said Sal, who probably knew more than he was willing to admit, but Amanda didn't want to push him. She could use her own grapevine.

As the taxi wound its way through the late lunchtime traffic, which was almost as heavy as the two traditional rush hours, Amanda was glad she'd decided not to take her own car. For once, she had listened to her inner voice (*Take a cab; that's what a rich husband is for!*) and had avoided driving through this mess. The cabbie, one of the few in the District who spoke English, cursed under his breath as they hit a pothole. Amanda laughed and said, "You must not have paid your taxes this year, and now the mayor can't fix the streets!"

Immediately she regretted having said anything, because the cabbie began a loud and vituperative diatribe against the District government. It lasted all the way to the main entrance of the hospital and prevented Amanda from losing herself in thought. She tipped the man less than she would have ordinarily and slammed the door of the cab unnecessarily hard. She valued peace and quiet while spending time in taxicabs and this man had been too garrulous. She supposed that driving a taxi was a lonely and sometimes dangerous job—and disappointing when someone as well-dressed as Amanda ended up being such a bad tipper.

You're doing it again, said the voice, which was trying to be helpful. *Stop feeling guilty. Tipping is not even required, and a big tip is certainly not called for if the guy won't leave you alone after you made a little joke. So stop thinking about it.*

She walked into the outer office of her suite and flopped down in one of the visitors' chairs next to Louise's desk. "My God, this heat is beastly," she said. "I don't think I can stand it much longer."

"But at least you can go home and jump into your own swimming pool," said Louise. Amanda couldn't tell if her secretary was jealous and annoyed and thought that Amanda had no right to complain about the heat, or if she was simply making an observation.

Amanda decided to ignore the remark. Everyone is touchy today, she thought. Aloud she asked: "Any disasters? Any phone calls?"

"No disasters and only one call," replied Louise, handing Amanda the pink message slip that said to call Betsy Murdock.

Amanda looked up Betsy's beeper code, punched it into her phone along with the required access numbers, and waited for the supervisor to reply.

"Amanda, I couldn't find any connections about what we were discussing the other day," said Betsy. "I didn't want to be too obviously nosy, and there may be something I don't know, but nothing overt. And there was another similar incident two nights ago."

"Okay, thanks," said Amanda. "I'll try to talk to Townsend this afternoon. We can't let this go on. Did the incident involve one of our three friends?"

"Yes," replied Betsy.

"Thanks for doing the legwork. I'll let you know what Townsend decides," said Amanda. She disconnected without putting the receiver back onto the cradle and immediately dialed her boss's office.

Amanda watched David Townsend's face as she told him what Betsy had discovered and what the two of them had done so far about the discovery. She liked Townsend. Sometimes his pomposity irritated her, but then too, sometimes Ken got a little carried away with his own importance, and she had to stick pins into his shirt when it got too stuffed.

Townsend had many of the same qualities she admired in her husband. He listened carefully to what she had to say, he respected her ability to think through a problem and to offer suggestions about solving it, and for the most part, he left her alone to do her job. But he demanded that she—and every other department head at J. F. K. Memorial—do her job well. David Townsend did not tolerate many screw-ups.

Now his patrician face with the hooded dark grey eyes was more annoyed than angry. Townsend did not take the theft of narcotics as personally as Amanda did, nor did he suffer her sense of outrage that patients were being denied pain relief. He saw it as one more administrative hurdle to be jumped, not much different than a mix-up in garbage collection days or a snowstorm that created a nightmare of staffing logistics.

"How long has this been going on?" he asked.

"We don't know exactly, because we went back through old charts for only a month," replied Amanda. "Two of the nurses have been here for about a year, and one is a real old-timer—four and a half years."

"Do you mean someone could have been stealing narcotics for four and a half *years*?" he asked. Anger was rising now.

"That's possible but not very likely," Amanda assured him. "It would have been just as obvious then as it is now, and someone would have noticed it—just as Betsy noticed it now." She chose not to add that Betsy's predecessor on the surgical units could have been in cahoots with the staff nurses and said nothing.

Townsend did not like to waste time with might-have-beens and could-have-beens; he concentrated on the present. That's what made him a good administrator, and it was another reason that Amanda liked him. "So what do you think we should do?" he asked.

Amanda was not surprised that he was asking her advice. It was a good managerial tactic: it puffed up the egos of his subordinates—and it saved him from having to solve all the problems himself.

"I think we should get some decoy nurses—private investigators—to work the same shifts as the suspects," she said, and added that it might not be easy to find real nurses who were also detectives.

"Why would they have to be real nurses?" asked Townsend. "Just dress them up in white pants and whatever else you're letting them wear these days."

What the nurses at J. F. K. Memorial wore was a constant source of low-key friction between Amanda and Townsend. She thought he would be happy if her staff dressed in full nun regalia, complete with chastity belt. Most of the staff would wear jeans and Nikes if they had their way, and Amanda sometimes was driven crazy trying to keep the two factions happy. For the most part the dress code that Amanda had established worked fairly well, but there were occasional lapses.

One morning about a month ago, Townsend had stormed into Amanda's office, something he never did. It was always she who was summoned to his office. "I saw a woman who I thought was a hooker in the parking garage this morning," he said, his face suffused with rage. "Then later when I went up to Center Wing Six, I saw her wheeling the medicine cart around. She's a nurse—in my hospital! Do something!" he had shouted. "And do it now before I fire her myself."

Amanda had leaped out of her chair, and with no trouble at all, picked out the nurse that had so offended David Townsend's sartorial sensibilities. She did indeed look like she was ready for a day of strolling the boardwalk at Ocean City. Townsend had not exaggerated.

Amanda took the young woman into the staff bathroom, turned her toward the mirror, and said, "Look at yourself."

The nurse, her jaws moving rhythmically on a wad of chewing gum, stared at her reflection and said, "Yeah?"

Amanda was furious. "Your hair isn't combed, you have on enough makeup to sink a battleship, your earrings are vulgar and much too big, your shoes are dirty, your skirt is so short that you look like a streetwalker, and your blouse is open two buttons too far. And if I catch you chewing gum on duty again, I'll fire you on the spot."

The staff nurse was speechless at Amanda's outburst. She simply stared at herself in the mirror, her face registering incomprehension.

"Where do you live?" asked Amanda.

"What?"

"I asked where you live," she repeated. "I need to know how long it'll take you to go home, change your clothes, wash your face, and come back to work."

"Now?" asked the nurse, incredulous that Amanda was making such a big deal out of what she was wearing.

"I'll give you two choices," said Amanda, more furious than ever at the denseness of this woman. "Leave now and take half a vacation day to go shopping for something appropriate to wear to work, or take two hours and go home and change into something that makes you look like a professional nurse. But you're not staying here one more minute looking like that."

The woman shrugged. "I'll take the vacation time."

"Fine," snapped Amanda. "Stop by my office before you leave and I'll give you a shopping list."

Amanda had left the nurse staring at herself in the mirror and had told the head nurse on Center Wing Six what she had done and why. "If this is going to leave you short-handed for a while, I'll do Linda's patient care," said Amanda. The head nurse, too, was shocked, but said they could manage. She did not want the director of nursing on her unit when she was that angry.

Amanda went back down to her office and wrote a memo about appropriate dress. She asked Louise to distribute it to the entire nursing staff, but she knew it was unnecessary because within an hour the story of what she had done would be all over the hospital, and the nurses would look like Florence Nightingales for a long time.

Now Amanda said to Townsend, "It doesn't matter what the decoy wears. She'll be spotted by my staff in two seconds flat if she doesn't know what she's doing for patients."

"True," admitted Townsend. "So what do you suggest?"

"Maybe there are detective agencies that have nurse-investigators," said Amanda. "Let me call a few and find out. Or if they don't have nurses, maybe they have other ideas."

"Okay," agreed Townsend, "but let Mark Sullivan know what you're doing and ask him who to call. He knows about this sort of thing. Keep me posted."

As Amanda left Townsend's office, she wondered what the hospital had been up to in the past that would make Mark Sullivan "know about this sort of thing." Public relations people, as scummy a bunch as ever there were, were probably into all kinds of things that Amanda would prefer not to know about.

Probably the PR people at Naylor-Noyes, with all those computer secrets to protect, knew about private detectives too. She would ask Ken.

═══ CHAPTER 16 ═══

Joseph Krahl, M.D., F.A.C.S., was a very handsome man. He was a charming man as well. In fact, the amount of charm and good looks floating out from Joseph Krahl's side of the desk made it hard for Amanda to concentrate.

"Transplant patients die sometimes, and we never know why," he said with a sad smile liberally laced with sexy, boyish appeal. Amanda could easily imagine, when the news was imparted with that smile, that the families of patients who had died would accept the death as a mere inconvenience or a piece of bad luck.

"I realize that," Amanda replied. "And I'm sure that Bill Zyrwynsky knows it too. It's just that . . ."

"Bill is one of the finest transplant surgeons on the East Coast," said Krahl. "J. F. K. is lucky to have hired him away from Hopkins."

"I know he is," said Amanda, "but I don't know him very well, and you can understand why I didn't want to have this conversation with him. He feels bad enough about these deaths, and I thought that if I talked to someone who has absolutely no stake in all this, it would be easier for me. I just feel so bad for him . . ."

Had Amanda been totally honest with Joseph Krahl, she would have told him that sparing William Zyrwynsky's feelings was not the only reason she had asked to see him. The problem was that she wasn't sure of her own motives.

Why had she driven all the way across town to St. Jude's Hospital, which had the only other transplant unit in Washington, to talk to a man she had never met, about a series of suspicious and embarrassing deaths in her own hospital?

True, she knew less about the transplant process than she probably should, but that would have been easy to rectify. Bonita Elliott or any of the nurses on the unit would have been happy to fill her in. She could have gone to Eddie, who was always willing to give her an impromptu medical lecture. And she had all the textbooks and medical journal articles she could possibly want right at her fingertips. But here she was, sitting in front of a stranger—a competitor in a way—admitting that she knew less than she should about what went on in an important unit in her hospital.

"Everyone metabolizes drugs differently," said Krahl, "and antirejection drugs are no exception. You can have what you think ought to be the best match in the world, and then sometimes the body goes crazy to get rid of the new organ—the foreign invader. And if, at the same time, the drugs don't behave the way you thought they would—boom. You strike out."

Amanda sighed. "I understand that. And I suppose I can understand that about the two men who died so soon after their surgery, but Roberta Garfield is another story." She wondered briefly if she should—in all fairness—eliminate Aaron Zurman from the discussion because his death had nothing to do with his kidneys or J. F. K. Memorial or Bill Zyrwynsky.

Don't shoot your mouth off any more than you have to, warned the voice, which didn't approve of her being here in the first place.

"I don't think you do understand the rejection process," said Krahl with just the slightest trace of a sneer in his voice. "Not many people do. And you *did* come here asking for my help with the problems you people are having over there."

Now he really did sound scornful. What a bunch of pompous jerks doctors were. They weren't happy unless they knew more than everyone else and were in total control of every situation.

Let him talk, said the voice. *Stop being a smart-ass and saying you understand when you really don't. That's what you came for, isn't it?*

Krahl continued. "The success of an organ transplant depends on our ability to suppress the body's immune response just enough so that the new organ isn't rejected, but not enough so that the patient dies of a massive infection or cancer that took the opportunity to attack while the immune system was 'down.' We walk an immunologic tightrope—with no safety net."

Krahl looked pleased with himself, and Amanda had the impression that the immunologic tightrope, which she had to admit was a neat metaphor, was part of his stock lecture. "Do you know how the immune system works, Amanda? May I call you Amanda?" he asked, flashing that neon smile.

She bristled, but when the voice hissed, *Let him call you King Kong if he wants to*, Amanda smiled at him and said, "I'm flattered, Joe."

She wondered if they were flirting with each other as she added, "I probably have an educated layman's idea of B cells and T cells and all that."

"Then let me refresh your memory," he said, knowing that she wouldn't recognize a T cell if it jumped up and bit her in the nose. "The immune system has several major components, among them white blood cells known as lymphocytes. Two types of lymphocytes, T cells and B cells, are especially important. Helper T cells promote the immune response and suppressor T cells reduce it. There are normally about twice as many helper cells as suppressors. All clear so far?"

"This is all familiar from what I've learned about AIDS in the past few years," she replied.

"The same cells are involved. The same system is involved, and the more we learn about AIDS, the more we can learn about how to prevent organ rejection. Many things in medicine are interconnected, you see." There was that smirk again.

Krahl continued. "B cells, and to some extent, T cells, produce antibodies, which you know are cells manufactured specifically for the purpose of destroying foreign or alien cells."

"Like a foreign or alien organ," said Amanda.

"Precisely. So when the immune system senses the presence of a foreign invader, such as a virus or a piece of tissue from another body, it produces antibodies to attack the invader. In addition, in ways we don't yet fully understand, the immune system protects the body against the too-rapid proliferation of certain cells that can become cancerous.

"When the system is not functioning at full capacity, the person becomes vulnerable to a wide range of infections and malignancies—like a medieval knight suddenly stripped of armor in the midst of battle."

Another wonderful metaphor. Who wrote this man's dialogue?

But the light was beginning to dawn. "So the immune response to organ transplantation is a kind of irony," said

Amanda. "You deliberately suppress the mechanism, thus creating vulnerability to one set of diseases, while treating another."

"You've got it," said Krahl, pleased that she was turning out to be such a good pupil. "Following transplant surgery, a normal immune system will recognize the cells of a new heart or kidney as 'foreign,' and will gear itself up for action by producing antibodies to kill the invader. So we prevent the body from sabotaging itself, and give the patient drugs—prednisone, Imuran, and cyclosporine—to put the immune system on 'hold' until it gets used to the new organ and adopts it as its own."

"I thought that transplant patients have to be on immuno-suppressive drugs for the rest of their lives. Expensive ones too. One of the nurses told me that cyclosporine costs about twelve thousand dollars a year," said Amanda.

"That's true," replied Krahl. "And that's where the tightrope comes in. We give the drugs in pretty high doses immediately after surgery; that's why everyone in the intensive care part of the transplant unit wears gowns and masks—because the patients are so vulnerable to infection. But gradually we reduce the dose. If we didn't, patients would die of viral infections every time someone sneezed on them. What we try to do is balance rejection prevention and too much vulnerability to infection and cancer. Most of the time we do a good job. Sometimes the process fails."

He shrugged, and Amanda noticed his use of language. When everything went well, Krahl said "we." When the patient died, he talked about "the process." Like all doctors, he wanted full credit for success and no connection with failure.

Amanda remembered some reading she had done several years earlier in an effort to understand the causes of AIDS and the opportunistic infections it produces. The article in the medical journal quoted a researcher at the Centers for Disease Control. He had ascribed the sudden huge increase in the number of cases of PCP entirely to the advent of AIDS. He had said that previous to the existence of AIDS, PCP was seen only in severely malnourished and debilitated patients—and in patients who had received transplants. But that had nothing to do with the subject at hand. "Tell me about rejection," she asked.

"I hardly know where to begin," he said. "Do you know about HLA matching?"

"Vaguely," replied Amanda.

"HLA stands for the 'human lymphocyte antigen' chromosome. Each one contains about two hundred different genes. Take the number of chromosomes in the human body and multiply each by two hundred, and you start to see the enormous difficulty we have in establishing histocompatibility."

"Histocompatibility means the degree of compatibility between a donor and recipient, right?" asked Amanda, annoyed with herself for wanting to please this man with the little shred of knowledge she had on the subject.

"Right again," he said. "The more of these hundreds of thousands of antigens we can match, the better the chance of success, which is never totally assured even with a transplant between identical twins.

"But if the new tissue releases antigens that are recognized by the host (that's the patient) as foreign, then the host's own immune system gears up and destroys the graft. If the process were left to its own devices, the destroyed transplanted organ will become necrotic and send out toxins that will eventually kill the patient."

Amanda thought about Aaron Zurman. "But if the new organ, say a kidney, fails and begins to be rejected, and the patient is still in the hospital, wouldn't you see what was going on and do something?"

"Of course," said Krahl. His sneer was definitely back. "We don't just stand around and let a kidney shrivel up and kill the patient. We take it out and put him back on dialysis until we can try again.

"Naturally, in the case of a heart, it's not that simple. When a heart is rejected, you don't have a lot of room to maneuver, you understand."

Amanda was positive that Bill Zyrwynsky didn't "just stand around" and let Aaron Zurman die. Something else was going on, but she couldn't discuss that with Joseph Krahl.

"I'm actually most interested in unexplained, immediate post-op rejection," she said.

"Like the three you've had recently," said Krahl, watching the expression of surprise and dismay cross Amanda's face. "Oh, I know about those," he said. "The network of transplant teams is very tight. And in a political place like Washington, you can imagine . . ."

Amanda could well imagine, and she felt humiliated for Bill Zyrwynsky, who had years of transplant research under his belt. He wasn't used to having patients die practically on the operating table, and it wouldn't do his reputation any good. In a sense, brilliant surgeons were like actors and movie stars: only as good as their latest hit. Two flops in a row and they were no longer good box office.

"I'm glad you came to discuss this with me instead of Bill," said Krahl. "There's no point in rubbing his nose in it. He probably feels bad enough as it is. I appreciate the fact that you're a sensitive woman."

The words were appropriate, but something in Krahl's tone, even with that brilliant smile, set Amanda on edge.

Silly! You've been with Ken so long that you don't even know when someone's coming on to you, said the inner voice, which this time didn't know what it was talking about.

Krahl may indeed have been flirting—Amanda was married, not dead—but there was something else in his manner that made her nervous. Perhaps it was just that he was one of the dozens of men she had run across over the years who had loads of charm but no substance.

She looked at Krahl. He was handsome, all right, with very full, sensuous lips in the kind of face that was often used to model men's clothes for successful mid-forties executives. But a closer inspection revealed features that appeared almost indistinct and unformed, more like a five-year-old child's innocent beauty than a full-grown man whose character was reflected on his face. There was a certain blurriness of features that gave him an immature cast beneath the surface good looks. It reminded Amanda of a sculpture that had been put aside before the finishing touches had been added.

This was a child in a man's body. He looked as though he would throw a temper tantrum with very little provocation. She could imagine the way he behaved in the operating room.

Krahl watched her eyeing him and mistook her interest for sexual quickening. He preened, which was his usual response to women who took more than a casual interest in his face and body. He was fully aware of his attractiveness and magnetism and took full advantage of it.

Joseph Krahl operated with more than his hands.

He now began what he liked to think of as the exploratory examination. He leaned across his desk, looked at his watch, and said, "It's almost noon. You'll join me for lunch, won't you? St. Jude's has a medical staff dining room that serves quite decent food."

"I really ought to get back," Amanda replied, not wanting to go back at all.

The smile flashed. "Please stay and eat with me. I've eaten lots of meals at J. F. K. Memorial—if you can call them meals. I want the opportunity to make you jealous of our chef. And we haven't even begun to talk about preventing organ rejection. Please."

Amanda Knight, age thirty-eight, a grown woman with a husband she loved and a responsible job, turned into an adolescent. She felt her knees go weak and other parts of her anatomy blossom with desire.

"Thank you, I'd like that. Just let me call my secretary and let her know that I'll be later than I thought," she said, ignoring the voice that was telling her what a damn fool she was.

"All right, here's how we prevent rejection," said Krahl as he and Amanda sat facing one another in the doctors' dining room at St. Jude's Hospital.

There was starched pink linen on the table. The flowers were real and the cutlery did not look like it belonged in a prison. Amanda had just taken a bite of a surprisingly good roll, slathered with real butter. No cholesterol-free margarine for the doctors here. And no mystery meat on the menu. She and Krahl had both ordered grilled swordfish from the waitress. No schlepping plastic trays to a cafeteria table, either. She *was* jealous.

She made an effort to appear more interested in rejected organs than in her elegant surroundings and listened to what Krahl was saying: "Up until late 1983, we had to use very crude drugs to prevent rejection. Imuran and prednisone were all we had."

"I remember reading once that in the early days of organ transplants patients were given total-body irradiation to suppress the immune system," said Amanda, refusing to admit that she was showing off.

The smile blinked on. "I'm surprised you know that," said Krahl. "Most people don't. So of course, you know that it didn't work at all; the patients died of massive X-ray poisoning, just as they died of the huge doses of various cancer drugs that were also tried at that time.

"But now we have cyclosporine, which has made all the difference in the world. It seems to work mainly on the T cells by suppressing rather than killing them, and it inhibits antibody formation. Thus, the new organ is not attacked."

"If cyclosporine is so great," asked Amanda, "why do you continue to use the other two?"

"Good question," replied Krahl. "It's really a matter of covering all the bases just in case a patient doesn't react well to one or another of the drugs, like putting up a net under the tightrope. Gradually, though, we withdraw all but the cyclosporine, and after a time we reduce the dose of that, monitoring the patient carefully for the rest of his life."

Amanda smiled at Krahl, not knowing what to say next. She thought of the way Bonita had described Roberta Garfield: healthy and functioning well for three years with a transplanted heart. That woman bore no resemblance to the one Amanda had seen less than two weeks ago in the ICU—desperately sick, dying of a massive infection that struck AIDS patients in huge numbers.

AIDS patients were otherwise healthy people who suffered sudden, massive breakdowns in their immune systems. What the hell did they have to do with Roberta Garfield?

"You look puzzled," said Krahl. "Haven't I been a good teacher?" He knew he was an excellent teacher.

He hoped Amanda Knight was thinking about something other than organ transplants and faggots dying of AIDS. He had already checked out her left hand and had noted the wedding band behind the emerald-and-diamond engagement ring. The fact that she was married made no difference to him. If Joseph Krahl wanted a woman, he went after her, no matter how many rings she wore.

He usually got who he wanted, and he was starting to want this woman. However, in the long run, she might be more trouble than she was worth. Although . . . the director of nursing at the hospital with the only competing transplant unit in town might be worth a try. Bagging her would be a coup.

He was good at coaxing pillow talk out of his lovers. He knew no better way to collect gossip.

Amanda Knight was a good-looking woman, with those green eyes and full-lipped wide mouth. She could stand to lose ten pounds, but her legs weren't bad, and her tits swelled pleasantly under the peach-colored linen blouse. Oh yes, he could enjoy making this one lose her composure. He smiled his perfect smile and put special softness in his voice. "Tell me what's on your mind."

Amanda was trying to think of a diplomatic way to say what was on her mind. She knew—she was convinced—that William Zyrwynsky did not "just stand around" and let those patients die of massive and unexplained rejection. Yet, wasn't there *something* they could have tried? Some last-ditch, desperate measure? But how could she ask this without letting Joseph Krahl think that she had less than absolute confidence in J. F. K.'s transplant chief, a man who had won a position coveted by many other prominent physicians. A man who was also the competitor of Joseph Krahl—who was now making no secret of the fact that his interest in her was more than professional.

So use it, said the voice, which sometimes egged her on to things not 100 percent kosher. *You're good at this. It's how you got a corporate executive type like Ken James to fall in love with you. Joseph Krahl is your kind of guy.*

"The thing that frustrates me so much, as a director of nursing, is that the nurses who work on the transplant unit are starting to become disheartened. They work so hard to help these patients recover, and then despite everything they do, all the good care, the patients just fade away. . . ."

Amanda allowed her voice to fade away too, and she lifted her hands from the pink linen napery in an echoing gesture of helplessness and frustration. "I just wish there was something more we could do," she said, looking directly into Krahl's eyes, thinking that she ought to nominate herself for an Oscar.

Krahl reached across the table and put his hand on Amanda's. Just for a second, just long enough for the gesture to be interpreted as pure sympathy for her professional concern—or just long enough for her to interpret it in another way.

"I understand how you feel," he said with no hint of anything more than doctorly feeling in his voice. "But you must not blame yourself or your nurses. There was nothing they could have done to prevent these deaths."

Did that mean that there was something that Zyrwynsky could have done?

"There was nothing that *anyone* could have done," he said in response to her unspoken question. "At least until the FDA gets off its butt and starts approving some of the new antirejection drugs that we *know* are more effective than cyclosporine. Or at least until the damn feds let us widen the scope of our human trial experiments. Until then, people like the ones in your hospital will keep dying."

There was a double meaning in what Krahl had just said. First he blames the Food and Drug Administration, thought Amanda bitterly, but he can't resist getting in a dig at another hospital. I'd like to know what's going on in the transplant unit right here.

She hoped there was no trace of the flash of anger she felt as she asked Krahl to explain.

"You know about monoclonal antibodies, of course," he said.

Oh God, he would ask me about that, she thought, trying not to feel like a fifth-grader who's been called on to recite the homework left undone the night before.

Monoclonal antibody research was hot now, and it was impossible to be alive and functioning in the health care system without having heard of it, but how the antibodies worked and what they did—that was beyond her. She decided to be honest. "Oh, I've heard about them, all right," she said. "But understanding them is another story."

Krahl smiled. "I like you, Amanda. And what's more, I respect you. Most women in your position would have tried to bluff their way through to impress me with what they know. You have enough ego strength not to need to do that."

Sexist pig. Condescending egomaniac. Shithead of the highest order. Charming, handsome devil who was churning up those disturbing places in her lower belly. Images of those full lips, parted, tracing the line of her body down to . . .

And you're calling him a pig! said the voice, which was dead right, as usual. To Krahl, she smiled, shrugged, and said, "Tell me how monoclonals are going to be used to save transplant patients."

"You probably know that monoclonal antibodies are cloned antibodies that recognize only one antigen," he said.

That at least sounded familiar.

"Normally, antibodies attack any and all foreign matter: viruses, bacteria, protozoa—anything," he explained.

"Including tissue from another person," Amanda said, to make sure she understood.

"Right. Each antibody that the immune system produces is matched to a special site on the antigen's surface and attaches itself to that antigen. The antibody marks the antigen and makes it a better target for other antibodies of the same type."

"Sort of like a dog peeing on bushes and trees to let other dogs know it was there?" she asked.

Krahl looked annoyed. Apparently he was the only one allowed to use metaphors. "Sort of," he said. "Anyway, the onslaught of antibodies destroys the antigens—the foreign invaders, if you will—and the infection abates. This is what happens naturally. The immune system, when allowed to go its own way, summons up many different types of antibodies when only one specific type is needed to repel one specific antigen. The others are wasted."

"So if you could manufacture 'designer' antibodies to attack only one type of antigen, the immune system wouldn't have to tax itself so much," said Amanda, impressed with the elegance and simplicity of the monoclonal antibody idea.

"Correct," said Krahl. "I'm not going to bore you with how scientists make them. It's complex and time-consuming and involves laboratory mice and cancer cells and several steps in the production process."

Amanda knew instinctively that he didn't understand the process himself but couldn't admit it. Few physicians understood much of what went on in the laboratory, and there was no need for them to. Their role was to take the fruits of those labors and use them to cure patients. But Krahl was the kind of man who wanted everyone to believe that he understood everything.

"That's okay," she said. "I wouldn't know what you're talking about anyway. But tell me how monoclonals can be used in transplants."

"It's all in the T cells, the heart of the immune system," said Krahl. "In a transplant, you remove some of the patient's own T cells and manufacture monoclonal antibodies from them. In other words, make more 'designer antibodies' in the laboratory. Then you take blood samples and count the cloned antibodies to keep track of the number of T cells, in order to monitor the immune system's function.

"Monoclonal antibodies also mark the T cells for destruction by the body's own immune system. Thus, they act in two ways: by halting the rejection process itself and by allowing us to keep an accurate T-cell count so that immunosuppressive drug dosage can be calibrated precisely."

"How close are you to being able to use monoclonal antibodies in clinically useful ways?" asked Amanda. She had no idea why she was asking a question like this since it had absolutely no bearing on her work, but for some reason that she did not fully understand she wanted to keep Krahl talking about transplants. Maybe a mental bell would ring somewhere, and she would be able to make a connection between treatment and research and why the patients at her hospital had died. Or perhaps she would learn something useful that she could bring back to the transplant nurses at J. F. K., who were starting to doubt their ability to keep patients alive.

"Researchers are doing whatever the FDA lets them do, but you know what conservative pansies they are," said Krahl. "There are lots of drugs in the pipeline, and some of them seem to work. Some are really good. But the frightened little politicians over there are scared to approve anything unless it's been tested for a hundred years."

Krahl talked for a while longer about transplant research, but it soon became obvious that nothing he said would be of help to her. She looked at her watch and was genuinely surprised to see that almost two hours had passed since they sat down to lunch. There were only a few other people left in the dining room. "I have to get back," she said, gathering her purse and rising.

"I'll walk you to your car," he offered.

"You may change your mind when you step out the front door," she said. "It's beastly out there."

He took her arm as they walked through the maze of St. Jude's corridors, and Amanda could see that the women employees they passed took note of the proprietary way in which Krahl steered her to the main lobby. A few people, men and women, greeted him, but he ignored them all.

Amanda thought that Krahl wanted her to believe that he was so enchanted by her company that all others ceased to exist for the moment. She just thought he was rude.

═══ CHAPTER 17 ═══

Evelyn Portman was exhausted this morning, but it wasn't just the sex that had tired her out. True, she was not as emotionally drained as she used to be when the sex was new and what she had chosen to think of as romantic. Now she performed without putting much of herself into the act.

What caused her bleary eyes as she unlocked her office, was fear.

She was afraid he would leave her if she stopped doing the things that he expected and had now come to need. In the beginning, she had done them out of love, but now that the bloom was off the sexual rose, the demands were becoming more difficult, more repugnant.

It wasn't that she had so many moral compunctions. It just seemed so unnecessary. How many times did he have to prove he could do it?

She was also afraid of the *way* in which he might leave her. They both had a lot at stake here, and her lover was a determined man. She didn't think that he was in love with her any longer (be honest with yourself, she thought, he probably never was), and he must know that her feelings had changed as well. Men had less power over women who were not in love with them.

That disappointed them and made them dangerous.

She was also afraid of being left without the extra money that she had grown to love—to need. "Reduced circumstances," her mother would have called it. As far back in her childhood as Evelyn could remember, her mother's circumstances had been reduced, but there had never been the total humiliation of absolute poverty. "On the public dole," her mother used to say during the rare moments that she could bring herself to discuss their financial situation. But the fear of disaster was always there. They were forever on the edge—

160

the way Evelyn was now.

Without her lover's contribution to her coffers, Evelyn would not be able to afford the upkeep, fees, and taxes on the California Street flat. If she lived solely on her salary as director of pharmacy, she would have to move to a smaller place in a less impressive neighborhood. She would not be able to shop for clothes at Saks and Neiman-Marcus, and would have to start watching the papers for sales. She might even have to do what so many other women did—go to discount stores and hunt for bargains. She shuddered.

Last night's scene with her lover scared her, too.

"Do you think we should stop for a while?" she had said tentatively. Very tentatively.

"Stop?" he had asked. His voice wasn't exactly what you could call menacing, but there was something there.

"Why? Don't you want me anymore?" His hand ran along her thigh, around her buttocks, across her belly, and then down to the place where all her weaknesses lay. She had put her hand on his then, just to stop him for a while so they could talk. So she could talk. So she could think. His grip when he removed her hand was firm. It had frightened her.

"Yes, I want you," she had said. "I love what you're doing to me." And she did. She loved it. She needed it. She was afraid of it.

"Then, what's wrong?"

"Your wife. You know what she did before. Maybe we should stop for a while until she cools off."

"Don't worry about my wife," he said, his hands insistent now, doing the things that drove reason away. "I have my wife under control. My wife is not your concern. I am your concern. We are each other's concern. What we need from each other. What we do to each other." He had entered her by then, and the rhythm of his words matched the thrusts of his body, and she forgot to be frightened.

But this morning, the fear was back in full force. She knew she didn't look well; two of the pharmacists had stared at her curiously when she filled her cup from the communal coffeepot. She regretted now not having taken the trouble to be more friendly to them and to the pharmacy aides. If she had established an atmosphere of camaraderie, she could have made a joke out of her exhaustion and the fact that her hand shook when she poured the coffee. She could have brushed it off lightly, the way everyone else did.

But she was not like everyone else. She never had been. She had always been more serious of purpose, more dedicated to her job, more clear about her goals.

And she had achieved them. She was director of pharmacy in a major medical center and she had more than enough money now for her purposes. She had status and position and power—all of which could be taken away in a single stroke by the man who had given them to her. She had no control. Therefore she had nothing.

Evelyn Portman took her purse out of her desk, left her office, and walked carefully to the ladies room just off the entrance to the emergency department. She chose that one because it had no stalls and offered total privacy.

J. F. K. Memorial was a big hospital, and the distance between her office and the bathroom in the northernmost wing of the building was about a quarter of a mile. She walked slowly and deliberately, and by the time she got to her destination, she had a headache. But her face registered nothing, as she locked herself into the tiled room.

She turned on both water taps full force. Then she sank down onto the cold floor in front of the toilet and howled out her terror and rage.

Len Agostino was not crying, but he felt damn close to it as he sat at his desk and finished typing the paperwork that would close out the Aaron Zurman case. There was no case. Even though he knew there was.

Yesterday he had indeed taken his $2,000,000 dump, but it had given him no pleasure, and as he was sitting in the palatial bathroom, which he figured was about the size of his own living room, he felt as though he were desecrating this man's memory.

It seemed as if this bathroom had never been used for anything as ordinary and human as defecation—or for showering, shaving, putting on clean socks, indulging in a long satisfying fart, searching for grey hair, squeezing a pimple—all the hundreds of things that people did with the bathroom door closed.

The bathroom looked as if its sole function was to look

pretty, as if at any moment photographers would reveal it to the world. The entire apartment looked that way. Like an incredibly expensive hotel suite.

Agostino had seen neat homes before, certainly not belonging to any member of his family, but in his years on the force he had been in places where the little woman would get an A-plus for housekeeping. But nothing like this. This was pathological, and Agostino wondered what filth lay in the heart and soul of a man whose liquor bottles were arranged in perfect rows, organized alphabetically, carefully dusted—and hidden away on a closet shelf.

Lots of people faced all the hangers in the same direction—Agostino himself did that to avoid the annoyance of tangles, but Zurman's clothes were hung in a bedroom closet at precisely the same distance from each other, arranged according to color. Agostino thought that was still within the bounds of normalcy. Incredibly fastidious and compulsively neat, but still normal.

What was really scary, though, was the piece of paper attached to each hanger. Written on it was the date and the place that each shirt had been purchased—and the dates it had been worn and the occasion.

Zurman had bought a white cotton broadcloth shirt with maroon stripes at Joseph A. Bank last year in October, and he had worn it to work six times and to a party at the home of someone named Gary Appleman in April. It had not been worn since then—probably too heavy a fabric for summer, Agostino thought.

What kind of person did this? Who had the time and inclination to keep track of this sort of stuff? Agostino saw an anal-compulsive personality run amok, and he wondered just how far off the beam Aaron Zurman had gone with the rest of his life.

Gerald Miller had said that Zurman had been unable to make and keep close human relationships, and Agostino could see why. Any woman coming into this apartment and seeing the precise order in which the knickknacks were arranged on the tabletops, and the pathological neatness of the kitchen, would go screaming into the night. What woman would feel comfortable putting on makeup in that bathroom? Who would not be able to read the message shouted from this home: "I care about my things more than I could ever care about a person."

Agostino did his search and found nothing. There was no personal correspondence. Checks for the past several months had been made out to utility companies, a mortgage holding company, Visa, MasterCard, American Express, a variety of charities, a few stores—nothing that disclosed more than the routine of a seemingly ordinary existence.

Zurman's dresser drawers and kitchen cupboards revealed the same compulsive behavior: socks and underwear arranged by color and fabric, dishes stacked according to pattern, glassware blindingly clean, cookbooks protected by plastic guards, a list of dinner parties over the years with neat notations about who had attended and what had been served. The whole thing exhausted Agostino and made him unaccountably sad. What kind of man devoted this much energy to meaningless effort? What kind of man derived so little pleasure from life that he required so much artificial satisfaction?

The bookshelves were slightly more interesting in that Zurman read in languages other than English. There were books in French, German, and what looked like Hebrew but, Agostino knew, could also have been Yiddish. The two languages were written with the same letters, but Yiddish sounded like German when it was spoken—an irony since he could not imagine Jews wanting to sound even remotely like Germans.

But a facility for languages did not constitute a motive for murder. Not even being irritatingly, pathologically neat and clean was a motive for murder, although if he were going to follow through on this case, Agostino would have a talk with Ziggy about how people hid inner slime with outer cleanliness. But he was closing this case, so there would be no talk with Ziggy—at least not officially. There was no reason why he couldn't call the psychologist and invite him for a friendly, nonofficial lunch.

Lunch was what Amanda and Ruth Sinclair were having, in the farthest corner of the hospital cafeteria. Even so, they had little privacy because the room was packed.

"The lettuce is particularly delicious today," Amanda said to Ruth. "And the tomatoes are exquisite specimens of plastic food."

Ruth said nothing. She was used to being teased, tortured even, over the consistently bad hospital food. If the people who worked here thought that Intercontinental provided bland, tasteless food, they should have tried the other catering companies. But she wished Amanda and everyone else would shut up about the meals at the hospital. Maybe it wasn't exactly delicious but it consisted of high-quality nutrition, and Ruth knew that the ingredients were top-grade and fresh. So the chefs that worked for Intercontinental would never get jobs in three-star restaurants. So what? They did their job and no one ever got food poisoning.

But Amanda persisted. "This is the height of the tomato season," she complained. "Why can't you buy real tomatoes from local growers instead of using these pale, awful things?"

"Amanda," said Ruth in a voice tinged with sarcasm, "why don't you bring your own tomatoes from home? In fact, why don't you bring your own lunch?"

Amanda immediately felt terrible. She had pushed Ruth too far. Everyone pushed Ruth too far about the food. "I'm sorry," she said. "I shouldn't tease you. I know you do a good job, and I've eaten too many meals at other hospitals not to know that we're lucky here. Well, relatively lucky," she said and smiled at Ruth, hoping a little humor would smooth things over.

Ruth smiled back. "Just don't bug me about the tomatoes. Everyone bugs me about the tomatoes. You don't see me eating them, do you?"

Amanda laughed and picked the tomatoes out of her own salad and pushed them to the edge of the plate. "I want to bug you about something else, but first I have to tell you where I was yesterday for lunch—St. Jude's Hospital medical staff dining room."

"Ooh la la," said Ruth, fanning her face with her hand in mock awe. "That's a real restaurant, not a hospital dining room. It's actually a branch of Dominique's."

"No kidding?" said Amanda in real surprise. "Isn't that kind of unusual?"

"It is," replied Ruth. "But I think that Dominique is big buddies with one of the directors at St. Jude's, and anyway, that hospital has tons of money. What were you doing over there, looking for a job?"

"No, but I bet they pay a lot more than I'm making here," said Amanda, who had not thought of changing jobs—until this very moment. "I went over to talk to their transplant guy; his name is Joseph Krahl, and he's one of the most arrogant bastards I've ever run across. He also thinks he's devastatingly sexy. I didn't have a stitch on by the time his X-ray eyes got done with me."

"All men think they're devastatingly sexy," replied Ruth. "They can't help it. Why did you go over there? How come you didn't talk to what's-his-name here? And if you tell me you dragged all the way across town in all that traffic on the hottest day of the year just to get a decent lunch, I'll put those tomatoes right where they'll feel real icky!"

Amanda explained why she had gone to St. Jude's.

"Do you think he bought it?" asked Ruth.

"Bought what?" said Amanda. "That really was why I went. What other reason would I have?"

"Listen, Amanda, I believe you, and I know you have a good heart, but going to St. Jude's was not the most diplomatic thing you could have done. He'll think that Zyrwynsky is screwing up, which he might be—who knows?—and then you'll have played right into Krahl's hands."

"What do you mean, played into his hands?" asked Amanda.

Ruth shrugged. "I heard that Krahl wanted the job here, but that the search committee chose Zyrwynsky because he's a big gun in transplant research and had been at Hopkins for a long time. You know how excited these guys get over a hotsy-totsy place like Hopkins."

"But why would Krahl want to leave a cushy hospital like St. Jude's to come here?" asked Amanda.

"Sometimes you're so naive, Amanda," Ruth replied. "St. Jude's *is* a nicer physical plant, but you know as well as I do that the medicine they practice isn't nearly as good as it is here."

"That's true," said Amanda. "And St. Jude's doesn't have a medical school or university affiliation. So what else do you know about the fight between Krahl and Zyrwynsky?"

"Not much," said Ruth. "I didn't exactly have a palpitating interest in who got hired."

The last part of that statement was true; Ruth had almost no interest in medical staffing and personnel at J. F. K. Memorial

Hospital. Her own doctors were at other hospitals. But the first part was a big lie for which she felt not the slightest shred of guilt.

Ruth Sinclair knew much more than she was willing to let on to Amanda Knight about why Joseph Krahl hadn't gotten the job he coveted. But she wasn't about to tell. Amanda was too nosy for her own good—and sometimes for the good of the hospital. Like this business of rushing off to St. Jude's just to satisfy her own curiosity, without considering the political ramifications of what she had done.

As it turned out, this was not a good time to have kept the knowledge to herself.

Amanda went back to her office more frustrated than ever. Ruth knew something she wasn't telling, but there was no point in pressing her. She had to talk this over with someone. Despite what Sal had said, Lydia probably would think her suspicions were completely off the wall. Besides, it wouldn't be fair to the detective to create problems for her at work.

Ken would tell her to mind her own business and stick to running her department. (*He has a point, you know*, said the voice, which always made sure to let her know when Ken made sense and she didn't.) Ruth might be correct in accusing her of political naiveté, but Amanda certainly wasn't stupid enough to tell anyone else in the hospital.

Well, maybe Eddie. No, he had enough to worry about without being a party to her suspicions, and he would agree with Ken. "Butt out, Amanda," he would say. "Stop looking for trouble."

So she called Glencora and arranged to have dinner with her friend that evening. "Where do you want to eat?" asked Glen, who could agonize for a half hour over the choice of a restaurant.

"You choose," she said.

"I'll have to think about it and call you back," said Glen.

When Amanda called Ken at his office to tell him that she wouldn't be home for dinner, he was relieved not to have to be in Glencora's company, but he complained about having to eat alone. "What is there to eat in the house?"

"I'm not sure," said Amanda, who was used to this conversation. "Look in the fridge or get Chinese takeout. Don't forget to feed Shadow."

"That mountain lion could live on her own blubber for six weeks," he said.

Amanda laughed in spite of herself. "If you don't feed her, I'll tell her to take a lion's bite out of your ass!"

Glencora had decided on the Two Quail restaurant on Massachusetts Avenue near Union Station, and she was waiting at a choice table near a window when Amanda arrived at seven o'clock. Glen was wearing what she had worn to work: a hot pink silk dress with a silk scarf wound around her tiny waist as a belt. Her shoes were white sling-back pumps with a tiny strip across the toe that exactly matched the pink of the dress. Amanda bet that Glen bought the shoes for the dress and didn't wear them with anything else.

Amanda was dressed more casually. She had gone home after work to get out of her hot pantyhose, shower, and change her clothes. She had fed Shadow and left a note for Ken taped to the cat's bowl. "I changed my mind," the note said. "*I* want to bite your ass. I'll be home by 10 P.M. XOXO."

Now she wore an orange cotton skirt that came down almost to her ankles, multicolored flat sandals on her bare feet, and a white cotton blouse. Around her waist she wore a fringed belt made of black cotton with orange and green stripes. She had on minimal makeup and huge dark brown sunglasses.

"Are you competing in the Miss Mexico contest?" asked Glen.

"Cha, cha, cha," said Amanda, who thought they were both well turned out. She had long ago stopped being envious of her friend's way with clothes. "Are you running for the Miss Upwardly-Mobile-Magazine-Editor award? What are you drinking?"

"Gin and tonic. What else does the trendy young executive drink on Capitol Hill in the summer twilight?"

"I'll have the same—with English gin," said Amanda to the waiter who, Amanda was pleased to note, did not introduce himself to the women. "Actually I could put away about a bottle of gin," she said.

"Are things that bad?" asked Glencora.

"No, actually things are quite good," replied Amanda. "But I have this one little problem that I want to talk to you about— but not now. Let's just sit in peace and drink for a while. Tell me about the new guy, the one with the giant . . ."

"He's out," said Glen. "Too stupid. Too boring. A great fuck, but nothing upstairs."

"Glen, how can a man be a great fuck and stupid at the same time? It takes intelligence to be a good lover. Don't you want something more than the "get-it-up, get-it-in, get-it-over-with" brand of lovemaking?"

Glencora sighed and said, "You're right. Something between the ears is more important than something between the legs. I'll just keep looking. Tell me what's bothering you."

"I will," replied Amanda, "but first I have news for you. Lydia and Sal are getting married on New Year's Eve."

"How cute," replied Glencora in a voice that could have sliced the bread she was buttering. "How just adorably darling."

Amanda was surprised. You have to be really miserable to be that jealous. There must have been something serious going on beneath Glen's surface, and Amanda felt her friend's pain in amounts equal to her own anger at Glen's reaction to the news.

"Glen, Lydia's happiness doesn't take away anything from you. You wouldn't be less lonely if Lydia were miserable too."

To Amanda's great surprise, Glencora's eyes filled with tears. Glen never cried in front of anyone, even her best friend. Amanda put her hand on Glen's arm. "Tell me what's wrong."

Glen immediately jerked her arm away, sniffed, and said, "Nothing drastic. Just the usual post breakup blues, and I'm due to get my period. Tell me what's going on at the hospital that's got you in a stew."

Bullshit, thought Amanda. But she said nothing. Glencora had never used her period as an excuse for anything, and she always derided women who did.

"Just let me decide what to eat," said Amanda, "and I'll tell you the whole story, but you have to promise not to tell *anyone*."

"I promise," replied her friend, crossing her heart and raising her right hand in the universal childhood gesture for a promise. Her eyes were dry now. "By the way, how's that narcotics-stealing stuff going?"

"Actually, we're making progress with that," Amanda told her. "We're taking some action and we're going to catch whoever's doing it.

"I'll have the roast duck," she said to the waiter. Glencora ordered pork with plum sauce.

"Our arteries are probably hardening right now before we even eat anything," said Amanda.

"Who gives a shit!" said Glen and put an extra heavy layer of butter on her bread.

"I love it when you're in such a positive frame of mind," said Amanda. "But maybe your cynicism will give me a new perspective on my problem." Then she told everything: the four deaths and her talk with Joseph Krahl, with a side trip into his personality and sexual come-on.

"Is he good-looking? How old is he?" asked Glen.

"Jesus, you have a one-track mind," said Amanda. She admitted that Krahl was handsome and about the right age for Glen. "But he's probably married," she added. "And he's a real shit."

"How do you know he's a shit?"

"Because my instincts tell me so, and I'm never wrong about those things. You know that," said Amanda.

"Will you at least find out if he's married?"

"No, find out yourself. You're the one with all these great contacts in high places. Now will you let me finish the story?"

"Go ahead. I'm sorry."

But there didn't seem much more to say beyond the fact that there was nothing on which to base her suspicions.

"Okay, so what have we got here?" said Glen. "Three deaths from the same thing in a relatively short time. Another death from something else—different but related—during the same time. And one accusation of murder."

"Right," said Amanda.

"What do they all have in common?"

Amanda ticked off on her fingers: "One, they all had transplants. Two, they were all taken care of by the same doctor."

"Except for the heart transplant woman," said Glen.

"Well, her original surgery three years ago was done by someone else, but when she got sick Bill Zyrwynsky was her doctor."

"So she's a wild card in two respects," said Glen. "What else do they have in common?"

"They were all treated at our hospital. Same nursing staff, same food, although I don't think any of them ate much real food. They breathed the same air," said Amanda, her mind soaring off into all sorts of nosocomial infections, the ones picked up in a hospital and caused by something *in* the hospital. "But all the other deaths at J. F. K., the ones not in the transplant unit during that time, were not related in any way."

"Are you sure?" asked Glen.

"Actually, I am," replied Amanda, "because I checked. There were a few trauma deaths in the emergency room, two cardiac arrests in the intensive care unit, and a few cancer deaths—people who had been dying for a long time."

"Is your new doctor, Zimecheck or whatever, killing his patients?" asked Glen.

"Zyrwynsky. Why would you ask a question like that? What on earth possessed you to think that?" said Amanda, who was afraid to think it herself.

"Listen, stranger things have happened. Remember that nurse a few years ago in Prince George's County? Who knows, Amanda. Maybe one of your nurses did it."

Amanda remembered the nurse at P.G. County Hospital only too well, and it had occurred to her that a similar person worked at J. F. K. "That woman," she said to Glen, "was nuts. She injected something or other—I forget what she used, potassium chloride probably—into patients in the ICU so they would have cardiac arrests. But she didn't give them enough to kill them, and then she rushed over and did cardiac resuscitation and made this heroic effort to pull them through. Sometimes they lived. Sometimes not."

"And why did she pull these little stunts?" asked Glen, who remembered the incident because she had written a cover story about it in *Style and Sense*.

"Because she was bored with the routine in ICU and wanted some excitement. And because she wanted to be a hero. We're talking about a *really* fucked-up person, Glen. A true whacked-out crazy. That was nothing like what I'm dealing with now."

"Maybe the situation isn't exactly parallel," said Glen gently. "But why couldn't you have a crazy running around your transplant unit: a nurse *or* a doctor. Someone, say, who disapproves of organ transplants, maybe a religious nut—or just an ordinary nut."

Amanda sighed. What Glen was suggesting made perfect sense. Hospitals often attracted weird employees. Several years ago, before she had become director of nursing, there had been a staff nurse at J. F. K. Memorial who believed that cancer was a failure of the patient's "will," and she went around forcing critically ill patients to get out of bed, sink to their knees on the floor, and accept the incantations she muttered over them. Luckily, she was caught and fired quickly, but not before she created an incredible amount of trouble.

Such a person could have forced the patients to drink something just as easily as she prayed over them. Most hospital patients will do just about anything that a person in a white uniform tells them to.

Amanda had heard even worse stories from colleagues, and if she was going to be realistic, she had to acknowledge that she might have a nut case on her hands. "Okay, let's assume that we have a zombie running around," she said to Glen. "Why these patients? And did she—or he—deliberately murder them? Maybe it was something less active than actual killing but that would cause death anyway? If so, what was it?"

═══ CHAPTER 18 ═══

Amanda was driving along Baltimore Pike marveling at the ugliness of the scene. Even the red brick University of Maryland in College Park was one of the most unattractive state universities she had ever seen, except in the spring when even the meanest of buildings was hidden behind a profusion of azalea, dogwood, redbud, rhododendron, and all the other flowering vegetation that made Washington a joy for a few weeks around income tax time.

But it wasn't spring now. It was the heaviest part of summer, the last gasp, when it was easy to believe that there would never again be a breath of fresh spring air or the refreshing crispness of autumn.

Amanda felt claustrophobic cooped up in her car with all the windows closed and the air conditioning on, but when she had opened the window a few blocks back, a huge truck belched diesel fumes in her face, and she held her breath until she closed the windows.

She wanted to move to Montana.

But you'd be snowbound eleven months of the year, said the voice, which immediately recognized Amanda's periodic frustration with Washington's political, personal, and meteorologic climate. *And after you had read all three books in the library, what would you do? Besides, Shadow would probably get eaten by a bear!*

Bears don't eat pussycats. They like blueberries, she retorted. But at least I wouldn't have to go hiring private detectives to catch nurses stealing narcotics.

She recognized her faulty logic at once, and knew that there were thieves all over. And there was probably a Mark Sullivan in the tiniest hospital in Missoula, Montana.

"Amanda, for God's sake, why can't you keep your nurses in line?" he had asked when she told him about the narcotics

173

thievery and what David Townsend had suggested.

Amanda never knew how to react when someone attacked her without warrant. In social situations she was very good— too good sometimes—with a quick, sarcastic rejoinder. But this was work, and although Mark Sullivan was not her superi- or, it would do no good to insult him in return. He was a public relations person and thus knew every single trick of revenge and back-stabbing that existed in Washington. And he wouldn't hesitate to use them.

So she ignored his sarcasm, which Ken had told her was the best way to handle it. "Respond only to the business at hand," he had said, "and you'll force the other guy to do the same." The technique worked—when she had the presence of mind to use it.

This time she did. "Mark, I don't know diddly about detec- tives, and since you know everyone worth knowing in this town, you might have to make fewer phone calls than I would to find someone. Besides, David wants to keep this as low-key as possible."

"I can't imagine why!" said Sullivan, the sarcasm in his voice thickening.

Now Amanda was angry and her palm itched to smack him across the face. Instead, she stood up and said, "Do you want me to find a detective, or will you?"

"Come on, Amanda, don't be so touchy," the PR man said, suddenly afraid that perhaps he had pushed her too far. He knew that David Townsend liked and respected Amanda Knight, and maybe that was one of the reasons he himself disliked her so much. But there was no point in risking trouble over something so trivial.

Even so, he felt a wave of hatred wash over him as he watched her sit back down and cross her legs. Her cream- colored linen suit and cocoa silk blouse probably cost enough to cover a whole month's payment on his BMW, and he recalled that she had not dressed that well before she married Ken James.

"Who's being touchy?" she asked, letting her anger peek out now that he had backed down. "I came in here all polite, and you made snotty comments about my nurses. If I were you, I'd keep my fingers crossed that I'm never a patient here, Mark."

She smiled brilliantly as she made the threat.

Vicious fucking bitch, he thought. He held up his hand, palm out, in a gesture of submission. "Truce?"

Amanda made the same gesture. "A temporary one," she agreed, but she smiled in a way she hoped was less nasty this time.

"I do know a few discreet detective agencies," Sullivan said. "Let me make the initial contact, tell them what's happening, and then you can fill them in on the details. Is that okay with you?"

"It's perfect, Mark, thank you," she replied. As she left his office, she wondered, as she always did, why a transaction that should have taken no more than a minute to complete had lasted a quarter of an hour, and why fourteen of those fifteen minutes had been filled with anger and hostility.

She wanted to move to Montana.

Instead, she brought her mind back to Prince George's County, Maryland. The university grounds gave way to a row of automobile dealerships, interspersed here and there with McDonald's, Burger King, and a few other fast-food emporiums. She almost missed the small "Welcome to Hyattsville" sign, hidden as it was in the forest of road signs, billboards, orange construction warnings, no parking admonitions, and all the other reading material that littered American highways.

Get off your high horse and look at the map, said the voice, which always recognized the view from that horse. *And don't be surprised if this woman slams the door in your face. There's no reason why she should be overjoyed to see someone from the hospital that killed her husband.*

Amanda ignored these admonitions, which she knew were well advised, and concentrated on finding Carol Court. It was, as she had thought, in a townhouse development in which all the streets had girls' names: Ann, Diane, Laura, Julie, and Simone.

Simone?

Were Carol, Ann, and the others the developer's daughters and Simone his wife? Or was Simone his mistress and the other women the wives, or mistresses, of his financial backers? Gimme a hundred grand for start-up costs and you can have the lady of your choice immortalized on a green street sign.

How romantic!

Shut up and rethink this. What are you going to say to this woman? asked the voice, which knew that too often Amanda flew by the seat of her pants.

This was one of those times.

Amanda got out of the car, locked it, and stood for a moment on the sidewalk. The townhouses, like hundreds of others in suburban Washington, were arranged in a U around a central grassy area, bordered by parking spaces. At the open end of the U was a shaky-looking pole on which rested the steel mailboxes for the two dozen or so houses on Carol Court.

Some of the houses had fake brick facing on the first-floor level and aluminum siding on the upper floor. Others were made entirely of siding. The colors were probably designed to blend in with the scenery—light blue, beige, a sort of middling green—but they succeeded in blending only with the depression that was rapidly enveloping Amanda. Even at the twilight hour, her favorite time of day, especially in summer, the development looked grim and seedy. It was probably no more than two or three years old.

Amanda walked to Number 5, rolled a plastic tricycle out of her way, and rang the bell. The small front lawn needed cutting and edging, and the shrubs, which still looked fragile in their infancy, were badly in need of care. Perhaps, thought Amanda, the people in this household had divided the chores according to longstanding tradition: outside work was always the man's job. And now that the man was dead . . .

The door opened to reveal a young woman with dark auburn hair and a face full of freckles. She's probably always hated those freckles, thought Amanda in the second of silence before the woman spoke, even though they're her most attractive feature.

"Yes?" the woman asked, in a cautious but not hostile voice.

Amanda handed her a business card as she introduced herself and said, "Mrs. Sherwood, I'm probably coming at a terrible time, but I was afraid that if I called first, you wouldn't agree to see me."

The woman's face softened at Amanda's admission of insecurity and she said, "What do you want?"

Again, Amanda was tentative. "I'm not sure. Some strange things have been happening at the hospital and your husband's death may have been a part of them, and I just wanted to talk to you a little."

Lynn Sherwood opened the door. "Come on into the kitchen. I'm just feeding the baby." She led Amanda through the house and into the kitchen. At the table, strapped into a plastic highchair, sat the most gorgeous baby Amanda had ever seen. He was about eight or nine months old, chubby, giggly, and seemingly delighted with his entire world, especially this new surprise that his mother had delivered for his amusement. Amanda could see his legs dangling out of his diaper, the rolls of baby fat on his thighs matching the three distinct rolls under his chin.

His eyes were huge and intelligent, and when his mother introduced him as Jack junior, the baby seemed pleased to make Amanda's acquaintance.

"What a beautiful and charming child," said Amanda, really meaning it. "He's so squeezable and huggable."

"He looks just like my husband," said Mrs. Sherwood as she tried to fight back the tears that poured down her cheeks. "He has exactly the same personality as Big Jack did."

She was crying in earnest now, and the baby suddenly got a worried expression on his face, puckered up, and began to wail. "Excuse me," she said, gulping sobs, and ran out of the room, leaving Amanda with a screaming baby and a dish of mashed carrots.

During Amanda's infrequent contacts with children, she had no idea how to talk to them, so she treated them all as if they were very short adults. She did that now. "How can you eat carrots when you're crying so hard?" she asked Jack junior in much the same way that she talked to Shadow, to whom she sometimes spoke as if she were a four-pawed, furry person.

He continued to cry, but the question in her tone got his attention, and the volume diminished slightly. "If you stop crying and eat your carrots, maybe your mom will give you a cookie," she said, as if she were discussing a year-end evaluation and raise with one of her staff nurses. "Do children your age eat cookies or do they eat pâté de foie gras?"

The baby's tears stopped as he tried to follow the nonsense conversation, and his eyes opened wide again, as if he were making a difficult decision between carrots and pâté. His mouth opened as well, and Amanda shoved in a spoonful of carrots. He swallowed it and then banged on the highchair tray for more.

"Delicious, huh? It looks kind of yucky to me, and you strike me as more the caviar type," she said.

"He'd better not develop a taste for caviar. We can barely afford carrots," said Lynn Sherwood as she came back into the kitchen. Her eyes were red, but she had brought herself under control, and she did not apologize for her burst of tears. Amanda liked that.

"Do you want some coffee?" asked Lynn. "I made it this afternoon, but I can heat it up in the microwave." Neither did she apologize for not making a fresh pot.

Amanda accepted, even though she hated warmed-over coffee and would have preferred an iced drink. The baby crowed, and Amanda gave him another spoonful of carrots since Lynn made no move to relieve Amanda of her temporary role as baby feeder.

At exactly the moment the buzzer on the microwave oven went off, a small boy of about two years old walked into the kitchen. He was stark naked and had obviously just awakened. His face had that baby-sleepy look that made children look so vulnerable and precious. His thumb was securely plugged into his mouth, and his other arm was holding a floppy-eared stuffed rabbit.

"When is Daddy coming home?" he asked, removing his thumb only long enough to get the question out.

Lynn Sherwood's eyes closed in pain, but she did not cry.

"Do you remember what I explained to you about Daddy?" she asked the little boy.

"Uh-huh," he said, his eyes puzzled. But at the same time he stared at Amanda, who felt that her presence saved the child's mother from having to repeat whatever she had told him about his father's death.

"This is Ms. Knight and she's come to visit me," Lynn said. "I'll make you a sandwich, but first I want you to go up to your room and get your underpants out of the drawer and bring them down here. I'll help you put them on."

To Amanda she said, "He asks all the time about his father. He can't remember from one minute to the next."

Amanda had no idea what two-year-olds were able to understand about death. Not much, she thought, which made it hard on whoever had to keep explaining it to them.

"I've obviously come at a bad time," she said to Lynn Sherwood. It seemed likely that no time would have been better.

"I'd like to know what you want," said the woman. "When Joey comes back, I'll send him out on the deck to eat his sandwich and then we can talk. But we have to stay in the kitchen so I can keep my eye on him."

Amanda had no choice but to agree, so she continued to feed baby Jack while Lynn made the little boy a sandwich and cut up some carrot sticks for him. Finally, the older child was dressed and settled on the deck with his picnic supper, the baby's face and hands were wiped clean, and he lay in his mother's arms suckling at her breast.

"You said you wanted to talk to me about my husband's death," said Jack Sherwood's widow. She seemed calm, as though she knew that his long-standing kidney disease would one day come to this.

"Mrs. Sherwood, I've probably come out here on a wild-goose chase, and all I'll succeed in doing is upsetting you even more than you are already, but your husband wasn't the only one who died of acute rejection reaction. Two other patients died of the same thing within a very short time, and the situation is so unusual that I wanted to talk to you about it."

"I'm not sure what you're getting at," said Mrs. Sherwood. "What do the other deaths have to do with my husband?"

Good question, said the voice, which implied that Amanda should never have come here. *You're in for it now. You'll have to tell her everything.*

Amanda did. Without mentioning their names, she described the deaths of Billy Ockerson and Aaron Zurman and said that, in one case, the possibility of murder had been raised. She said nothing about Roberta Garfield because there seemed no reason to.

"Are you saying that you think my husband was murdered?" Mrs. Sherwood's voice rose to a surprised squeak, and the baby raised his head from her breast and seemed to ask, with his great round eyes, what was wrong.

She kissed him and cooed to him as she put him to her other breast.

"I don't know, Mrs. Sherwood," said Amanda miserably. "I'm not sure what I think. Except that I know there is something very strange going on in my hospital, and I'd like to get to the bottom of it—if there's a bottom to get to."

"Have you talked to the police about this?" asked Mrs. Sherwood.

A reasonable question, thought Amanda. "I haven't," she replied, "but a relative of one of the patients who died did go to the police. Nothing came of it."

She knew this because Lydia had called her today to tell her what Len Agostino had done—and what he had concluded.

"Then what do you want me to do?" asked Mrs. Sherwood. *Another good point. She's scoring them all, and you're getting yourself in deeper and deeper*, said the voice, which added that she should get the hell out of there before she did any more damage.

But Amanda sometimes refused to listen to reason, even when the source of caution was her own mind. She was also guilty of jumping in with both feet when an experimental toe in the water might be more appropriate. This was one of those times.

"Do you know of anyone who might have wanted to murder your husband?"

Mrs. Sherwood's eyes opened wide and for a moment she looked remarkably like the baby who was now asleep in her arms. Then she got angry. "No, I don't," she said. "And you have some nerve suggesting that my husband had any enemies. No one would have wanted to kill him. He was a wonderful man. Everyone liked him." She began to cry again. "I think you'd better go."

Amanda put out her hand to touch the woman's arm. "I'm so sorry," she said. "I didn't mean to upset you like this."

"Just leave," said Mrs. Sherwood.

"Well, what did you expect?" asked Ken later that evening as they sat at the side of the pool eating a supper of grilled Italian sausage, and tomatoes from their own garden. "No one wants to believe that the person they loved could have been murdered. That would mean that someone hated him enough to kill him."

Part of Amanda regretted telling Ken about going to see ynn Sherwood, because she knew that he would say precisely hat he was saying now. But part of her wanted his advice bout what to do next.

"Don't do anything," he said in answer to her question. Lydia told you that no murder took place, and she strikes ne as a competent person. So leave it alone. You'll just wind p getting yourself into hot water."

"In the first place, Lydia didn't do the investigation; she nly told me what the other guy had said. And furthermore, he didn't say that Zurman wasn't murdered, only that no one ould prove anything. There was no real evidence."

Ken sighed. He knew his wife very well. Her stubbornness as one of her most endearing qualities—except when it drove im crazy, as it was beginning to now. He wanted to tell her hat had happened during his board meeting today, the one e had spent weeks preparing for. The tension of the prep- ration and the meeting itself was gone now, and he wanted er to listen.

"Honey, I don't know what to tell you," he said. He really idn't. "I know you're going to keep poking your nose where doesn't belong, so my telling you to leave it alone won't do ny good. Just be careful and don't get yourself fired."

"Why, do we need the money from my job?"

Ken laughed, relieved that she wasn't going to push this. Without you, I'd be in the poorhouse—emotionally—if not nancially."

"Do you want anything else to eat?" she asked.

"I'm stuffed. That was delicious."

"You grew the tomatoes," she replied. "Let's take a little alk and you can tell me how the board meeting went."

Their usual after-supper walk took them down Huntington arkway, a wide residential street with a divider strip down e middle. On that strip were some of the most beautiful ees in the neighborhood, planted by the county years ago. Fall's coming," said Ken as he looked at the top of the ige trees and saw the rich green of summer beginning to ull.

"And none too soon," Amanda said and took his hand. "So ll me everything, Mr. Corporate Executive. Did you knock m dead?"

As a matter of fact, he had, and as they strolled dow Huntington Parkway toward Old Georgetown Road, he de scribed how the board had reacted to Naylor-Noyes plans fo development of a new series of computers and faster-than-eve software to go with it.

Amanda was not particularly interested in computers (ar although she would never admit it to him, she was somewh afraid of hers), but she loved her husband, and she learne a lot from his mastery of corporate politics, so she listene carefully to everything he said.

Their neighbors' gardens were suffering from the sam end-of-summer exhaustion that theirs was and nothing wa in bloom. Most of the vegetables had already been harveste and people left everything else alone until it was time for fa cleanup. Consequently there were few people out in the yards, and she and Ken had the street to themselves. It wa peaceful and quiet, and she felt good being out in the Frida evening air with the man she loved.

They came to the corner of Old Georgetown Road an waited for the light to change at the always busy six-lane high way. On the other side of the street, also apparently waitir to cross, was a woman with her hand on a baby stroller. Th woman looked middle-aged, and Amanda thought she must b the baby's grandmother.

When the traffic halted, she and Ken crossed the street, b the woman didn't move. As they approached, Amanda saw th she was in her mid- to late-fifties and the baby was less than year old. Amanda and Ken nodded and said good evening the woman, and Amanda waved her hand at the baby, wh waved back. The woman said nothing, but after a time sh nodded briefly, as if unsure of the proper response.

She had a broad Slavic face and was dressed in clothes th were European in style and cut. The black coat was too war for the mild evening. She made no move to cross the stre but stood at the corner in an attitude of hesitation and anxiet Her face had a worried, uncertain look, and Amanda felt th strength of her unhappiness. When she and Ken reached th end of the Temple Beth El parking lot, with the sounds the chanted prayers coming through the open windows, sh turned around and saw that the woman was still there, he body leaning slightly toward the street.

"That woman looks as though she's trying to make up her mind whether or not to throw herself and that baby into the traffic," said Amanda.

"Jesus, Amanda, what on earth makes you say something like that," Ken asked, truly shocked.

She shrugged. "I don't know. This really strong feeling came over me, and I wouldn't be surprised to read about it in the paper tomorrow."

Ken changed his mind. He did not know his wife nearly as well as he thought he did.

CHAPTER 19

That night, Amanda lay in bed, unable to sleep. Shadow knew she was awake and purred softly into her woman's ear perhaps in an effort to comfort and soothe.

Amanda couldn't shake the image of the woman they had seen on their walk that evening, and she felt ashamed of the genuine horror she had heard in Ken's voice when he reacted to her observation. He never had thoughts like that, or at least she didn't think he did. But then, if he was surprised at her reaction to the woman on the corner, maybe she would be surprised at some of his thoughts.

Ken had never been as open or as emotionally giving as she wanted him to be, but he had relaxed his guard over the years as he came to trust her. She knew that no one person could meet all of anyone else's needs, but right this minute she wished that he understood her loneliness and depression.

If she were to wake him now and ask him to hold her in his arms, he would. But he was obviously exhausted and would fall asleep again right away. Or he would force himself to stay awake because he would sense that his presence was important to her. But he would resent having his sleep disturbed and would be tired and grumpy tomorrow.

Or, perhaps worst of all, he would misinterpret her need for physical contact as a need for sex and would try to accommodate her. She smiled at that. He was so tired that it would take him forever to get things rolling, and then he would feel inadequate, and his ego would be wounded. She would have to pet him and say it was all right, that she hadn't actually wanted to make love in the first place, and he wouldn't believe her and then it would be his needs that they were concentrating on, not hers.

Amanda sighed. Feeling lonelier than ever, she reached up for the cat, who had given up on purring her woman to sleep and had fallen asleep herself. She pulled the cat out of her accustomed place in the valley between the pillows, dragged her under the covers, and hugged the fat, furry body. Shadow lay still for a moment, then meowed in an irritated, grouchy way, struggled out of Amanda's arms, jumped over Ken's sleeping body, and stalked out of the bedroom.

Tears pricked Amanda's eyelids as she let herself sink down into the abyss of self-pity. Rejected by both her cat and her husband!

Try to get a grip on reality here, said the voice, which hated it when Amanda behaved like this. *Your husband didn't reject you. He just went to sleep because he's had a hard day and he's exhausted. And you can't say he rejected you, since he doesn't even know what you need. And crying because your cat behaved like a cat is disgusting and stupid.*

I suppose you're right, Amanda replied.

Of course, I'm right. Now, what's really the matter? Why did you see a woman thinking about suicide when all that was there was a grandmother standing with a child in the pleasant evening air, perhaps waiting for someone? Maybe the child's parents were at services in the synagogue.

That was pretty fucked-up thinking, wasn't it?

So what's really the matter?

The matter, Amanda realized, was the deaths at the hospital and the fact that she had no control over what had happened.

Christ, Amanda, since when have you needed to control life and death? Who do you think you are?

But that wasn't the type of control she meant. She had long ago accepted the fact that death was sometimes better than lingering illness and suffering, and she herself was not afraid of death—only the agony that often preceded it.

Loss of control over what you want and need *to control*, said the voice, which knew her better than she knew herself.

Was that the real issue? She knew that the deaths had not been caused by the failure of care at the hospital. No nurses were at fault.

That's what you really care about, not the people who died.

True. She was always sorry that people had died needlessly, but she could not mourn for these four particular people because she didn't know them, and she had never subscribed to John Donne's poetic but not very realistic belief that any man's death diminished him.

Well, Amanda, said the voice, which sometimes didn't know what the hell she was talking about. *If the theory that no man is an island, is a crock of shit, why do you care so much about these deaths?*

I didn't say it was a crock of shit. For God's sake, if I really thought that, I wouldn't have chosen nursing as a profession, would I? It's just that I can't help but come back to the idea that these deaths really were needless. They weren't natural. The whole thing is just too coincidental.

So where does that leave us?

Murder!

Okay, let's say it was murder, said the voice of practicality. *Who did it? Why did they do it? Why four seemingly unrelated people? And now the biggie—how was it done?*

Oh, and one more question for you to go to sleep on, said the voice that never liked to leave well enough alone. *How come you're the only one who thinks it's murder?*

But Amanda was *not* the only one. Bonita Elliott wasn't sleeping either. She was trying to banish the growing fear that Roberta Garfield had been murdered. She was positive that Caspar Torrey knew more about her death than he would be willing to admit. No man cries like that over a woman unless he had been in love with her—or unless something very serious had been going on—or both.

The fact that Bill Zyrwynsky had trivialized her idea that the minister had been Roberta's benefactor simply hardened her conviction that it was true.

But so what? That didn't mean that he had killed her. Life was not the movies, and every affair where one of the parties was married did not end up in death. If that were true, the population explosion problem would be solved, she thought grimly.

What if Mrs. Minister had found out? Could she have killed Roberta in a fit of jealousy? *That* happened all the time—in the movies *and* in real life. But how? Roberta died of massive PCP infection; the autopsy had been unequivocal about that. Not exactly your basic murder weapon, she thought.

Stop being silly, she told herself. Go to sleep. Roberta was not murdered. She probably *had* been having an affair with the minister and made jokes about being horny all the time to cover up what she was doing. That wasn't so terrible. Bonita was not a close enough friend for Roberta to have confided something like that to her. And even if the minister had been giving her money, so what? Lots of women took money from lots of men.

But where would a minister get several hundred thousand dollars to pay for the most expensive medical care there was?

That was the question that *should* have been on Leona Torrey's lips as, once again, she screamed hysterically at her husband. The Reverend Caspar Torrey was grateful that money was not the subject of this most recent in a series of increasingly vituperative outbursts about what people would think.

They were sitting at the kitchen table having a late cup of tea. Or at least they had started out sitting at the table, but each of them in turn got up to pace the floor, to shout and gesticulate more freely, to walk off the worst of the anger.

He had not admitted his affair with Roberta to his wife, but neither did he deny it any longer. He was too tired. He was too panic-stricken over what he had done. He was too frightened that Leona would find out about the money.

He needn't have worried about that. Most men worry about the wrong things when it comes to the women they love. Caspar should have listened more carefully to the true hysteria in Leona's voice. Instead, he argued with the content of what she was saying.

"I keep telling you, Leona, that no one knows. No one even suspects. Everyone thinks I'm a caring and humane pastor to have broken down in tears over one of my flock."

"Flock, my ass," she hissed. "That bitch was nothing but a horny goat and you were happy to ram your thing into her."

Leona was not a punster, Caspar knew. In fact, a sense of humor was not one of her strong points, and most of the time when other people punned, she didn't catch it. He understood this, and he realized that his wife had no idea of what she had just said. He also knew that he should let it go by, but his mind had become unhinged enough to latch onto the horny goat-ram pun, and he realized his mistake even as the laughter bubbled up against his will.

Her eyes opened wide with rage and hatred, and her lips parted as if to speak. No words issued from them, but Caspar heard a low, keening wail that raised the hairs on the back of his neck. The wounded cry of pain and anguish could have come from a wild animal. Indeed Leona had become a wild animal.

Caspar held up his hand in a placating gesture. "I'm sorry, Leona. I didn't mean . . ."

He felt a whoosh of air near his hand.

Nothing else.

But there had been something else. There *must* have been something else. Otherwise, his hand would not be lying on the kitchen floor. If only a gust of air had gone by his hand, why was there nothing but a bloody stump at the end of his arm? Why was Leona holding the cleaver, staring at it?

Caspar Torrey believed that his mind was still working clearly, and that surprised him because it was obvious that something momentous, shocking even, had happened. The only difference now was that his thought processes were slow. Terribly slow.

That's a good thing, he thought. Because I have a real problem here. He stared at the place where his hand had been and saw the blood pumping out of the severed radial artery. It really does pump out in time to my heartbeat, he thought.

He knew that he was in shock, which was why he felt no pain. He also knew that when the pain finally registered, it would consume him totally.

So I should plan for that, he thought. I should plan for the pain and prepare for it. But of course he couldn't, and very soon, when enough of his life's blood had gushed down his arm, the Reverend Caspar Torrey sank to the kitchen floor. He landed in such a way that his outstretched arm came to rest next to the severed hand. From the perspective in which he was lying, it appeared that the hand was not in fact disengaged.

He was relieved. Thank God, he thought. It had seemed so real, staring at that bloody stump, wondering why he hadn't felt Leona slice his hand off. He laughed again. Because she didn't, he thought. It was just an hallucination.

And because he believed that his mind was still working clearly, he thought about why he should have had so horrific an hallucination. He tried to think of biblical parallels, but none came to mind.

Of course. This wasn't a religious or philosophical issue, it was a psychological one. He was consumed by guilt over what he had done, and God was punishing him.

If thy right eye offend thee, pluck it out, and cast it from thee: for it is profitable for thee that one of thy members should perish, and not that thy whole body should be cast into hell. Whosoever shall marry her that is divorced committeth adultery. If thy right hand offend thee, cut it off.

So it was a religious issue, after all. The Book of Matthew, Chapter V, was quite clear. There was no question now. He had offended God, his wife, his parishioners—himself. And he had offended his beloved Roberta. The offense to her was the greatest of all, and Caspar knew now, with what remained of his consciousness, that his right hand was indeed gone. He deserved to have lost it. As he saw the cleaver descend, he knew that further punishment would be forthcoming.

As the first stroke crushed his rib cage, the pain of his severed hand, as well as the sheet of white fire in his chest, burst upon him and he welcomed it. As he saw the hand raise the cleaver yet again, the Reverend Caspar Torrey felt something that he believed was the ecstasy that Our Lord Jesus Christ experienced on the Cross.

Just before the final stroke of the cleaver smashed into his heart and lungs, Caspar Torrey was happier than he had been in years.

CHAPTER 20

Lydia Simonowitz had never seen so much blood in her life.

She knew that the average human body contains about six quarts of it. A gallon and a half. Six cardboard milk cartons. It didn't seem like so much when you thought about it that way.

But the kitchen of this modest parish house in Gaithersburg was awash in blood. There were gallons and gallons and gallons of it. It was on the ceiling and walls. It seeped into the seams of the tile floor and spread out under the stove and ran under the refrigerator. There was blood in the sugar bowl sitting in the middle of the kitchen table, and the paper napkins in their holder next to the sugar were soaked through with the red liquid. There was blood all over the counters, and it had splattered onto the pitcher of wooden spoons that Leona Torrey kept handy near the stove.

Lydia had a jar of the same kind of spoons and spatulas next to her own stove.

And there was the smell. She would never, if she lived to be one hundred and stayed on the force as many years, get used to the heavy, brackish-sweet smell of blood that had been spilled in death.

It was not the smell that had become somewhat familiar to her from spending time with Sal in his morgue. This was different. This was something still alive and menacing, and she felt engulfed by it—and in a way that she would not come to understand for years, she was afraid of it.

The smell was on Leona Torrey too. Oh my God, there was so much blood on that woman. When she and Bandman had arrived on the scene in response to a call from the Montgomery County Police, the county detective had said that at first the men in the patrol car hadn't been certain which one was the victim.

190

When Lydia walked into the kitchen, she could see why. The woman, whose name she now knew was Leona Torrey, wife of the victim Caspar Torrey, sat on the floor not far from her husband. Her back rested against a row of drawers and her legs were spread out in front of her, the way children sometimes sit when they play jacks.

The cleaver was in her hand, and when Lydia looked carefully, she could see that the woman was breathing in slow, shallow breaths. But that was the only sign of life. In all other respects, Leona Torrey was dead, and Lydia did not think that all the psychotherapy in the world, nor an entire truckload of drugs, would ever bring her back.

Just as well, Lydia thought. Better to be dead inside after you had done something like this.

Paul Bandman saw how ashen and sweaty his partner had become. "Outside," he said.

Lydia focused on the man's long, sad face and thought once again how much he looked like an amiable and rather lazy basset hound. He seemed awfully far away, and her own voice which said, "I'm okay," came through a long tunnel.

"No, you're not," said Bandman. "Go outside and sit down."

Lydia opened her mouth to protest again, and he leaned into her ear—apparently he wasn't far away, after all—and said, "If you pass out, it's not me who'll be embarrassed. Besides, you'll get blood all over your new dress, and then you'll be mad at me because of it."

She smiled in spite of herself, tottered through the living room and out the front door, where she sank down onto the brick steps and concentrated on deep breathing and not fainting.

In a very few minutes she felt better and was heartened to see a Montgomery County patrolman emerge from the bushes wiping his mouth with a handkerchief. He walked toward her, the sun shining on his blond hair, and sat down on the steps next to her. "You look as green as I feel," she said.

"But you didn't toss your cookies," he said miserably.

"How do you know?" she said.

The young man, who looked no more than fourteen years old, seemed relieved to hear that he wasn't the only one who might have been sick. "Did you catch the call?" she asked.

"Yeah," replied the patrolman whose name tag said his name was Thomas. For some reason, perhaps because her mind had not fully recovered from the horror in the kitchen, she remembered a dinner several years ago with three other women. Several bottles of wine had been consumed and Jocelyn had said, "There are three types of men to stay away from: men who live at home with their parents, men who have just broken up with someone, and men who have two first names."

They had shrieked with laughter. The wine in their bloodstreams had made it logical to equate the last restriction with that of the first two. Lydia wondered now if Officer Thomas had suffered much because he had two first names. She thought she might ask Amanda if Ken had ever said anything about bearing such a burden.

It occurred to her then that she was feeling a good deal better and would gain nothing by sitting here in the sunshine next to this impossibly young police officer. But neither did she want to go back inside to all that blood.

Luckily she didn't have to. Bandman and the two county detectives emerged from the house. Hands were shaken all around, and no one mentioned what Lydia had almost done in the kitchen. There were no expressions of sympathy or empathy and no solicitous questioning to see if she felt better. Lydia understood their silence on the subject. It wasn't because she was a woman and this was some sort of macho test, since they ignored Officer Thomas in the same way they ignored her. Neither was it because cops were any more hard-boiled or insensitive than anyone else. They felt things just as strongly.

Rather, they believed that if they acknowledged her faintness and queasiness at the sight of worse horror than most people could imagine, then they would have to acknowledge that it could happen to them too. Indeed, that it had happened in the past. That was what was so intolerable.

That was the worst thing about most of her colleagues on the force—their unwillingness to talk about what they saw and did all day. Or if they did talk about it, they turned almost all of it into a lewd or otherwise inappropriate joke. That's why they turned into drunks in record numbers. That's why they divorced at an astoundingly high rate. That's why so many of them ended up eating their guns. That's what scared her most about being on the police force.

"If we hear anything else, we'll give you a call," said the taller of the two county detectives. "But I don't think anyone needs to be Sherlock to solve this one."

"No, but you're not going to close the books on it so fast, either," said Bandman. "That woman's not going to say *bubkes* for a long, long time."

The county detectives sighed at that observation and thought about the mountain of paperwork that lay ahead. In the State of Maryland, it was no easy task to get someone committed to a mental institution, even for someone as obviously bat-shit as Leona Torrey.

"Tell me again why we schlepped all the way up here," said Lydia when they were in the car headed down Interstate 270 back toward Washington. It crossed her mind that a year ago she would never have used the word "schlepped." She hadn't even known what it meant. Now she was beginning to talk like her partner. Maybe in time she would grow to look like him too. God forbid!

"Just to quell any doubts you might be harboring that life—and death—exist beyond the Beltway," replied Bandman.

Lydia laughed at the reference to the strip of traffic-choked interstate highway that encircled the capital. It was an old joke that Washington powerbrokers had no idea, and cared less, about what went on beyond that highway.

"Gaithersburg," she said. That's pretty far beyond. I'm surprised we didn't have to stop at the health department and get shots!"

Bandman laughed at her response, grateful anew that he had lucked out with his new partner after Peters had gotten blown away, right in front of his very . . . He shook off the image and stopped himself in time—this time.

"The county police got an anonymous call from a woman who had heard the news of the murder on the radio this morning," Bandman told her. "Apparently she was hysterical—"

"Which means that she was probably mildly upset," interrupted Lydia with an acid tone in her voice. "How come they never describe men as hysterical?"

"Now, do I get an explanation of the Greek root of the word 'hysterical'?" asked Bandman.

"How many times have you heard it?"

"Two million and three, not counting the times I tuned out," he replied.

"Okay, I guess you've got it by now. Sorry for the interruption."

"So this mildly upset woman told the operator that Caspar Torrey deserved to die because he had killed her friend. Naturally, the operator's curiosity was piqued."

"Naturally," replied Lydia.

"So the operator asked the woman for more details."

"The operator deserves a commendation from the commissioner."

"Indeed," replied Bandman. "But the woman, who grew slightly more upset as the conversation progressed, would say nothing more than the fact that this alleged murder had taken place at J. F. K. Memorial."

"So I get three guesses where we're going now," said Lydia.

"Don't strain your brain," said Bandman. "It's too hot."

As Paul Bandman and Lydia Simonowitz were fighting the increasingly heavy traffic on Wisconsin Avenue, Amanda Knight was in her office doing something she had never been taught in nursing school. In graduate school, either. She was hiring a private detective.

The woman who sat across the desk looked more like Harvard Business School than a former nurse. She had a $75 haircut, a $300 Coach handbag, nail polish that precisely matched the color of her lipstick, and a demeanor that was so supercilious that Amanda wanted to punch her in the nose. Hard.

The fact that she was doing this on a Saturday did not endear Amanda to this perfectly groomed detective.

But Rosalind Smythe ("It's Smythe, S-M-Y-T-H-E, not Smith," the woman had said even before she took the proffered seat. That's when Amanda had started hating her.) was a detective as well as a nurse, and probably knew judo and fist-fighting and groin-kicking and all that other stuff, so Amanda simply smiled and returned to Smythe the photostat of her license to practice nursing in the District of Columbia.

"Thank you," said Amanda. "I was burned once by hiring an imposter, and now I look at the actual license of everyone who works here as a nurse."

"This could be a forgery," said Rosalind Smythe.

"It could," agreed Amanda, "but I'll find out if it is when my secretary calls the licensing board to verify your registration number."

Smythe's face softened a little. "Very good," she said as if speaking to a pupil who had performed better than expected.

You ought to slap her silly, said the voice that, once in a great while, said something that was not in Amanda's best interest. Amanda ignored her itching palm and asked the detective how she planned to go about catching whoever was stealing narcotics.

"We generally don't like to discuss our techniques with clients," said Smythe. "I know what you've told me—what you've found out so far—and now we'd like to take it from there."

Amanda didn't know what to say. This woman came from the Steelman Agency, which Ken had told her was one of the best in the country. "Very discreet, very efficient," he had said. On one hand, that's all she needed to know, but something seemed incomplete about this process. Perhaps it was the idea of letting this woman loose at night in a hospital filled with sick people. Her hospital and her sick people.

"When was the last time you gave actual nursing care to actual patients?" asked Amanda.

"Are you worried that I'll screw up somehow?" asked Smythe. That damn smirk was back on her face.

"The thought crossed my mind," replied Amanda.

"You can rest assured that I'm up on all the latest techniques and procedures, and there's not a machine that I don't know how to operate," replied Smythe.

But what about the machines that lie under your breastbone and inside your skull? wondered Amanda who thought she would rather have her call bell remain unanswered forever than be cared for by this hatchet-faced bitch. "I'm sure you do," she said. "I'm sure you could run circles around me when it comes to that sort of thing. I don't spend a lot of time with patients anymore."

"Then what are you concerned about?" asked Smythe, who seemed genuinely puzzled by Amanda's lack of enthusiasm.

"I'm not sure. Perhaps it's having you here pretending to be something you're not," replied Amanda.

"I'm not *pretending* to be anything," replied Smythe, clearly offended now. "I *am* a nurse and I *am* a private investigator. It's simply that I'm not revealing everything about myself to the people I'm going to be working with for the next several nights. Do you reveal everything about yourself to every person you come into casual contact with?"

Amanda conceded the point and acknowledged that the detective couldn't do her job if the staff knew what she was up to. That was only logical. Still . . .

Her intrahospital line buzzed and Amanda had to pick it up. Louise didn't work on Saturdays. "Two police detectives are here to see you," said the receptionist at the entrance to the locked administrative office suite. "A Detective Bandman and Ms. Simo . . . Uuh." She swallowed the last part of Lydia's name.

Now, what the hell did these two want? Her immediate thought was that somehow their visit was connected to the reason Rosalind Smythe was here, and not for the first time, Amanda wished she had a back door to her office to prevent embarrassing traffic jams in front of Louise's desk.

"Okay, ask them to wait in my outer office," she said.

Amanda was not enjoying this meeting with Rosalind Smythe. In fact, she was more uncomfortable than she had been in a long time, and she supposed she ought to feel grateful to Lydia and Bandman for giving her an excuse to end the meeting. At the same time, she felt a clear sense of unfinished business. But what that business was, she had no idea, and the interior voice that often offered advice was silent.

"I know you don't like having me here," said Smythe. "None of our clients does. It makes them feel incompetent, as though they should have been able to solve the problem themselves. Our presence is a reminder that they had to ask for help. And we're very expensive. No one likes that." The detective smiled, a little wolfishly perhaps, but nevertheless she made the effort.

Amanda felt herself soften just a little at the smile, and she was forced to admit that this woman had put into words what she had been feeling but didn't understand. However, that did not make Amanda like the detective any better.

"Will you trust me to do my job?" asked Smythe.

"I will," said Amanda, who decided that she had no other choice. She paged Betsy Murdock so the two of them could work out the details of the undercover operation.

Amanda and Rosalind Smythe chatted about their respective nursing schools, a safe and boring enough subject so that each woman felt at ease, until Betsy arrived. As Amanda opened her door to the reception area, she saw Lydia's eyes widen in surprise when she saw who was right behind Amanda. Bandman's face was as impassive and sad as she remembered from the Leo McBride murder investigation last fall. But she also remembered that behind that droopy expression was an intelligence that could melt lead.

Lydia and Rosalind Smythe greeted each other with a bare minimum of cordiality, and Amanda introduced the latter to Betsy, who took the detective off to the third-floor office that the supervisors shared.

"So who spilled the beans?" asked Amanda after the two police detectives had seated themselves in her office.

"That's what we're here to ask you," said Bandman. "Do you know who made the anonymous call?"

"What call?" said Amanda.

"The call about Caspar Torrey," said Lydia.

"Who's Caspar Torrey?" asked Amanda. "The only Caspar I know is a ghost in movie cartoons."

"This Caspar is a ghost now, too," said Bandman.

It dawned on all three of them at about the same time that no one knew what anyone else was talking about, so Bandman explained to Amanda about the butchering in Gaithersburg and the anonymous phone call about the death at J. F. K. Memorial.

"Who died?" asked Amanda.

"We don't know," said Bandman. "We hoped you might be able to shed some light on this mystery. All we know is that a woman placed an anonymous call to the Montgomery County police saying that Caspar Torrey deserved to die because he had killed her friend who died at this hospital."

"We average about ten deaths a week," said Amanda. "Don't you have any other information? Was the friend a man or a woman? When did the death take place?"

"We don't know anything else," said Lydia and spread her hands, palms up, in a gesture of futility and frustration.

"Anyway, this is really Montgomery County's case, not ours. But they called us out of courtesy because of the connection with J. F. K. Memorial."

"Which we are lucky enough to have in our very own precinct," added Bandman. "Can you tell us anything that we can give to the county that might help them?"

Amanda felt something happen to the hairs on the back of her neck. All these deaths were just too much. There *had* to be some connection among them. "No," she said and opened her hands to reflect what Lydia had expressed. "Why don't you stay for lunch?" she added.

"The last time I ate lunch here, I spent a week's salary on antacids," said Bandman.

"That's because you ate the mystery meat and not the salad bar," said Amanda. "I warned you."

"You did indeed," he said. "This time I'll take your advice and eat rabbit food." Paul Bandman hated salad but figured he could drown it in enough dressing to make it palatable. He recalled that the hospital's desserts were edible.

"What was Rosalind the Royal doing in your office?" asked Lydia after they were seated in the cafeteria, which was much less crowded and noisy on the weekend.

Amanda watched in amazement as Paul Bandman stirred five heaping spoons of sugar into his coffee. "Do you want me to run to the pharmacy and get you a shot of insulin?" she asked him.

"Huh?"

"All that sugar, how can you stand it?"

Bandman rolled his eyes. "Don't start on me, okay? Everyone gets on my case about the sugar. My wife nags me about it. My partner nags me about it. The guys in the squadroom . . ."

Lydia made a sign with her eyes to drop the subject of the sugar and repeated her question about Rosalind Smythe.

Amanda sighed. "It's confidential."

Bandman's head snapped up and he came to attention exactly as Amanda knew he would at her refusal to answer. She sighed again.

"Not in a million years would I even remotely consider asking you to violate your ethical principles by divulging confidential information about patients," he said, with perhaps just the slightest tinge of sarcasm. "But if this has anything at all to do with the death of Caspar Torrey and the 'murder' that may or may not have taken place here, and if you know something you're not telling us . . ."

He let his voice trail off because he didn't want to threaten Amanda Knight, not after what had happened in the Leo McBride case, but he had a very strong feeling that she knew more than she was letting on.

"It has nothing to do with anyone's death," said Amanda and was relieved that she could tell the truth about that. "But you seem well acquainted with Rosalind Smythe," she said to Lydia. "She does think she's a princess, doesn't she?"

"She's a snotty bitch," replied Lydia. "But she's very, very good at her job. Very discreet. Very efficient."

Exactly the words Ken had used to describe the Steelman Agency.

It wasn't so much that Amanda *knew* something that she was hiding from Bandman and Lydia, because God knew she was more confused than ever. But her radar was on full alert—the same radar that she and Glen had taught themselves to use to ferret out men who were married or otherwise bad news. This time her radar was directing her toward something, but she didn't know what. She had agreed to listen to the police tape recording of the anonymous caller to see if she recognized the voice. The problem was that she was pretty sure she would.

The moment she had returned to her office after saying goodbye to the two police detectives, she had called the transplant unit and found out that Bonita Elliott had called in sick that day. That was when she realized that she would know the voice on the tape.

Could Bonita have had anything to do with the deaths on the transplant unit?

What a stupid assumption to make, said the voice, which tried not to jump to conclusions. *If she had, why would she deliberately focus attention on herself by calling the police?*

It was an anonymous call, replied Amanda. Maybe she's having a guilt attack, and she's desperate. Maybe that's why she came to you with that story about Mrs. Zurman.

That makes no sense at all. You're the one who's desperate, said the voice of reason. *In the first place, anyone who watches the news on television knows that all calls to the police are recorded. They play the screw-ups often enough on the eleven o'clock news. In the second place, what motive would she have had? In the third place, how does this Caspar person fit into all this? In the fourth place, you don't know what the hell you're talking about.*

You're right, of course, Amanda thought. There's no possible connection among all four of these people. It's just that . . .

Just what? asked the voice, which made Amanda sigh heavily as she opened her purse and took out the article she'd clipped from *The Washington Post* that morning.

It's just that there is a connection. They all died here. They all died for no apparent medical reason. There was every reason to believe that all four of them would be successful organ transplants. You know as well as I do that organ transplantation isn't experimental anymore. The patients are very carefully evaluated; all four of these people should have survived in the best possible shape.

So?

So they were all murdered. They were murdered here. At my hospital. And they were murdered by someone who has easy access to the very tightly controlled transplant unit.

Bonita Elliott did not kill anyone, said the voice, which knew how much Amanda liked and respected the transplant nurse.

How do you know?

This time the voice of logic had no adequate response and said instead, rather lamely, Amanda thought, *It could have been any one of them up there.*

Then how come Bonita called in sick after making an anonymous call to the police? Amanda replied.

You don't know that she made the call, and people do *get sick.*

She made the call, all right. I'd bet money on that, but you're right that any of the nurses or doctors could have killed those patients.

Or a janitor or a nurse's aide or one of the consulting doctors who are in and out of there all the time. Even Eddie Silverman could have done it, said the voice, which liked to tease sometimes.

Don't start that again, she replied. But you're right. It could have been anyone.

Of course, I'm right, said the voice. So damn smug.

About two hours later, a Montgomery County police officer, whose name was Thomas, and who looked as though he might have been playing hooky from high school were it not for the pistol and about ten pounds of other equipment hanging from his belt, played the recording for Amanda. She recognized Bonita's voice almost immediately, but she listened to the entire tape before she made the identification.

When Officer Thomas left, Amanda sat at her desk and watched her hands shake. There was no mistaking Bonita's voice, but what had shocked Amanda and had left her feeling sick and lost was the venom she'd heard in the nurse's voice.

This was not the Bonita Elliott whom she had seen a hundred times speak quietly and calmly to frightened patients. This was not the Bonita who would spend an hour explaining a fifteen-minute medical procedure. This was not the Bonita who spoke eloquently, even passionately, to school and community groups about the desperate need for organ donors.

The Bonita that came through the tape was a snarling Doberman pinscher. Not the smiling cocker spaniel that Amanda knew. Thought she knew.

Evelyn Portman was in disarray again. Her hair was messed up. Her makeup was smeared. Her eyes were red and puffy— from crying and from fear. The navy silk dress with the wide lapels, the one that Amanda Knight had so admired that day in the ladies room, lay torn on the living-room floor, the buttons scattered every which way.

"You'll tear my dress," she had said about an hour ago shortly after he had rung her doorbell. He had been hard and insistent, not wanting to make even a pretense at affection. She shrank away.

"I paid for it, and I'll tear it if I want to," he had said, his hand grasping the fabric at the V-neck, and for one terror-filled moment, she had thought he meant to strangle her.

Now, the two of them lay spent on her bed. She wondered again, as she had so many times in the past, at the paucity of his seminal fluid. And she wondered again if it had anything to do with the changes that came over him so often. The charm that turned into rage with no warning. The teasing flirtatiousness that became sexual frenzy. In the beginning, it had fascinated her. She'd been flattered that so public a person would let his guard down to such an extent in her presence.

But now as she lay next to this man, her vagina throbbing with pain from the battering it had just received, she wondered if she had made the biggest mistake of her life.

It had been a long time since college psychology, but it didn't take a professional to realize that she was lying in bed next to a thoroughgoing schizophrenic.

As soon as she said the word to herself, Evelyn felt panic-stricken, and at the same time, calmer than she had been for months—ever since this affair had begun. The fact that he was completely crazy explained the mood swings, explained both the tenderness and the savage rages, the exquisite lovemaking, as well as the attacks that now she could admit to herself were rapes.

It also explained why he wanted the things he wanted. And that was what scared her half to death.

It now came to her as a whole and complete thought that his mental illness explained both his brilliance and fame, as well as the needs he revealed to her only after he knew that he held her in thrall.

Evelyn Portman was one of the many people who believed the myth that all crazy people were brilliant, that beneath their mania lay a crafty shrewdness that made them even more dangerous when they went out of control.

The thing was that in this case she was correct, and she knew it as she lay next to her lover watching his face in repose as he slept. She ran one fingertip gently over the full lips that had provided her more sexual pleasure than she had ever had in her life, more than she would probably ever experience again. She knew that lovers like this man didn't grow on trees, and she hated the thought of giving up all that pleasure.

Even now, watching him sleep in a shaft of late-afternoon sunlight, knowing what he was, still in pain from what he had done to her so short a time ago, she wanted him. Does this make me crazy too? she wondered.

The answer didn't bear thinking about, so she continued stroking his lips with her finger until he awoke and began to respond. This time he was patient with her. He gave her everything she asked for, and he gave it lovingly and passionately. He gave it over and over again, as much and as little as she wanted, and when it was over, when her heart was beating normally once again, she smiled to herself at the power she could exert on him. He needs me as much as I need him, she thought as she let herself drift off into sleep.

CHAPTER 21

Amanda and Glencora were in Glen's apartment near DuPont Circle, happy and exhausted from four hours of shopping. They had been to both Syms and Loehmann's that Sunday morning and were pleased with their bargains.

"You're a real barracuda when you shop," said Amanda.

Glencora grinned. "You should talk. I thought you were going to kick that woman in the shins when she got too close to your purple jacket."

Amanda wasn't even slightly ashamed. "I need that jacket to go with the skirt. There would have been no point in buying the skirt and the blouse if I couldn't put together the entire outfit. Besides, the color would have been all wrong for her."

"Sounds reasonable to me," said Glen. "What do you want to do about lunch?"

"I want to eat something, and I want to do it soon. I'm starving. What have you got?" she asked, opening Glencora's refrigerator. "God, I should have known," she said, staring at the plastic bag of limp carrots, two six-packs of lime-flavored Perrier, and several mystery packages wrapped in tin foil.

Glencora shrugged. She was not embarrassed that her friend saw the condition of her refrigerator. "What about City Lights of China?" she asked. Even though she knew Amanda didn't like to eat Chinese food at lunch, there was always the chance that she'd change her mind.

"I don't like to eat Chinese food at lunch," said Amanda. Neither woman commented on the number of times they had had this conversation during the nearly twenty years of their friendship. "I'll go anywhere that's not Oriental as long as it's air-conditioned."

"Grim, isn't it, trying on wool clothes during the middle of a blasting heat wave?" asked Glencora, knowing that both of them would try on bathing suits outdoors at the South Pole if he sale were good enough. "How about Childe Harold?"

"Okay, but let's go now before it's overrun with yuppies out looking for a late brunch," replied Amanda.

"What do you think we are?" asked Glen. "What did we spend the entire morning doing?"

"That's different," said Amanda. "We went to discount stores. Real yups buy everything at Britches." Glen rolled her eyes, and the two women giggled at their own silliness as they walked over to Connecticut Avenue.

"Amanda!" shouted a masculine voice from across the street. She looked up and saw Donald Tannenbaum waving to her.

"That's Eddie's lover," she explained to Glen as the women walked to the corner of Q Street and waited for the light to change. "Speaking of yuppies and shopping and Britches, those two make us look like rank amateurs."

Amanda and Donald kissed hello and Glencora was introduced. "We're just going to eat lunch," said Amanda. "Why don't you join us?"

"Actually, I have a huge salad in the fridge at home," said Donald. "Come and eat with us. I'm just waiting for Ed to finish his turn in there." He gestured toward the unisex hair salon behind him.

The three chatted idly on the sidewalk until Eddie emerged from the salon and registered surprise and pleasure at bumping into Amanda. "Come home and eat with us," he said.

"We've already accepted," said Glencora as she linked her arm through his and the four of them walked off down Q Street.

"If I didn't know that she knows that Ed is gay," said Donald to Amanda as they strolled a few paces behind, "I'd think she was on the make."

Amanda laughed, but she could see from Glen's body language that Donald was right. "She just broke up with someone, and I think she wants a little masculine company right now. You know, Glen was the one who told me that Eddie was gay when I was too dense to see it."

"I know," replied Donald. "He told me how nervous he was when he decided to come out to you and how relieved he felt when you told him that you had always known and that it didn't make any difference."

"Glen gets a little pissed when she sees gorgeous hunks like the two of you 'going to waste,' as she calls it," said Amanda. "Actually, I think most straight women feel the same way."

"Do you?" asked Donald, surprised. "Were you disappointed when you found out about Ed?"

"A little," she admitted, and remembered how bitterly disappointed she had been at the time. "But it all worked out well didn't it?"

"What worked out?" asked Eddie as he unlocked the door to their house on Corcoran Street and they all breathed a sigh of relief at being in an air-conditioned place.

"It worked out that I made such a big salad and that we bumped into two hungry women," said Donald, signaling Amanda to be silent. She winked at him, a promise that their brief conversation would remain private.

"Did you see the article in the *Post* yesterday?" Donald asked Eddie when they all had plates of salad and glasses of cold white wine in front of them. There was a loaf of homemade bread on the table but no butter. "I forgot to mention it before now."

"The one about steroids being effective against PCP?" Amanda asked. That was the article she had cut out of the paper and put into her purse.

"Yeah, so?" said Eddie, who was tired of everyone treating him as if he were an expert on AIDS. Just because he was a doctor and a gay man didn't mean that he was a research scientist. He knew little more about using prednisone for AIDS-related pneumonia than what he had read in the paper yesterday. He had not yet read the issue of the *New England Journal of Medicine* in which the studies had been reported. It was in his mile-high stack of medical journals waiting to be read.

"So do you think this could be the cure?" asked Donald.

"No," replied Eddie. Then he must have realized how snappish he sounded, so he added, "Look, Donald, I know how anxious we all are to end this scourge, but I keep telling you not to get your hopes up about every new treatment wrinkle that comes along. Most of them end up being a big zero." He squeezed his lover's hand across the table to soften the harshness of the words.

The article had reported on five studies which suggested that prednisone, a steroid that had been around for years and vas almost as common as aspirin, significantly increased the urvival rate of AIDS patients who were hospitalized with PCP pneumonia.

Amanda had torn the article out because she remembered hat Roberta had died of PCP, and she knew that organ trans-plant recipients often received prednisone during the first few veeks after surgery, among several other antirejection drugs. 'he wondered if a renewal of the drug would have helped Roberta. She wondered if the woman had been taking it, and f so, why the drug had not prevented her death.

"Eddie," she asked now. "Remember Roberta Garfield?"

"The heart transplant patient who died so mysteriously? Vhat about her?"

"Was she getting prednisone?"

"We gave her about three times the usual dose," he replied. 'Listen, Amanda, just because the paper said it improves sur-vival rates, doesn't mean it's a miracle, and that everyone will uddenly arise from his bed of pain. Or her bed of pain.

"And Roberta didn't have AIDS. We didn't know what was vrong with her until it was too late. She could have been ejecting the heart for all we knew." He shook his head in emembered frustration. "I've never seen anyone get that sick hat fast," he said, echoing Bill Zyrwynsky's words.

"Is she one of the patients you were telling me about the ther night?" asked Glencora.

"Yes," replied Amanda, who knew, after long years of trust nd friendship with Glen, just as Eddie knew about Donald, hat she could discuss patients without fear of having the tories leave the room. Even so, she always felt a little prick f guilt whenever a patient's name was revealed, even a dead atient, and she betrayed the confidentiality that she was sworn o maintain. And this time she had only herself to blame. She vas the one who blurted out Roberta's name.

"But was she taking prednisone before she got sick? Don't hey still give that to transplant patients even now that there's yclosporine and Imuran and everything else?" Amanda asked.

"I don't know," replied Eddie. "I never saw her before. I ever got a chance to read her old chart. I was called to see er when she was brought into the ER, because technically he was a medical not a surgical patient. The people in the ER ad me paged, and we admitted her to the transplant unit only

because of her past history—and because they had an empt
bed where they could put her on infection precautions.

"But I doubt that she was taking prednisone so long after
transplant," he added.

Eddie looked hard at Amanda. "What's cooking in there?
he asked, tapping his own forehead.

"It feels like Hungarian goulash," she replied, and the othe
three laughed.

"You're so funny, Amanda," said Donald. "I love the thing
you come out with."

She smiled at him. People often told her she was funny
sometimes in all the wrong places. But Amanda believed tha
life was so absurd most of the time that a sense of humor wa
an absolute necessity to hold the pain at bay. She also knev
that her sense of humor was one of the things Ken loved bes
about her. About a year after they met he'd told her that h
hadn't laughed so much in his whole life as he had in th
time he had known her. He had started to fall in love wit
her then.

"Thanks, Donald," she replied. "But this goulash isn't rea
appetizing. It's kind of a mixture of dead bodies and hug
pieces of a puzzle."

"Let's not talk shop," said Eddie. "At least not while we'r
eating."

"Okay with me," she agreed, "But you asked what wa
going on in my mind."

"And I know that's often a mistake," he said, and everyon
laughed again, but Glen winked at her across the table t
let her know that they would continue the conversation th
minute they hit the pavement outside Eddie and Donald'
house.

And they did. "So what has this Roberta's death to do wit
the others?" asked Glencora. "This is the woman who yo
think had a sugar daddy?"

"The answer to the second question is yes," replied Amand:
"And the answer to the first is I don't what, but something sur
as hell is going on."

"All right," said Glen. "Let's think this through. All th
patients died in your hospital, and that's their only connectio
to each other, right?"

"Yes, but that doesn't mean they *were* connected."

"But you said that this is more than a coincidence," Glen pointed out."

"I could be wrong," said Amanda, who knew that she was not.

You're lucky I don't report you to Miss Manners, said the voice, which just seconds ago had bawled her out for yet again planning to visit someone without an invitation. *Look what happened last time; you got thrown out on your ass.*

But Mrs. Sherwood was a stranger. I know Bonita.

But that doesn't mean that she's going to be thrilled to have you ring her doorbell on a Sunday afternoon and listen to you accuse her of murder.

I'm not going to accuse her of anything. I just want to talk to her, replied Amanda with a lot less confidence than she pretended. Why *was* she going to this much trouble—in the middle of a killer heat wave? Any normal person would be floating on her back in the middle of her delicious blue swimming pool, maybe taking a nap after the exertion of spending all that money this morning.

Instead, she had left Glen's, stuffed her purchases in the trunk of her car, driven to her office, looked up Bonita Elliott's home address in her files, and was now on her way to Bailey's Crossroads, Virginia. She had exited the Beltway and was now driving west on Route 7, through a traffic jam from Hell.

Amanda gritted her teeth and refrained from giving the finger to a driver who had cut across two lanes of traffic and missed her bumper by inches. If her window had been open, she would not have stopped herself.

Then he would have taken out his pistol and shot you in the face, said the voice, which had warned her many times about the bad temper that came over her when she got into a traffic mess.

She pulled into the parking lot of a group of high-rise apartment buildings which she knew without being told was a "singles complex." Amanda shuddered at the thought of all those young men and women in their twenties and thirties living in identical one-bedroom apartments waiting to meet the person who would provide an escape from the hideous yellow brick buildings.

Don't be such a snob, said her conscience. *People like to live in groups. Lots of people think this is fun. There's a ready-made social life here. They probably don't sit at home nearly as many Saturday nights as you did.*

Amanda rode to the eighth floor in an elevator lined with fake paneling and walked down a corridor covered with brown industrial-grade carpeting. There was no answer when she rang the doorbell of Apartment 816. Well, what did she expect? It was only in the movies and detective novels that people were home all the time, waiting around for unannounced visitors to accost them with unpleasant conversations.

Don't you dare do what you're thinking of doing, said her conscience as Amanda stood in the parking lot listening to the voices from the swimming pool located in the central space between the three buildings of the apartment complex.

Amanda sighed, got into her car, and headed back out toward the Beltway and home. By the time she pulled into her own driveway, she was sorry she had not gone to the pool to look for Bonita. So what if she embarrassed the woman? She had information that could be connected to a murder.

You don't know that, said the voice of reason for the hundredth time that week.

Yes, I do, she muttered to herself as she walked through the house looking for Ken. She went into the kitchen and hugged the grey cat, who was both happy at being in her woman's arms and disgruntled at having her nap interrupted. Her need to express both emotions resulted in one annoyed squawking meow followed by thunderous purrs.

Amanda smiled when she finally found her husband—doing exactly what she had been thinking about an hour ago: he was on his back on a plastic raft in the pool. His eyes were closed and one hand dangled in the water. His novel, reading glasses, and a can of beer lay on a poolside table.

She went upstairs, dropped the cat on the bed next to her clothing purchases, and changed into her oldest and most comfortable bathing suit. As she slipped into the pool and swam toward her husband, she thought about the rest of the day that lay, deliciously empty, ahead. "Hi, lazybones," she said.

Ken smiled without opening his eyes. "Do I have any money left at all?" he asked.

"Nope," she said. "You're broke."

"That means that we have to spend the afternoon doing things that don't cost money," he said. "Can you think of anything?"

"My mind's a blank," she replied and tipped him off the raft.

As Ken and Amanda were demonstrating to each other the economical ways to while away a summer Sunday, Bonita Elliott sat in her apartment, paralyzed with fear and remorse.

How could she have been stupid enough to call the police? There was no such thing any more as an anonymous telephone call to 911. She had found that out last year when she had seen smoke pouring out from under the hood of a car parked in the apartment lot. She had called the fire department, and the dispatcher had responded to her by name. "How do you know who I am?" she asked the emergency operator.

"We have a system that automatically traces the phone number, address, and the name of the person to whom the phone is listed," said the woman at the fire department.

"Wow," Bonita had replied. "Big Brother is all over the place, isn't he?"

"It's for your own protection, ma'am," said the woman huffily. "If you were in a real emergency situation, you might be glad we know where you are."

Bonita had acknowledged, at the time, that the trace might come in handy one day. But now that safety net would backfire, and it was only a matter of time before there was another knock at her door and she would have no choice but to respond. She had ignored the earlier knock this afternoon because she had been staring blankly out the window and had seen Amanda get out of her car. She had no desire to talk to her boss, and at the time had been angry at the unwarranted intrusion.

But now, as she sat alone, she was sorry that she had not let Amanda in—at least to find out what she wanted. Amanda Knight did not seem the type to drive all the way out to Bailey's Crossroads to make an unannounced visit to a staff nurse at home unless there was something serious on her mind.

Bonita Elliott was pretty certain what was on Amanda's mind, so perhaps it was just as well that she hadn't answered the door.

What Amanda wanted to talk to her about was the same thing the police would want when they came. Maybe she should just leave now and avoid the whole mess, get in her car and go. But where?

If she ran, it would look like she had something to hide. But if she stayed, how would she explain the phone call, as well as the anger and fear in her voice that must have come through clear as a bell on the tape recording that she knew was made of all calls to the police.

But perhaps no one would replay the tape. Bonita's hopes soared as she forced herself to be calm and go back over the events that had led her to make the call in the first place. The radio reporter had said that Caspar Torrey, a minister—they leaned heavily on the word minister, as if it conferred automatic sin proofing—in Gaithersburg had been found hacked to death in his kitchen. The wife had the murder weapon in her hand, so it was an open-and-shut case, right?

Right. If the police had already solved the murder because it had been solved for them, then they had no need to look for clues or whatever they did in murder cases. Right?

Right. So they wouldn't go back over the tape of an anonymous caller. They must get dozens of anonymous calls every day. Maybe hundreds. Right?

Right. So there was no need to worry that anyone would come knocking at her door. Right?

Wrong. Someone already had, and others would too.

═══ CHAPTER 22 ═══

Sunday night at J. F. K. Memorial Hospital—or early Monday morning—it didn't matter to Rosalind Smythe. She didn't want to be here, whatever day or time it was. She didn't want to be wearing these stupid white running shoes and the white skirt that made her hips look fat. And she definitely didn't want to be in this utility room dumping shit-covered sheets into the laundry hamper.

This is the main reason I left nursing in the first place, she thought grimly as she soaped her hands with PhisoHex for the second time in an effort to wash off the feces. She shuddered and forced herself not to feel anger at the patient whose bowels had let go when he thought that all he had to do was fart. It happened all the time to post-op patients. She remembered it well from when she did this for a living.

Rosalind dried her hands, inspected them carefully, and then sniffed. Good, no shit smell. She walked down the darkened hallway, grateful at least that the shoes were comfortable—so much better than those heavy white oxfords that she remembered from her nursing school days—and that white stockings were no longer required, at least at this hospital. How to have fat legs in one easy step, she thought as she remembered the ugly white hose.

She unlocked the narcotics cabinet, quickly checked the remaining supply against the list of drugs used that shift and found nothing missing. But there would be no discrepancy this early in the shift, not with a new nurse on duty. She drew 100 mg of Demerol into a 1 cc syringe with a number 22 needle, forced a smile onto her face, and gave the injection to the man who had just shit in the bed.

He was a tall man in his mid-fifties, and when his face wasn't contorted in pain and humiliation, he was probably handsome. There was a leather Coach briefcase on his over-the-bed table. Next to it was a cellular phone. Did this idiot think he was going to work the same day he had his belly cut open and half his stomach removed? No wonder he had a perforated ulcer. Another fat-cat executive who thought the world couldn't get along without him for five minutes—and that everything he said was too important to risk going through the hospital switchboard.

Rosalind pulled the clean sheets and light blanket over the man's shoulders and said, "I'm going to put your briefcase in the closet. There are plenty of people here who would like to rip off a few hundred dollars' worth of leather goods."

The man gave her a sly look, and Rosalind knew immediately that she had said the right thing. Acknowledging that he could afford such an expensive briefcase took away some of the sting of having lost control of his bowels. She hated him for that. She hated them all for all things like that.

Rosalind broke the needle off the syringe and placed it and the syringe in separate locked, one-way receptacles. In theory, the receptacles were to prevent thievery of used needles and syringes, which in any case were of no use one without the other. She looked at the locks and smiled sardonically. Naive assholes! She could have the lock picked in about two seconds flat, and one drop of Krazy Glue was all a junkie needed to have a perfectly usable way to shoot up. Most of them made do with equipment a thousand times more primitive and dangerous than a factory-fresh sterile syringe used only once to pierce flesh that was free of viral and bacterial diseases.

Used, glued-together drug apparatus stolen from a hospital would be a luxurious bonanza for a junkie.

"Sorry you had to get such a messy one your first night here," said the other nurse on the unit—Lisa something-or-other. Rosalind couldn't remember the girl's last name (and she *was* a girl, probably no more than twenty-two) because she had not memorized it instantly when they were introduced by the night supervisor. Rosalind memorized what she had to, but only what she had to.

"I would have helped you," said Lisa, "but that woman who was screaming ended up pulling out all her lines, and she has veins the size of sewing thread, so it took three of us to get her all straightened out. How's the gastrectomy?"

Rosalind didn't know it, but she shared at least one thing

with Amanda Knight: she hated to hear the patients depersonalized, even the ones she took an instant dislike to, and especially by a nurse as young and inexperienced as this one. "He's okay," she said. "Shitting in bed probably took him down a peg. Guys who have expensive Coach briefcases and cellular phones aren't used to losing it in front of strange women!"

Rosalind watched the young nurse's eyes for a telltale widening of pupils in response to the knowledge that there was something expensive and easily hockable in a patient's room, especially a patient who was now in a deep narcotic sleep.

Lisa's eyes remained as they were, but she laughed. "We get a lot of people like that up here—women too. It's all private rooms on this floor, and nice ones too. The Gold Coast everyone calls it."

"Not very original," said Rosalind. "That's what it's called in every hospital in the country."

A mistake. Lisa looked petulant, as if Rosalind had insulted her entire linguistic capabilities. She tried again: "I'm new in Washington, and I understand that's what they call upper Sixteenth Street, where all the rich blacks live. Where I come from, I'm not used to *any* rich blacks!"

"Well, we've sure got a lot of them here," said Lisa. A statement, a neutral observation—had it not been for the note of scorn that crept into the young woman's voice. Not outright hostility, not a voice that would burn a cross on anyone's lawn, but racist nevertheless. It was probably racism born of a lifetime of unquestioned belief rather than a true bias. But there it was.

Rosalind Smythe didn't care one way or the other. She herself had no great fondness for blacks, but neither did she hate them with the single-minded passion that so many of her colleagues did. However, she always liked to know the kind of people she was dealing with, and she had learned that the way white people discussed black people, especially when the discussion was among white people who were strangers to each other, offered a window into their personalities. It was the same way when Gentiles talked among each other about Jews.

Rosalind couldn't explain the phenomenon, but it worked every time. And in her profession, in her real profession, her very life could depend on knowing immediately who she was dealing with.

She shifted gears. There was no point in wasting time, because the longer it took to find out who was stealing the narcotics, the longer she had to wear this stupid white skirt. "A guy like Mr. Singleton doesn't like it when people see him not on top of things," she said. "It makes me mad when they take out their embarrassment on the nurses. I'll bet he treats me like dirt tomorrow night when he's more alert."

"Who's Mr. Singleton?" Lisa asked.

Jesus Christ, what a numbskull, she thought. Aloud she said, "The gastrectomy who just crapped himself." Talk to her in language she was used to, that was the best way to get through to this bimbo.

"Oh," said Lisa. She had nothing to say about the way people handled pain, vulnerability, and embarrassment. It seemed unlikely to Rosalind that she gave it any thought whatever. It was beginning to seem unlikely that Lisa whatever-her-name-was gave any thought to anything. But she was careful not to let her annoyance show. "What I meant was," she continued, trying a different approach, "it's easy to get really mad at patients like him."

Lisa shrugged. "That's why I like working nights," she said. "Even the jerks have to fall asleep some time."

Rosalind didn't push the conversation. There would be time enough for that another night. She moved to safer ground. "What do you do for food on nights? I assume the cafeteria is closed."

Lisa perked up. "There's a snack bar with machines next to the cafeteria, but it's all junk food. Most of us bring something from home, and once in a while we send out for pizza." She made no offer to call other units to see who was interested in pizza, nor did she ask if Rosalind had brought a meal from home. She hadn't bothered to explain the rules about the communal coffeepot in the nurses' lounge. Rosalind was on her third cup already and had decided not to chip in unless she was asked.

"Where do you keep the flashlights?" she asked.

"Why do you need a flashlight?"

Rosalind could hardly believe her ears. "Don't you make rounds every hour?"

Lisa shrugged again. "I do it when I get a chance. But what's with the flashlight?"

"So you can see the patients without turning on the overhead light and waking them up," replied Rosalind.

And that director of nursing was worried about *her* proficiency, when she hired fucking idiots like this one to be in charge of a post-op unit. Jesus!

Rosalind Smythe never eliminated even remote possibilities until she was sure she had solved whatever she was hired to solve. But if this child nurse, who seemed to care about nothing at all and understand even less, could get it together to steal medium-sized quantities of narcotics from a relatively controlled environment, Rosalind would wear the white shoes and the ugly white skirt into her office at the Steelman Agency.

Hell, she'd eat the damn shoes.

═══ CHAPTER 23 ═══

On Monday afternoon, Amanda once again sat across the desk from Dr. Joseph Krahl, and once again his charm and goodwill engulfed them both. His smile was steady and calm. Hers was nervous and insecure.

"I need to have your word that you will treat this conversation as privileged doctor-patient communication," said Amanda. "You can have your secretary send me a bill if that would help convince you that I really need your trust."

That last remark sounded silly and childish, even to her. She shuddered inwardly with embarrassment over how it must have fallen on this physician's ears.

Joseph Krahl stepped up the wattage of his smile and thought about how much he would like to do a *very* complete physical examination on this woman. He felt her discomfort and tried to put her at ease. "A bill!" he said and laughed. "What an idea. What's on your mind?"

"Do I have your word?" asked Amanda.

Krahl leaned forward, rested his elbows on his desk, and clasped his hands just under his chin. He arranged his face in an expression of helpfulness and concern, turning down the power of the smile somewhat, but still remaining open and friendly. He did this unconsciously, as a result of years of developing what used to be called a bedside manner. He hadn't heard that term in ages, probably because doctors now spent so little time at bedsides.

"Cross my heart and hope to die," he said and noticed the slight frown that crossed her face. There was something wrong here and it was a mistake to use levity, even the slightest bit. No flirting either—for now. "Sorry," he said, matching her demeanor. "I didn't mean to make light of your request. You have my word, as a physician and as a person."

218

He stopped himself from saying, "Trust me." Even some-one as obviously naive as Amanda Knight no longer fell for that line.

"To tell you the truth, I feel like a complete idiot," she said. "But I need some advice, and I don't know where else to go." Even as she spoke the words, Amanda could hear how trite they sounded. A cliché right out of some vapid romance novel.

But the truth was that she really did not know what to do. She and Ken had spent the remainder of yesterday reading, swimming, and eating cold-cut sandwiches and raw vegetables from their garden. The answering machine had been on the whole time, and they never even bothered to listen to the messages. Last night, after the sun had gone down, they made love at the shallow end of the swimming pool and then discovered that a neighbor's dog had watched the whole thing.

The dog, a Dalmatian, lived next door. His official name was Fireplug, but everyone called him Pluggie, so that was the only thing he answered to. Ken threw a stick for him for a while as Amanda, wrapped in a towel, lay in a lounge chair watching her husband play with the dog. Once again, she thought about buying him a puppy for his birthday.

This morning they had made love again, this time with Shadow supervising from a windowsill. "Between Pluggie and the grey horse that lives here, we're going to have to check into a hotel if we want privacy," Ken said, pushing the cat off his chest where she had leaped the minute her woman and man had settled down and stopped shaking the bed.

It had been a lovely day and would have been perfect if Amanda hadn't thought almost constantly about murder. Obsessed with the four deaths, she thought about what she had read in the charts and autopsy reports, and went back in her mind to the three morbidity and mortality conferences she had attended. The one for the child had not yet taken place.

The patients had only one thing in common: they had all had organ transplants at J. F. K. Memorial Hospital, and if they had indeed been murdered, someone at the hospital had done it.

She said all this to Joseph Krahl, and as she told him the story and concluded with her questions and suspicions, his eyes widened in surprise and shock. "I can't believe that Bill Zyrwynsky would kill his patients," said Krahl. "I've known him for years. He's a dedicated doctor." He shook his head as if to clear it of the thought that she had planted there. "No," he said again. "It's impossible."

"It doesn't necessarily have to be Bill," said Amanda, afraid now that she had gone too far, sorry that she had come here, stuck with the realization that she could not retract her damning words. "It could be anyone who works there. Another doctor. One of the nurses." Her voice sounded lame and weak, even to her.

Again, Krahl shook his head in disbelief. "Why would anyone do something like that? What reason could any sane person have for mass murder—in a hospital?"

Amanda felt a chill wash over her, and she wondered if Krahl realized what he had said. A sane person. What if there really was a madman loose in the hospital, sneaking into the transplant unit in the middle of the night and injecting the patients with some deadly dose of something? The possibility could not be ruled out. People who ran hospitals knew that these things happened—and knew also that there was very little that could be done to prevent it.

"What poison could be used to mimic the rejection response?" she asked.

"What?"

She related the fantasy of a crazy person killing patients. "I know I sound as though I've been up too many nights watching horror movies on television," Amanda said. "But do you know a poison that could do that?"

"I don't," he said. "You'd have to ask a toxicologist. But even if you're right and there is a madman loose in your hospital, why these particular patients? Why a little child?"

So he had heard about Billy Ockerson. "The transplant community is a tight little world," said Krahl in response to the look of surprise and dismay that crossed Amanda's face. "We don't miss much.

"But to get back to your original premise, what makes you think that it's murder?" he asked. "I should think that a woman in your position would look for mistakes in medical care first. Mistakes among the nursing staff. A less-than-adequate infection control procedure."

He raised his eyebrows quizzically, hoping to steer this crazy lady's mind into more productive and realistic channels.

Joseph Krahl did not want to think about murder at J. F. K. Memorial Hospital's transplant unit. In fact, he did not want to think at all about transplant patients dying.

Amanda forced herself to remain calm, to hide her annoyance at the way he was patronizing her. *A woman in my position—what bullshit!* She smiled in what she hoped was a self-deprecating manner. "I thought of that," she said. "I've been through all four charts with a fine-tooth comb and have read the three autopsy reports several times. I went to all the M and M conferences. No one screwed up. For once," she added.

"Only three autopsies?" asked Krahl.

Amanda explained about how Aaron Zurman's body had been whisked out of J. F. K.'s morgue the minute the Jewish Sabbath was over.

"Ah, yes," said Krahl. "I know well the Orthodox Jewish reluctance to permit autopsies. In that regard, they're as stubborn and ignorant as Catholics. A lot of perfectly healthy organs are lost to us because of religious fanaticism."

Amanda agreed with him, but she wasn't about to let the conversation go off on a tangent of his choosing. So she described Mrs. Zurman's accusations and her original conversation with the Chinless Wonder. She omitted the story of her fruitless jaunt to Leisure World.

"So, even though I still think that Mrs. Zurman is a senile old lady, I can no longer discount what she said as off-the-wall ramblings. Not with three other patients in the same boat."

"But they're not in the same boat," replied Krahl. "They didn't all die of hyperacute rejection." He could hardly believe that he was allowing himself to be caught up in this mess. He wanted to get this woman out of his office (his sexual desire for her had dried up the minute she started talking about murder), but at the same time he was almost compulsively fascinated by what she was saying. It was like driving past a car wreck on the highway: knowing that what you would see was nothing that you'd want to look at, but being unable to avert your eyes. Joseph Krahl was unable to stop himself from probing into Amanda Knight's obviously crazy assertions.

"I've thought about that," she said. "And at first, the differences in the deaths threw me for a loop, but now I'm beginning to believe that it doesn't matter. I think they were all poisoned, and I think the fact that they were transplant patients was what they had in common. That they received different organs, and that one of them was transplanted three years ago, makes no difference.

"It's too great a coincidence," she continued. "Less than one percent of all transplant patients die of hyperacute rejection, and here we have *three* in about as many weeks—all in the same hospital. That's no coincidence—is it?"

He stared at her. He had no idea what to say, and wished that Amanda Knight, who was an uncomfortable reminder of the choice position that he had lost to Bill Zyrwynsky, would take her bizarre notions and leave his office.

As if sensing what he was thinking, Amanda stirred in her seat and picked up her purse from where it rested next to her on the floor. "I've taken up enough of your time," she said. "I'm sure I'm on a wild-goose chase, but I thought maybe if I told you what's been happening . . . and with your expertise in transplants . . . that maybe you could shed some light on our problem. . . ." Her voice weakened as she ran out of steam in the face of Krahl's continued silence.

"Well," she said and stood up and walked toward the door. It was quite a hike. The man had a huge, imposing office, complete with two sofas and a few armchairs arranged around an elegant coffee table. There was an oil painting of an impressionistic beach scene on the wall behind the couch. Probably someone famous and expensive had done it, she thought.

When Krahl realized that she was leaving, he snapped himself back into his charm mode, walked with her to the door, and said, "I know how you must feel. I'd feel the same way if this horrible thing were happening here at St. Jude's. I wish I could help you." His smile was again firmly in place. "But all I can suggest is that you talk to a toxicologist or a pathologist. If you want, I can put you in touch with some of our people."

"No, no," Amanda said in a rush. The one thing she did not want was to have anyone else from St. Jude's poking around in this mess. "And please," she added. "I must have your absolute assurance that this will go no further."

Joseph Krahl held up his hand as if he were about to take an oath. "You have my word," he said.

• • •

A half hour later Amanda walked back into her office. Louise greeted her cheerfully. "That's a pretty dress. Is it new?"

Louise knew Amanda's wardrobe as well as she knew it herself, and was aware of Amanda's propensity to shop. She had never before seen this pink- and white-striped linen outfit with the big mother-of-pearl buttons.

"Can I help it that when Glen and I went looking for fall clothes, there was a gigantic sale on summer things?" asked Amanda, pretending indignation.

Louise laughed. "It was a moral obligation to take advantage of it. That way, next summer no one will have to wear last year's clothes—because you'll have bought them all!"

Amanda blushed and took the stack of message slips that Louise handed her. "There's nothing very urgent," the latter said. "But the report from Rosalind Smythe came by messenger a little while ago." Louise came out from around her desk, unlocked the steel filing cabinet, and handed her a sealed envelope. "I didn't want to leave it lying around in case I had to run out to the john."

Amanda leafed through the message slips and decided that Louise was right. None of them required her immediate attention, so she unglued the flap of the white manila envelope and began reading.

The first thing she did was raise her eyebrows in admiration for the obvious nursing competence that Rosalind Smythe displayed, while she swallowed annoyance and chagrin at being wrong about the woman. Then she screwed up her face in anger at the comments about Lisa Pardoe. What the hell were they teaching, or not teaching, in nursing school these days? And hadn't Betsy Murdock ever seen her make rounds by snapping overhead lights on in sleeping patients' rooms?

Maybe she didn't do it when Betsy was around. But Smythe had specifically said that Pardoe didn't even seem to know where the flashlights were kept.

On the other hand, maybe Betsy knew and didn't care. But that couldn't be right. Betsy had gone to nursing school when there were still standards about treating patients with kindness. Now it was all high technology, as well as bullshit like nursing diagnosis and nursing histories and meaningless crap like that.

Amanda would bet a month's salary that not one nurse in America under the age of twenty-five knew how to give a decent back rub.

You're getting off the subject, said the voice that always tried to make her stick to business. *Even though you'd probably win your bet!*

So what did you learn from this?

Nothing, replied Amanda, who decided that she would say nothing to Betsy about Lisa Pardoe. But she would watch carefully to see if the supervisor had a reaction to what Rosalind Smythe had written about the nurse.

You're wrong, said the voice, which sometimes read things more carefully than she did. *You learned something else. Something verrrrry interesting!*

Amanda read the report again, and once again was grateful for its brevity and succinctness. Not only that, everything was spelled and punctuated correctly, which raised Rosalind Smythe yet another notch in Amanda's opinion. Too many people these days couldn't spell c-a-t, let alone d-i-a-r-r-h-e-a and c-h-o-l-e-c-y-s-t-e-c-t-o-m-y.

But there it was. The brief sentence, almost an afterthought that didn't register on Amanda's mind during the first read-through. The comment surely had no meaning to Rosalind Smythe, who didn't know any of J. F. K. Memorial's staff from a hole in the wall. So she included the observation as simply that: an objective observation that may or may not have a bearing on the series of narcotics thefts.

Kind of unusual, isn't it, for her to be in the hospital at that hour of the night? asked the voice, which wasn't usually so sarcastic.

I often come in at night to check up on things, said Amanda. To catch the evening and night shifts in acts of stupidity—like waking up patients unnecessarily.

But you have a legitimate reason to wander around the hospital at all hours. That's your job.

She wasn't wandering around the hospital. She was in her office where she belongs.

At two-thirty on a Sunday morning?

Amanda conceded the point but refused to believe that it had anything to do with the narcotics thefts. It was a coincidence.

Not an hour ago you were in Joseph Krahl's office making an ass of yourself carrying on about not believing in coincidental deaths on the transplant unit. And now you're trying to convince yourself that this is a coincidence?

This time, Amanda listened to the voice that liked consistency of thinking. She had to acknowledge that the narcotics thefts could be originating from somewhere other than staff nurses. Betsy and she could be barking up the entirely wrong tree.

I thought you'd never figure that out, said the part of her mind that had known it from the moment it read the report.

She picked up the phone and dialed the Steelman Agency.

═══ CHAPTER 24 ═══

Bonita Elliott's body was at work, but her mind was not. By yesterday afternoon, she had begun to relax. She had not worked for three days, and her doorbell had not rung again. No police had been around to ask why she had called them. Now it was midafternoon on Monday, and she was once again sitting in the staff lounge with her shoes off and feet up on a cracked, fake leather chair.

There were only two patients on the unit and one was almost ready to be discharged. He'd had a heart transplant two weeks ago and by now was pedaling the stationary bicycle for twenty minutes at a time, with no ill effects.

His one minor rejection episode had been fully reversed within a day by a moderate increase in cyclosporine and Imuran. It had been a perfectly normal and routine thing—practically every transplant patient has one or two such experiences during the first three months. It was simply the body's way of getting adjusted to the new organ, but both she and Bill Zyrwynsky had almost panicked when it happened.

The doctor and the nurse had years of experience with this sort of thing, and each knew what the other was thinking during the hours that they waited for Mr. Levinson's immune system to right itself. But neither could talk to the other about it.

The other patient on the floor had had a routine surveillance biopsy of his heart that morning and was peacefully sleeping off the anesthesia. He would be discharged tomorrow morning.

"It's awfully quiet around here lately. Not like the usual hustle-bustle in a hospital."

Bonita looked up, and there was Mr. Levinson standing in the open doorway of the staff lounge. He had on khaki Bermuda shorts and a short-sleeved plaid madras shirt. On

226

his feet he wore brown Docksiders and cotton argyle socks that picked up the colors in the shirt. His hair was combed, his face was shaved, and his expression was open and cheerful. He looked not even remotely like the grey-faced man who, three weeks ago, hadn't had enough energy to shave the stubble from around his blue lips.

Three weeks ago, Mr. Levinson had been among the walking dead. Now the only outward sign that he had ever been ill was the white gauze bandage on his left forearm which covered the plastic tube that ran into his basilic vein. One vein was kept open for emergencies while transplant patients remained in the hospital.

"You look like you're ready for a round of golf," she said to him and patted the chair next to her. "Come on in and talk."

The transplant unit was one of the very few places in the hospital where nurses invited patients into the staff lounge, which everywhere else, was a safe haven to escape for a few minutes from the insistent needs of sick people.

But the transplant unit was a different ball game; it was why Bonita loved her job. The patients here were people in a different way than they were on the regular floors. Here, the staff and patients got to know each other, and the relationship went on for years. Sometimes, they got to be friends, the way she and Roberta Garfield had.

Bonita closed her eyes in remembered grief, and Mr. Levinson said, "Hey, Bonnie, you look like the one who needs some tender, loving care right now."

She smiled and Mr. Levinson noticed how little of her usual ebullience there was in it. He imagined that any nurse would be upset to see so many of her patients die, and once again he was grateful that his surgery had gone without a hitch. But if he had known beforehand the recent failure rate at this hospital, he might not have embarked on this adventure. . . .

What the hell was he talking about? If he hadn't been lucky enough to get a donor heart the day he did, he would be sitting in the staff lounge in a hospital run by St. Peter—or maybe the person sitting next to him would be holding a pitchfork and sporting a long red tail. He smiled at his own imagination and then told Bonita what he had been thinking.

That brought a real smile to her face. "Believe me," she said, "I've sat next to some real devils in staff lounges in my day!"

"But not here?" asked Mr. Levinson.

"No, not here. We've got a good crew. Everyone gets along, and I think we really do work as a team."

"You sure pulled me through," said Mr. Levinson. "I would have died without all of you."

"That's true," Bonita said. "But if it hadn't been for another person who really did die, a hundred transplant teams wouldn't have been able to save you. The gift came from outside this hospital. We only wrapped it and made sure the tissue paper didn't get all wrinkled."

"The gift of life," said Mr. Levinson.

"To the gift of life," said Bonita and raised her coffee cup.

The two sat in companionable silence for a while staring absently at the monitor above their heads. The black screen had a number of wavy lines running across it, as well as a series of numbers flashing at the bottom of the screen.

"I passed by that guy's room just now," said Mr. Levinson, inclining his head in the direction of the row of monitors, all of which were turned off except for that one. "He was sawing wood like crazy. You could hear him two doors away, and it's funny to see what's going on inside his body while he's sleeping so soundly.

"All this high-technology stuff is what saved my life, but still—it gives me the creeps a little," he said.

"If you want to know the truth," said Bonita, "I think it gives us all the creeps. Things in medicine are advancing so fast that sometimes it's hard to remember that these are people we're healing, not just bodies and pieces of tissue.

"That's one of the reasons I like working up here. The patients are all people. Take Mr. Borodin, for instance." She waved her hand in the direction of the number 4 monitor. "He's had his new heart for five years now, and every six months he comes in for his surveillance biopsy. Each time, he says that he comes back here to old friends who know him and care about him. About *him*, not just about his new heart and his immune system.

"Later, when he wakes up, he'll go in on the pizza order with the evening shift, and then he'll sit by the elevators and wait for the Domino's guy and pay for the whole thing. And the nurses won't feel patronized when he pays because they know him and like him—and because he makes tons more money than they do. He treats them like the professionals they are.

"It's funny," added Bonita with a smile. "I remember once when I was working evenings, the Domino's guy took forty-five minutes to get here, so we got two free pizzas, and no one was more jubilant than Mr. Borodin. He said it was the best one he had ever eaten!"

"Maybe I should talk to him about what it's like to get the surveillance biopsies," said Mr. Levinson.

"That's a good idea," Bonita replied. "Actually it's the same as the one you had last week, but the other ones won't feel like such a big deal because you'll be in better physical shape—and you won't have just started to recover from major surgery.

"But go and talk to him later. He can tell you a lot of stuff about what it's like to live with a heart transplant. He's very open about his feelings—for a man!"

The patient and his nurse smiled at each other. "So do you want to tell Uncle Barney why you're so down in the dumps?" asked Bernard Levinson. When he saw the cloud pass over Bonita's face, he patted her arm and said, "I've overstepped my bounds and stuck my foot in my mouth again. Now that my heart condition has been fixed, I'll probably die of hoof and mouth disease!"

She laughed, but she didn't volunteer any further information, and she didn't take Mr. Levinson up on his offer. Mentally, Bonita shook off the depression and got back into her nurse role. "Mr. Levinson . . ." she began.

"Barney," he said.

"Barney. *Uncle* Barney, I know you're feeling chipper, like a whole new person. You *look* like a whole new person, but don't start thinking about your heart condition as 'fixed,' as if it were nothing more complicated than the plumbing under the kitchen sink."

"I know, I know," he said. "I understand that I have to cut out practically all cholesterol and caffeine and that I have to exercise and do all that stuff. At least I don't smoke!"

And he did understand. Bernard Levinson was a smart man, and he was a grateful man—now. But Bonita wondered how long it would last. She had seen more than one cardiac transplant vow to change his lifestyle, to eliminate stress, to live on boneless, skinless chicken breasts and broccoli stalks for the rest of his life. But within a few years, too many of them were back to swilling down ten cups of coffee a day, working hectic schedules, and eating McDonald's french fries and greasy hamburgers in airport corridors.

They always had the best intentions that first year because they had been so scared. Of course, they couldn't change their genetic endowment, and if someone's parents and grandparents had all dropped dead in their fifties of cardiovascular disease, the future didn't hold a lot of promise for them. But there was no need to help nature along the road to disaster. That road was paved with the kind of good intentions that Mr. Levinson was vowing at this very moment.

"Well then, see that you do it," she said as the patient left the staff lounge. She tried to be severe with him but failed utterly as she always did. Bonita believed that you could do only so much for patients—and then they were on their own. But she made a note to see if Mr. Borodin was awake on her way out of the unit this afternoon. If anyone could get across the message about follow-up care, he could.

So could Roberta, and look where she was. Tears threatened again, so she sniffed them back and bent over to tie her shoes. As she straightened up, Amanda Knight walked into the lounge.

Shit!

Amanda closed the door, walked over to the coffeepot without being invited to, looked into the murky depths, and said, "How long has this been sitting here?"

Bonita knew she meant it as a lighthearted introduction to whatever it was she had come up to the unit to talk about. Hospital coffee brewed by the staff was a constant source of material for bad jokes about skin preps, cheap disinfectants, and natural corrosives. Ordinarily, she would come back with a remark like, "We made it fresh only a week and a half ago," and Amanda would say, "I didn't need my stomach anyway," and pour herself some. Today, though, Bonita wasn't up to jokes. She shrugged and said, "Have some." She remained standing and thus forced Amanda to do the same.

"How are you feeling?" asked Amanda.

"Fine," replied Bonita. "Why do you ask?"

"You were out sick on Friday. I came up to see if you're better."

Bullshit, thought Bonita. The director of nursing did not go over the attendance records of every single nurse in the hospital. That was the job of the supervisor and the personnel department. Amanda found out about nurses' sick days only if they were really very ill, or if they were taking too many days, or if something else unusual happened. The fact that Amanda was up here nosing around about Bonita's one day off (well, not counting the day she had told Bill Zyrwynsky about in advance, but she didn't think Amanda knew about that—or cared), *and* the fact that she had made that unsuccessful visit on Sunday, meant only one thing. Trouble.

Trouble, with a great, big, capital T.

The two women stared at each other, and Bonita could see Amanda trying to decide something. Amazingly, the transplant nurse felt nothing. Not fear. Not sadness. Not the heart-pounding anxiety that had been her constant companion for almost three full days. She simply stood patiently and waited for Amanda to do whatever she was going to do.

"Sit down," Amanda finally said. She, however, remained standing. Not a good sign.

"I have to get back to the floor. I've been in here talking to a patient for almost a half hour now," she said.

"You're not alone up here, are you?" asked Amanda.

"No, Sue is out there with the patients."

"And your census is down to two, right? So nothing will fall apart if we stay here and talk for a few minutes. Right?"

Bonita sat down and Amanda followed suit. "Why did you make an anonymous call to the police?" she asked.

Bonita's mouth dropped open. "No one could ever accuse you of beating around the bush," she said.

"That's true," Amanda agreed. When Bonita remained silent, she repeated the question.

Bonita took a deep breath. She might as well say it straight out. "Because I think that minister murdered Roberta Garfield. I've thought so for a long time, but I never said anything to anyone, and now I'm responsible for his death."

She burst into tears.

Amanda watched Bonita cry for a while. Although the tears were obviously genuine and heartfelt, she had a strong impression that the transplant nurse was crying for the wrong reason.

"Caspar Torrey murdered Roberta Garfield?" she asked incredulously. "Do you want to tell me why he did it? Not to mention how, where, and when." Now there was sarcasm in her voice which she didn't bother to hide. "Or better yet," she added, "why don't you tell the police?"

Bonita continued to cry, and Amanda stared at her, not knowing what to do or say.

The staff lounge was quiet except for Bonita's now-subsiding sobs. The plastic armchairs were as ugly as ever. The coffeepot was as filthy as all the others in the hospital's staff lounges—as filthy as hers would be if Louise had allowed it.

No one would disturb the two women. People had seen Amanda walk into the room and close the door, so Bonita would be free of interruptions unless there was a genuine emergency. When she and Bonita finally emerged, the other staff on the unit would see the nurse's red-rimmed eyes and think she had been chewed out by the boss. The minute Amanda left, they would pounce on Bonita to find out what had gone on behind the closed doors.

Amanda never bawled out nurses on the floors, nor did she fire them there. Well, there was that one time that, in a fit of rage, she had canned a night nurse when she had made one of her "sneak attacks," an inspection visit at one-thirty in the morning and had found the woman sound asleep with the patients' call-bell board lit up like a Christmas tree.

She always made it a point to give bad news or hold unpleasant conversations in her own office, so that a nurse could stop in the john and pull herself together before going back to face her compatriots.

Amanda had made a mistake this time, but she told herself a lie. How was I supposed to know she'd begin to cry after a simple question like, "Are you feeling better?"

You're forgetting the other little question about the anonymous call, said the voice, which hated it when Amanda lied to herself. *But never mind that now. Just get on with it.*

But get on with what? she wondered. Amanda was in way over her head here. She believed that Bonita Elliott was genuinely upset over Roberta Garfield's death—frantic even. But what else was going on?

She looked at the nurse, who had calmed down now and was fishing through her purse for a mirror to check the damage done by the tears. A woman who cared about what tears had done to her makeup was definitely finished crying. It also usually meant that she was finished dealing with whatever had prompted the tears in the first place.

"Let me ask you again," she said to Bonita. "Why haven't you gone to the police? Why didn't you go the minute you suspected that Roberta had been murdered?"

Bonita was calm now. Almost matter-of-fact. "Because no one would have believed me. I'm not even sure I believe it myself. Because there was that whole business with Aaron Zurman and his mother carrying on about murder—and no one believed her. Because it's too much coincidence."

There was that word again. Coincidence.

The trouble was that Amanda didn't believe Bonita any more than anyone else would have.

Speaking of going to the police, that was exactly what Mark Cipriotti was thinking about doing.

He hadn't had more than two or three hours of sleep in a row since the death of Aaron Zurman, and he couldn't keep telling his wife that his insomnia was "nothing." Nor could he keep pretending that his increasingly haggard appearance had only to do with the lack of sleep. When he looked at himself in his shaving mirror every morning, he saw a haunted man, a man who has seen something that has shaken him to his very core.

Cipriotti knew that people here at the office were beginning to gossip about him, and he didn't blame them. He hadn't done any productive work in weeks, and his boss had suggested very strongly that either he get a grip on himself or take a vacation. Either that or get his ass kicked out.

It wasn't as if he had committed first-degree murder. He had not actually done it. Hell, he didn't even know how it had been done. "Leave everything to me," Sarah Castle had said. "The less you know, the better off you'll be afterwards."

At the time, he'd been angry that she had treated him like a child, that she hadn't trusted him enough to tell him the details. Now he was grateful. It meant that whatever shit came down on the three of them, Castle and Allen Hackett would have the biggest load dumped on them. He couldn't be convicted of anything more than being an accessory. Shit, he thought, as he watched his hands shake, an accessory both before and after the fact.

He helped plan it. Well, at least he knew about the plan. They hadn't liked any of his suggestions, so you couldn't actually say that he had planned it. But he did nothing to stop it from being carried out, and he hadn't said or done anything after Zurman was dead.

If that's not first-degree murder, I don't know what is, he admitted to himself. I am totally fucked whatever I do.

If he said nothing and simply continued the way he was, he would go completely crazy. He was halfway there already. But if he went to the police and ratted on the other two . . . Jesus Christ, he thought. "Ratted!" I'm talking like Jimmy Cagney in a thirties gangster movie.

Nevertheless, if he ratted, squealed, or told on the other two, they would get him. Especially that Castle woman. Sarah Castle wouldn't rest until Mark Cipriotti was chopped liver all over the sidewalk.

The prison yard.

Cipriotti thought of all the stories he had read about how men like him were raped in prison. He believed every one of the stories, and he knew there was no way he could protect himself or prevent that from happening. That's the way it would be for the rest of his life. Whatever he did, he would spend the rest of his life in jail. Hulking men coming after him . . .

Stop it, he told himself. You're not going to jail. If there's one place on God's green earth that you're not going to live out your days, it's a state penitentiary. So get a grip on yourself. This may be your last chance to turn things around.

And amazingly, his hands stopped shaking, his eyes cleared, and the fog in his brain lifted so that he could think clearly about what he had to do.

CHAPTER 25

When Amanda returned to her office, Louise told her that Rosalind Smythe had returned her call. "She said she'd be at Steelman until five o'clock, or you can call her at home this evening," said Louise. "Maybe she's found something," she added.

"I doubt it," replied Amanda. "Absolute zip happened in the hospital this weekend."

"Usually you're delighted to hear that," replied the secretary.

"I know," said Amanda. "Ironic, isn't it? Secretly hoping for a drug-war-style shootout in front of thirty-five patients recovering from heart attacks!"

"Oh, Amanda, you're such a riot," said Louise, who turned to answer the ringing telephone.

Great, she thought as she went into her office and closed the door. Someone else thinks I'm funny—just when a thief is stealing narcotics right in my very own hospital.

Don't forget the serial killer who's running around loose, said the voice that was the source of the humor.

Jesus Christ! Could that be? Does that account for the fact that all these deaths had one thing in common—and *only* one?

Amanda's entire store of knowledge about serial killers came from what she'd read in novels and newspaper articles, and about the only thing she knew about them was that they usually targeted people who had one thing in common. Sometimes it was age. Sometimes it was hair color. Sometimes it was occupation.

Could it be the fact of an organ transplant?

If that's true, then there isn't one patient in the transplant unit that's safe, said the voice, which was just as surprised as she at the thought that popped into both their minds at the same time.

235

Maybe the killer is someone who's been denied a transplant and is angry. Very, very angry.

Okay, let's go with that line of reasoning for a while, said the voice that knew when Amanda was on to something. *If you're right, how is he getting into the transplant unit?*

He doesn't have to get in, said Amanda. He—or she—is already there. It's a hospital employee.

You just made your first mistake. No one who works here is that ill. There's no one with serious kidney disease or liver disease—or whatever disease.

Amanda was undaunted. Okay, an employee who has a close relative who's been denied a transplant. Or one who had a transplant here and died anyway.

Or one who had a transplant anywhere in the world and died anyway, said the voice, which sometimes liked to complicate things.

Then why pick this hospital?

To complicate your life, said the voice. *Because he moved here recently—just like the thousands of other people who move to and from Washington every year.*

But the deaths just started this summer, said Amanda. So it has to be someone who's a new employee.

Bill Zyrwynsky.

Evelyn Portman drummed her fingers impatiently on the desk blotter while her lover's secretary took her own sweet time locating him.

"He's not in his office, Evelyn," she had said a minute ago. The bitch had started calling her by her first name when Evelyn left St. Jude's and took the job at this hellhole.

"Well then, find him," Evelyn had snapped. "It's important." Now she sat waiting while the secretary kept her on terminal hold, probably on purpose. Jealous bitch!

Evelyn looked around her office and saw that it was pretty crummy compared to the one she'd left at St. Jude's. But she had to admit that it was better than what she would have had if she'd either gone into business for herself, as so many of her classmates at the Philadelphia College of Pharmacy had done, or taken a job at one of the big drugstore chains.

Compared to that life, this was phenomenal. She didn't have to spend ten or twelve hours a day on her feet counting out two dozen Valium tablets or generic penicillin into little plastic bottles. She didn't have to concern herself with employee theft and bottom-line profit statements and worry about whether property values were going up, down, or sideways.

Best of all, she didn't have to assume that any second some drug-crazed kid would come into the store and shoot the place up looking for whatever they were on these days. Two of her classmates had died that way.

Here she had her own office, and little by little she was softening its institutional tone by hanging prints on the wall and covering the windowsills with plants. Maybe this evening she would go to White Flint and look for an area rug to relieve the beige monotony of the hospital-issue carpet.

Oh yes, there was a lot to be grateful for, and she'd been lucky to get this job after the fiasco at St. Jude's. Her lover had pulled a lot of strings so she could sit here instead of pounding the pavement asking for a job at People's or Rite Aid, or God forbid—a supermarket pharmacy.

She owed him one. She owed him more than one. She owed him about a million.

Then why was she calling him now to say that she didn't want to be with him anymore? Why was she giving up everything that had become so important—so necessary—to her? If she broke it off, he would pull more strings, and she'd find herself on the unemployment line. She had no doubt that his influence reached that far.

Because the stress was killing her, that's why. It's not that she had any moral compunctions about screwing a man like that. After all, it was the best sex she'd ever had. It was just that she couldn't face another scene like the one in the St. Jude's pharmacy when his wife had come in and torn the place apart.

But that wasn't the worst of it. It was all the other stuff, like owing him so much, and being afraid of him so much of the time. It was the emotional roller coaster. It was making her sick. She had to get off before it killed her. She would do it tonight, without . . .

"Evelyn, what's the matter? You got me out of an important meeting." His voice at the other end of the telephone wire was angry, impatient—and worried. She never called him at work.

"I just wanted to tell you . . ." Evelyn stopped, her heart pounding. She looked around her office and then her gaze fell on her shoes. They were made of soft taupe leather, and she had bought them last Saturday at Nordstrom's, a department store famous for its incredibly expensive shoes. These had cost $245, and she had paid without a qualm. He had paid.

She gulped. "I just wanted to tell you what I would do to you if I had you in my office right now, with the door locked."

He was still angry at being dragged out of his meeting, but his ego swelled, along with other body parts, as he listened to what Evelyn was describing.

She knew exactly what he liked. For some reason, he had not hesitated to ask her for what he wanted. He had never been so sexually frank with a woman before. But then, he had never met a woman who was so sexually insatiable and who was more than willing to fulfill any and all of his requests. Evelyn Portman was a natural slave, and he was not about to get unduly angry and give all that up.

Besides, she was useful in ways that went way beyond the sexual, and now he was committed.

"I'll be at your apartment between six-thirty and seven. Be ready for me," he said. And then he told her precisely what she was to do to get ready for him.

Evelyn assented and hung up the phone. She had failed again in her resolve to end it, but as she stroked the leather of the beautifully made shoe, she rationalized it to herself. I'd have to be crazy to give all this up, she thought. I *can't* give it up.

The phone jolted Amanda out of her reverie. It was Louise. "Rosalind Smythe is on line two," she said. "This episode of telephone tag is over."

"Thanks," replied Amanda, who smiled at Louise's comment and looked at her watch before punching the button that would connect her to the detective. She was surprised to see that more than an hour had passed while she sat at her desk lost in thought.

"This is Amanda Knight," she said.

Who else would it be, dummy? asked the voice who knew that Amanda didn't know whether to call the private investigator by her first name or not, so she took the easy way out and avoided the issue.

"I'm about ready to leave my office for the day," said Smythe. "I assume you received the report. Did you have a question about it?"

Amanda assured her that she had read the report. "I don't think I have any questions," she said. "Although it's embarrassing to know that Lisa Pardoe behaved so badly. I appreciate your being frank about that." She hesitated to tell Smythe why she had called in the first place.

"Okay," said the investigator. "I'll be there for the next three nights in a row and will write a comprehensive report at the end of that time—unless something happens, in which case I'll call you right away."

"That's fine," said Amanda. "But I wonder if you could . . . um . . . uh, never mind."

"What?" asked Smythe.

"Nothing," said Amanda. "It's not important." She swore she could feel the detective's contempt for her silliness come through the phone line as the latter said goodbye and hung up.

She couldn't possibly let that woman know what she was thinking, what she deeply suspected. She would simply hunt around on her own.

Hunt around on your own! said the voice, which knew what was coming. *What did Ken tell you about this?*

To mind my own business, Amanda admitted.

What did Eddie tell you about this?

To mind my own business.

What do you think you ought to do about this?

Mind my own business.

You're not going to, are you?

Amanda smiled, got her purse out of the bottom drawer of her desk, locked the office, got in her car, and drove home through rush-hour traffic. You never want me to have any fun, she told her conscience.

When she got home, she rummaged around in the freezer looking for a plastic container of pesto that she had made a few weeks ago from her herb garden's bumper crop of basil. She checked the cupboard to make sure there was enough fettucini and took the makings of a salad out of the refrigerator crisper. From the kitchen window, she could see dozens of ripe tomatoes on the vine. "Time for a harvest and an evening at home making spaghetti sauce," she said to Shadow, who was rubbing against her legs, meowing and pretending she hadn't eaten in weeks. "But not tonight," she said, picking up the cat and rubbing her cheek against the soft fur. "How would you feel about getting a puppy?" she asked. "Ken still thinks dogs are better, but of course we know he's wrong," she explained to the cat, who purred her agreement.

She and Shadow went upstairs to the bedroom, where she gratefully stripped off her dress and pantyhose while the cat curled up in an armchair. "Want to go swimming with me?" she asked. Shadow opened an eye, blinked once, and then tucked her nose under her paws, heaved a huge contented sigh, and went to sleep.

"I didn't think so," Amanda said as she stroked the cat's fur once again and went outside to swim twenty laps before Ken came home.

CHAPTER 26

Rosalind Smythe was up to her elbows in shit again. At least it seemed that way as she carried yet another bedpan to the utility room and emptied it into the hopper. Where were all the nurses aides who were supposed to do the dirty work? she wondered.

"None of them wants to work nights," the head nurse on the surgical step-down unit had said in response to Rosalind's tired query a half hour ago. "Sometimes when people call in sick at the last minute, I'm here all alone," she had said. "So you can't imagine how happy I was when Betsy told me she had hired a new float. You're a real godsend."

Rosalind felt an unaccustomed twinge of guilt at her deception. There was no way she could tell this beleaguered nurse that she would be out of here the minute she caught the thief. Nor was there any way she could reveal her true identity, although this one had a brain and could probably have been of some help. She could only smile and say, "I don't know how you manage it. I'm pooped, and the night isn't even half over."

That part was true enough. She had forgotten the sheer physical exhaustion that came with nursing. Her feet throbbed already, despite the comfortable shoes, and she thought longingly of the empty bed next to a patient who was sleeping like a stone. No more spending all day in the office, she thought, and promised herself an entire day of sleep the minute she left the hospital later this morning.

Amanda yawned widely enough to almost dislocate her jaw as she unlocked her car door and began the drive to J. F. K. Memorial. At least at one-thirty in the morning, there won't be any traffic, she thought.

She also thought yearningly of Ken curled up on his side of their bed, fast asleep. Shadow had stayed downstairs in the

241

den with her while she sat reading in Ken's big leather chair. Amanda had thought about going to sleep and setting the alarm, then decided that she didn't want to fight the temptation to go back to sleep when it rang. So she had made a pot of coffee and almost finished John Steinbeck's *Sweet Thursday*. She was slowly working her way through all of Steinbeck— even those novels she had been forced to read in high school and college, when she and her classmates had been much too young to appreciate the power and beauty of his writing.

Since the covered parking garage was deserted and spooky at this hour, Amanda pulled into an empty space in the doctors' reserved lot adjacent to the emergency entrance. She locked the car and walked around to the main entrance, the sandals she had bought in Israel four years ago making pleasant little squeaking sounds as she walked. She had on jeans and a light cotton sweater because of a distinct chill in the night air. She shivered a little as she cut across the lawn in front of the hospital, hoping that perhaps this meant a break in the heat wave.

A uniformed security guard was sitting on a chair just inside the front entrance. He was reading the newspaper, but he looked up as he heard Amanda's keys rattle outside the door. He jumped up and opened the door for her before she had a chance to put her key into the lock. "You're quick, Joshua," she said as he held the door for her and then made certain that it was locked behind her. "Thanks."

"Evenin', Miz Knight," replied the guard whose iron-grey hair and genial face reminded Amanda of Uncle Remus. She always half expected an off-screen orchestra to accompany him in a rendition of "Zippity Doo Dah" while he danced down the lane gathering flowers, with bluebirds hovering around his head. Just like in the movie her mother had taken her to when she was about four or five.

"You here to shape up them nurses?" is what Joshua said. No bluebirds appeared.

Amanda smiled and started to say something, but clapped her hand over her mouth when what came out was another jawbreaker yawn.

"You want a cup a coffee?" asked Joshua. "I got plenty right here in my Thermos. The wife always gives me more than I can drink."

"Thanks, Josh," she said, "but if I drink another cup, I'll go right through the roof. Maybe I'll find another patient hanging from his Posey, and that'll wake me up!"

"Lawd, remember that?" the security guard said, shaking his head at the folly and stupidity of what he saw all around him.

Amanda did remember, only too well. It was just about a year ago that she'd made another one of her middle-of-the-night inspection tours. Someone else had been on the front door that night, but Amanda knew that none of the security guards would call around to the patient units to warn them that the boss was on her way up. That's why she always walked around to the front entrance, even though going through the emergency department would be quicker and more efficient. The nurses there would get on the phone the second they saw her coming, and would warn as many of their compatriots as they could.

That night she had chosen two medical units to visit. She could do only two or three units on each visit because within an hour every nurse in the hospital knew she was there.

She had found everything fairly quiet and routine and was beginning to feel good about the way things were going—until she got down to the end of the hall on East Wing 7. There, in a private room, she saw something that had disturbed her sleep for many weeks afterwards. One of the patients, a young man who was dying of AIDS and was in the final stages of dementia, was hanging by his throat, caught in the canvas restraining straps that were used to prevent him from hurting himself, slowly turning blue. His ghastly gargling noises were growing fainter by the second.

Amanda had yelled, "Help me," before she rushed into the room. The person who came to her aid and helped get the man back into bed was Joshua, who had been coming up the fire stairs at the end of the hall.

All hell had broken loose then, and Amanda still wasn't sure of the sequence of events. She knew she had slapped an oxygen mask on the patient's face and had turned the supply of the life-giving gas up full blast. She had pushed the signal bell to summon a nurse.

In about a minute and a half, the patient had revived enough to commence screaming and raving and making superhuman efforts to leap out of bed. Amanda's arms were strong from years of swimming, but she thought they would be pulled from their sockets in her efforts to hold the patient down, even with Joshua's help. But she remembered thinking at the time that she would rather have a broken arm than a patient who had strangled to death on his own Posey.

The demented man had gotten a shot of Valium big enough for a herd of elephants, but even so, it had taken an hour for him to finally fall asleep. He died three days later with no memory of what had happened to him.

There was no lawsuit, since no friend or family member had been around to witness the debacle, but the incident had been written up for the record. Even though the patient had been dead for a year and the report of his near-strangulation was now safely buried among the boxes of old patient records in a warehouse in Poolesville, Maryland, Amanda carried with her the nagging fear that it—and all the other hospital disasters that the public never knew about—would come back to haunt her one day.

Now she grinned at Joshua and said once again, "I don't know what I would have done without you." She really meant it. "Have a good night, Josh," she said. "I'll go out through the ER, so don't wait up for me."

They smiled at each other because they both knew that Joshua Pitkin was the last person on earth who would ever sleep on duty.

Amanda decided, for sentiment's sake, to go back to East Wing 7, where she found everything quiet and peaceful. The nurse who had been on duty that night a year ago was just finishing rounds—with a flashlight.

The nurse greeted Amanda warmly, which was a good sign. That meant that the nurses knew they were doing a good job and were proud of it. "Liz and I were just going to call Domino's," she said. "Do you want some?"

"No thanks," said Amanda who, in truth, was hungry again and could easily have polished off two or three slices of pizza. "What did night nurses do before there was pizza?" she asked and wondered fleetingly how many slices she had consumed during her tenure as a staff nurse.

"I didn't know there was life before pizza!" said the nurse, who had on a blouse with brightly colored little people embroidered down the front. Her lipstick was the exact shade of the

ostume of one of the figures, and she had on small button
arrings that picked up the other colors in the blouse. If it
veren't for the regulation white pants and shoes—and the
tethoscope draped around her neck—she could have been on
er way to a summer patio party. Amanda thought she looked
heerful. She said so.

"Thanks," said the night nurse, "although whenever I wear
his blouse, I'm always afraid that some poor drugged patient
vill wake up and go bonkers when he sees all these wild
eople leaning over him!

"They're representations of Guatemalan worry dolls. The
tory is that each doll represents one of your worries, and if
ou line them up next to your bed as you sleep at night, in
he morning, the dolls will have absorbed your worries, and
hey won't bother you anymore."

"That's a nice story," said Amanda. "It's a perfect outfit for
night nurse to wear. Enjoy the pizza," she said and went off
n a brief inspection tour, looking into the utility room as well
s four or five patients' rooms, where everyone was sleeping
eacefully. She was leaving the wing, headed for the stairway,
vhen she saw light coming from under the closed door of the
ame room where the AIDS patient had been a year ago. She
apped gently and went in when a pleasant male voice invited
er to do so.

Amanda introduced herself and asked the man if everything
vas all right, although she could see at a glance that it was.
Ie was lying comfortably in bed, and as she entered he tucked
finger inside a book to mark his place. He removed his
arphones and shut off the small radio.

"I'm a night owl," he explained, "and the older I get, the
nore owlish I become." He smiled and his face changed
ompletely, the way Ken's did when he smiled. In fact, this
nan reminded her a little of Ken—or at least what he might
ook like in about twenty-five years. He had the same formal
ignity about him, which was not diminished in the least by
he tailored blue- and white-striped pajamas. He could just as
asily have been wearing a three-piece worsted suit. Although
a fourteen years, Amanda had never seen Ken in pajamas, she
new that he looked just as dignified in swimming trunks—or
tark naked—as he did in full business armor.

"I won't disturb you further," she said and turned to leave.

"You're not disturbing me," he said. "I'd be pleased if yo
stayed and chatted for a few minutes." Although the invitatio
was formal and the tone soft, even courtly, Amanda sense
that he needed, rather than wanted, her company. He wasn
just being polite, so she sat down and didn't leave the man'
room for an hour.

Amanda paused on a landing of the steel-and-cement stai
well. Going down long flights of stairs always made her dizz
but she hadn't wanted to take the elevator for fear of runnin
into someone she knew. Even in the middle of the night,
large hospital was never silent, nor did it sleep.

She needed these few minutes to collect her thoughts an
refocus her mind on the task at hand. She knew, howeve
that the hour she had just spent with the seventy-eight-yea
old gentleman with lymphocytic leukemia was one of th
most important of her life. She knew it would take lon
hours alone thinking about what they had discussed to full
understand what he had said. She also knew that she ha
learned something that would be of immense use to her i
the future, perhaps when she faced her own death—if she wa
lucky enough to have the time to face it squarely.

Amanda Knight wanted very much to have the opportunit
to face her death, to watch it coming and to meet it with a goo
heart. She believed that death was the most important journe
she would ever take, although she also believed that it was
journey to nowhere. Sometimes, though, when she was feelin
lonely and a little irrational, as she was right now, she thoug
that perhaps she would be reunited with her mother at the en
of that journey.

Then the journey will have a destination, won't it? asked th
voice, which had asked the question before. *And you won't l
nowhere when you get there.*

Don't start this again, Amanda retorted, and shook her hea
to clear it of thoughts of death. She walked quickly dow
the remaining flights and pushed open the heavy steel fir
door marked "G" in bright orange paint. J. F. K. Memorial'
basement was not nearly as depressing as some hospitals sh
had worked in. The cinderblock walls were painted in a no
too-ugly cream color, and the multicolored stripes were colo
coded to direct visitors to various departments. The stripe

nade an attractive and functional design on the wall, and here
nd there groups of pictures were hung. The pictures, which
vere changed periodically, were lesser works of whatever local
rtist was featured in the main corridor upstairs.

Amanda followed the blue stripe, which led around three or
our corners until it stopped with a stylized arrow pointing to
he door of the pharmacy. Next to the door was a window, now
huttered for the night, where patients could have prescriptions
lled. She tried the pharmacy door and found it locked.

Well, what did you expect? asked the voice, which had told
er in the car driving over here that this would be a wild-
oose chase.

She ignored that perfectly reasonable question and pressed
er ear against the door, listening for what she didn't know.

*Think about what an asshole you're going to look like to
vhoever comes around the corner next,* said the same damn
oice, neglecting to warn Amanda of the footsteps that were
ndeed approaching.

"What are you doing here? And what are you listening
)?"

Amanda's heart lurched against her rib cage and then
ounded painfully. For a moment, the rush of adrenaline sent
red haze across her field of vision. When her sight cleared,
he saw Rosalind Smythe standing in front of her, dressed in
white poplin skirt and a yellow- and white-checked cotton
amp shirt with the elbow-length sleeves rolled up two jaunty
irns to form a neat cuff. Very cute.

All of a sudden, Amanda's jeans seemed a little rattier than
iey did when she had put them on two hours ago, and she felt
strong need to put the cotton sweater in the giveaway basket
iat she kept at the top of the cellar stairs for when AmVets
r the Purple Heart solicited used clothing.

When she felt Smythe's gaze travel to her sturdy Israeli
andals, she felt herself flush. Her toes, the nails of which
ad been freshly polished just this evening, felt naked and
ulnerable. A wave of hatred for Rosalind Smythe washed over
er, and she didn't need her conscience to tell her that she was
ngry at herself for being found in a compromising position.

"I do periodic inspections at night to keep the nurses on
ieir toes and to satisfy myself that everything is going as

it should," she responded in a voice that sounded prim an
self-righteous even to herself. "After all, I'm the one who'
ultimately responsible," she finished, even more acidly.

"Is there a lot of nursing care being given in the pharmacy–
in a locked pharmacy?" asked Smythe.

Amanda's mouth opened to make a cutting retort, but noth
ing came out, so she closed it again, looking, she imagined
like a dying flounder. There was no excuse whatever for he
being here.

Wait a minute, what's this about excuses? asked the voice
which finally brought Amanda to her senses. *You're the bos
here.* You *hired* her. *You're allowed to be anywhere you war
in the hospital at any hour of the day or night.*

Right. Of course. But she still couldn't think of anythin
to say.

"Look," said Smythe. "I think I know what you're up tc
and that's why I'm down here too. There's no reason why th
narcotic vials couldn't be altered right here in the pharmacy
In fact, it makes more sense than a nurse doing it on the floo
when the big boss might come sneaking around the corner a
any time." She smiled a little as she said this, and Amand
realized that Smythe was trying to put her at her ease. Sh
responded by involuntarily relaxing—just a fraction.

"Do you think one of the pharmacists is stealing narcotics?
asked Amanda.

"I don't know," replied Smythe, "but I'm going to make i
my business to find out. I think it's exceedingly strange that a
administrator of a department comes to her office in the middl
of the night when there's no reason for her to be here, so
thought I'd see if she's here again tonight. Is there a legitimat
reason for the chief of pharmacy to behave so strangely?"

Amanda said that she couldn't think of one, and explaine
that all the night nursing supervisors had keys to the pharmac
in the unlikely event that a patient needed a drug that wasn'
stocked on the units or in the various emergency carts locate
throughout the hospital. The medical and surgical intensiv
care units, as well as the cardiac care unit, had what amounte
to small pharmacies of their own. The supervisors almost neve
went to the main pharmacy at night.

"So Evelyn Portman could count on a clear coast and n
one around to ask questions," said Smythe. "I have to get bac

upstairs," she added, "and then when my shift is over, I need to go home and get some sleep. But before I do, I'll call the office and have one of the assistants start a background check on Evelyn Portman. Can you tell me anything about her?"

"She used to work at St. Jude's," said Amanda, "and started here only a few months ago."

"Anything else?"

"The rest is just nasty gossip and speculation."

"In my business," said Smythe, "you learn very quickly that most gossip, nasty or otherwise, has a basis in fact. It wouldn't exist otherwise. So tell me what you've heard, and leave it to us to separate fact from fiction."

Amanda related the story that Ruth Sinclair had told her about the debacle in the pharmacy with the surgeon's wife, and she also told the private investigator about the lunch she had with Evelyn Portman and how secretive the pharmacist had been about where she lived. "She's kind of icy and aloof," added Amanda. "But that may be just because she's shy."

"Do you believe that?" asked Smythe.

"No. I think she's a mean bitch who's convinced that she's better and smarter than everyone else. But underneath, she's as shaky and insecure as the rest of us."

Even you, sweetheart, Amanda added to herself.

"Okay, thanks," said Smythe. "I'll get someone on it first thing in the morning." She turned to go and then changed her mind. "Two more things. First, leave the snooping around to us. That's what we're paid for, and you might find that if you stick your nose where it doesn't belong, it could get bitten off.

"Second, where did you get those sandals? They're really great. Very serious, yet comfortable-looking."

Amanda was taken aback for a second. Rosalind Smythe was saying something pleasant to her. "I got them in Israel four years ago, and they *are* great. I wear them all the time, and they're as good as new. The Israelis make the best sandals in the world, probably because that's all anyone seems to wear over there."

Smythe looked disappointed, as if she had planned a sandal-shopping trip between her daytime sleep and her return to work tonight. But she just shrugged and said, "Too bad." Then she added, "I really do have to get back now. I'll call you the minute I find out anything."

• • •

There was nothing further Amanda could do in the hospital tonight, and now that the excitement was over, she felt suddenly exhausted, too tired even to drive home. She should probably call a cab, but then she would have to move her car from the doctors' lot into her reserved space in the enclosed garage, and that didn't appeal to her at all.

Screw it, I'll drive home with the radio blasting and the windows open, she thought, and began the long walk through the deserted basement corridors to the emergency department, which was in a fury of activity when she pushed open the double doors.

She flattened herself against the wall as an orderly she didn't recognize pushed a stretcher into emergency bay number three. Amanda couldn't tell whether the person on the stretcher was a man or a woman, so covered with blood was the patient, who was also screaming his or her lungs out. Two nurses and a doctor came tearing in after the stretcher and went to work.

Amanda left. There was nothing for her to do here, and she would only be in the way if she stayed. But as she pushed herself away from the wall, she heard one of the nurses say, "Goddamn fucking drunk drivers . . . ought to be shot."

"Right you are," she muttered as she went out to her car and began the drive home through the deserted streets of Washington.

=== CHAPTER 27 ===

But when she got there, she couldn't sleep. Part of what kept her eyes wide open was overexhaustion, but part of it was visions of the criminals that seemed to be stalking the halls of J. F. K. Memorial Hospital.

Stalking the halls! said the voice, which went on to accuse her of seeing too many horror movies.

I never go to horror movies, she retorted. There's enough real-life horror in the newspaper every day.

Could Bill Zyrwynski be a serial killer?

He seemed like such a nice guy. All the nurses liked him, and that was unusual. Nurses were prepared to automatically hate all doctors unless they proved themselves to be worthy of respect and admiration. Zyrwynsky had fallen into that category amazingly quickly. She remembered Bonita saying one day, "He treats us like adults who can think, and doesn't go around believing that he's the greatest thing since sliced bread."

That was high praise indeed.

But nice guys can be serial killers, said the voice, which always tried to make her deal with reality. *Look at Ted Bundy. He bashed women over the head and then had sex with them after they were dead.*

Okay, so he wasn't nice. But he had a lot of superficial charm. You have to acknowledge that.

Amanda turned over and punched her pillow into a fatter mound, and Shadow gave a squeak of disapproval at being disturbed. She turned around three times and then pressed herself against the back of Amanda's head and went back to sleep. The cat had begun to snore gently as she got older, and Ken had always made little buzzing sounds as he slept. Amanda asleep made more noise than her two bed partners put together, but she didn't know that. Right now, though, she was deathly quiet.

Nice girls can be serial killers too, said the voice, which

251

was in a mood to give reality its fair share.

There are no women serial killers, Amanda replied.

How do you know? You just don't want to think about that possibility. Have you been through all the FBI files? Do you know that for a fact?

No.

Well then, why couldn't it be Bonita Elliott? She has as much opportunity as Bill Zyrwynsky, probably more because she spends more time with the patients than he does.

What about motive? What reason could she possibly have to kill her own patients? Besides, serial killings always have a sexual component.

Well, there was no sex in these murders, and anyway, what reason could Bill Zyrwynsky have? Serial killers don't have logical reasons for what they do—at least not the kind of logic that would make sense to you.

Amanda had to admit that this line of thinking was going nowhere. Whoever was killing the transplant patients could be anyone at all. Most likely a hospital employee, but there was no reason why it couldn't be someone off the street. There also was no point in continuing to obsess about it. Go to sleep, she told herself.

You can't, said the voice, which was getting to be a real pain in the ass. *You're thinking that Evelyn Portman is stealing narcotics and that's how she can afford to buy expensive clothes on her salary, not to mention living in Kalorama. She's got a whole drug ring going on down there in the pharmacy.*

I don't give a flying fuck if Evelyn Portman is dealing in stolen TV sets, Amanda snapped back.

Yes, you do, said the voice of reality. *You hope that she's the thief, because that would take the heat off the nurses—and because you hate her and would love to see her carted off to jail in handcuffs. No designer dresses in the women's house of detention.*

Amanda grinned into her pillow at her fantasy picture of Evelyn Portman in handcuffs. God, what a treat that would be!

Go to sleep. The alarm is going to go off soon, said the voice that liked to see Amanda take care of herself.

This time she obeyed.

Two days later the call came from Kevin Hogwood at the

Steelman Agency. "I'm sending to you by special messenger the background report that you and Rosalind Smythe talked about," he said. "But she asked me to call you to see if you have any questions."

"I don't see how I can have any questions until I've read the report," she said as kindly as she could manage.

"Well, that's true," he replied and then paused, not knowing where to go from there.

"Is there anything dramatic that I should know about right now?" she asked.

"Uh gee, I don't know. I didn't actually read the report. I'm just doing what Roz told me to do."

Amanda wondered if the guy were stupid enough to call Smythe "Roz" to her face, and then decided that he probably was. She thanked him and said she would read the report and call if she had questions.

Not five minutes later, Louise came in bearing a large white envelope with CONFIDENTIAL stamped all over it in red. There was also a big blob of sealing wax covering the black flap. Imbedded in the hardened red wax was the Steelman Agency logo.

How medieval, she thought as she tore open the envelope, scattering flakes of red stuff all over her desk.

The report was three single-spaced pages, and Amanda read it with only casual interest until she came to the middle of the last page.

"Holy Christ Shit!" she said out loud.

Holy Christ Shit was one of Amanda's strongest expletives, used in moments of greatest agitation. Although Amanda knew how to curse like a sailor, Holy Christ Shit had great sentimental value. It had been the favorite expletive of Dickie Levine, her best and dearest friend of early adolescence. "Shit" and "turd" and the lexicon of other scatological synonyms were their worst language when they were kids. No one *ever* said "fuck." Neither she nor Dickie Levine were positive about the precise meaning of the word.

"Holy Christ Shit!" she said again. Evelyn Portman's surgeon lover at St. Jude's was none other than Joseph Krahl.

All at once things clicked into place, and Amanda could not believe the picture that emerged as her mind completed the puzzle. This isn't possible, she said to herself. No one would do what Amanda suddenly realized had indeed been done.

She put the report back into its envelope and placed it in her steel filing cabinet. As she pushed in the button to lock the drawer and checked to make sure that all was secure, she thought once again that anyone with a strong arm and a heavy hammer could open the drawer in two seconds flat.

Never mind that now, said the voice, which was as shaken as she. *Just get out of here and do some serious thinking.*

Amanda changed into her Easy Spirit walking shoes that she kept in the office for just this very purpose. She whizzed past Louise's desk. "Going out for a walk," she said by way of explanation.

Keep your mind a blank until you get across Reservoir Road, she told herself as she waited impatiently for a break in the heavy mid-morning traffic. She walked furiously for a few blocks until the huge many-winged hospital receded behind her and the noise of the main thoroughfare had given way to the quiet of the Georgetown streets.

Then she slowed her pace to a steady aerobic clip and acknowledged what she knew in her heart to be true: Evelyn Portman had killed the transplant patients at the direction of Dr. Joseph Krahl.

Even if you're right—which you may be, how can you prove it? asked the voice, which knew damn well she was right.

I don't have to prove it, she replied. Let Lydia and Paul Bandman do that. That's their job.

But when you tell Lydia about this—and you are *going to tell her; you're not going off half-cocked on your own the way you did last time. When you tell Lydia, how will you convince her? She's not going to buy feminine intuition and other assorted wild theories. She's the police. She needs facts.*

I don't have any facts, replied Amanda. I just know what I know, and when I'm this positive about a gut reaction, I'm never wrong. You know that.

It was true. Amanda had fantastic radar. She remembered a time not too long ago, walking these same streets, that another strong conviction had come to her all in one piece, neatly falling into place, as this one had.

It was when she was still assistant director of nursing,

biding time until her boss would finally give in to old age and incipient senility and realize that it was time to retire. The department of nursing was top-heavy with management then and had needed two secretaries to do all the unnecessary paperwork that her predecessor had generated.

One of the secretaries was Louise, as competent and efficient then as she was now. The other was a young black woman who had only one talent: polishing her fingernails, which she did to perfection at least once a day, sometimes more often. Sometimes right at her desk.

She didn't take accurate messages, and when she didn't feel like it, she didn't answer the phone at all. It would take her two days to type a one-page letter, which she filled with misspellings and sprinkled with commas in all the wrong places, as if she had shaken them on like salt. She spent hours on the phone with her friends and sometimes didn't come back from lunch until three in the afternoon.

The previous director thought she was a wonder. Everyone else hated her. And it was to Amanda that they complained. "Jacqueline isn't mine to fire," she had explained time and time again. "I didn't hire her, I'm not her boss, and besides, she's black."

The last part of the sentence usually ended the discussion. In Washington, D.C., it was almost impossible to fire a black employee. The federal government had set that standard—much to the chagrin of many black leaders who saw how affirmative action was beginning to backfire, creating increased racism—and private industry slavishly followed suit.

One day Amanda had watched Jacqueline ignore the phone for a dozen rings before she picked it up. She had told the caller, far too curtly, that the director was out. She didn't bother to ask for a message. That had been the last straw for Amanda. Her palm had itched to slap the secretary across the face; instead she changed shoes and took a walk.

It had been the height of autumn then, and Amanda weaved along the sidewalk looking for the biggest clumps of leaves to walk through, enjoying the crunchy, crackly sound. The squirrels were in the middle of their busiest season of the year, and many of them forgot their natural shyness in their zeal to prepare for the coming winter. It was while she was on her way back to the hospital that the puzzle completed itself.

The director of nursing was a racist, a serious racist, but she
was guilty about it and knew that the depth of her hatred was
no longer acceptable. So in order to assuage that guilt, she
let Jacqueline get away with her impossible behavior, making
everyone else in the department suffer as a consequence.

There was nothing Amanda could do then about this observation except to ignore Jacqueline as much as possible. But
she started to document all the secretary's atrocious behavior
and a year later when her boss finally retired and Amanda was
promoted, one of the first things she did was to fire Jacqueline
Gates.

Would you get your mind off that lazy bitch, said the voice
which knew that Amanda was avoiding thinking about what
she had come out here to think about. *She's out of your hair
now—you saw to that very neatly, and now you have a problem
on your hands that makes Jacqueline look like Rebecca of
Sunnybrook Farm.*

*You say that you know what you know, and you may be
right, but you have no facts to back it up, and you can't go
to Lydia with this wild-eyed story.*

Why not? asked Amanda. It's true that Lydia is the police
but she's also my friend.

*And that puts her in an awkward position. She'll feel obli-
gated to listen to your story out of friendship, and . . .*

She *ought* to listen to it out of professional interest, retorted
Amanda. After all, if I'm right, she gets credit for the arrest
and this is a big one. This will be on the front page for days.

All right, all right, said the voice, which had to admit that
Amanda had a point. *But keep walking until you know what
you're going to say to Lydia.*

It took Amanda almost an hour to decide how she was going
to present her case to her friend, the police detective. When she
had it figured out, she stopped at a pay phone and called Lydia
at the station house.

The detective knew immediately from the tone of Amanda's
voice that this was no social call. "Paul and I will come to the
hospital," she said.

"No, don't do that. I don't want *anyone* seeing me talk to
the police," said Amanda in a near panic at the thought of
what Evelyn might do if she saw Amanda with two police

detectives. It never occurred to her that Evelyn Portman had no idea who Lydia and Bandman were. "I don't want to meet anyplace in Georgetown, either," she added.

"There's a Hot Shoppes on the corner of East-West Highway and Wisconsin Avenue," said Lydia. "The food's bad, but the booths are private, and it has a big parking lot. We'll meet you there in fifteen minutes."

Amanda put another quarter in the pay phone and told Louise that she was going to lunch without returning to her office. Then she walked back out to Reservoir Road and hailed a passing taxi. There were always plenty of cabs near a hospital.

Lydia and Paul Bandman waved to her from a booth at the far end of the restaurant. The adjacent booths were empty, and Amanda wondered if Bandman had arranged the convenient privacy. She slid onto the seat opposite them and drank half a glass of ice water before she even said hello.

Amanda looked at Lydia and said, "That's a pretty blouse. Is it new?"

Paul Bandman knew exactly what Amanda was doing. He had dealt with this type of behavior many times before. He said, as gently and firmly as he could, "Lydia bought that blouse yesterday at some store that she said was having the sale of all sales, and I waited for her in the car in the boiling sun while she 'ran in just for a second.'"

Bandman smiled as he said the last part, but he also put up his hand, palm out, to prevent Amanda from asking Lydia where the sale was—to prevent her from asking anything. "The blouse was marked down from a thousand dollars to one dollar—and now that we have the important stuff out of the way, let's get down to brass tacks."

Amanda stared at Bandman in admiration. He had put her at her ease while at the same time letting her know that there was to be no messing around. This was strictly business.

She told them everything she knew and everything she thought.

Neither detective said a word during her recitation, which took a full twenty minutes, with a short break while the waitress served their sandwiches. Amanda bit into her tuna fish on whole wheat without giving a moment's thought to how it had gotten there or who had ordered it for her.

When she finished, she took another bite of her sandwich and looked at Lydia and Bandman. Neither had any expression on their faces, and Amanda was surprised to see how different her friend looked now that the topic under discussion was murder. Her usual open expression had hardened as she thought about multiple murder.

As if reading her mind, Bandman said, "You're talking about a woman who you think killed in cold blood four total strangers. Killings in which the motive cannot be tied to the victim in any way. Killings in which the autopsies revealed no obvious poisons. Killings in which there were no mortal wounds."

"Killings—deaths—in which you and a confused, grief-stricken, senile old woman are the only ones who are talking about murder," said Lydia gently.

Amanda's heart sank and she felt tears well up. Ordinarily she hated to cry in front of anyone. Even Ken was not often privy to her tears, but now she didn't care if she burst into wild sobs right here in this depressing restaurant, eating bland tuna fish salad made with too much mayonnaise on bread that tasted like Styrofoam.

"I should have known this was useless," she said bitterly, reaching for her purse. "Get the check. I'll pay for your lunches." Anger welled up now, along with the frustration that had been there for so long. The urge to cry disappeared in a flood of outrage and indignation.

Amanda slid out of the booth, and as she looked around for the waitress, she felt a hand clamp on her arm. It was not at all painful, but neither could she shake it off. "Sit down," said Bandman.

He was more excited than he had been for longer than he cared to remember. He knew instinctively that Amanda Knight was correct, although it was his job to remain cool—skeptical even—in the face of a story bizarre enough to be almost impossible to prove. He saw in his mind's eye the entire staff of prosecuting attorneys engaged in an ultimately futile effort to prove this. In fact, the entire trial flashed before his eyes, complete with Evelyn Portman walking out of the courtroom a free woman because reasonable doubt hung over the jury box like Olympian storm clouds.

None of this registered on his face as he said, "Tell me every single reason you can think of why this woman would murder four total strangers at the behest of a lover."

Amanda began to talk, and Bandman listened attentively as he always did. But his mind simultaneously shifted to another level, one that processed and analyzed everything he was hearing.

He knew without a doubt that a woman sufficiently in thrall to a man would do whatever he asked—even murder. It had happened before, and it would happen many times again. Although the circumstances were different in this case, the story was depressingly familiar.

Paul Bandman listened to Amanda Knight and thought about what she was saying. He believed every word of it, and he felt crushingly sad.

Ken James looked at his wife across the dinner table and realized that she wasn't there at all. He supposed that everyone took these little mental vacations every now and again, but she had been doing it a lot lately, and it worried him.

"My meeting on K Street this morning didn't last through lunch," he said to Amanda and watched her make the effort to snap back to the present. "I called your office, hoping you could meet me for lunch somewhere nice, but Louise said you were out and she didn't know where you were."

Amanda knew that her husband wanted to know where she had gone at lunchtime that was so secret she didn't want to tell her secretary. She also knew that he couldn't bring himself to ask the question directly. It was one of the things about him that irritated her the most, but she didn't have the energy to punish his reticence by pretending that she didn't know what he wanted. So she told the truth.

Ken was visibly annoyed. He sighed and said, "You're going to end up making a fool of yourself."

"I know," she replied. "That's what Lydia and Paul Bandman think too."

He was surprised that she admitted as much. Usually she was much more stubborn. "So now that you've put the whole thing on their plate, are you willing to drop it?"

Amanda looked her husband straight in the eye and said, "I have no choice."

He didn't believe her, and she knew it and didn't care.

CHAPTER 28

You lied to your husband, said the voice, which strongly disapproved of that.

I didn't lie exactly, she retorted. I just didn't tell him the whole truth.

Bullshit, said her conscience, really angry now. *But it's done and you can't take it back, so at least stop lying to yourself. Or better yet, go to the damn library, put John Steinbeck in the return slot, buy a quart of chocolate chip ice cream, and go home and sublimate your frustration by eating the whole thing yourself.*

That's disgusting, replied Amanda as she got back into her car in the library parking lot on Arlington Road in Bethesda, strapped herself in, and drove downtown.

It's better than doing what you're going to do, said the voice, which was getting scared as well as angry. It didn't like where Amanda had gone, and what she had done there, after lunch with Lydia and Bandman.

Amanda had accepted the detectives' offer of a lift back to the hospital and had waved cheerfully to them as she went in the main entrance. But instead of turning right and pushing open the heavy glass doors to the administrative wing, she continued down the main corridor, past this month's art exhibition and out through the door on the other side of the X-ray department.

For the second time that day, she crossed Reservoir Road, walked up to Wisconsin Avenue, turned left, and entered the Georgetown branch of the D.C. Public Library at the corner of R Street. She spent a half hour with the *Haynes Criss-Cross Directory* spread open on the oak table, and when she left, she knew Evelyn Portman's address and unlisted phone number. Kalorama was a small neighborhood with not more than two dozen streets, and it had required only patience to find out what she needed to know.

And what are you going to do when you get there? asked the voice, which was really frightened now.

Amanda didn't respond. Instead, she turned right onto California Street from Connecticut and found a parking place halfway down the block—an unheard-of bonanza in this neighborhood. She thought of it as a good omen.

Bullshit, said the voice, which was at a loss for anything more sensible to say or do. Amanda seemed to be operating on some sort of automatic pilot that excluded her rational self.

Another good omen came her way as she smiled politely and sailed through the open outer door of the apartment building, along with a tenant who was juggling three large sacks of groceries. She had been worried about the problem of figuring out Evelyn's Portman's door buzzer code, which in these buildings was never the same as the apartment number.

She entered the elevator with the tenant and his groceries and hung back to see which floor he pushed. He chose the third floor, so she pressed the button for eight. Evelyn Portman lived on seven. *Who do you think you are, a CIA operative?* hissed the voice sarcastically. Amanda smiled pleasantly at the tenant and said nothing.

The door slid open on Eight, and Amanda walked down the hall to the red exit sign and entered the concrete and steel stairwell, which looked almost exactly like the ones at J.F.K. Memorial.

"Holy shit," she said aloud, her heart lurching, as she grabbed the heavy steel fire door an inch before it clicked shut—and locked from the inside. The only door in these buildings that opened from the stairwell was the one that led to the street. All the others were locked for security reasons, and she would either have been trapped on the stairs or found herself back on the sidewalk, perhaps this time with no unsuspecting tenant to let her in.

She rang for the elevator and got off at the seventh floor.

"Who is it?" Evelyn Portman called out in response to Amanda's tap with the small brass knocker.

"It's Amanda Knight, Evelyn. I need to talk to you about something important."

The response was silence, deafening silence. It went on for so long that Amanda looked up and down the hall and then put her ear to the door, half expecting to see Rosalind Smythe interrupt her again.

What she heard sounded exactly like the squirrels in her backyard as they scurried around each autumn augmenting their nests and gathering acorns and dogwood seeds for the winter. Amanda heard scratching and rustling and, although she couldn't be certain, she thought there were high-pitched voices as well.

But she was evidently mistaken about the last because when Evelyn finally opened the door she was alone. The pharmacist was dressed in a lavender silk kimono, patterned with leaves of pale grey, peach, and aqua. A band of darker grey bordered the front edges and cuffs of the kimono. Amanda guessed that the garment had cost as much as she had spent on her shopping spree last Sunday with Glencora.

Evelyn Portman was not pleased to see Amanda Knight, and she made no effort to hide it. "This is not a convenient time," she said. "I was just about to go to bed."

Amanda was still standing on the other side of the doorway, and Evelyn had made no move to invite her in. "At nine o'clock in the evening?" she asked, not disguising her sarcasm. She put her foot onto the doorsill and shifted the weight of her body so that her shoulder bore most of the impact as Evelyn tried to swing the door closed.

Whatever misgivings Amanda might have had about her speculations and suspicions dissolved into absolute certainty as Evelyn made a futile effort to keep Amanda out of her apartment.

"I know Miss Manners wouldn't approve of my paying a visit without calling first, but when you hear what I have to say, you'll know why I didn't bother with the social amenities."

As she said this, Amanda moved to one of the couches that flanked the fireplace at a 90-degree angle. Evelyn had no choice but to close the door and follow. She had said nothing after her stated intention of going to bed, but she sat down on one of the couches and said, "As long as you're here, you might as well tell me what's so important that it can't wait until tomorrow."

Amanda looked around the living room and into the dining room beyond. The apartment was beautiful, furnished in exactly the style in which Evelyn Portman dressed—understated, in perfect taste, and terribly, terribly expensive. The hand of a $200-an-hour decorator was everywhere: in the matching crystal lamps with pale green silk shades, in the rich wool carpet, the color of which precisely matched the lamp shades and was picked up in the floral fabric of the two sofas.

"Did you do it just for money?" she asked. "Or are you so in love with him that you'll do whatever he wants?"

"What are you talking about?" Evelyn asked, but her voice was a shade more hesitant than it had been a moment before.

"I'm talking about killing four people. Taking four innocent lives, one of them a little child—a little helpless child whose mother gave up part of her own body to save his life," Amanda said. Then she stopped because the voice was telling her to cool it, to stay in control.

"You must be completely crazy," said Evelyn, standing up and pointing dramatically toward the door. "Get out of my house." Her voice was distinctly shrill now, and there was a splotch of bright red on each cheek. It made her look like a woman who didn't know when to call it quits with the rouge pot.

"Sit down and tell me how you did it," said Amanda. "You're a pharmacist. You must know all the good poisons. How did you make it look like hyperacute rejection? How did you manage to give Roberta Garfield PCP without her knowing?

"How could you have been so taken in by that man's pathological jealousy? Is he *that* good in bed?" asked Amanda. "Or are you *that* lonely and desperate?"

Evelyn Portman caved in. She said nothing, but right in front of Amanda's eyes, she aged fifteen years and visibly crumpled in on herself. The exquisite silk kimono now looked like a pathetic effort to hide decay, like a blanket of flowers on a coffin.

"Right on both counts."

The familiar voice came from behind her, and Amanda swung her head and upper body around on the couch to see Joseph Krahl standing in the doorway leading to the bedroom. He was stark naked.

Behind him, she could see the rumpled king-sized bed. She

realized that Evelyn Portman had not been getting ready *for* bed. She and her lover had been *in* bed.

And here he was, that arrogant son of a bitch, flaunting it all. He had had the nerve to suggest that a madman might be stalking J. F. K. Memorial. The madman was right here. Joseph Krahl had been talking about himself all the time she had been in his office Monday afternoon.

Why don't you drop the philosophy and psychology for now? said the voice of practicality. *You're in a pretty sticky situation here. You and the naked psycho.*

Amanda had to agree. The situation was worse than sticky. It was downright dangerous. She could feel the menace radiating from Krahl in hot waves.

There seemed to be nothing to say, so she stood up. In doing so, however, she had to turn her back on Krahl. That was a mistake. "Where are you going?" he asked.

"Home."

"I don't think that's the truth," said Krahl. "I think you'll drive straight to the police." His voice had lost none of its charm and casual elegance and authority. If she closed her eyes to shut out his nude body, the bed with the sheets all awry, and Evelyn Portman in her silk kimono, he could be lecturing medical students or addressing the department of surgery.

"No, I won't. I promise. I won't tell anyone."

Again, in that reassuring doctor's voice, Krahl responded: "You've been seeing too many bad gangster movies. All the female characters say the same thing when they're begging for their lives."

And the next thing she knew, Joseph Krahl was pointing a small but very serious-looking gun at her. Now, where the hell did that come from? Where had he been hiding it?

Here you go again with these stupid, meaningless questions, said the voice, which had noticed that Krahl was standing with one arm behind his back. But it didn't say this to Amanda. There was no point now in confusing her with details that no longer mattered. What was important was getting out of here alive. *Keep calm,* the voice said. *He's not on as even a keel as he looks.*

It didn't occur to either Amanda or her inner voice that a man who would face a woman accusing him of murder in nothing but his birthday suit, was no longer here with the rest of us in the world of reality. What occurred to Amanda was that from Joseph Krahl's point of view, he had no choice but to kill her. It made sense.

Then, for the first time, the fear that had been lurking around without quite touching her, reached her heart and grabbed it with such a strong icy-cold hand that Amanda gasped in pain and surprise. Her breath whooshed out of her chest, her knees turned to tissue paper, and she toppled backward onto the couch.

"That's better," said Krahl, a hard edge coming into his voice now. "I'm just an old-fashioned guy. I like my women submissive."

"You're going to kill me, aren't you?" Amanda croaked.

"Verrry good!" said Krahl. "Evelyn said you're a smart cookie, and I'm glad to see she was right. Evelyn is very often right."

"Damn straight I am. I told you she was dangerous." Evelyn Portman spoke for the first time since Joseph Krahl had entered the room. Actually, that wasn't quite right. He was still at the bedroom door, leaning against the doorjamb, gun in hand, in a manner that suggested insolence, arrogance—and total control.

Okay, said the voice. *Enough with the paralyzing fear. Start thinking how you're going to get yourself out of this mess.*

Oh Jesus, retorted Amanda. You're very funny. He's holding a gun on me. What am I supposed to do, get up and walk out the door?

She couldn't think of anything better to do, so she stood up again. Another mistake.

"Down!" barked Krahl as if he were talking to a dog.

The three of them, Krahl still in the doorway but standing straight at attention now, and she and Evelyn facing each other on the flowered couches, remained silent. Amanda could see Krahl thinking hard about what to do with her. She tried to think, but nothing entered her mind. Zero. Zip. Zilch.

Amanda didn't know what Evelyn was doing while Krahl was deciding her fate and she was gazing inward at the black hole where her brain used to be. The pharmacist had passed into the realm of supporting cast. Her usefulness to Krahl was obviously at an end, and he would probably have to kill her too. That made sense. However, it seriously compounded his problem. Killing one woman and getting rid of the body was not an easy task, but it had been done before. Killing two women and getting rid of their bodies was almost impossible, unless you were out in the wilds of West Virginia in the middle of miles and miles of silent forest. But here they were in crowded Kalorama where gunshots were not an everyday occurrence.

Don't tell anyone, but you're thinking, said the voice, which wasn't certain that Amanda realized her own strength and ingenuity. Therefore, a little encouragement might go a long way. *Try to prevent him from figuring out how to solve his little problem,* said the voice.

"What poison did you use?" she asked Krahl.

"Huh?"

"How did you kill all four?"

"You've already figured out the heart transplant woman," he said, but absently as if his mind were still elsewhere.

Amanda was genuinely puzzled. "You can't just *give* someone PCP infection," she said.

"Sure you can," said Evelyn. "You can spin the bacteria out of blood samples and mix it into any concoction you want. Roberta Garfield got her cyclosporine at the hospital pharmacy. All the transplant patients do. We're cheaper than a commercial drugstore."

Amanda was dumbfounded. "But how did you do all this?" she asked. "Where did you get the PCP? How could you have used the centrifuge in the lab without anyone seeing you? How did you know how to do it?"

Evelyn was angry now. "You're just like everyone else," she hissed. "You think pharmacists don't know anything beyond counting pills into little bottles and typing those stupid labels. But we're so much more than that. We're scientists. We're chemists. Any fool can use a centrifuge. Pharmacists make compounds. We create things. Don't ever make the mistake of selling us short!"

Believe me, I won't, thought Amanda grimly. Aloud, she said, "What about the other three? How did you simulate the rejection process?"

Evelyn Portman laughed merrily. "I didn't have to. They really did go into hyperacute rejection. There was nothing faked about it."

The light dawned on Amanda Knight. Nurses intent on stealing narcotics give placebos to patients in pain, and pharmacists intent on killing transplant patients give them placebos instead of antirejection drugs. How simple. How potentially foolproof. No pathologist in the world would think of looking for a drug that wasn't there. It was murder without a murder weapon.

Amanda stared at Evelyn Portman, who smiled back at her. "Good idea, wasn't it?" asked the latter.

"It was a great idea," replied Amanda truthfully. "Too bad you won't get away with it."

Joseph Krahl knew how empty and hollow her threat was. "We already have gotten away with it," he told her. "And we'll keep doing it until your hospital realizes how much it needs me. I wanted that position at J. F. K. I deserve it and I'm going to get it. I'm better than Bill Zyrwynsky. I always have been and I always will be. After all, his patients keep dying on him."

"His patients die because you're killing them," she retorted—and then when she saw his face, she was immediately sorry she had spoken.

Shut up, said the voice, which should have warned her a moment earlier. *This man doesn't seem to do reality very well. In fact, he seems to have left reality far, far behind.*

"Zyrwynsky's patients died because he's not as good a doctor as I am," said Krahl in a voice that Amanda had not heard before. It had all the charm that it usually did, but there was an automatic quality to it, sort of like a computer voice. "He has never been as good a doctor as I am. He's not as smart as I am."

Amanda said nothing. There was nothing to say. He had a gun. Her only protection consisted of a white polo shirt and a red Boston University sweatshirt, which would nicely camouflage her blood.

Don't start thinking like that, said the voice, which wanted to keep her spirits up but didn't have anything more constructive to offer.

What else can I thi . . .

The explosive pounding on the apartment door startled all three of them and froze them into a tableau of shock.

"Open up! Police!" The pounding increased in ferocity.

Two things happened simultaneously, and they happened

so fast that Amanda had no memory of the movements that caused her to end up where she did.

One of the things was that the apartment door crashed inward. It didn't just open. It was lifted off its hinges and lay on the living room floor completely severed from the doorjamb. There was a piercing odor.

The other thing that happened was that Joseph Krahl had one arm around Amanda's upper body pinning her to him. His other hand, the one with the gun in it, was pressed against her throat.

CHAPTER 29

A knowledge of anatomy comes in handy at a time like this, Amanda thought, even though she would just as soon not have thought about it. But there didn't seem to be anything else to think about.

If he shoots me in the throat, I'm sure to die. If he shoots me in the head, I may not be so lucky. I could wind up like Karen Quinlan.

She guessed she was over the edge, and had joined Joseph Krahl in a never-never land of insanity. It was quite liberating, really. At least she was no longer afraid.

Yes, you are, said the voice. *You're scared shitless. You just don't know it.*

It was true. Amanda was scared beyond mere fear, and she was most assuredly not insane. She watched what looked like dozens of policemen freeze in horror the instant they saw that she was being held hostage, their guns pointed at the ceiling rather than at her and Krahl.

Paul Bandman and Lydia Simonowitz pushed through the blue uniforms, their guns also held pointing up. If it hadn't been for the flaming red hair, she would hardly have recognized her friend Lydia. The soft-spoken young woman, who still believed what her mother had told her about getting drunk faster on red wine than white, was pale and grim. There was no trace of the relaxed person who, only a week and a half ago, had talked happily of wedding plans over pizza and beer.

Behind the uniformed policemen, Amanda could see Ken, his face a mask of pain and rage. I lied to him about where I was going, she thought. Now I'm going to die, and the last thing I will have said to the man I love was a lie. She began to cry.

Behind her, Joseph Krahl felt her body begin to shake with sobs, but since Amanda made no noise, he couldn't be certain what she was doing. So he pressed his hostage tighter to himself, and Amanda's buttocks ground into his pelvis. His penis began to harden.

As this fact penetrated her misery, guilt, and humiliation, she was engulfed by anger and disgust at a man who responded sexually to her helplessness. She tried to pull her lower body away from his erect penis, but he felt her struggle and tightened his grip.

"You pig," she said. "You're a disgusting swine."

Her practical self told her to shut the hell up and not make this man any crazier than he already was.

"Get out of my way," Krahl said to the uniformed police, to Bandman and to Lydia. Krahl began pushing Amanda forward, an inch at a time, his erection digging into her. The uniforms moved slightly as the gunman and his hostage crept toward them.

"You're not exactly inconspicuous, dressed like that," said Bandman in his calm, slightly droll way, which didn't even hint at the tension going on underneath the measured tones. "We have to let you out this door," he continued as though giving directions to a befuddled tourist. "But what are you going to do when you get to the street? Half the D.C. police force is out there waiting for you. They're going to laugh like hell."

They would indeed laugh like hell. But not until it was over. Then, the story of the naked gunman with a gigantic hard-on would circulate through the entire police department in less than a day. But right now, there would be no laughing. The police who responded to a hostage call were specially trained. The "shrink tank," as they were dubbed, consisted of a hundred or so officers who had more psychological training than some of the therapists whose shingles were hung out all over Washington's toniest neighborhoods.

Paul Bandman had not been through hostage training, but his natural talent for defusing potential disasters clicked into place almost automatically. Since he was the first one on the scene, the captain who headed the hostage unit left him alone. He was well aware of what Bandman was attempting, which was to make the gunman look ridiculous in his own eyes and thus take away his power to harm. Force him to think ahead to where he would be when this was all over. Protect the hostage.

Krahl hesitated for a moment, as if suddenly realizing that he was naked, and Amanda's hope soared. But only for an instant, because Krahl began his slow, insistent march toward the door. The sea of blue uniforms began to part, forming an aisle for the bride and groom from Hell.

Again, two things happened at once, and again Amanda did not know in what order they occurred, although everyone else in the room knew. There was a loud, snapping sound, exactly like the crack made when she stepped on a dead branch that occasionally fell out of the giant oak tree in their front yard.

Almost simultaneously, Krahl's grip on her loosened a little, and even before she had a chance to think about the possibility of escaping, his arm fell away completely, and he crumpled to the floor.

As Paul Bandman reached for her, she turned around to look, and saw the neat hole, hardly bleeding at all, in the middle of Krahl's forehead, just above his nose.

Only then, did she give in to the deliciousness of permitting herself to pass out cold.

Later, as she sat with Bandman in one of the most depressing rooms she had ever seen, he told her to try to drink the coffee. She held out her shaking hands and said that coffee wasn't exactly what she needed just now.

"It's decaf," he said. "Drink it."

She brought the cup to her lips and took a swallow. Then she sat up straight in the hard wooden chair and opened her eyes wide as the almost-straight brandy slid down her throat. It settled nicely in her stomach and then spread out in a warm, comforting glow. She smiled at Bandman and said, "Decaf is exactly what I needed. Thank you."

Bandman's basset hound face settled into more benign folds as he asked, "Are you ready to tell us what happened?"

She sighed. "Can I finish my coffee first?"

"Absolutely. Take your time," he said. "In fact, I'll leave you alone for a few minutes if you'd prefer." Amanda smiled gratefully, and he added, "I'll be right outside the door. Let me know when you're ready, and I'll bring in the stenographer."

He opened the door and slipped out. Before he closed it, Amanda got a glimpse of Lydia and Ken and three or four other people standing in the corridor outside the room in which she was sitting.

She sat quietly, not thinking of anything, not even having to try to make her mind a blank. From time to time she sipped the brandy and coffee, knowing that when the adrenaline wore off and the shock passed, the liquor was going to sneak up behind her and knock her block off. But for the moment, it had no effect other than the creeping warmth, and she was grateful for that.

In a short while, she went to the door and told Bandman that she was ready. Ken was still in the hall talking to Lydia and the other detectives, and they looked at each other for a long moment. She could not read the expression on his face and that frightened her.

Don't think about him now, said the voice, which this time was filled with compassion. *Yes, you lied to him, but for God's sake, you just escaped death by a hair . . .*

"I think we're ready now, Amanda," said Bandman, and she looked up in surprise. She was sitting at the scarred wooden table and had no memory of moving away from the doorway, pulling out a chair, and sitting down. The plastic foam cup was gone.

Lydia sat next to Bandman. A stenographer was at the end of the table, busy setting up his little machine. To Amanda's right, there was a middle-aged man who looked exactly like Amanda had always pictured Jay Gatsby—not like Robert Redford at all. To his right, there was a man with pockmarked skin. Everyone had blank expressions, like department store mannequins.

There was a large reel-to-reel tape recorder in the center of the table.

Bandman spoke again. "Amanda, this is Peter Abrahams, an assistant district attorney, and next to him is Len Agostino, one of the detectives here at the second district." Both men nodded gravely. Neither smiled. Neither spoke. The stenographer was not introduced.

"In a minute I'm going to turn on the tape recorder, make a few introductory notations, and then I'm going to ask you a series of questions. You are to answer them fully, completely, and briefly. At the end of your statement, you will be asked i you have any additional comments. Then, within a few days, I will ask you to return, read the typed statement, and sign it. Do you understand what I have just said?"

She nodded.

"Please say so in words."

"I understand."

"Are you ready to begin?"

"Yes."

Bandman turned on the tape recorder and said, "Today is Thursday, September 12, 1991. It is one forty-seven A.M. Present are Lydia Simonowitz, detective second grade, Second District, District of Columbia Metropolitan Police, Leonard Agostino, detective sergeant, District of . . ."

Amanda answered questions put to her by Bandman and Abrahams for more than two hours. She declined to add further comments. "I can't think of anything that you haven't covered," she said.

"Does anyone else in the room have anything to add?" asked Bandman, and when no one offered anything, he turned off the machine, and everyone around the table relaxed visibly.

"Thanks, Stan," said Bandman to the stenographer, who packed up his gear and left the room. No one said anything until the stenographer had closed the door behind him.

Paul Bandman got up and pulled the tape recorder plug out of the wall, coiled the cord neatly, and laid it next to the machine on the table. Still no one said anything.

"If you're not too tired, Amanda," said Bandman, "Len Agostino has a story to tell you."

Amanda was so exhausted that she felt as though she were seeing the activity in the room through a vat of thick Karo syrup. She knew she was part of the activity, and she realized that she must have been the central actor, but she could hardly find herself through the gooey syrup.

"I'm not too tired," she replied.

Agostino told her of his interview with Mrs. Zurman and Gerald Miller. "Who's Gerald Miller?" Amanda asked.

"Mrs. Zurman's nephew. Aaron Zurman's cousin," replied Agostino.

"Oh, the Chinless Wonder," she said, remembering.

Agostino smiled at that and then continued, telling her how he had searched Zurman's apartment and had been unable to find any evidence—anywhere—that a murder had been committed.

"But it bothered me," he said. "I knew I was missing something, but there was no evidence at all, so I had to close out the file. The captain wouldn't even let me put it in cold cases; he said there was no reason to keep it open."

The detective shrugged, accepting, as always, the vagaries of the bureaucracy in which he worked. "Then, this afternoon, a real nut case showed up in the squad room, saying that he knew who had murdered Aaron Zurman.

"Of course, I didn't know then that he was completely off his trolley, so I sat him down and let him talk." Agostino shook his head as he thought about the conversation with Mark Cipriotti and then later with Allen Hackett and Sarah Castle.

Politicians! He would rather talk for an hour with the stupidest, most docile, passive bureaucrat than spend five minutes with a damn politician.

"Those three assholes out there in Montgomery County . . . Sorry about the language," he said.

Amanda waved her hand as if to blow away the word. "Anyway," Agostino continued, "the three of them hated Aaron Zurman and had plotted to kill him because he opposed plans to build a huge office-retail-hotel complex in downtown Silver Spring. At least that's what this guy Cipriotti told me."

"They wanted to kill someone over a building?" asked Amanda, incredulous. She was awake now, no longer swimming through Karo syrup.

"Amanda, people kill for a pair of shoes," said Lydia. But she spoke the harsh words softly, seeing the ravages of the evening etched deeply into her friend's face.

Amanda sighed. "I know. But how could Zurman have been murdered twice? I don't understand."

"We're not sure we do, either," replied Agostino. "Cipriotti told me about this plot, crying like a baby the whole time, denying that he had anything to do with the actual murder, saying that the woman, Sarah Castle, had 'taken care of it.' Apparently she refused to tell Cipriotti and the other man exactly how Zurman had been killed or who had done it. Cipriotti thought that maybe she had hired a hit man."

"Jesus," said Amanda.

"Right. So we went out with arrest warrants and picked up the other two on suspicion of murder one. That's first-degree murder," Agostino explained.

Amanda smiled for the first time in many hours. "I know what murder one is. I watch TV."

Agostino tried to return her smile, but all he could manage was a grimace. He was convinced that too many people watched too much television, and then everyone thought they knew how to do a murder investigation. But, he had to admit, this woman seemed to have pulled it off. "Right," he continued. "So half the squad spent the day interrogating the three of them, and they all denied killing Zurman. Castle and Hackett denied even discussing the possibility of murder—although you could see the two of them thinking about knocking off *Cipriotti*.

"Anyway, about two seconds after we booked them, they clammed up and wouldn't say boo until they had their lawyers there. Since everyone denied everything and the two of them called Cipriotti a liar, and since we had no proof, nothing concrete to use as evidence, we had no choice but to let them go.

"The lawyers hustled them out, screaming about suing the department for false arrest and harassment and all the rest of that bullshit."

Amanda stared at him. "So what happens now?"

Agostino held out his hands, palms up in the classic gesture of futility. "Nothing much. I think the worst thing that those three are guilty of is being complete fuck-ups. When they left, the place was a mob scene of reporters, and the shit will hit the fan in the morning papers. Their political careers are over—thank God.

"Evelyn Portman admitted to everything, and unless she retracts her statement after her lawyer gets through with her, she probably won't stand trial. She's finished, too."

Amanda said nothing. There didn't seem to be anything to say. Even if she could have thought of something, she was too tired to open her mouth to speak. She crossed her arms on the conference table and laid her head down on them. She thought about the last time she had rested in this position.

She had been in fifth grade. She and her classmates had read *The Yearling* by Marjorie Kinan Rawlings. The teacher, whose name she no longer remembered, read the last chapter aloud to the class. When she got to the part about Jody's pet fawn, whose name she did remember—it was Flag—being shot by accident, Amanda had crossed her arms in front of her, put her head down on the desk in that fifth-grade classroom, and sobbed out her broken heart over the death of the little animal.

The teacher had berated and humiliated Amanda for her sentimentality over a wild animal, for lack of control over her feelings—and for crying in public. She remembered now how the other children had taken their cue from the teacher and had laughed at her, too. And she remembered how angry her mother had been at the teacher, and had marched off to the grammar school to bawl the hell out of every adult in sight.

Amanda cried now too—for the little dead fawn, for the cruelty of that fifth-grade teacher, for the cruelty of little children to one another. For all the cruelty in the world.

She cried for her mother who had died four years later and for the people who had died these last few weeks on the transplant unit.

Amanda sobbed in great wracking gulps and was unaware that the detectives and the assistant district attorney had left the room. She was aware, although only dimly, that her husband sat next to her with his chest pressed against her bent back, his arms enfolding her body.

She did not see the tears that streamed unchecked down his own face.

The sky was beginning to turn from its deep nighttime navy blue to a softer color that hinted at the freshness of the day to come. The stars were still visible but slowly fading into the background of the lightening sky when Ken helped his wife out of the bathtub and wrapped her in a soft towel.

She stood quietly and passively while he patted her dry and helped her slip a pale blue silk nightgown over her head. "You don't have to brush your teeth tonight," he said.

"Thank you, sweet love," she replied and laid her head on his chest.

He picked his wife up and carried her to their bed where Shadow was waiting for them. Amanda pulled herself to a sitting position, plumped two pillows behind her back, and

egan to stroke the cat, who had crawled into her lap. Ken
at down next to her and took her other hand. They looked at
ach other for a long time.

"I lied to you," she said. "I'm sorry for that. I am so very
orry for that." Her eyes filled again, but her gaze remained
teady. "Can you ever forgive me?"

"I do," said Ken. "I have. There is nothing to forgive. My
e of omission was far greater."

They looked silently at each other again, knowing that what
vas between them now created a bond so strong that only
eath could sever it.

Even death would not sever it.

"You never told me you had a gun," she said. "Has it been
n the house all this time?"

"Yes, sweet love. It has. I never told you about it because I
now how strongly you feel about guns. I've had it for almost
hirty years, and this is the first time I've fired it."

Again they looked at one another, and Amanda said, "The
un I would have hated and would have asked you to get rid
f saved my life. You saved my life. You killed a man who
vould have killed me."

"Yes, I did," said Ken. "I killed him because I couldn't live
vithout you."

Amanda did not thank her husband with words. There are
o words sufficient to express gratitude for the gift of life.

══ EPILOGUE ══

Amanda woke out of a deep sleep, wild giggles rising in he throat.

She had dreamed that she was in the bathtub and her to was stuck in the water faucet. Water dripped into the crevic between her first and second toes and tickled her unmercifully and the combined crud of years of mineral deposit buildu inside the faucet scraped her toe with sharp intensity. Th scraping didn't hurt exactly, but neither did it feel good.

She lay in bed for a moment, knowing she was awake, bu still trapped in the sensation of the dripping faucet and shar scraping. When she realized what was causing the sensatior she giggled outright and leaned over her sleeping husband.

"Your dog is eating my foot," she whispered in his ear.

"Mmmpfff," said Ken.

He neither moved nor spoke further, so she bit his ear lob just a little.

"Mmmpfff," he said again, louder and in a decidedly irri tated voice.

"Your dog is eating my foot," she repeated. She giggle again, and Ken woke up, went head first under the covers disengaged the black Labrador puppy from her toe—and the bit it himself, not at all gently.

"Ouch," she yelped and tickled the puppy under his fa chin.

"Come on, Windy," said Ken, getting out of bed with th puppy in his arms. "Back to your own basket."

Amanda smiled as she heard her husband talk to the dog and thought about the drive to the breeder's home two day before. She had told Ken that his birthday present would b slightly delayed, and when it was time, she had asked hir to cancel his tennis game and help her pick up the pres ent.

278

He had been a little grumpy over missing the game, but as they drove out into the Virginia hills with the car windows open to catch the breeze, fresh and dry with the beginning of autumn, he had gotten into the spirit of the occasion. When Amanda made the left turn into the winding lane with the neat white sign that said, LABRADOR RETRIEVER PUPPIES FOR SALE, Ken broke into a huge grin, took her hand, and gave it a squeeze.

The puppy that Amanda had picked out was the last one of the litter to leave his mother, and he scampered over to her in happy recognition because Amanda had already paid three visits to him and his mother.

The breeder came out of the house when she saw the car drive up and watched Amanda pick up the little dog and put it into her husband's arms. The mother retriever watched all this very carefully, but she made no move to interfere with this woman who had praised her so lavishly for producing such fine babies.

Ken, with the dog in his arms, hugged and kissed his wife, and at that very moment, the little black thing had emitted an explosively noisy fart that was about three times the size of himself.

The humans laughed in delight, and the puppy turned around in surprise, looking for whatever was behind him that had made such a funny noise. The people laughed again, and somehow the dog knew that they were laughing at him but in the kindest possible way, so he laughed too.

"Windy little fellow, isn't he?" said Ken.

That was all it had taken, and now Ken knelt next to the wicker basket and spoke gently to the animal, saying his name over and over again. He rewrapped the ticking clock in a terry cloth towel and placed it next to the dog's body.

Shadow watched all this from her accustomed place at the head of the bed. Her face registered feline disdain, as well as the security of knowing that she was, and would always be, queen of the household. She had established that in no uncertain terms this very morning, with two quick swipes of a paw and a no-nonsense hiss. The puppy had gotten the idea immediately, so Shadow was secure in her position and had no need to intercede in these shenanigans. She simply waited patiently for everyone to settle down in bed.

And soon they did. Ken and Amanda hugged each other. "Thank you again for Windy," he said.

She smiled and kissed him and said, "Happy dreams, sweet love."

The cat went to sleep right after her man and woman did, but the dog bided his time until he was sure that everyone's breathing was smooth and rhythmic. He lifted his nose from under his paws, rested it for a moment on the edge of his basket, and then sniffed the fragrance of the breeze blowing in through the open window, as well as the special smells of his new man and woman.

When he had committed all of this to memory, he got quietly out of the basket, waddled on his still-stubby legs to the rosewood chest at the foot of the bed. He gathered his hind legs under him, jumped, and landed on top of the comforter that was folded neatly in case the night air grew chilly. From there it was an easy hop to the foot of the bed.

He padded very softly up the middle of the bed and lay down with a satisfied little grunt on top of a tangle of legs. The man and woman, without waking from sleep, shifted slightly and made room in the big bed for the new family member.